O JOSEPHINE!

by Jason

FANTAGRAPHICS BOOKS

Fantagraphics Books
7563 Lake City Way NE
Seattle, WA 98115

Designer: Justin Allan-Spencer
Editor: Conrad Groth
Production: Paul Baresh
Publicity: Jacq Cohen
Associate Publisher: Eric Reynolds
Publisher: Gary Groth

ISBN: 978-1-68396-210-6
Library of Congress Control Number: 2018963700
First edition: June 2019
Printed in China

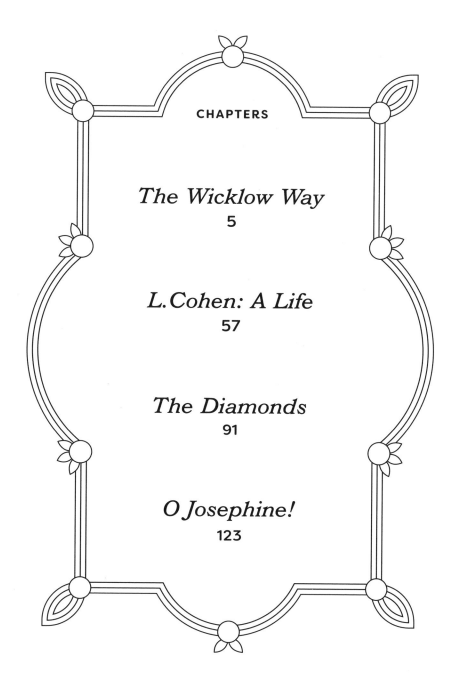

CHAPTERS

The Wicklow Way

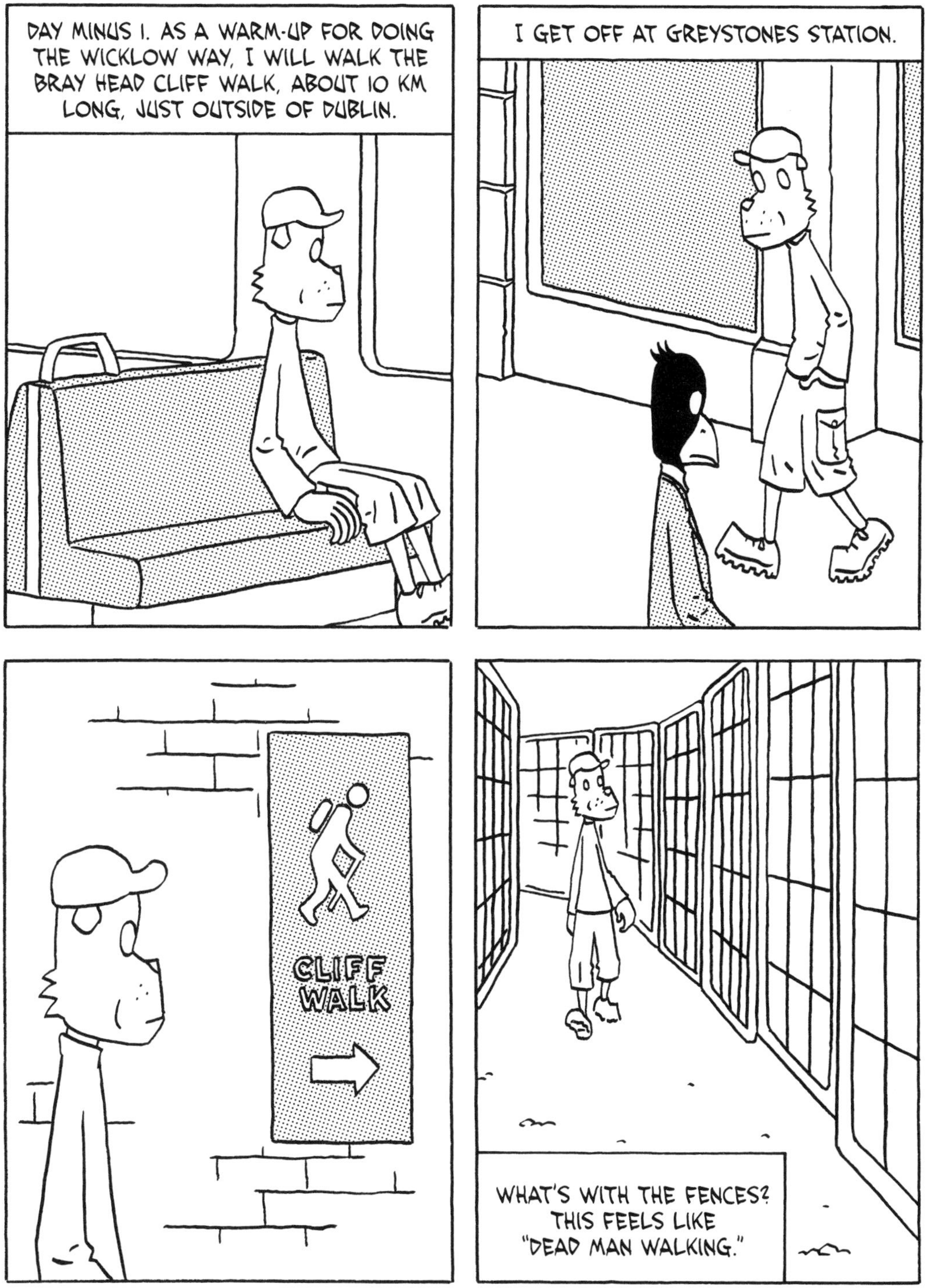
DAY MINUS 1. AS A WARM-UP FOR DOING THE WICKLOW WAY, I WILL WALK THE BRAY HEAD CLIFF WALK, ABOUT 10 KM LONG, JUST OUTSIDE OF DUBLIN.
I GET OFF AT GREYSTONES STATION.
CLIFF WALK
WHAT'S WITH THE FENCES? THIS FEELS LIKE "DEAD MAN WALKING."

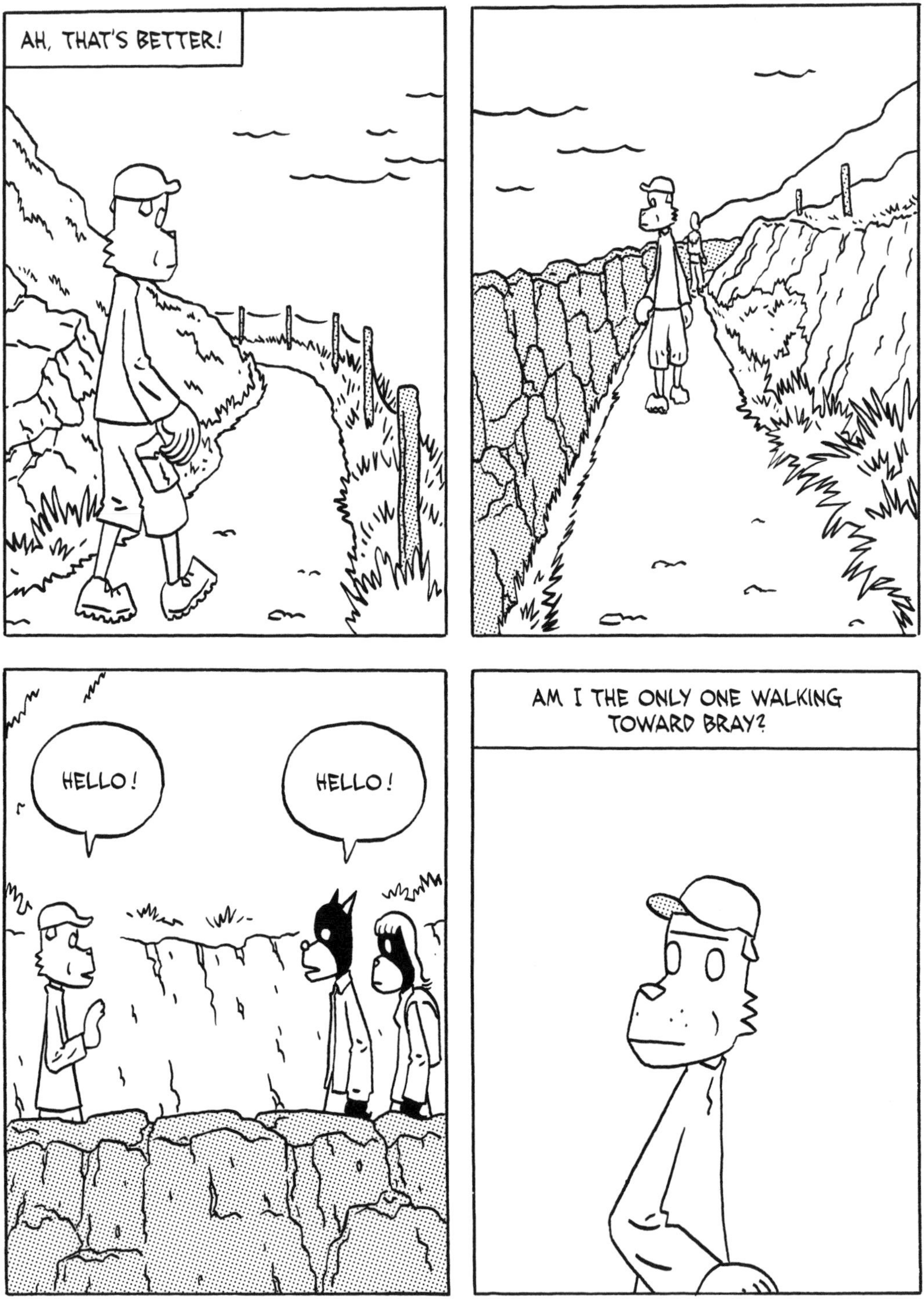
AH, THAT'S BETTER!
HELLO!
HELLO!
AM I THE ONLY ONE WALKING TOWARD BRAY?

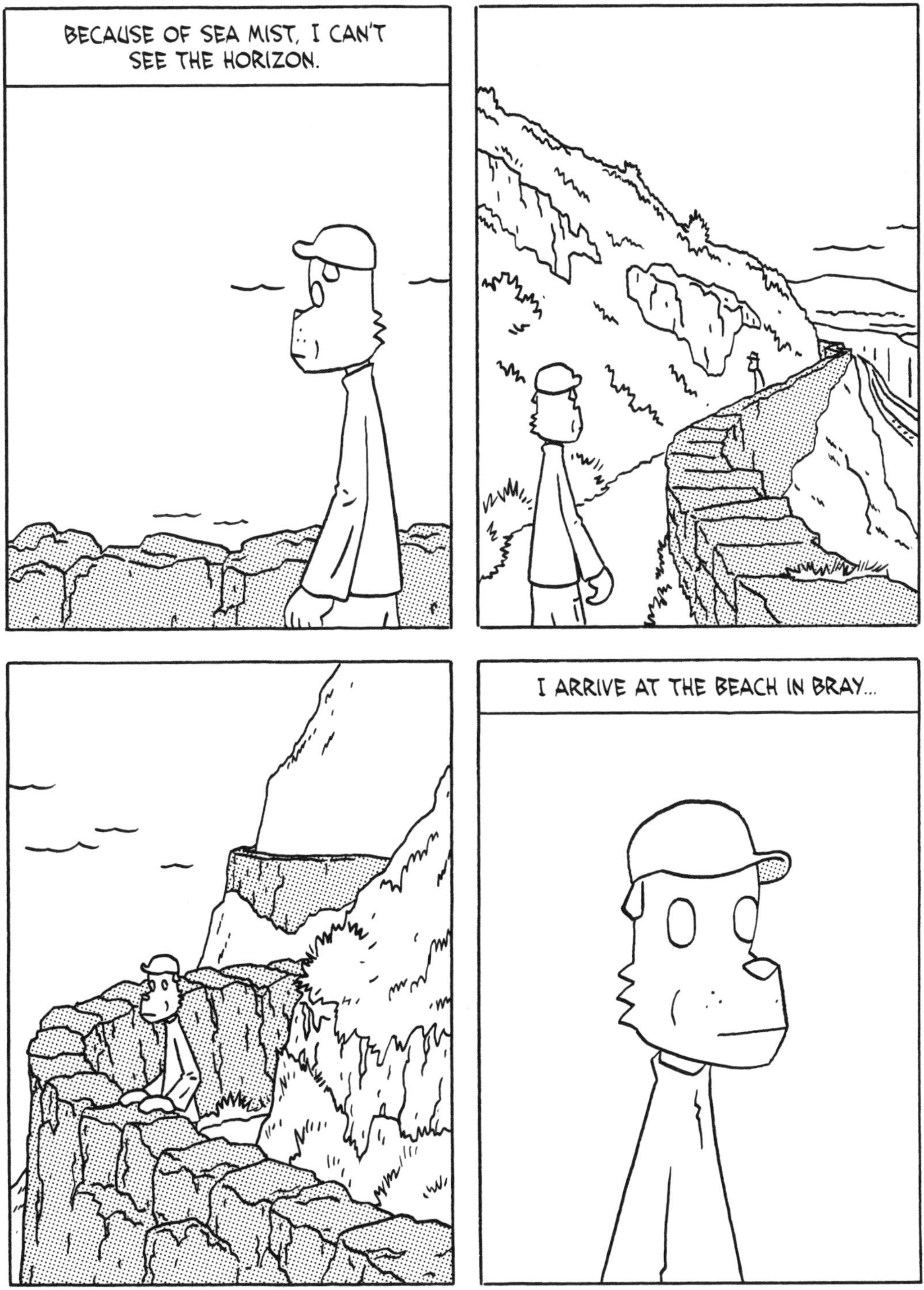
BECAUSE OF SEA MIST, I CAN'T SEE THE HORIZON.
I ARRIVE AT THE BEACH IN BRAY...

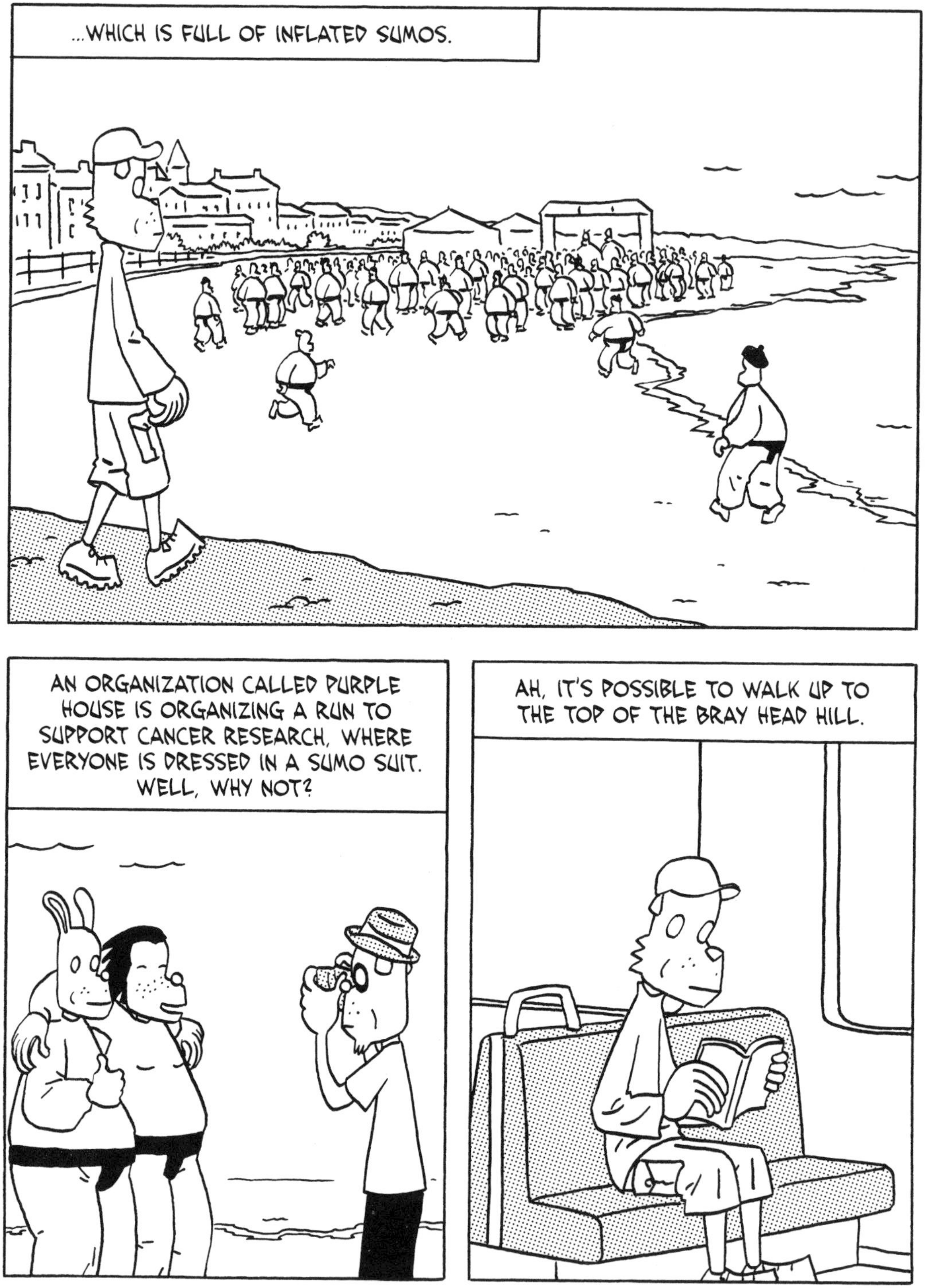
...WHICH IS FULL OF INFLATED SUMOS.
AN ORGANIZATION CALLED PURPLE HOUSE IS ORGANIZING A RUN TO SUPPORT CANCER RESEARCH, WHERE EVERYONE IS DRESSED IN A SUMO SUIT. WELL, WHY NOT?
AH, IT'S POSSIBLE TO WALK UP TO THE TOP OF THE BRAY HEAD HILL.

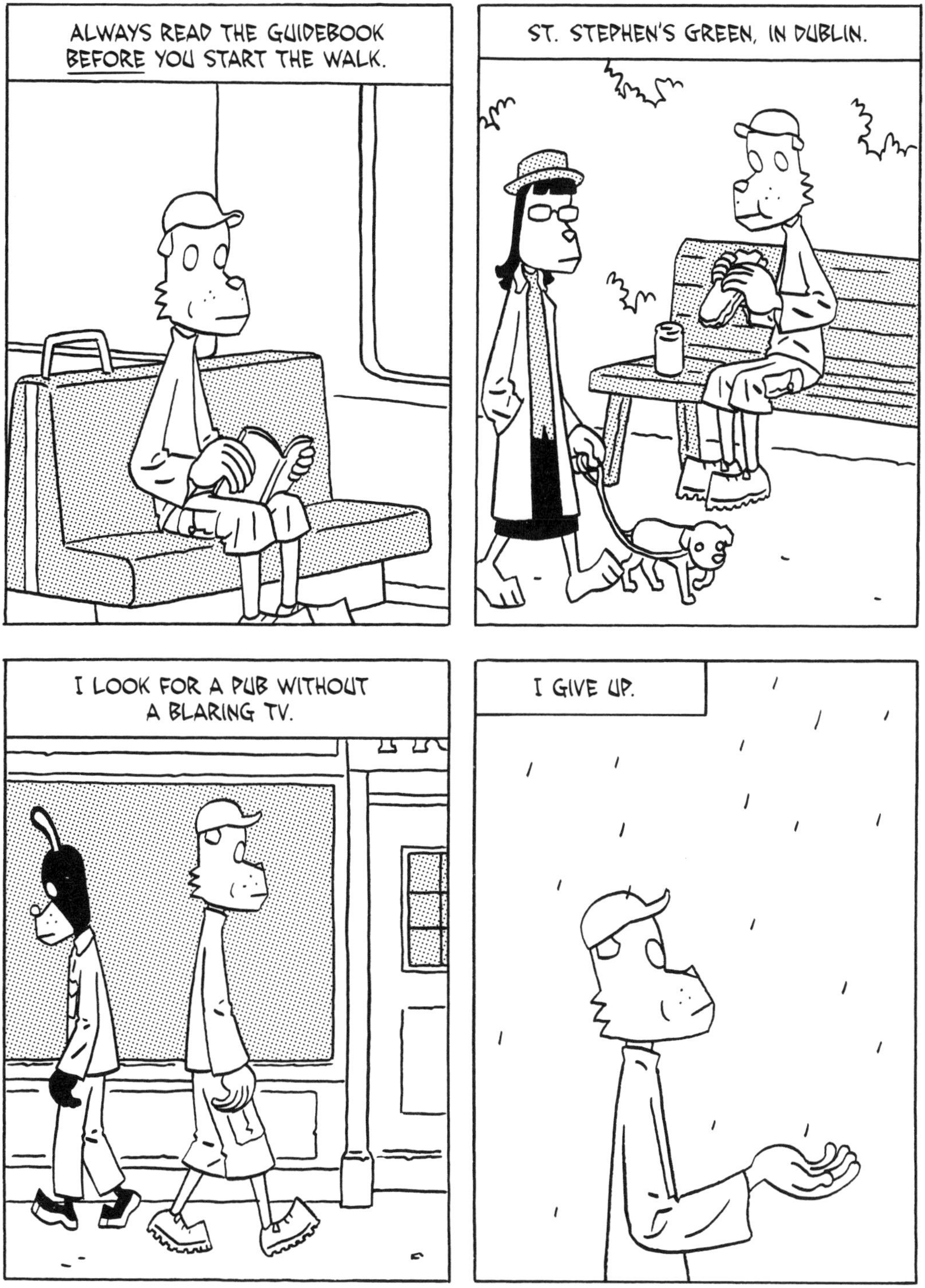
ALWAYS READ THE GUIDEBOOK BEFORE YOU START THE WALK.
ST. STEPHEN'S GREEN, IN DUBLIN.
I LOOK FOR A PUB WITHOUT A BLARING TV.
I GIVE UP.

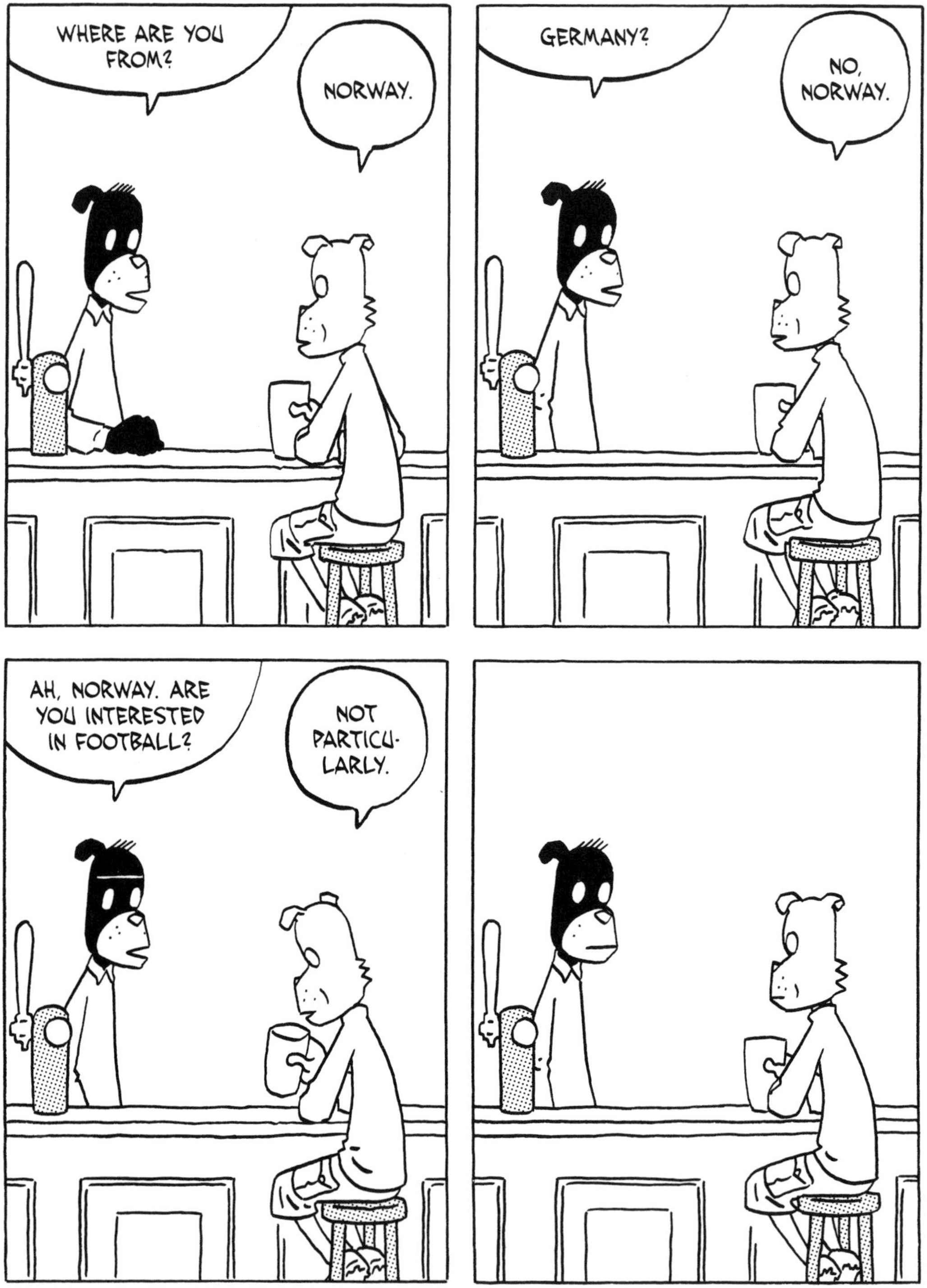
WHERE ARE YOU FROM?
NORWAY.
GERMANY?
NO, NORWAY.
AH, NORWAY. ARE YOU INTERESTED IN FOOTBALL?
NOT PARTICU-LARLY.

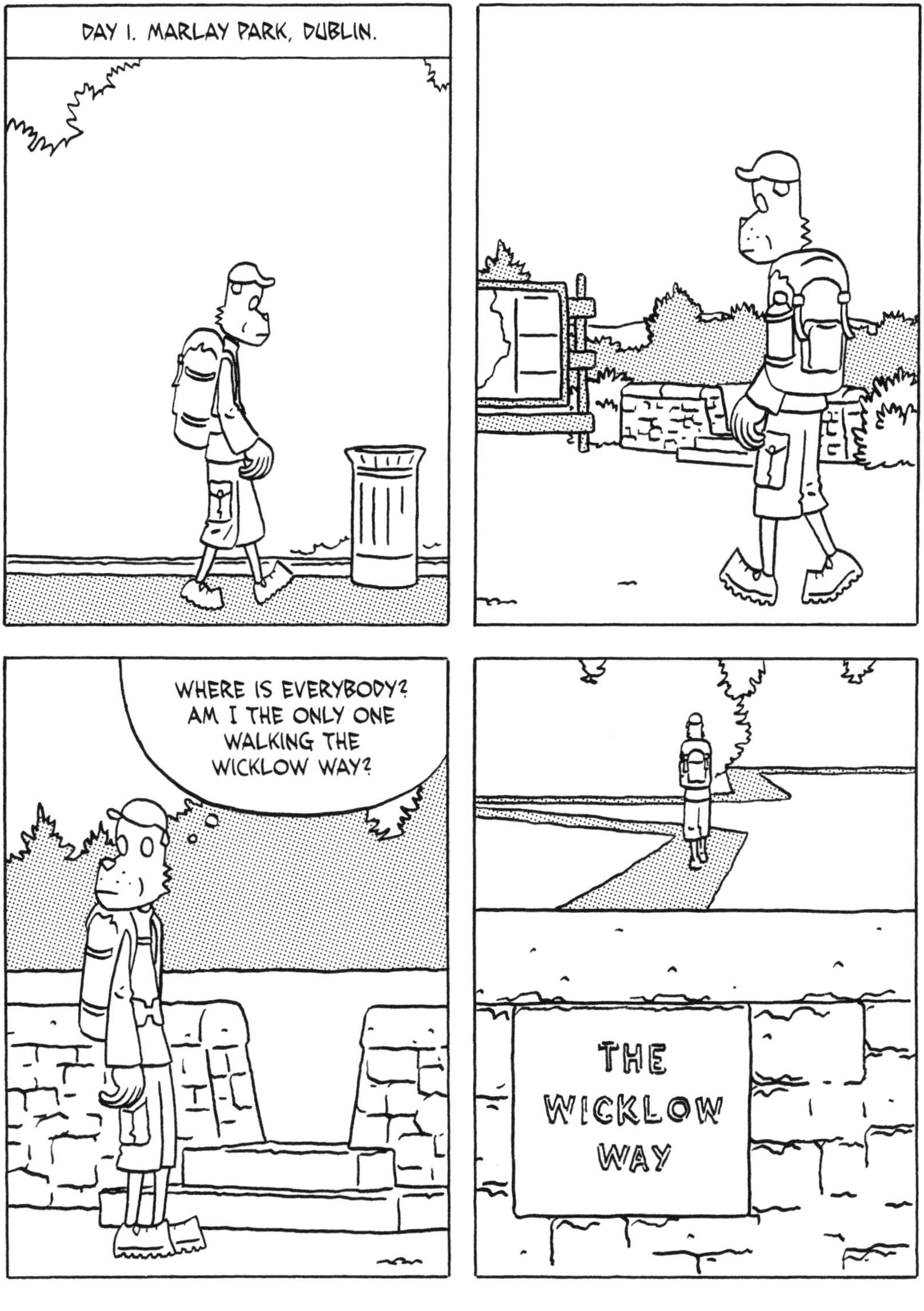
DAY 1. MARLAY PARK, DUBLIN.
WHERE IS EVERYBODY? AM I THE ONLY ONE WALKING THE WICKLOW WAY?
THE WICKLOW WAY

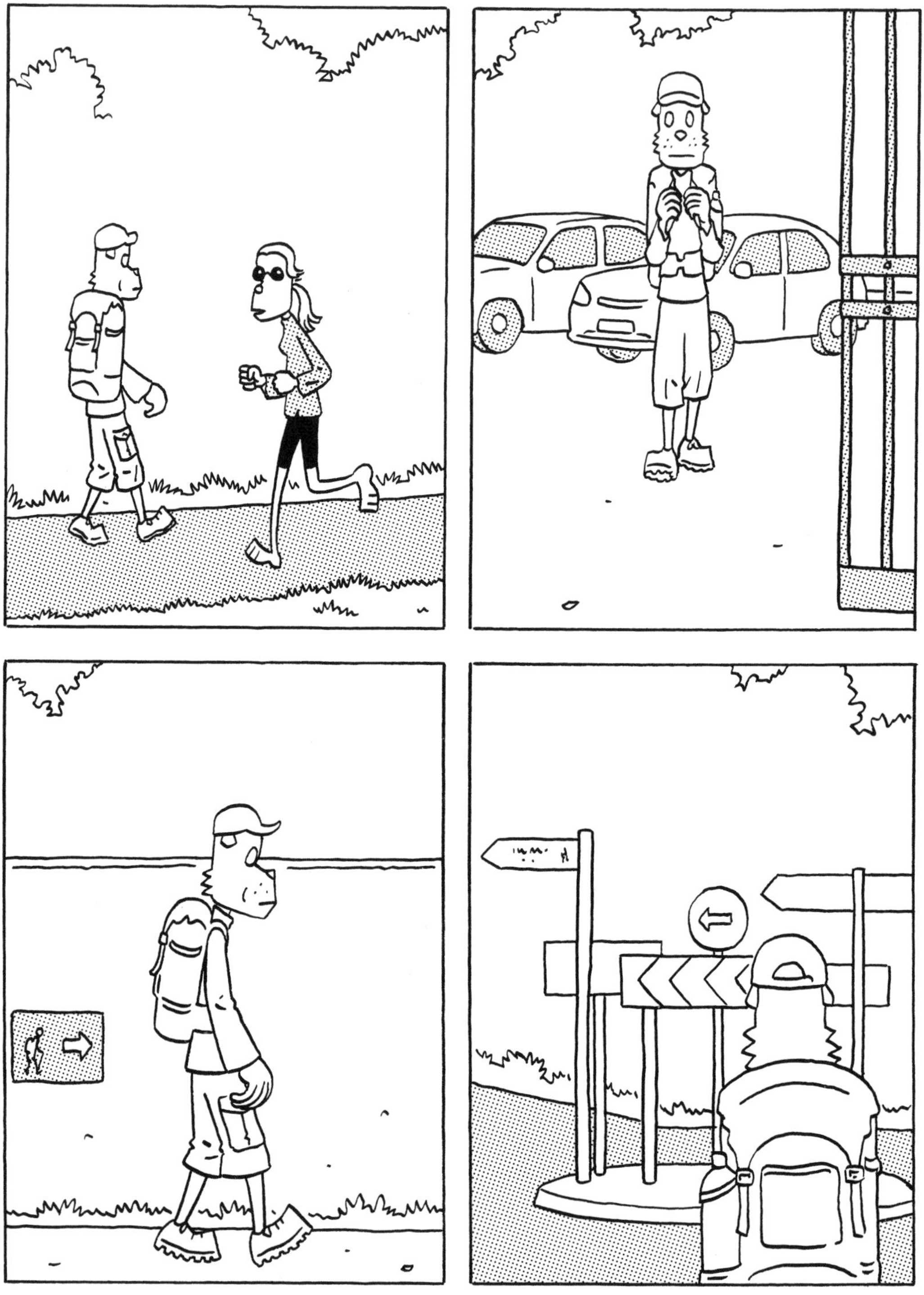

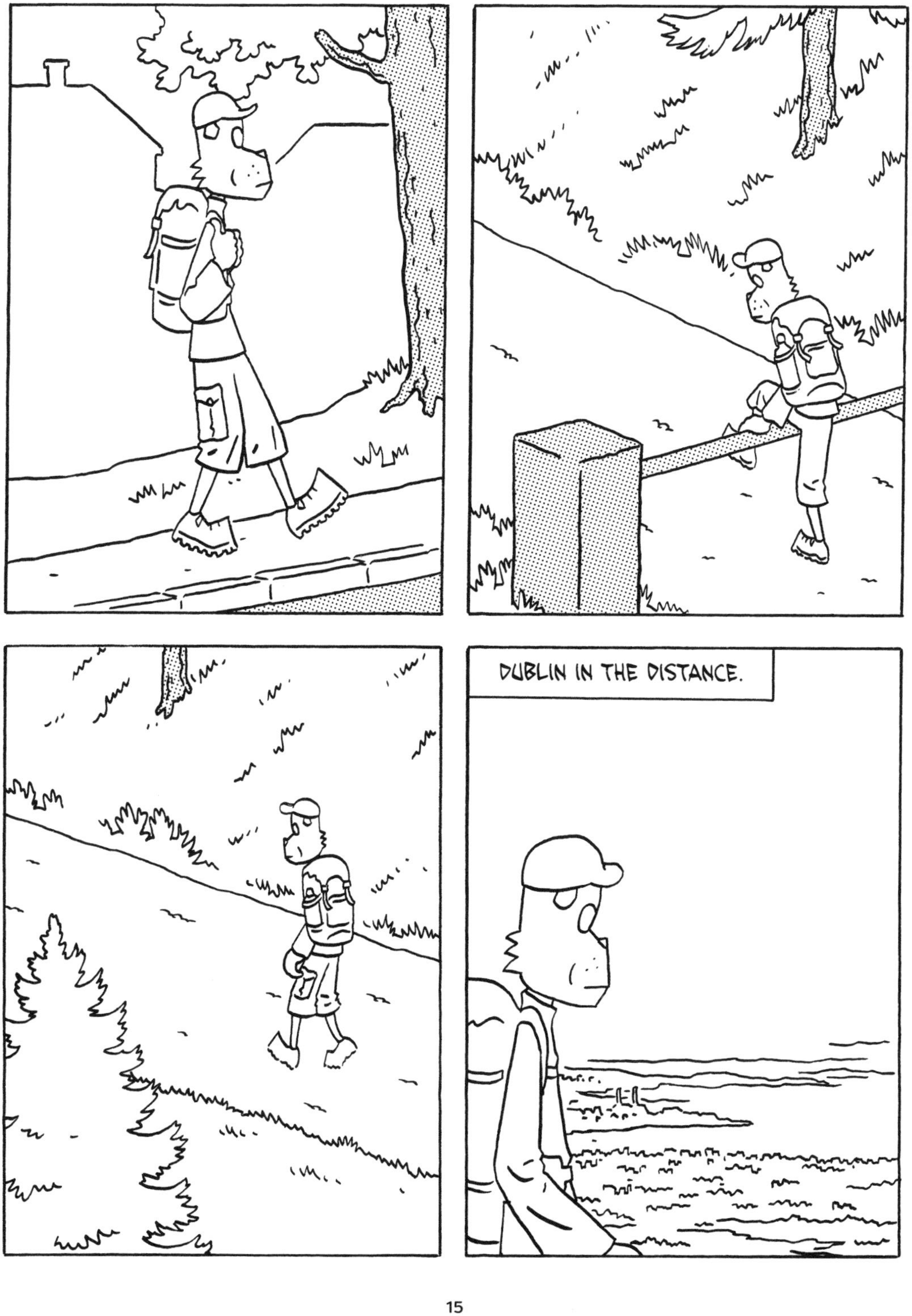
DUBLIN IN THE DISTANCE.

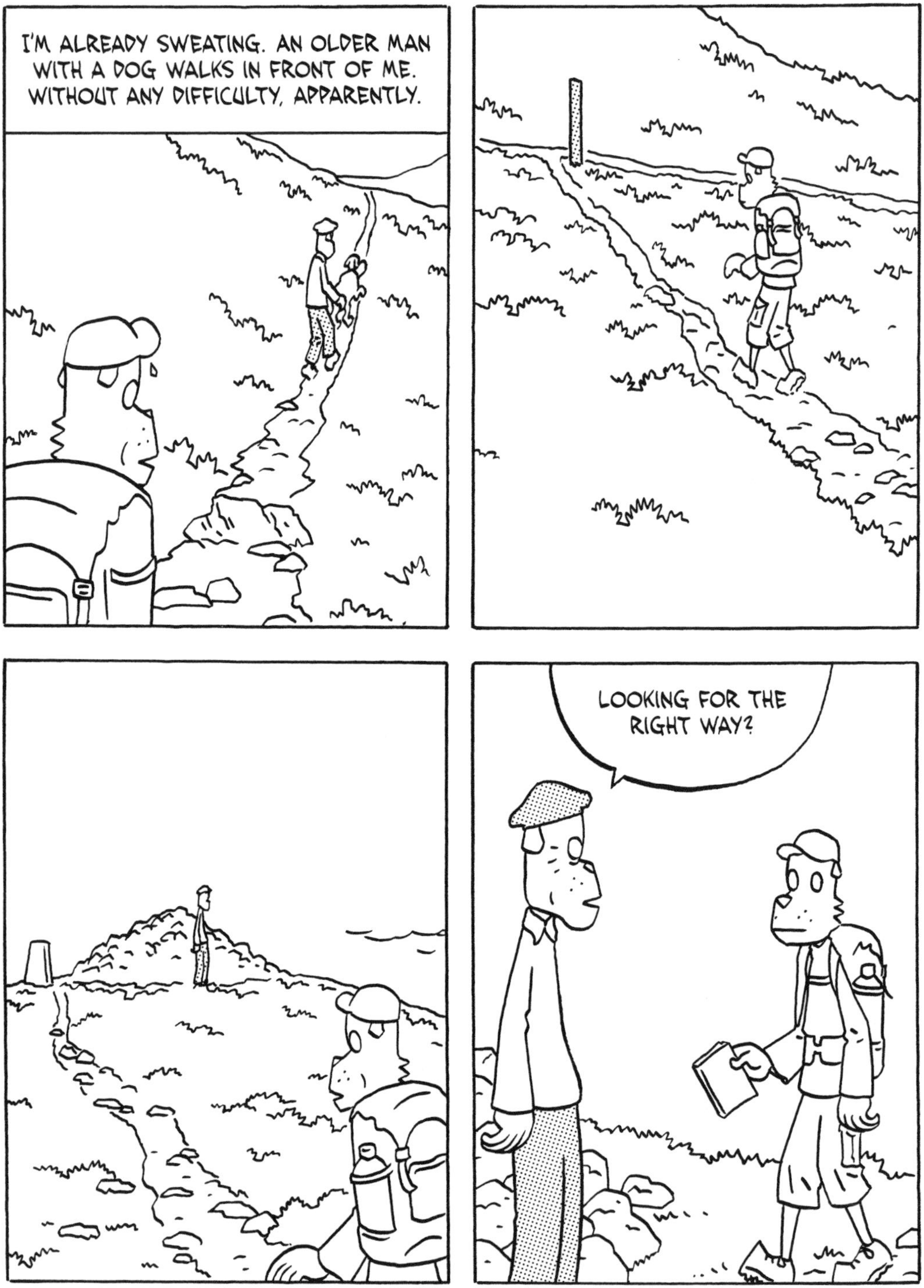
I'M ALREADY SWEATING. AN OLDER MAN WITH A DOG WALKS IN FRONT OF ME. WITHOUT ANY DIFFICULTY, APPARENTLY.
LOOKING FOR THE RIGHT WAY?

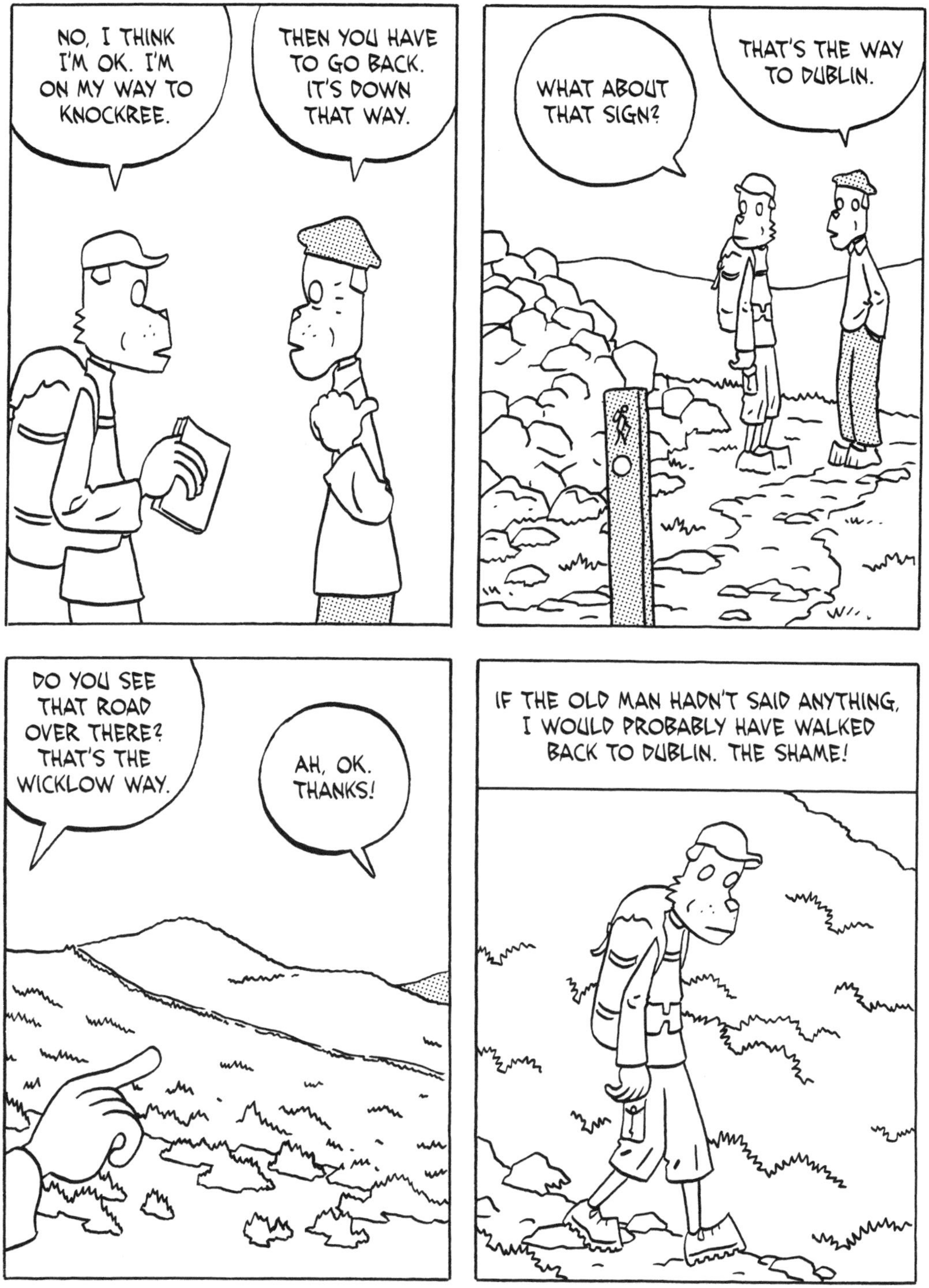
NO, I THINK I'M OK. I'M ON MY WAY TO KNOCKREE.
THEN YOU HAVE TO GO BACK. IT'S DOWN THAT WAY.
WHAT ABOUT THAT SIGN?
THAT'S THE WAY TO DUBLIN.
DO YOU SEE THAT ROAD OVER THERE? THAT'S THE WICKLOW WAY.
AH, OK. THANKS!
IF THE OLD MAN HADN'T SAID ANYTHING, I WOULD PROBABLY HAVE WALKED BACK TO DUBLIN. THE SHAME!

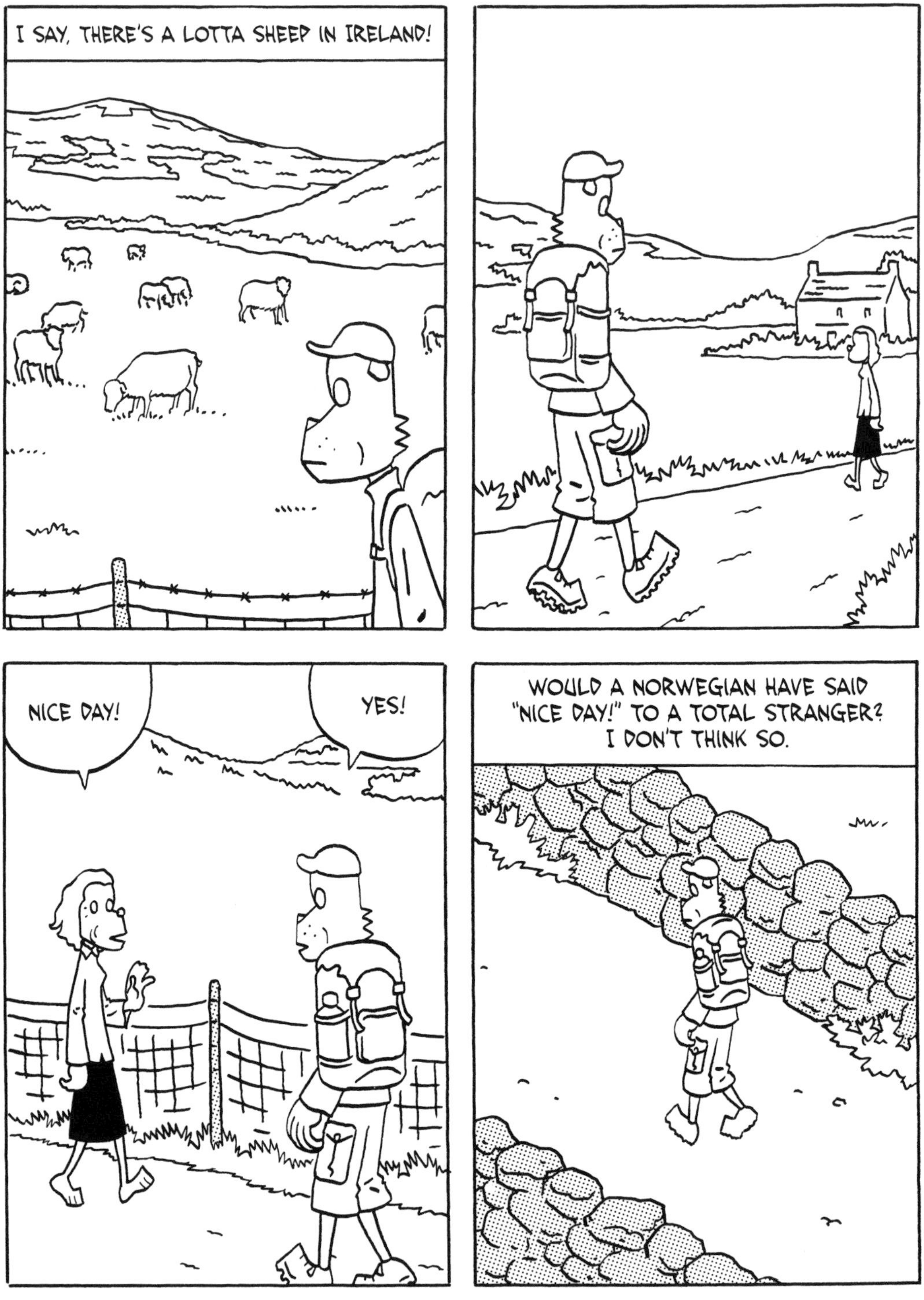
I SAY, THERE'S A LOTTA SHEEP IN IRELAND!
NICE DAY!
YES!
WOULD A NORWEGIAN HAVE SAID "NICE DAY!" TO A TOTAL STRANGER? I DON'T THINK SO.

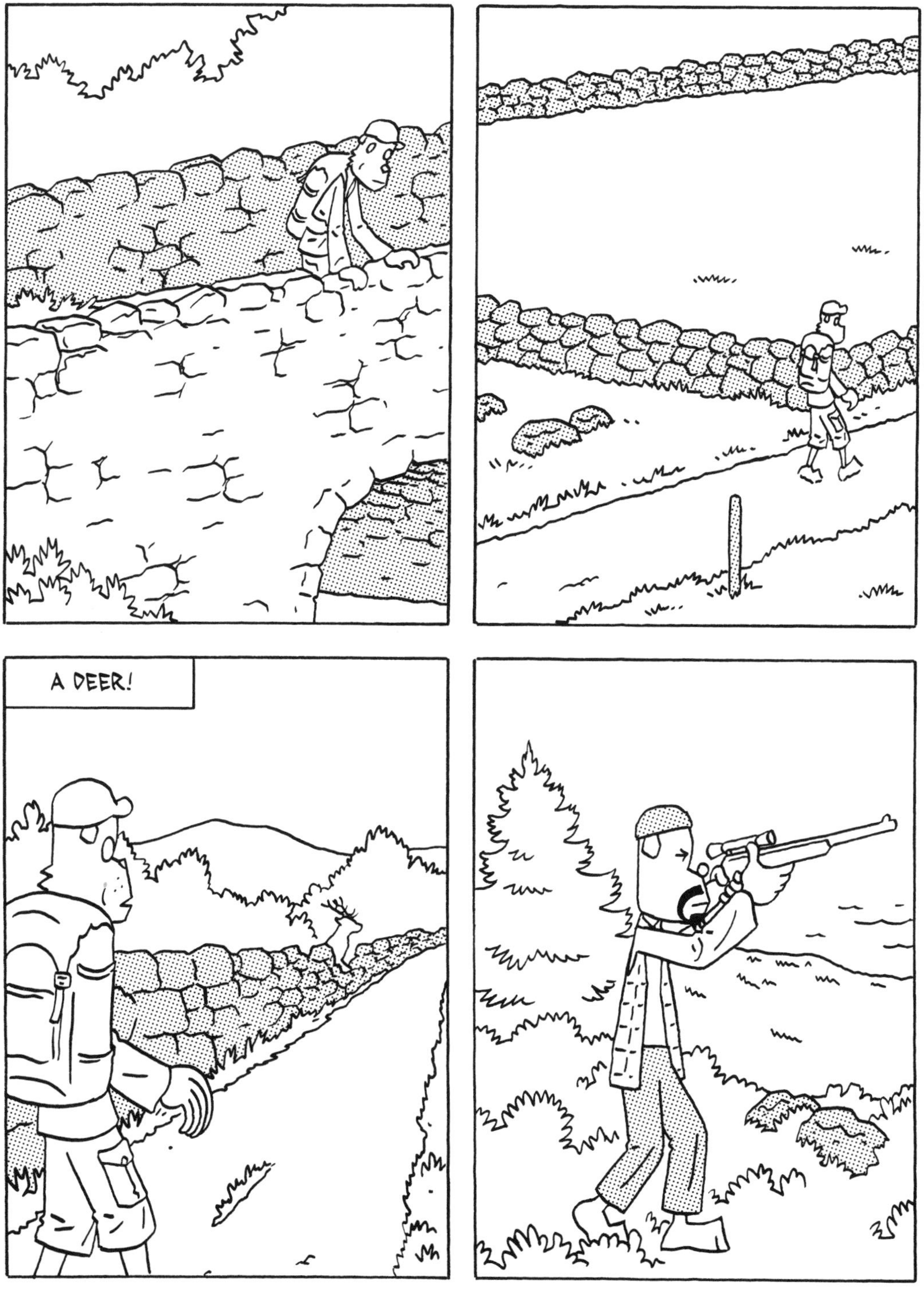
A DEER!

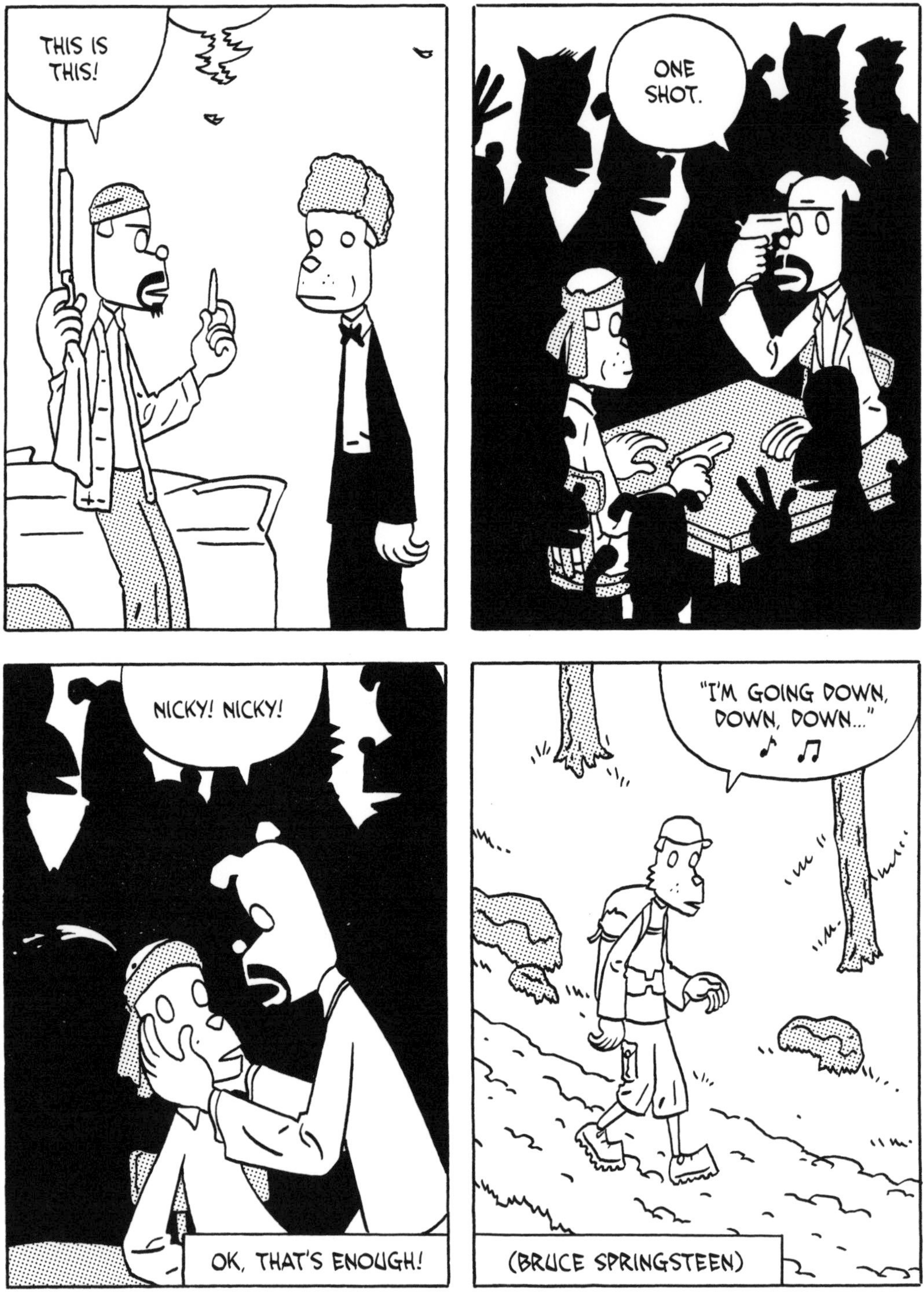
THIS IS THIS!
ONE SHOT.
NICKY! NICKY!
OK, THAT'S ENOUGH!
"I'M GOING DOWN, DOWN, DOWN..."
(BRUCE SPRINGSTEEN)

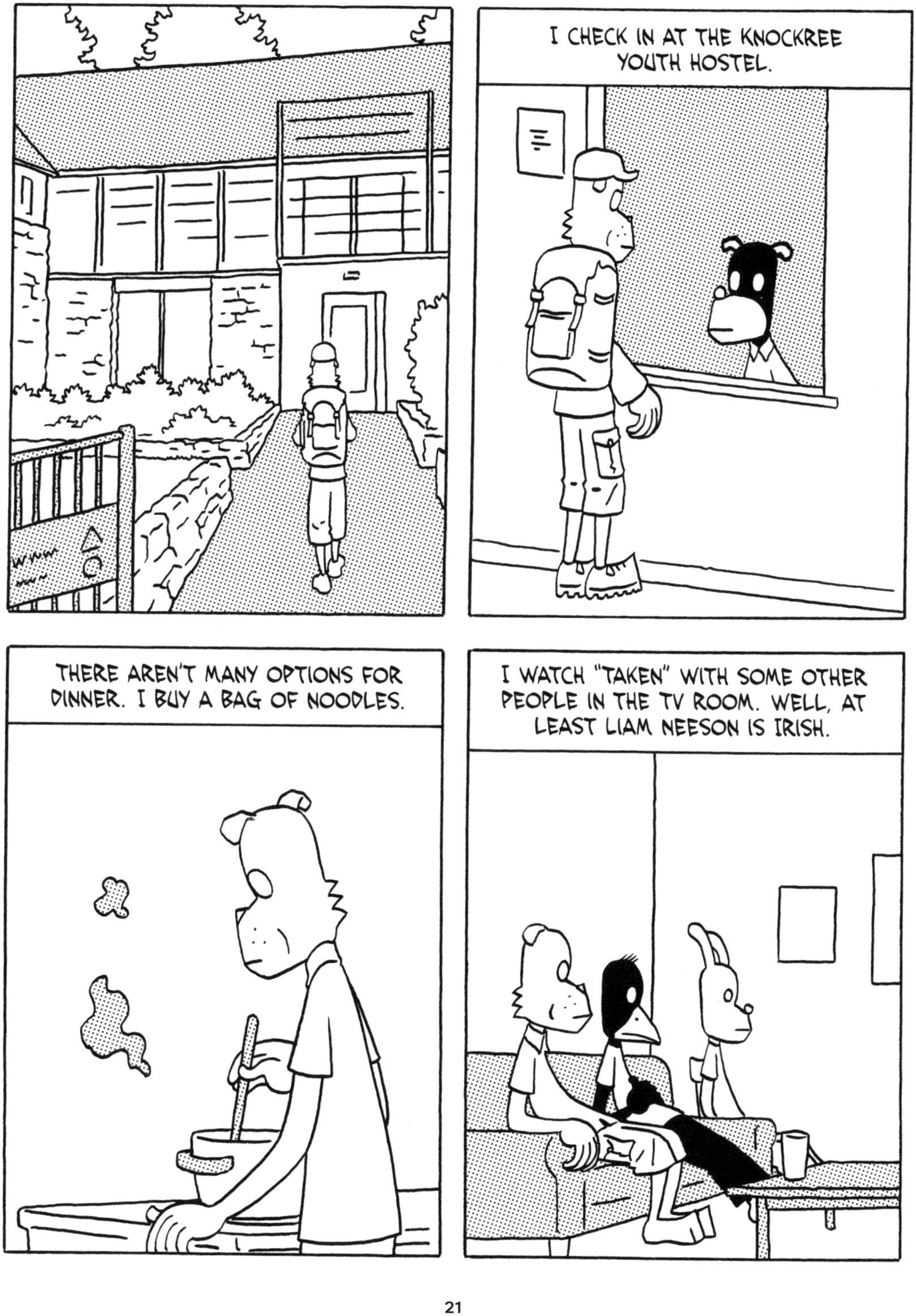
I CHECK IN AT THE KNOCKREE YOUTH HOSTEL.
THERE AREN'T MANY OPTIONS FOR DINNER. I BUY A BAG OF NOODLES.
I WATCH "TAKEN" WITH SOME OTHER PEOPLE IN THE TV ROOM. WELL, AT LEAST LIAM NEESON IS IRISH.

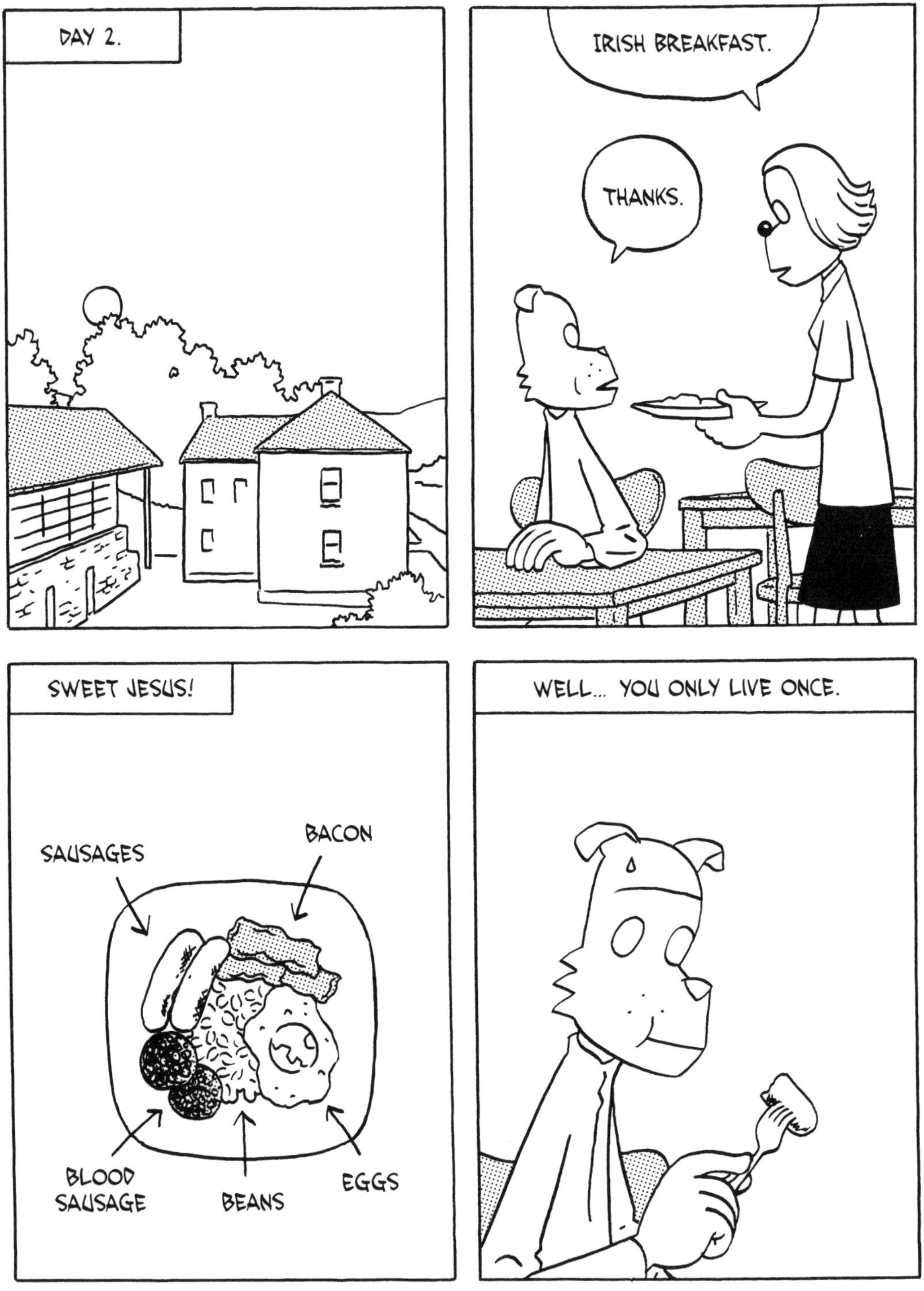
DAY 2.
IRISH BREAKFAST.
THANKS.
SWEET JESUS!
SAUSAGES
BACON
BLOOD SAUSAGE
BEANS
EGGS
WELL... YOU ONLY LIVE ONCE.

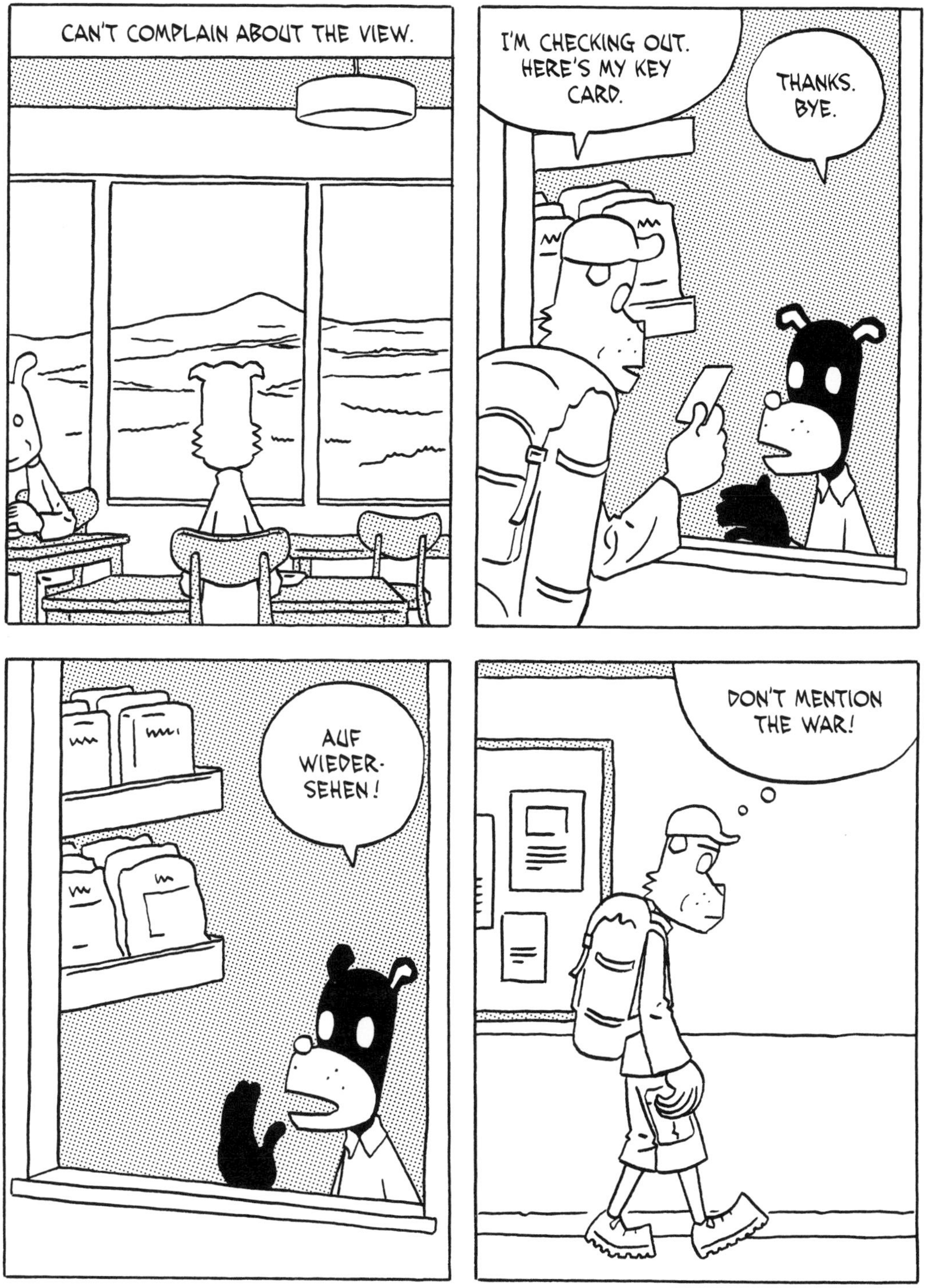
CAN'T COMPLAIN ABOUT THE VIEW.
I'M CHECKING OUT. HERE'S MY KEY CARD.
THANKS. BYE.
AUF WIEDER-SEHEN!
DON'T MENTION THE WAR!

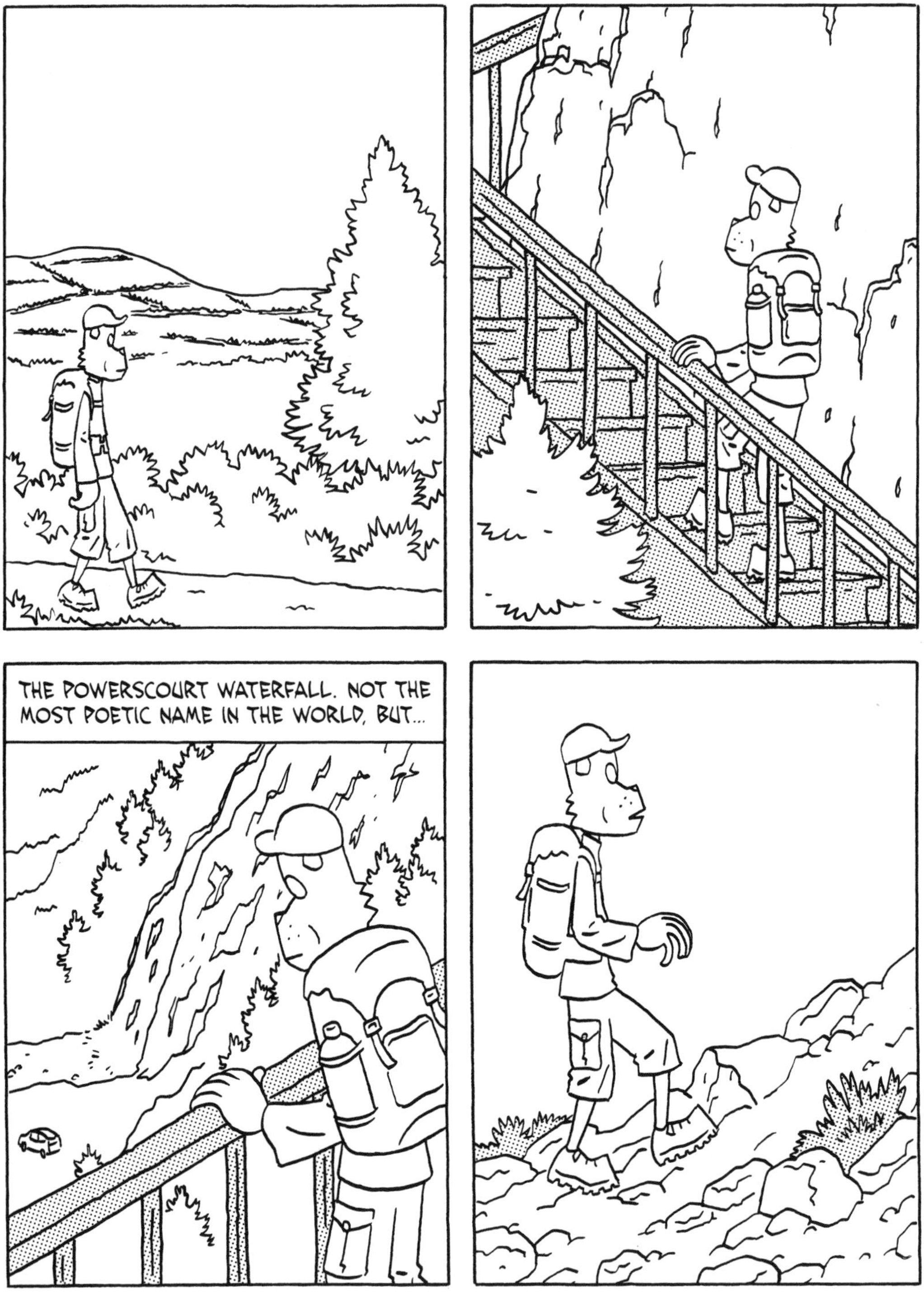
THE POWERSCOURT WATERFALL. NOT THE MOST POETIC NAME IN THE WORLD, BUT...

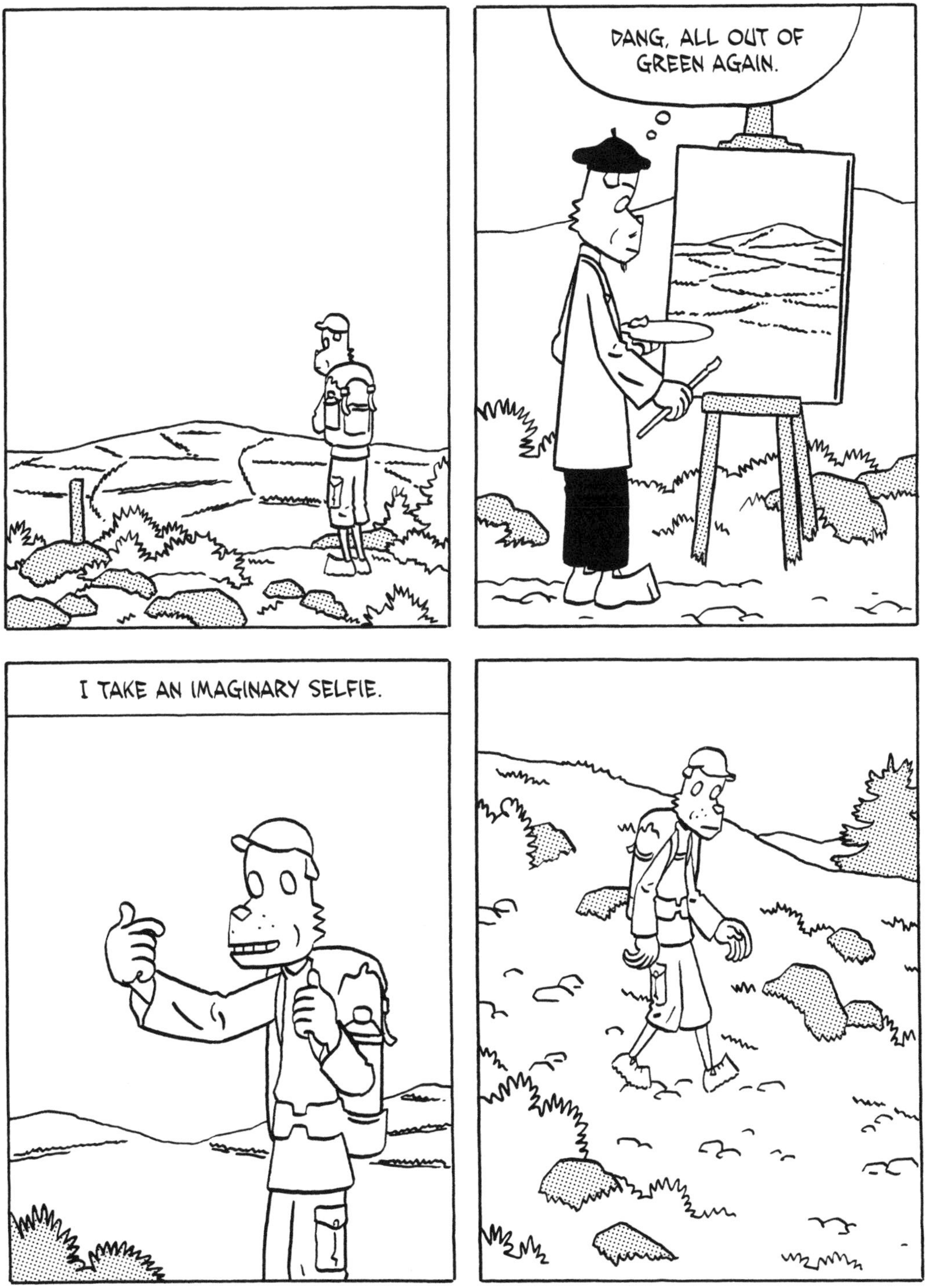
DANG, ALL OUT OF GREEN AGAIN.
I TAKE AN IMAGINARY SELFIE.

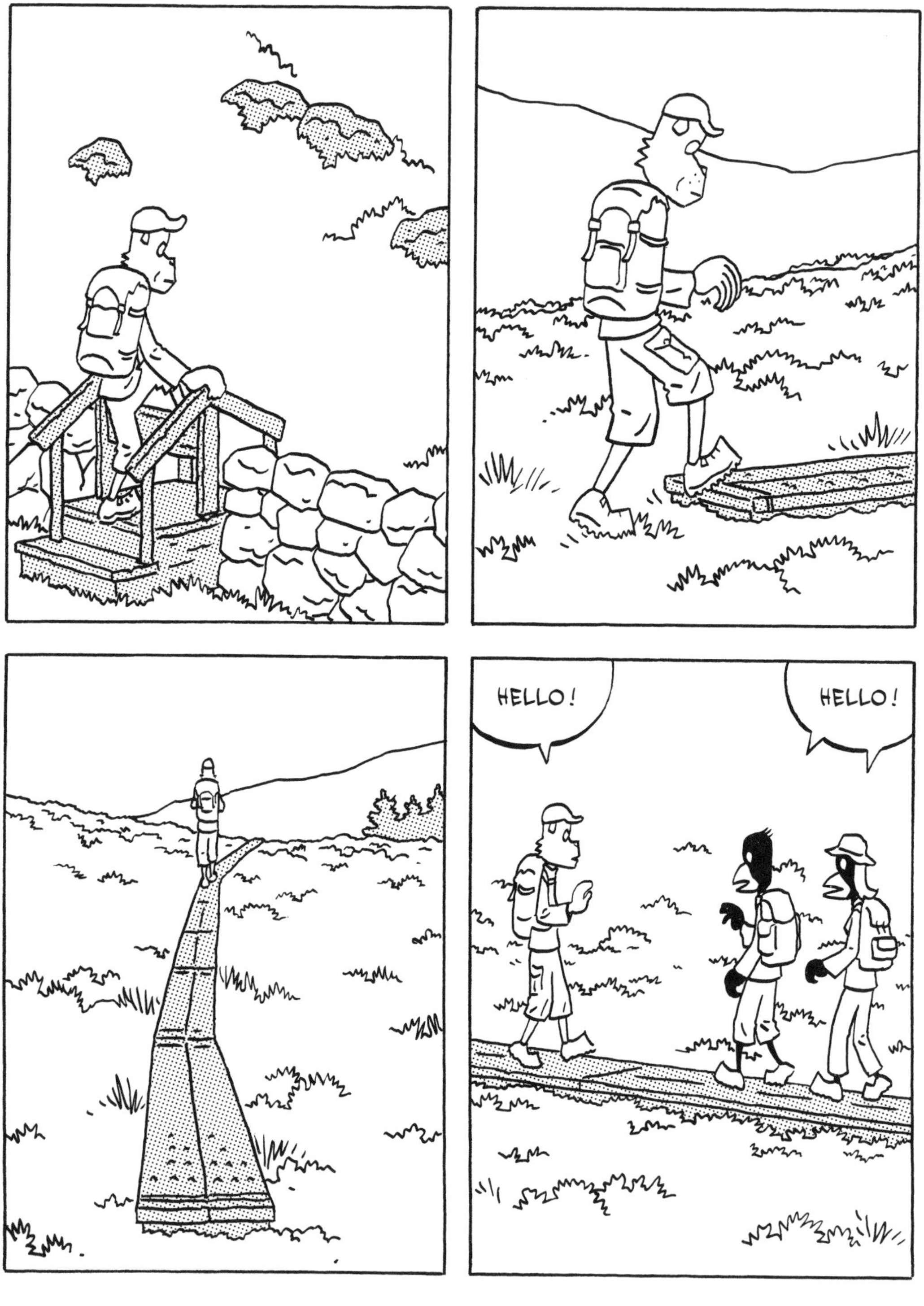
HELLO!
HELLO!

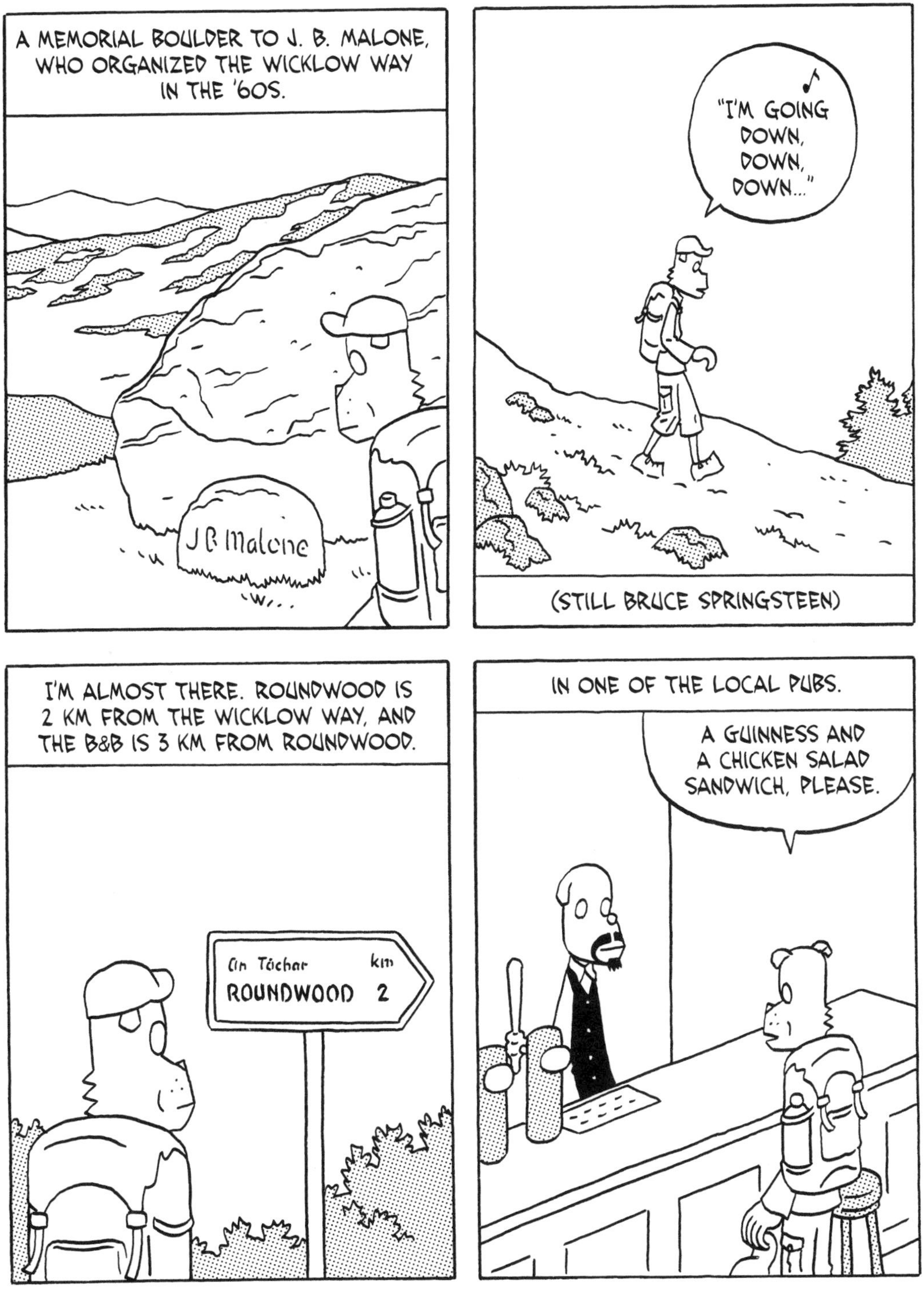
A MEMORIAL BOULDER TO J. B. MALONE, WHO ORGANIZED THE WICKLOW WAY IN THE '60S.
J B Malone
"I'M GOING DOWN, DOWN, DOWN..."
(STILL BRUCE SPRINGSTEEN)
I'M ALMOST THERE. ROUNDWOOD IS 2 KM FROM THE WICKLOW WAY, AND THE B&B IS 3 KM FROM ROUNDWOOD.
An Tóchar km
ROUNDWOOD 2
IN ONE OF THE LOCAL PUBS.
A GUINNESS AND A CHICKEN SALAD SANDWICH, PLEASE.

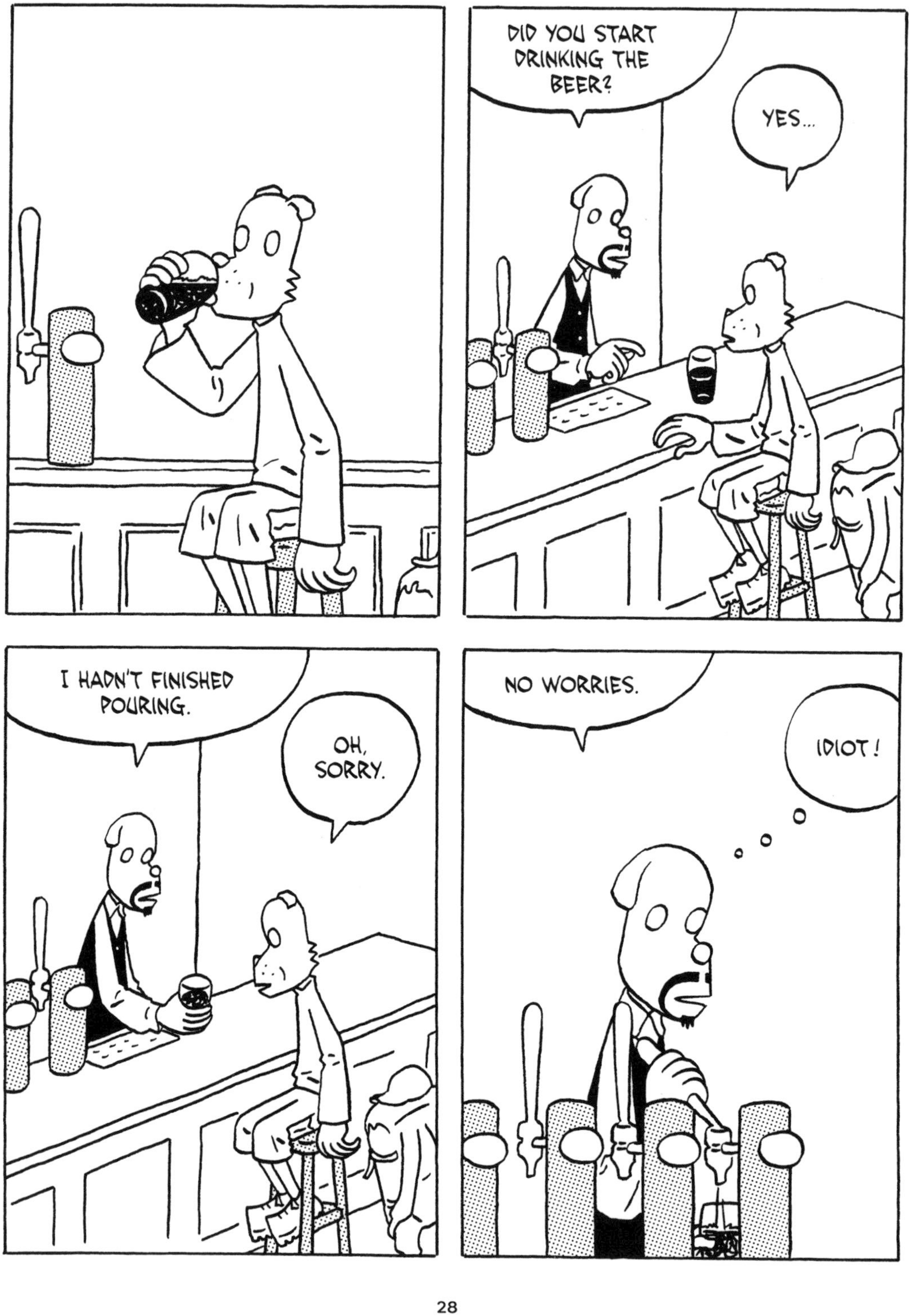
DID YOU START DRINKING THE BEER?
YES...
I HADN'T FINISHED POURING.
OH, SORRY.
NO WORRIES.
IDIOT!

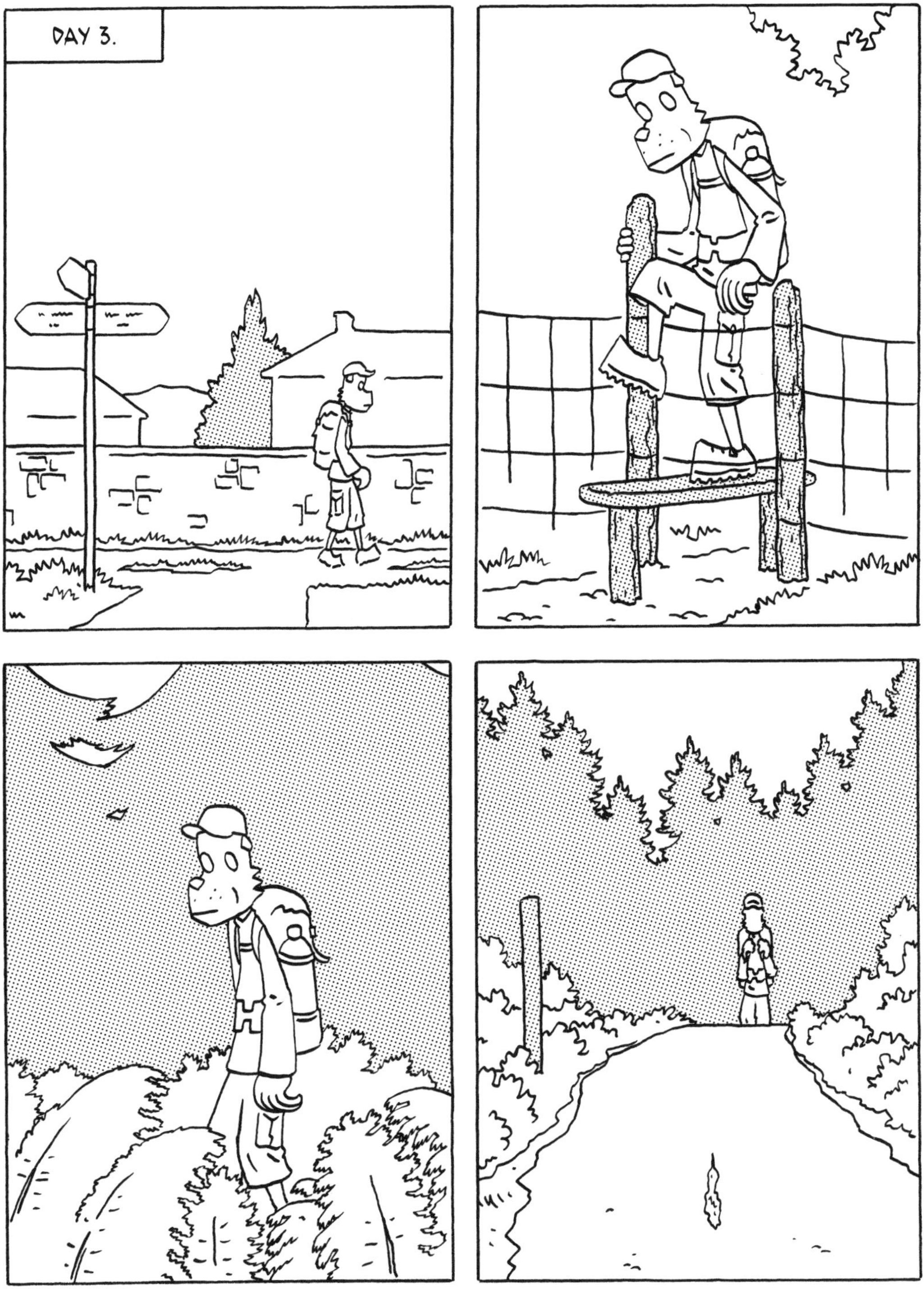
DAY 3.

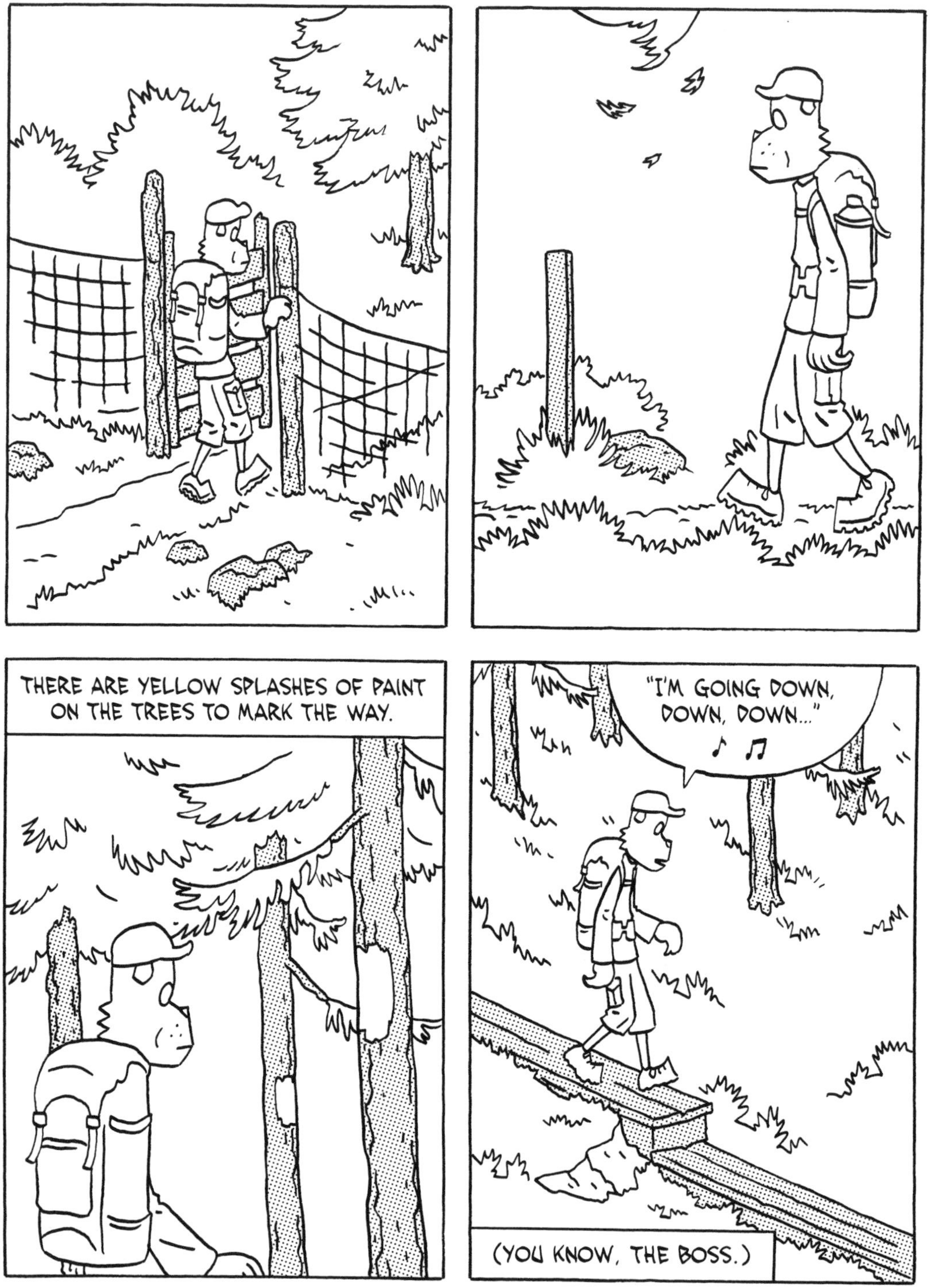
THERE ARE YELLOW SPLASHES OF PAINT ON THE TREES TO MARK THE WAY.
"I'M GOING DOWN, DOWN, DOWN..."
(YOU KNOW, THE BOSS.)

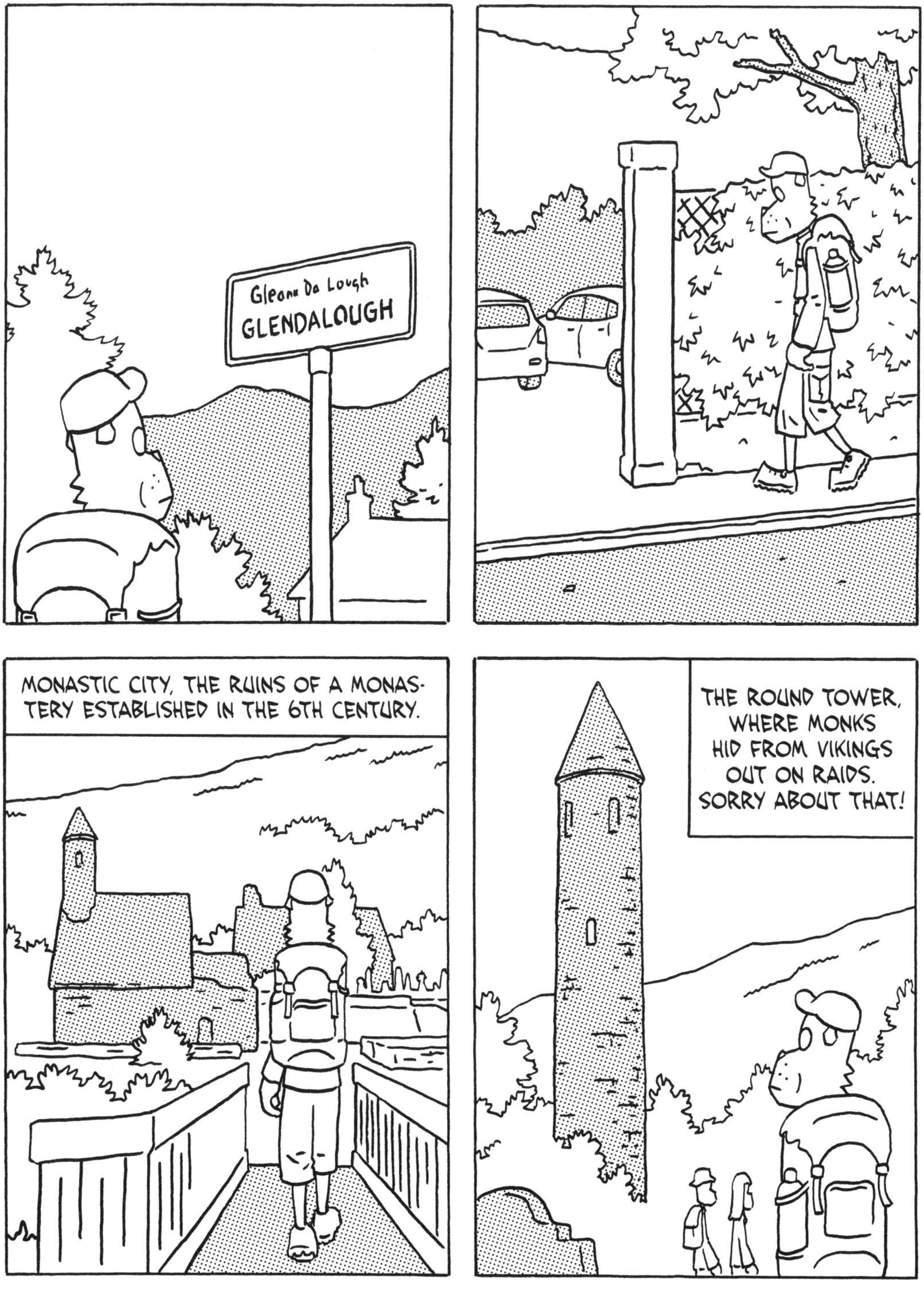
Gleann Da Lough
GLENDALOUGH
MONASTIC CITY, THE RUINS OF A MONASTERY ESTABLISHED IN THE 6TH CENTURY.
THE ROUND TOWER, WHERE MONKS HID FROM VIKINGS OUT ON RAIDS. SORRY ABOUT THAT!

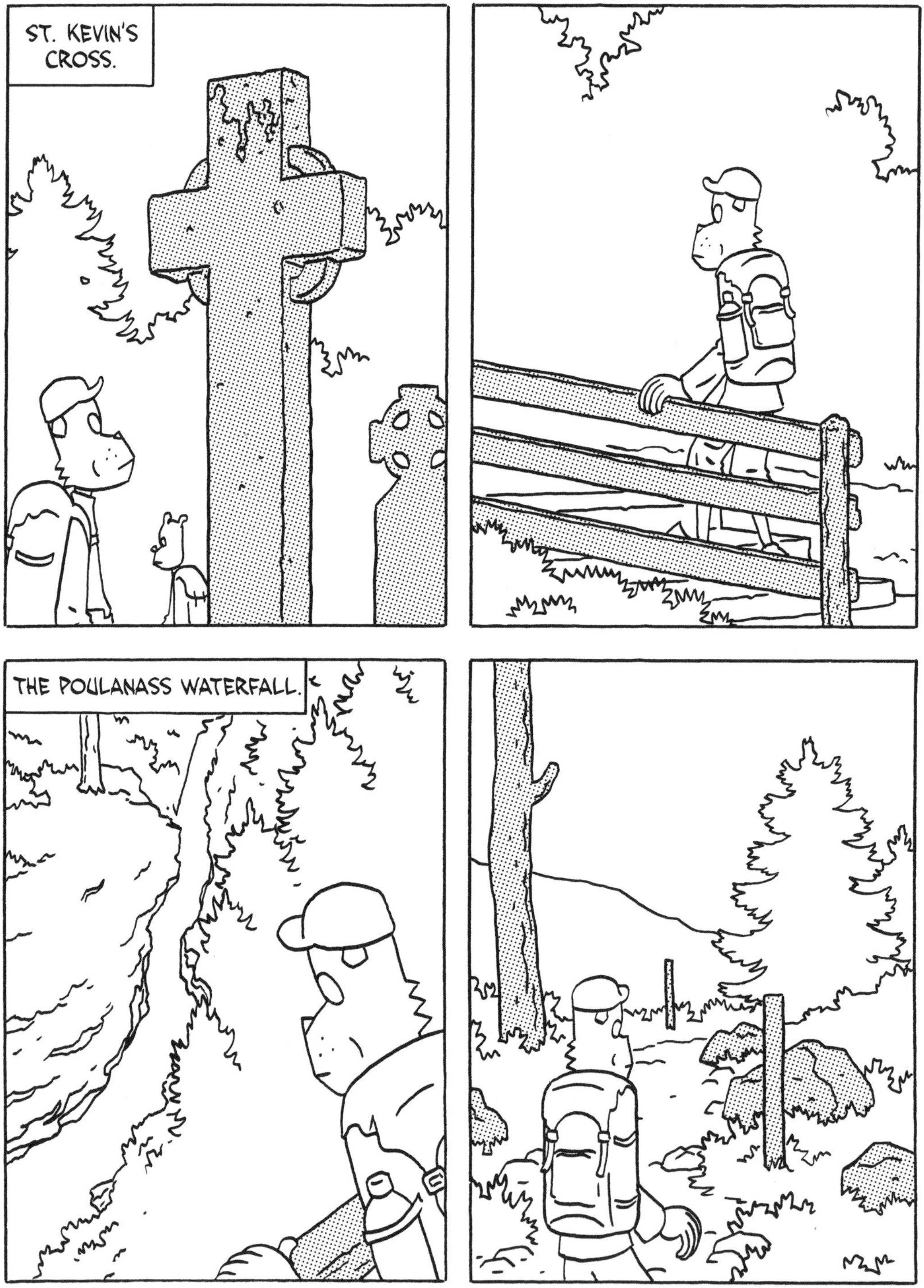
ST. KEVIN'S CROSS.
THE POULANASS WATERFALL.

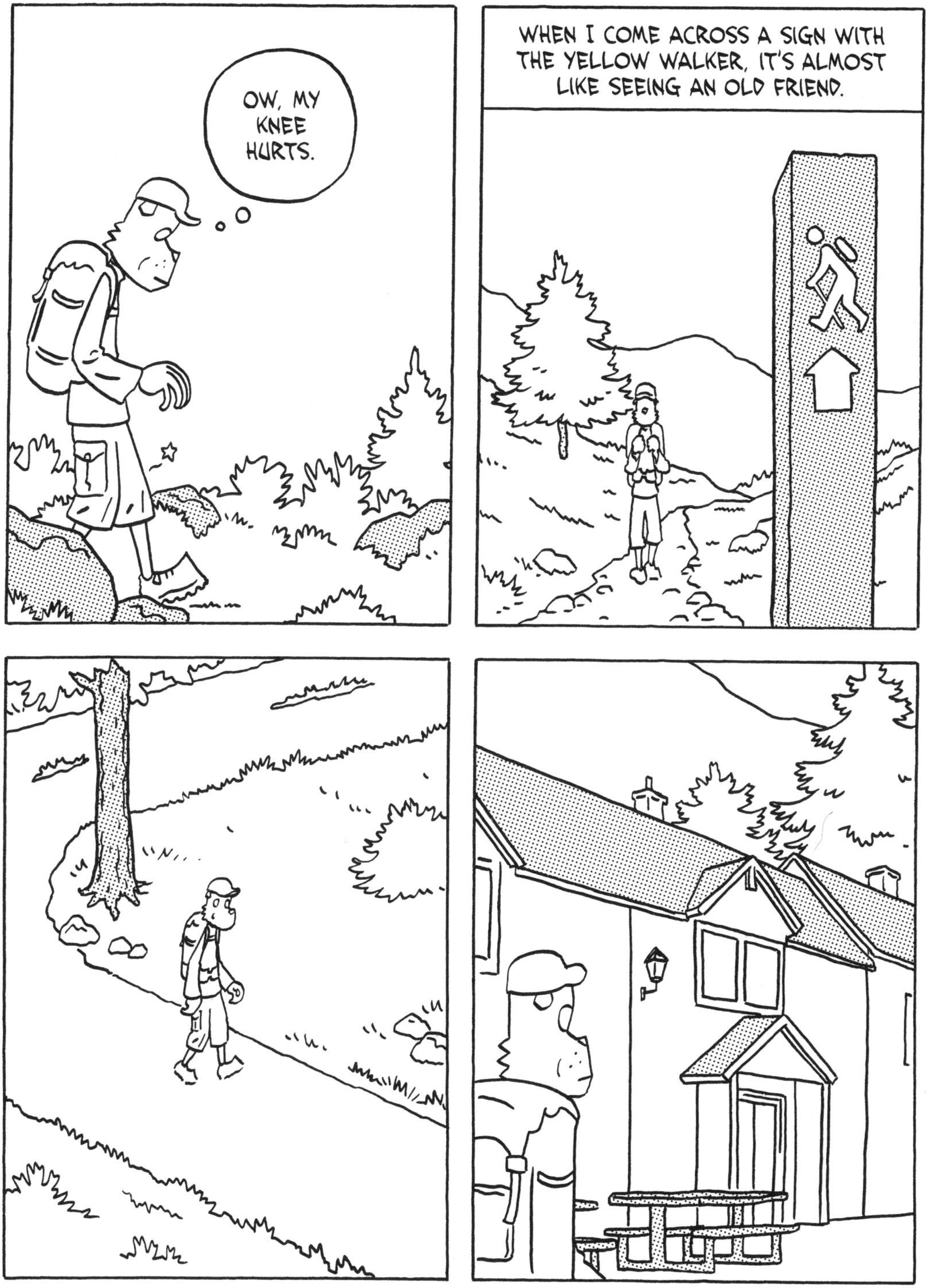
OW, MY KNEE HURTS.
WHEN I COME ACROSS A SIGN WITH THE YELLOW WALKER, IT'S ALMOST LIKE SEEING AN OLD FRIEND.

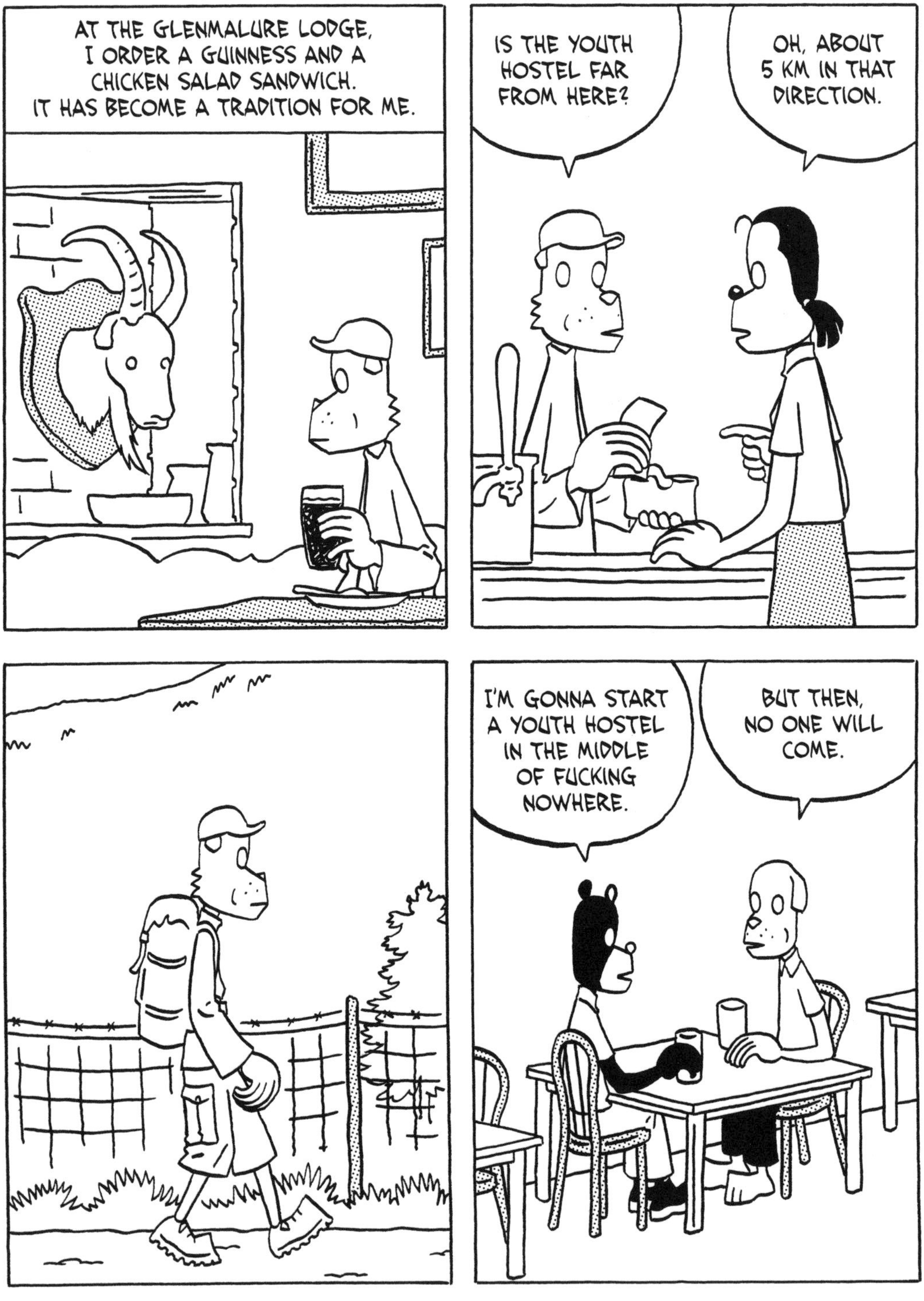
AT THE GLENMALURE LODGE, I ORDER A GUINNESS AND A CHICKEN SALAD SANDWICH. IT HAS BECOME A TRADITION FOR ME.
IS THE YOUTH HOSTEL FAR FROM HERE?
OH, ABOUT 5 KM IN THAT DIRECTION.
I'M GONNA START A YOUTH HOSTEL IN THE MIDDLE OF FUCKING NOWHERE.
BUT THEN, NO ONE WILL COME.

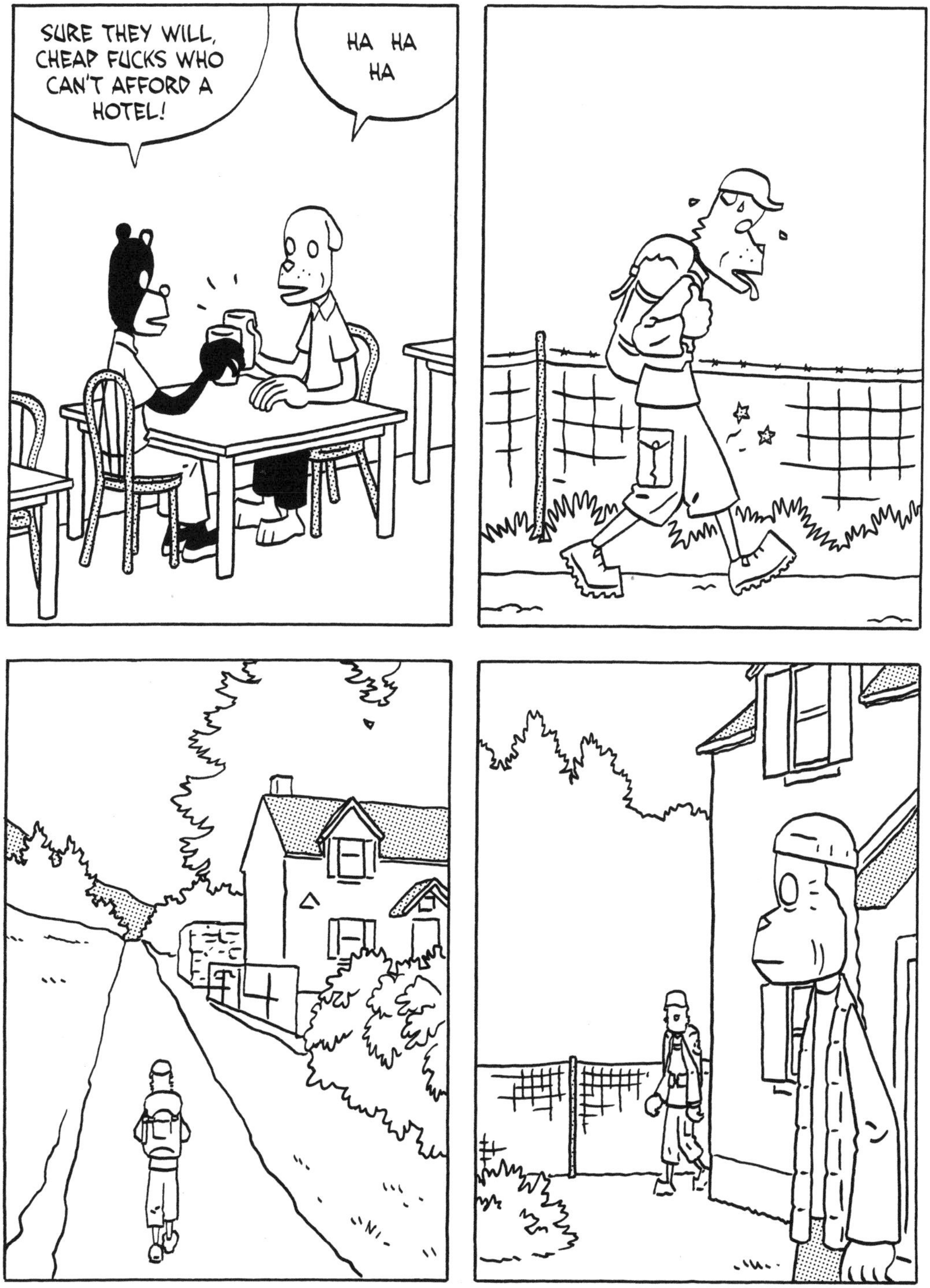
SURE THEY WILL, CHEAP FUCKS WHO CAN'T AFFORD A HOTEL!
HA HA HA

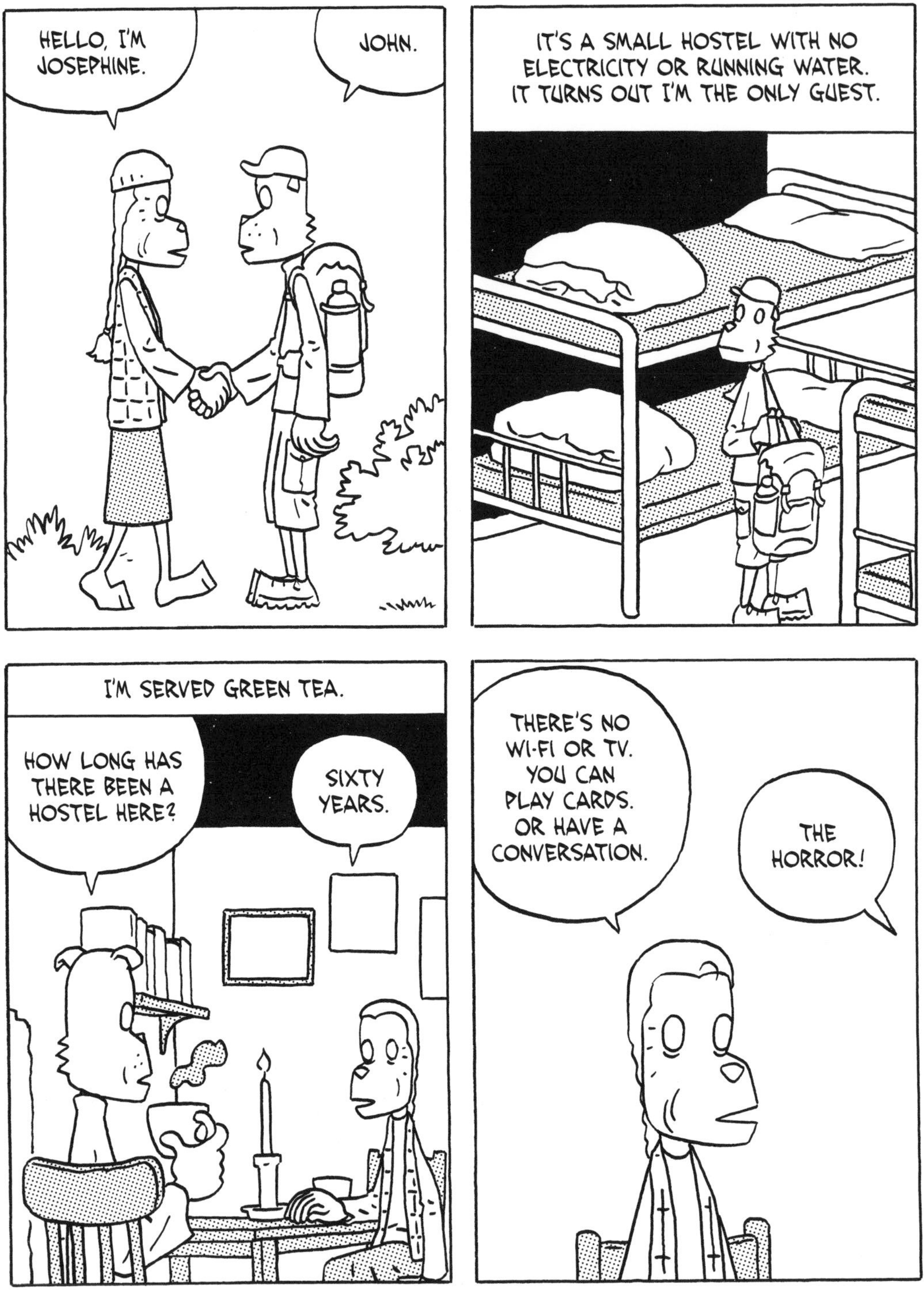
HELLO, I'M JOSEPHINE.
JOHN.
IT'S A SMALL HOSTEL WITH NO ELECTRICITY OR RUNNING WATER. IT TURNS OUT I'M THE ONLY GUEST.
I'M SERVED GREEN TEA.
HOW LONG HAS THERE BEEN A HOSTEL HERE?
SIXTY YEARS.
THERE'S NO WI-FI OR TV. YOU CAN PLAY CARDS. OR HAVE A CONVERSATION.
THE HORROR!

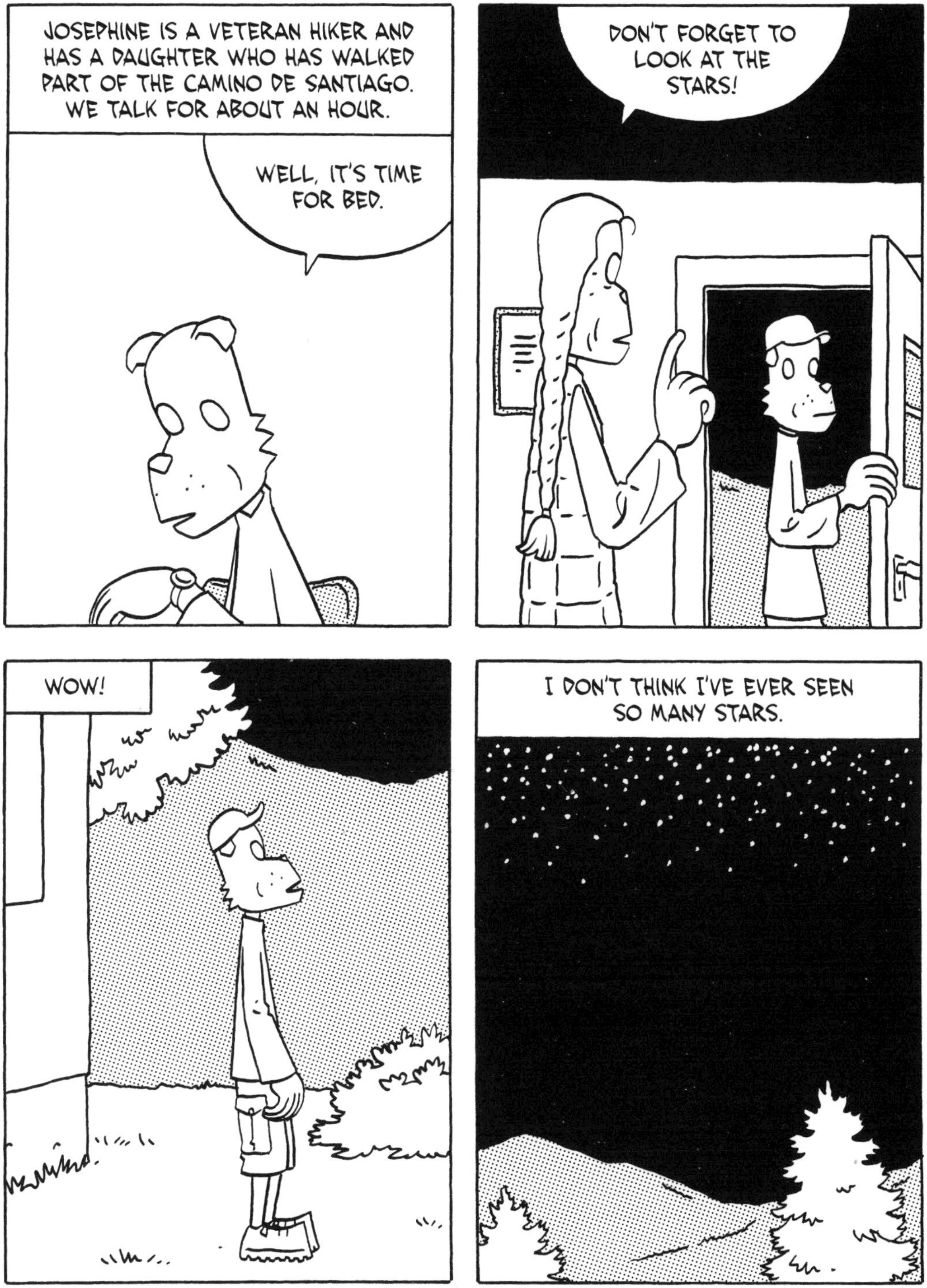
JOSEPHINE IS A VETERAN HIKER AND HAS A DAUGHTER WHO HAS WALKED PART OF THE CAMINO DE SANTIAGO. WE TALK FOR ABOUT AN HOUR.
WELL, IT'S TIME FOR BED.
DON'T FORGET TO LOOK AT THE STARS!
WOW!
I DON'T THINK I'VE EVER SEEN SO MANY STARS.

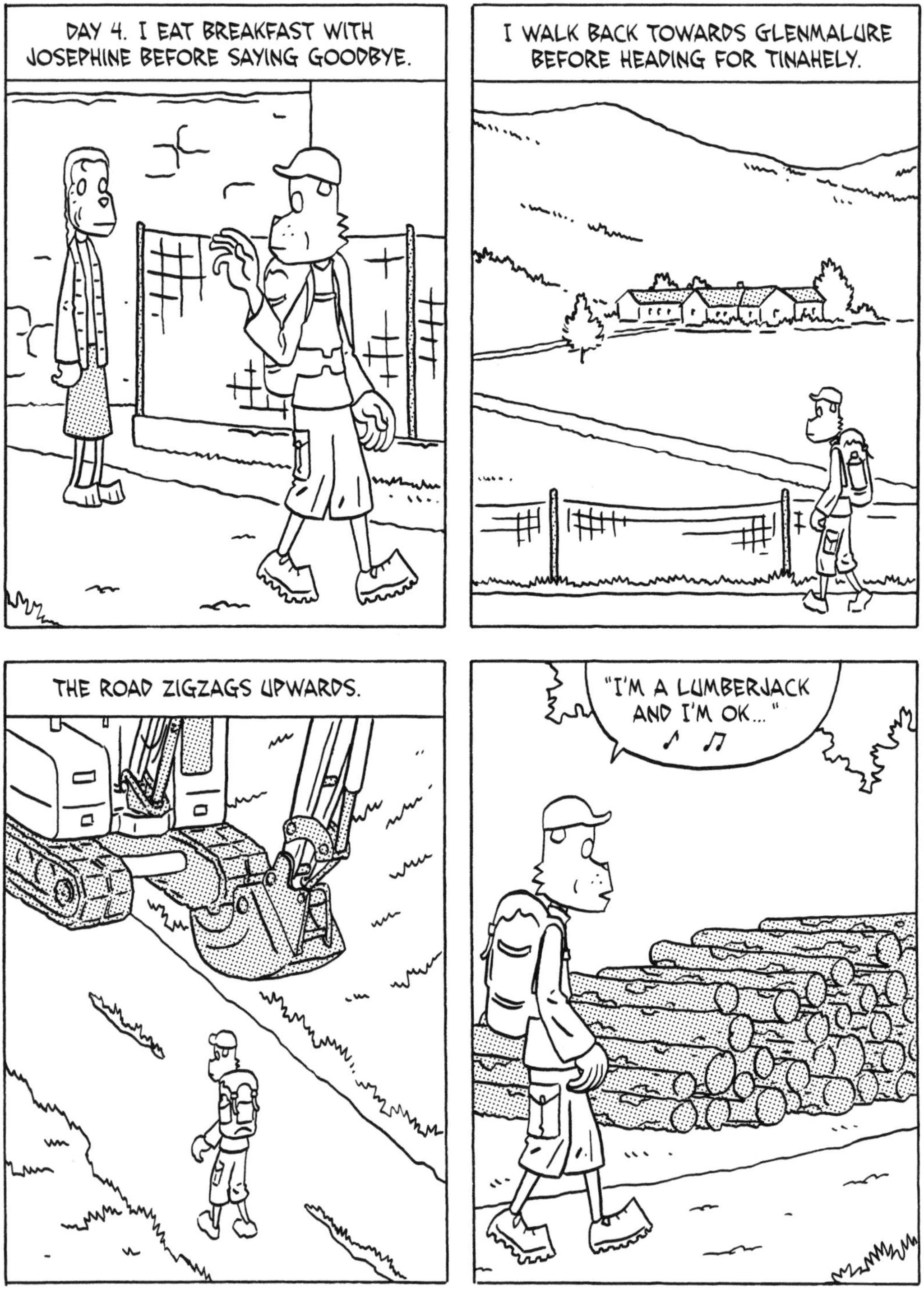
DAY 4. I EAT BREAKFAST WITH JOSEPHINE BEFORE SAYING GOODBYE.
I WALK BACK TOWARDS GLENMALURE BEFORE HEADING FOR TINAHELY.
THE ROAD ZIGZAGS UPWARDS.
"I'M A LUMBERJACK AND I'M OK..."

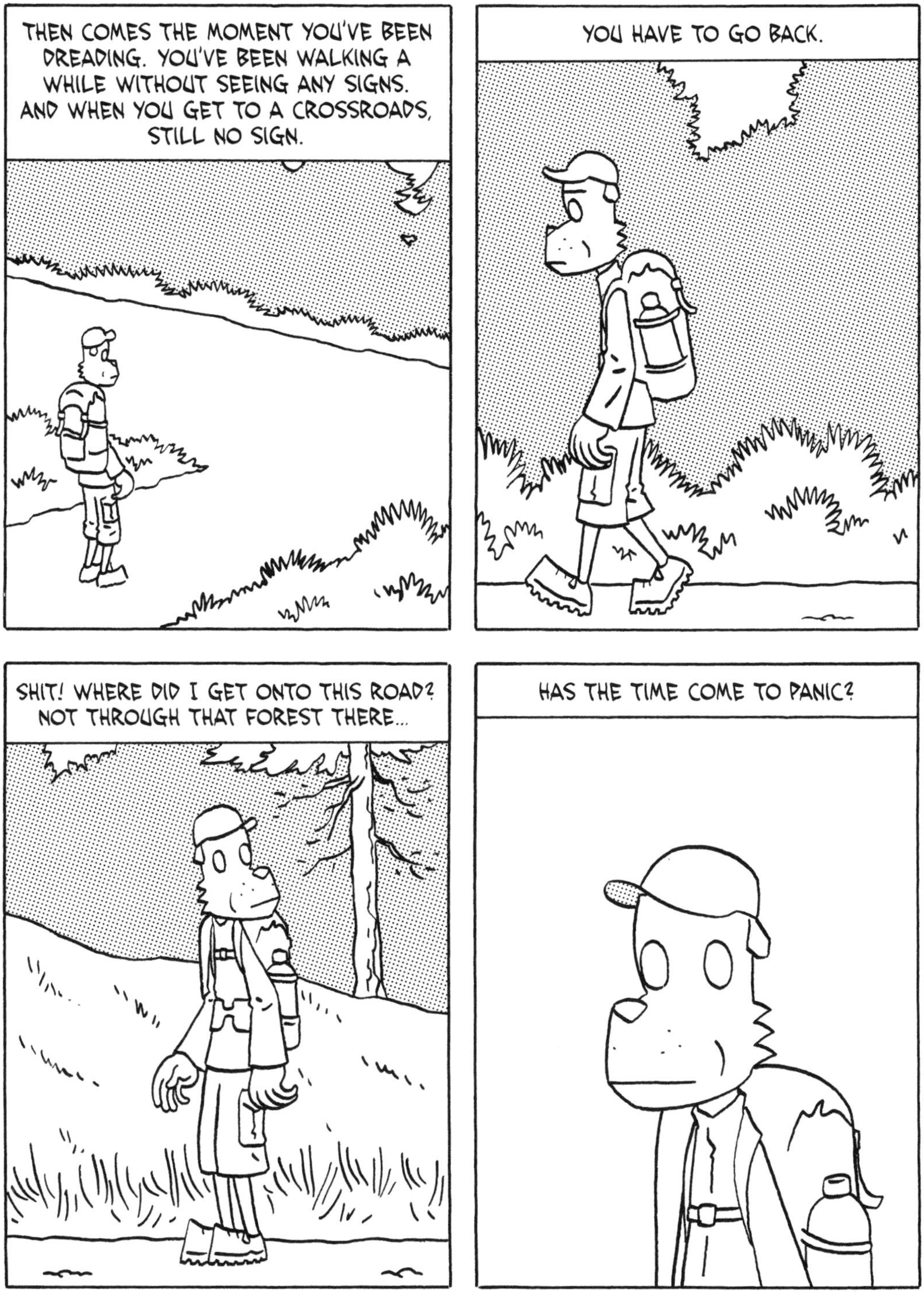
THEN COMES THE MOMENT YOU'VE BEEN DREADING. YOU'VE BEEN WALKING A WHILE WITHOUT SEEING ANY SIGNS. AND WHEN YOU GET TO A CROSSROADS, STILL NO SIGN.
YOU HAVE TO GO BACK.
SHIT! WHERE DID I GET ONTO THIS ROAD? NOT THROUGH THAT FOREST THERE...
HAS THE TIME COME TO PANIC?

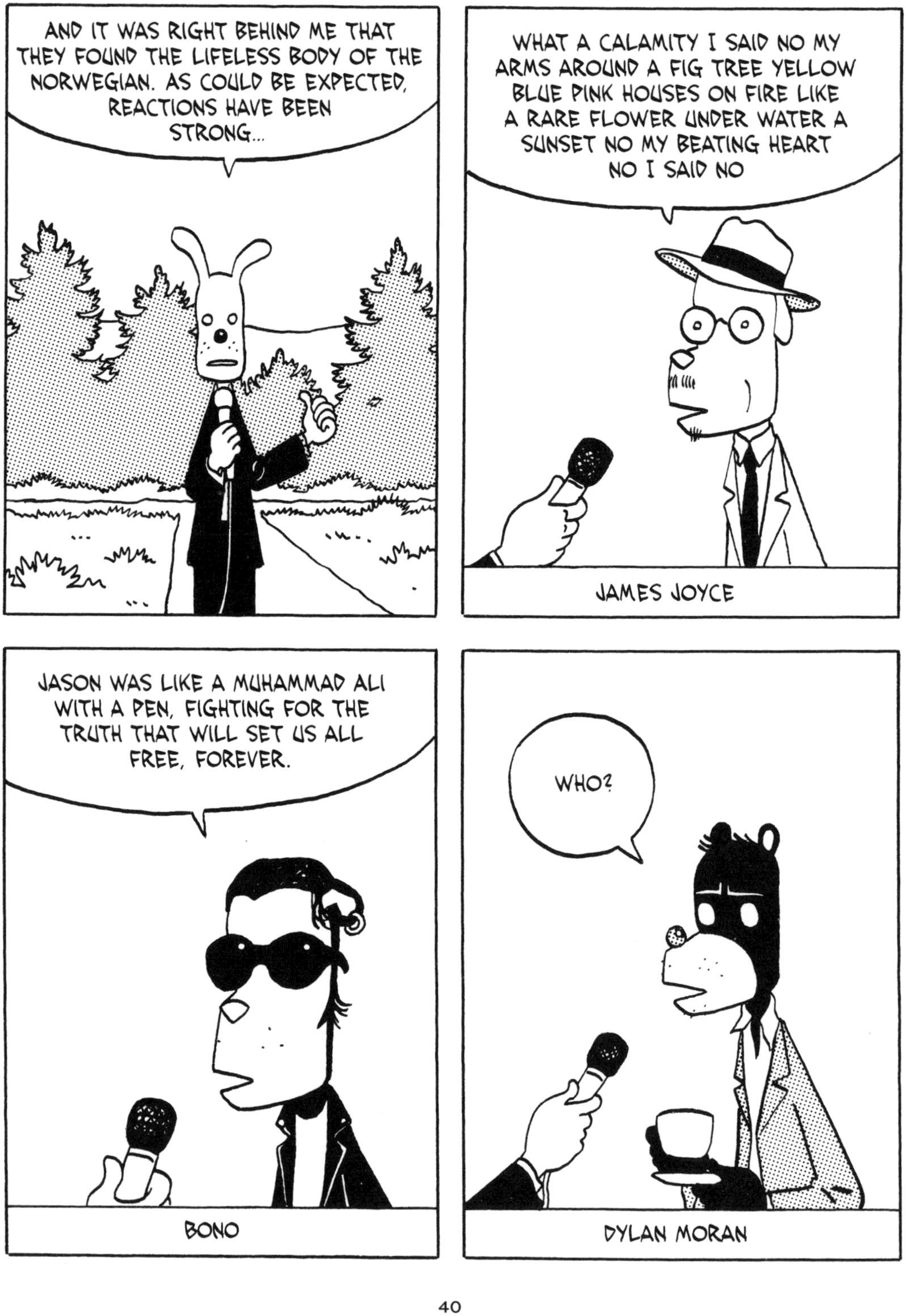
AND IT WAS RIGHT BEHIND ME THAT THEY FOUND THE LIFELESS BODY OF THE NORWEGIAN. AS COULD BE EXPECTED, REACTIONS HAVE BEEN STRONG...
WHAT A CALAMITY I SAID NO MY ARMS AROUND A FIG TREE YELLOW BLUE PINK HOUSES ON FIRE LIKE A RARE FLOWER UNDER WATER A SUNSET NO MY BEATING HEART NO I SAID NO
JAMES JOYCE
JASON WAS LIKE A MUHAMMAD ALI WITH A PEN, FIGHTING FOR THE TRUTH THAT WILL SET US ALL FREE, FOREVER.
BONO
WHO?
DYLAN MORAN

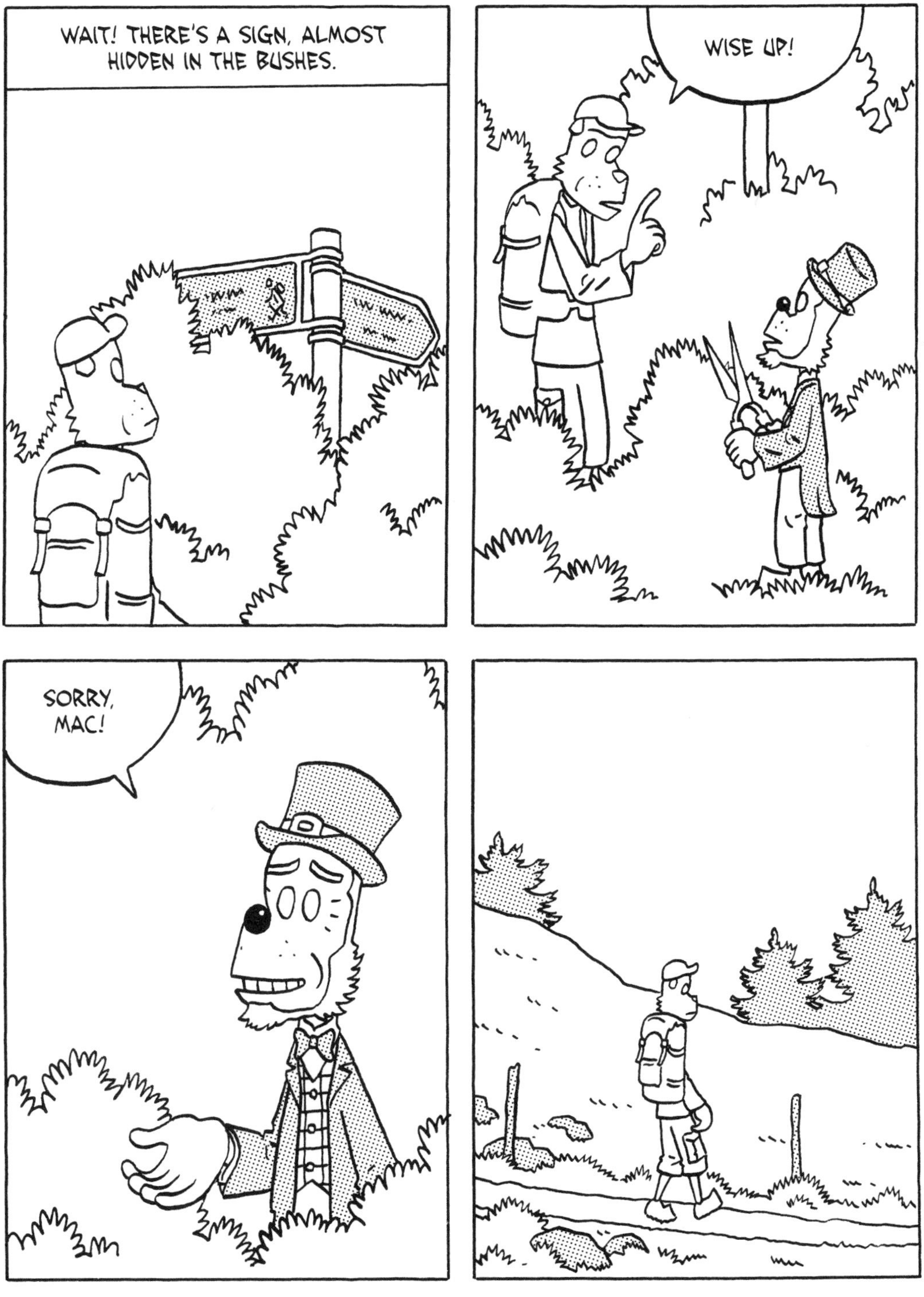
WAIT! THERE'S A SIGN, ALMOST HIDDEN IN THE BUSHES.
WISE UP!
SORRY, MAC!

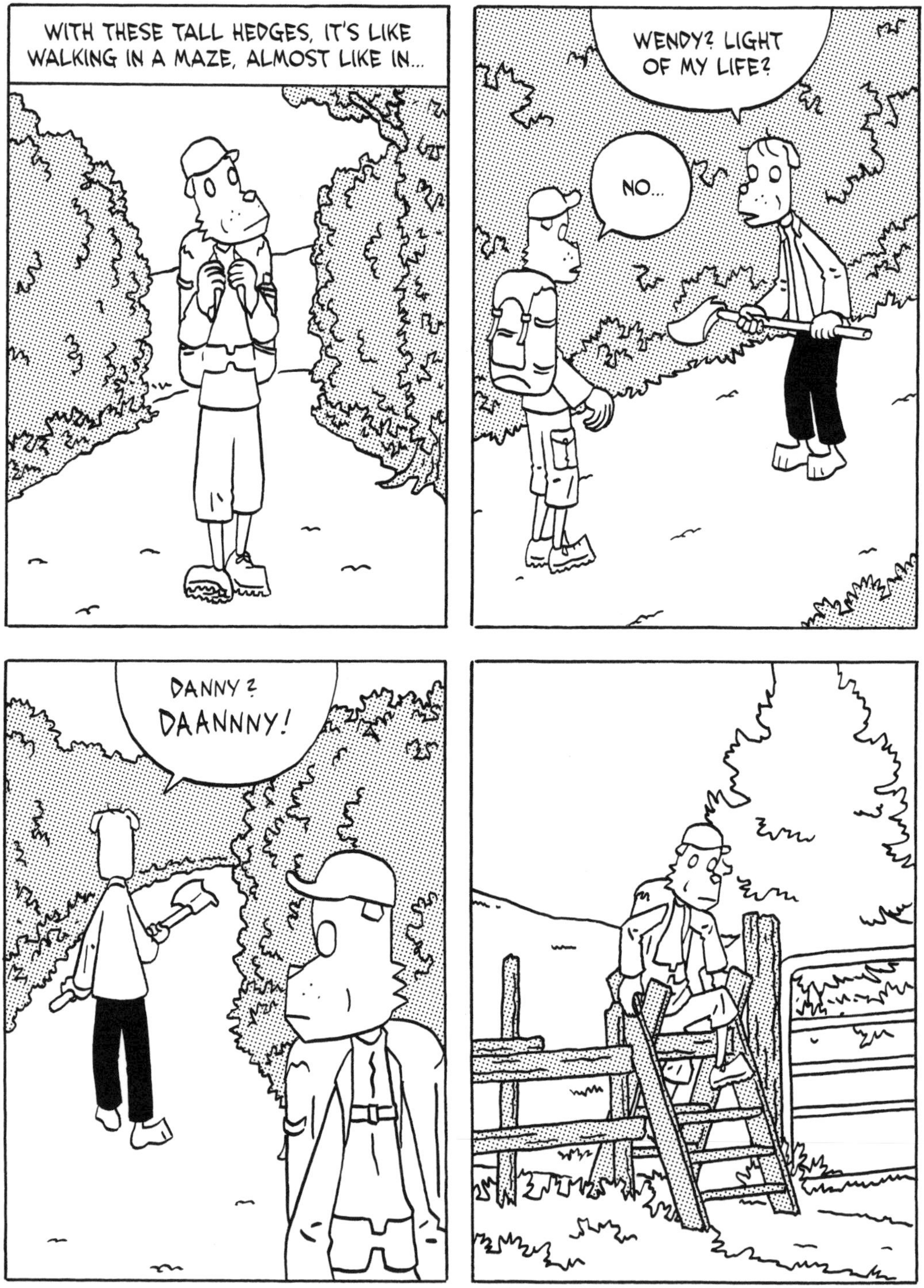
WITH THESE TALL HEDGES, IT'S LIKE WALKING IN A MAZE, ALMOST LIKE IN...
WENDY? LIGHT OF MY LIFE?
NO...
DANNY? DAANNNY!

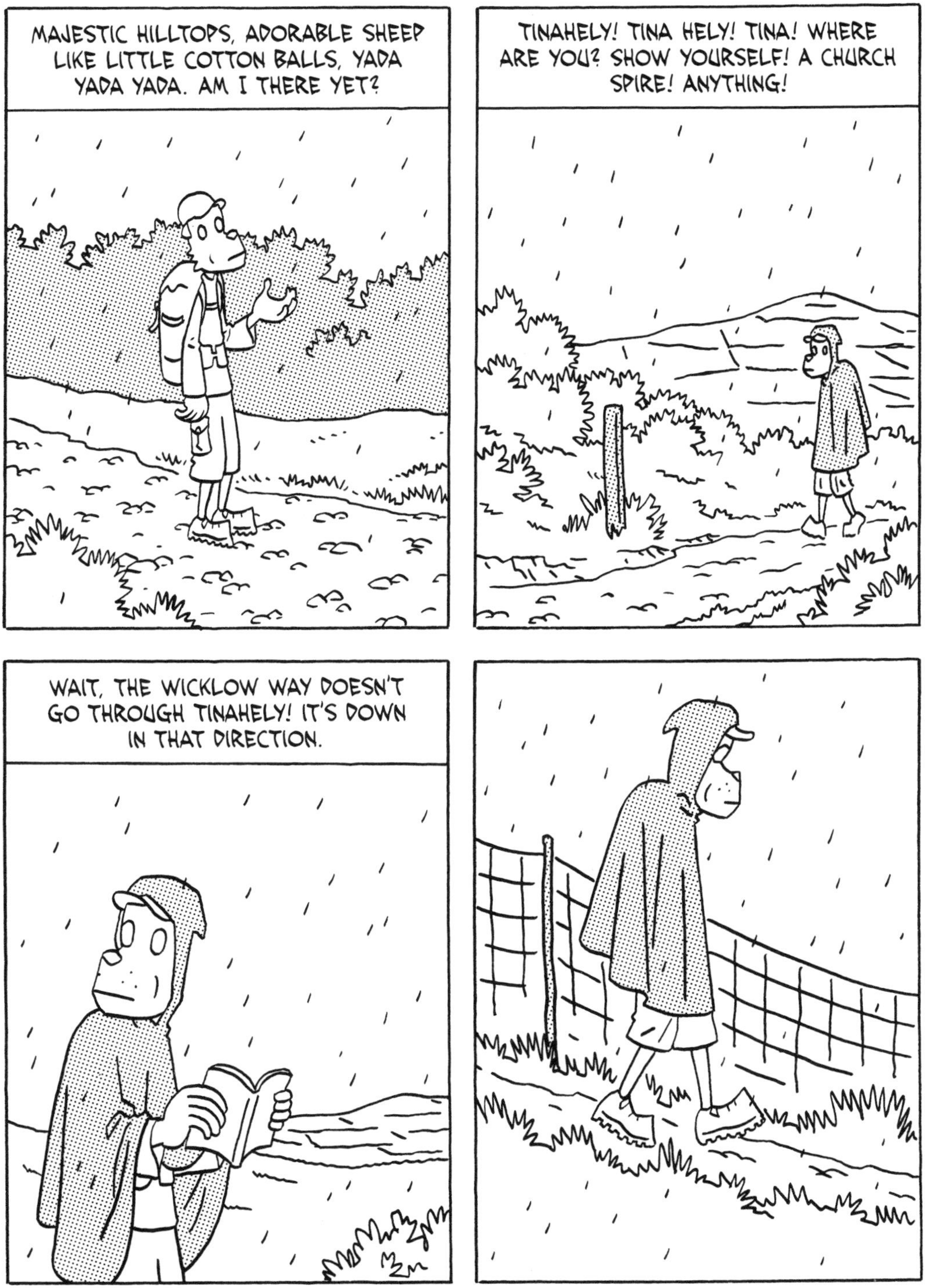
MAJESTIC HILLTOPS, ADORABLE SHEEP LIKE LITTLE COTTON BALLS, YADA YADA YADA. AM I THERE YET?
TINAHELY! TINA HELY! TINA! WHERE ARE YOU? SHOW YOURSELF! A CHURCH SPIRE! ANYTHING!
WAIT, THE WICKLOW WAY DOESN'T GO THROUGH TINAHELY! IT'S DOWN IN THAT DIRECTION.

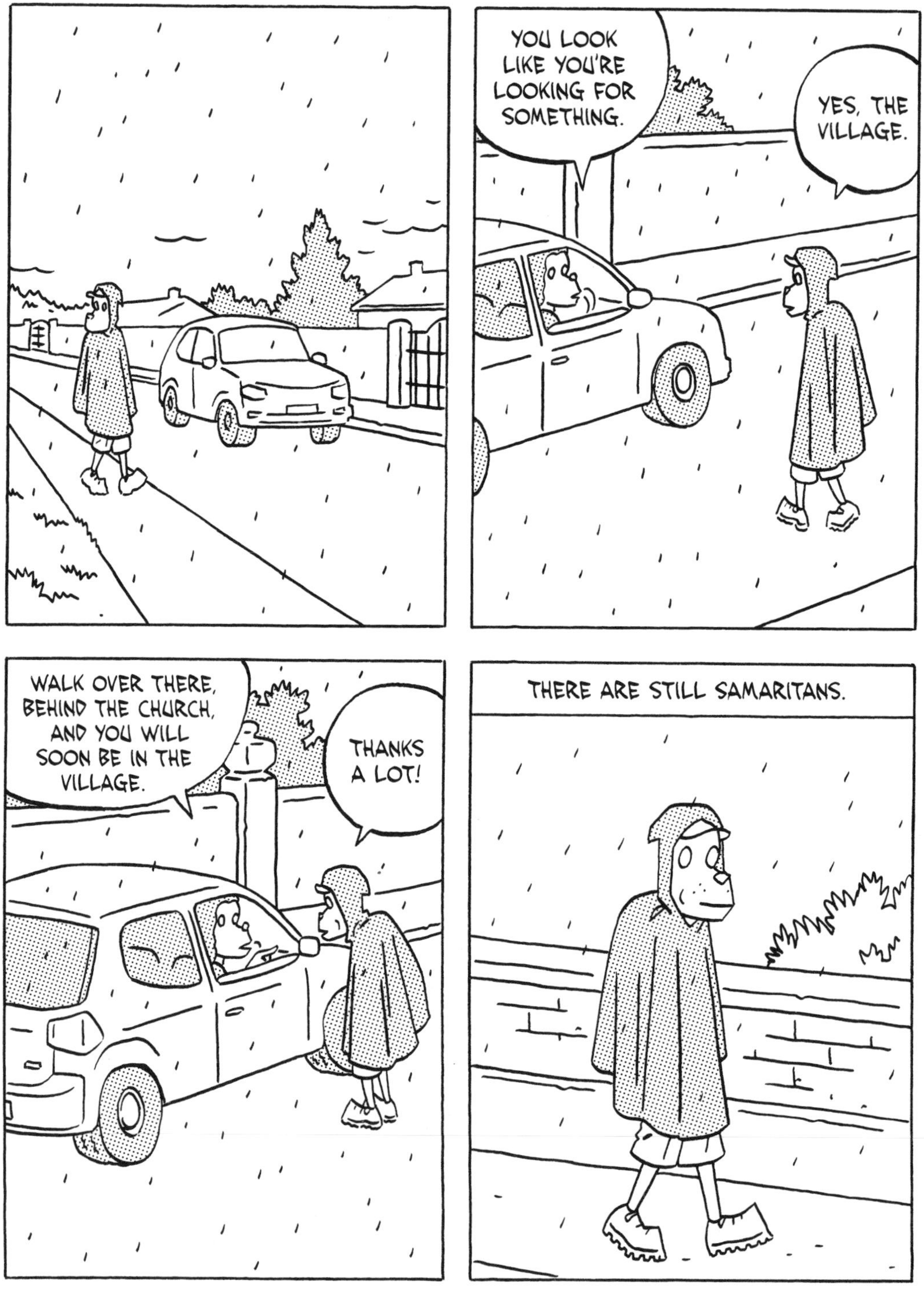
YOU LOOK LIKE YOU'RE LOOKING FOR SOMETHING.
YES, THE VILLAGE.
WALK OVER THERE, BEHIND THE CHURCH, AND YOU WILL SOON BE IN THE VILLAGE.
THANKS A LOT!
THERE ARE STILL SAMARITANS.

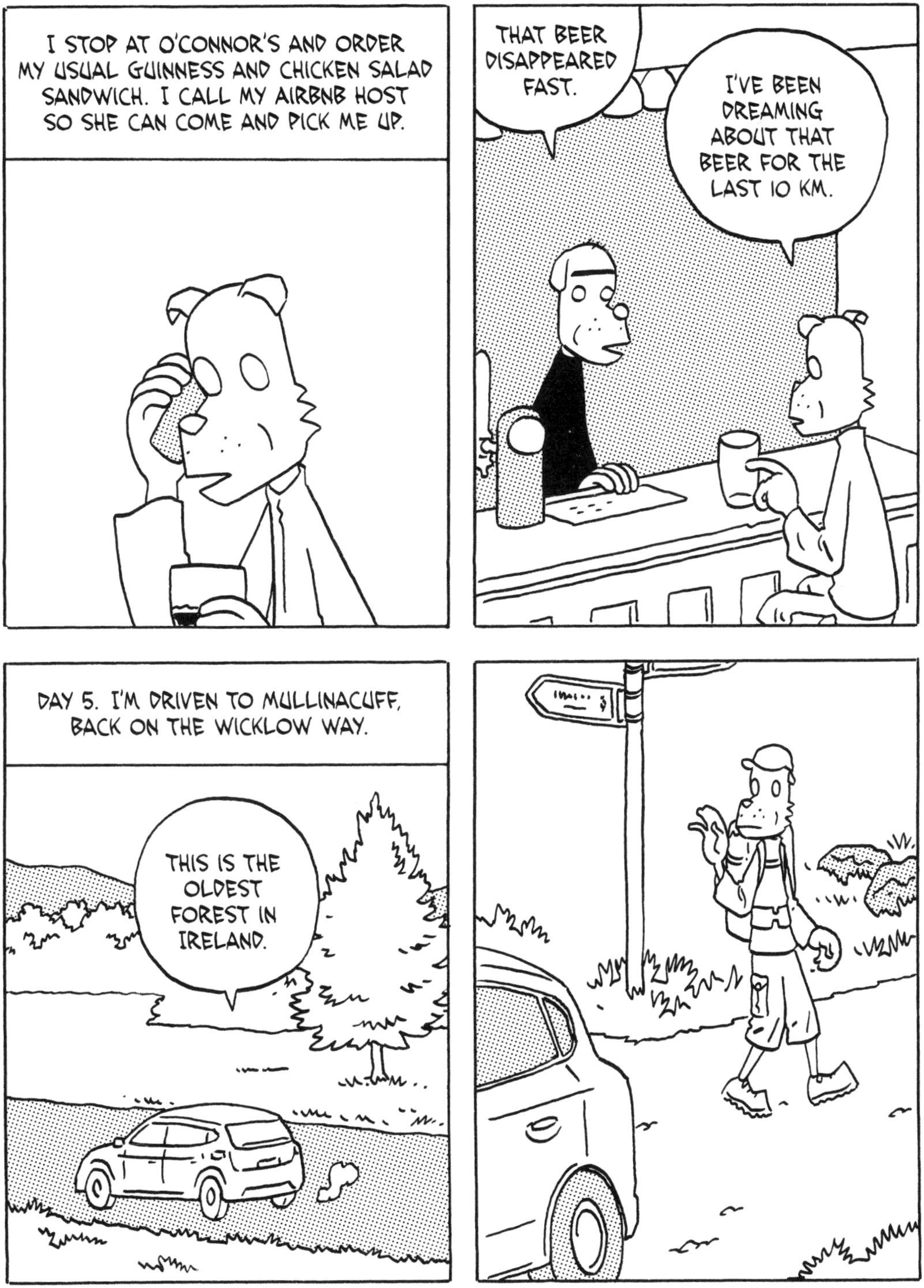
I STOP AT O'CONNOR'S AND ORDER MY USUAL GUINNESS AND CHICKEN SALAD SANDWICH. I CALL MY AIRBNB HOST SO SHE CAN COME AND PICK ME UP.
THAT BEER DISAPPEARED FAST.
I'VE BEEN DREAMING ABOUT THAT BEER FOR THE LAST 10 KM.
DAY 5. I'M DRIVEN TO MULLINACUFF, BACK ON THE WICKLOW WAY.
THIS IS THE OLDEST FOREST IN IRELAND.

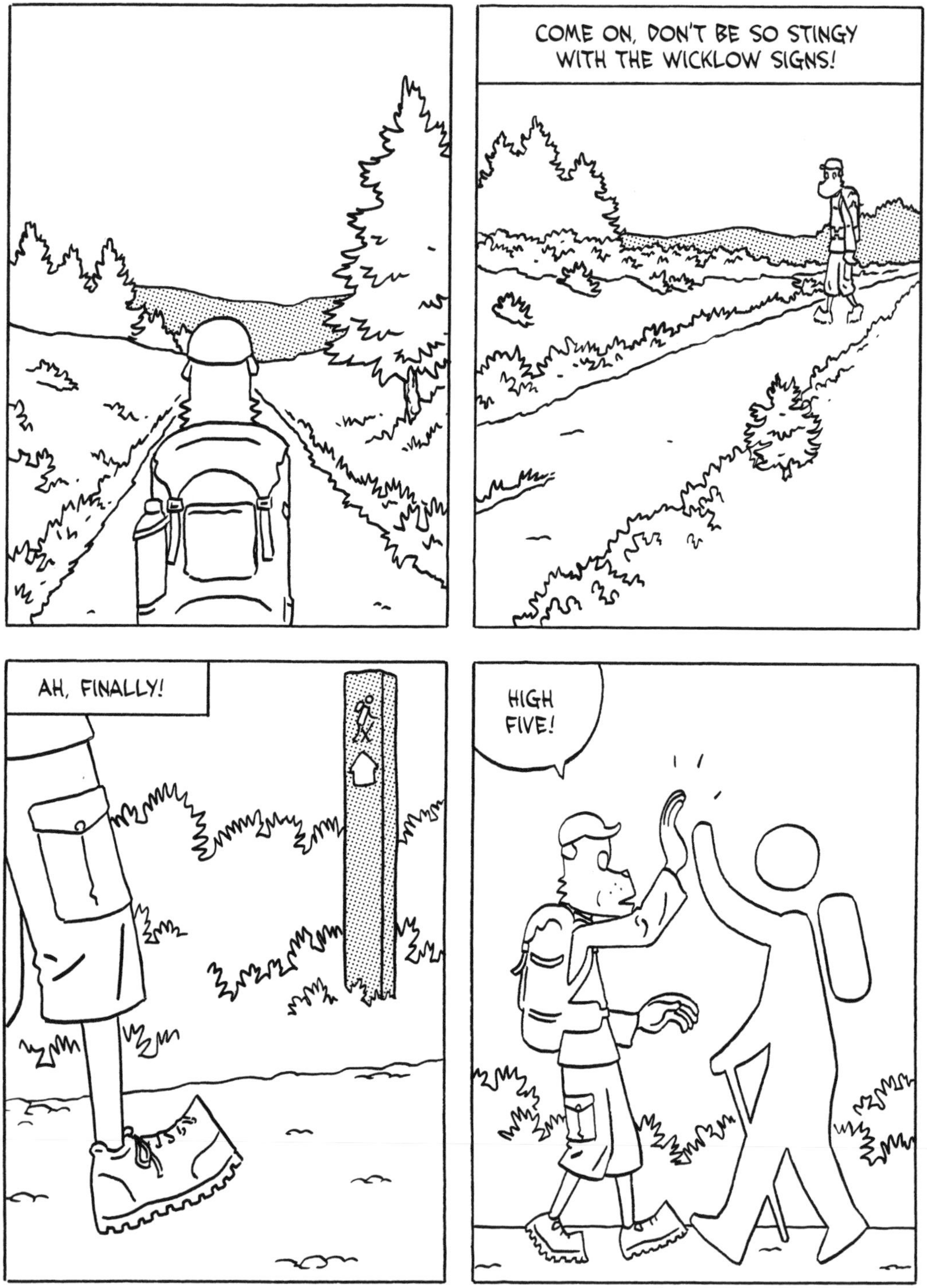
COME ON, DON'T BE SO STINGY WITH THE WICKLOW SIGNS!
AH, FINALLY!
HIGH FIVE!

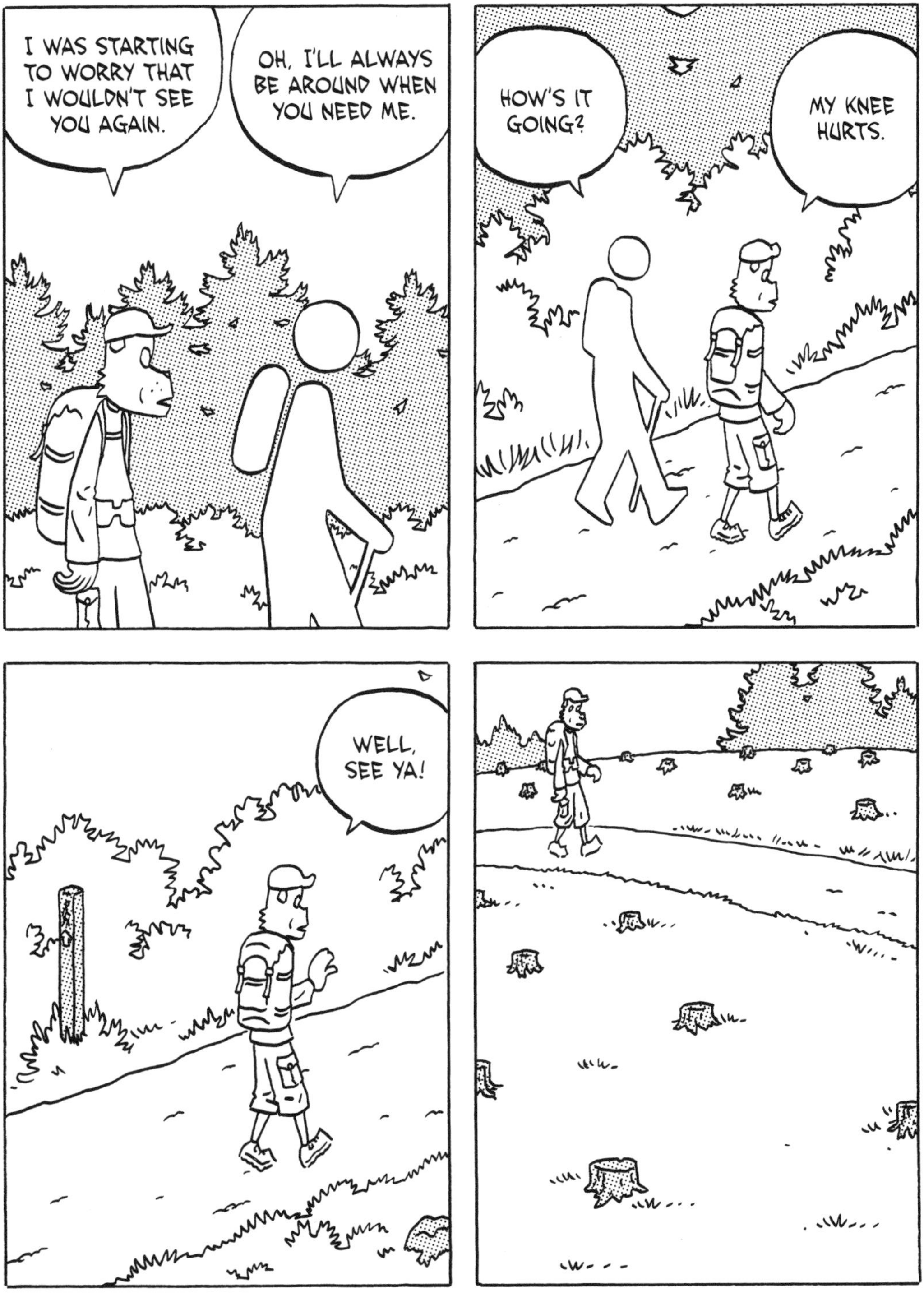
I WAS STARTING TO WORRY THAT I WOULDN'T SEE YOU AGAIN.
OH, I'LL ALWAYS BE AROUND WHEN YOU NEED ME.
HOW'S IT GOING?
MY KNEE HURTS.
WELL, SEE YA!

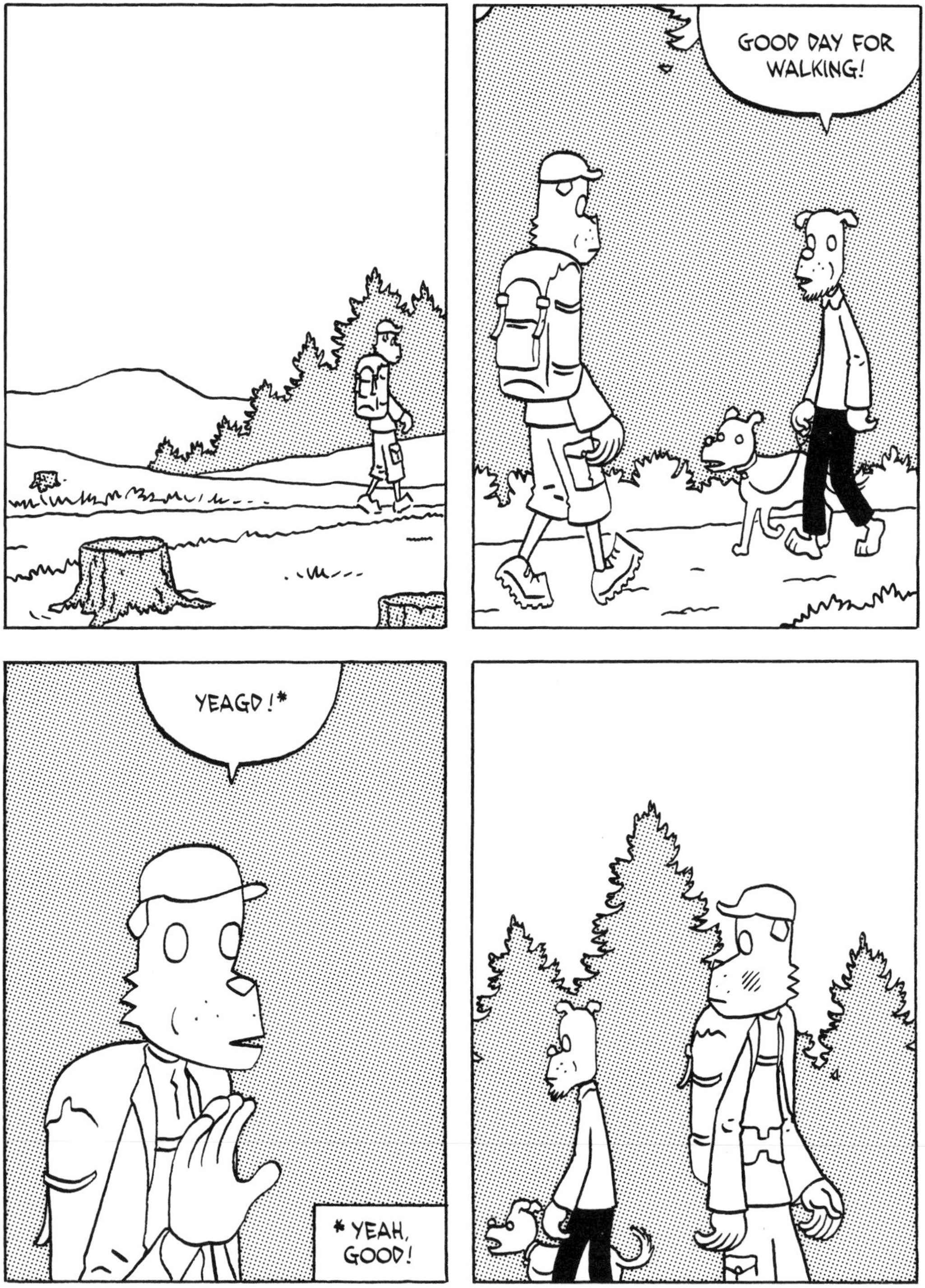
GOOD DAY FOR WALKING!
YEAGD!*
* YEAH, GOOD!

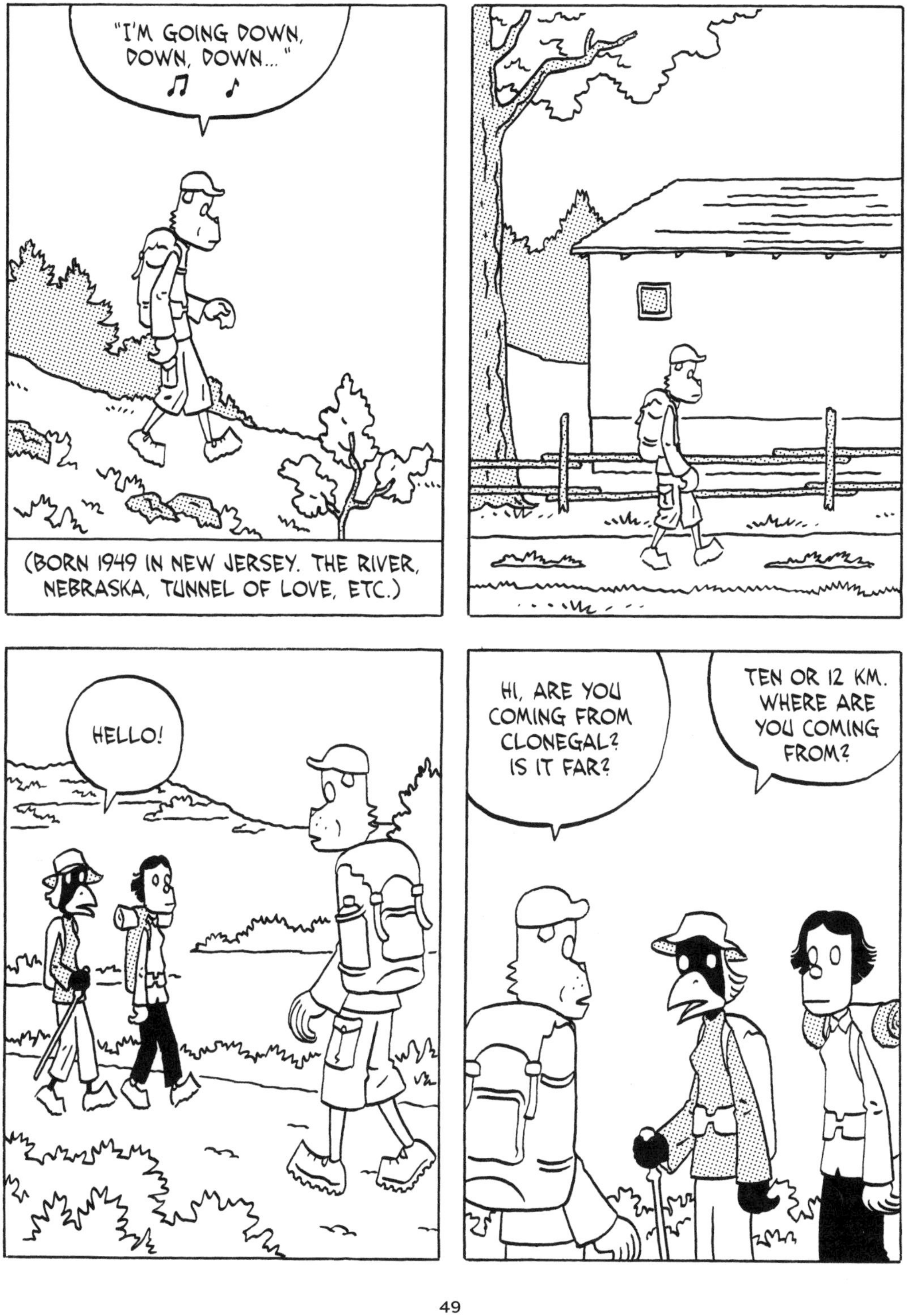
"I'M GOING DOWN, DOWN, DOWN..." ♫ ♪
(BORN 1949 IN NEW JERSEY. THE RIVER, NEBRASKA, TUNNEL OF LOVE, ETC.)
HELLO!
HI, ARE YOU COMING FROM CLONEGAL? IS IT FAR?
TEN OR 12 KM. WHERE ARE YOU COMING FROM?

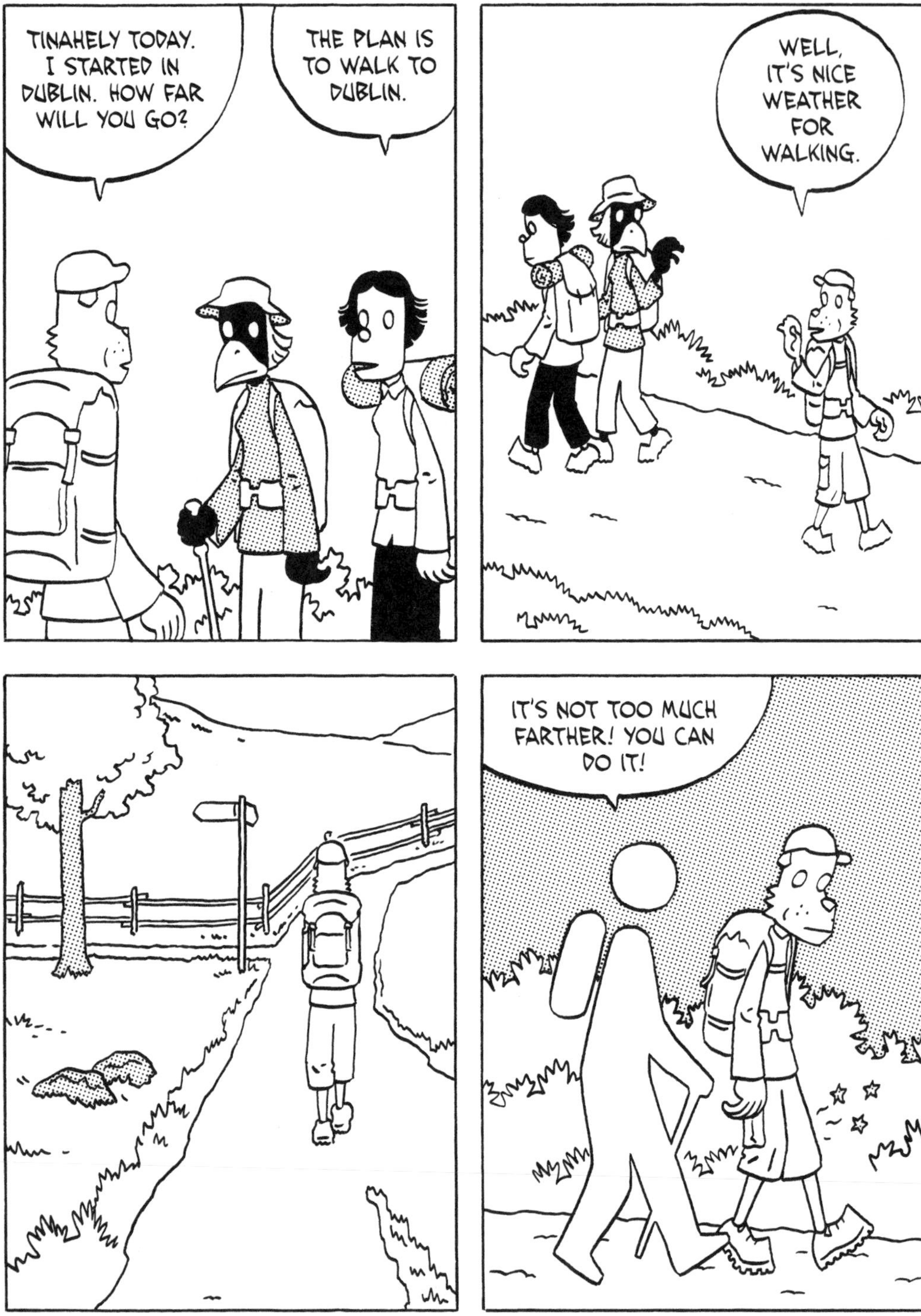
TINAHELY TODAY. I STARTED IN DUBLIN. HOW FAR WILL YOU GO?
THE PLAN IS TO WALK TO DUBLIN.
WELL, IT'S NICE WEATHER FOR WALKING.
IT'S NOT TOO MUCH FARTHER! YOU CAN DO IT!

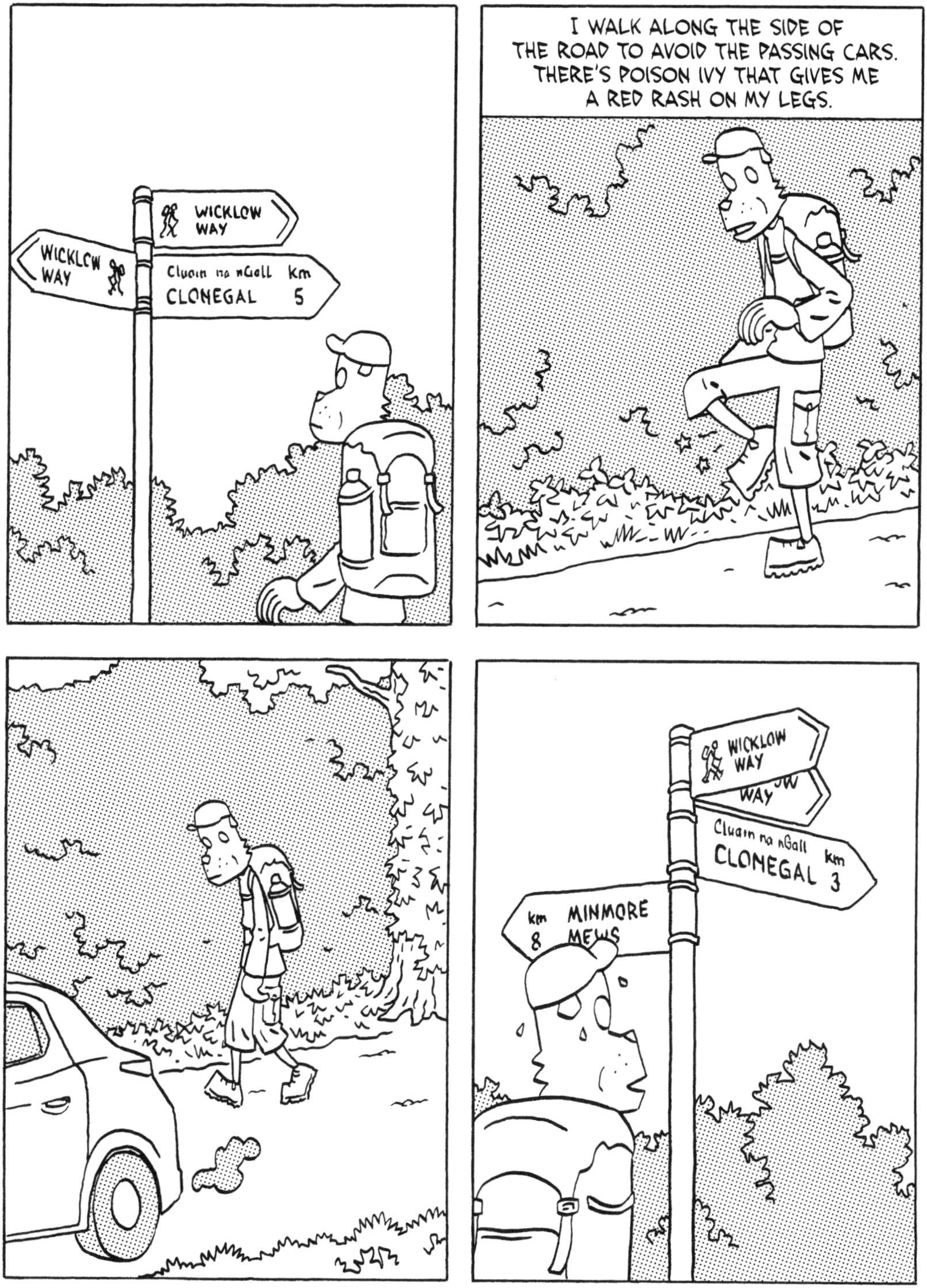
WICKLOW WAY
WICKLOW WAY
Cluain na nGall km
CLONEGAL 5
I WALK ALONG THE SIDE OF THE ROAD TO AVOID THE PASSING CARS. THERE'S POISON IVY THAT GIVES ME A RED RASH ON MY LEGS.
WICKLOW WAY
WAY
Cluain na nGall km
CLONEGAL 3
km 8 MINMORE MEWS

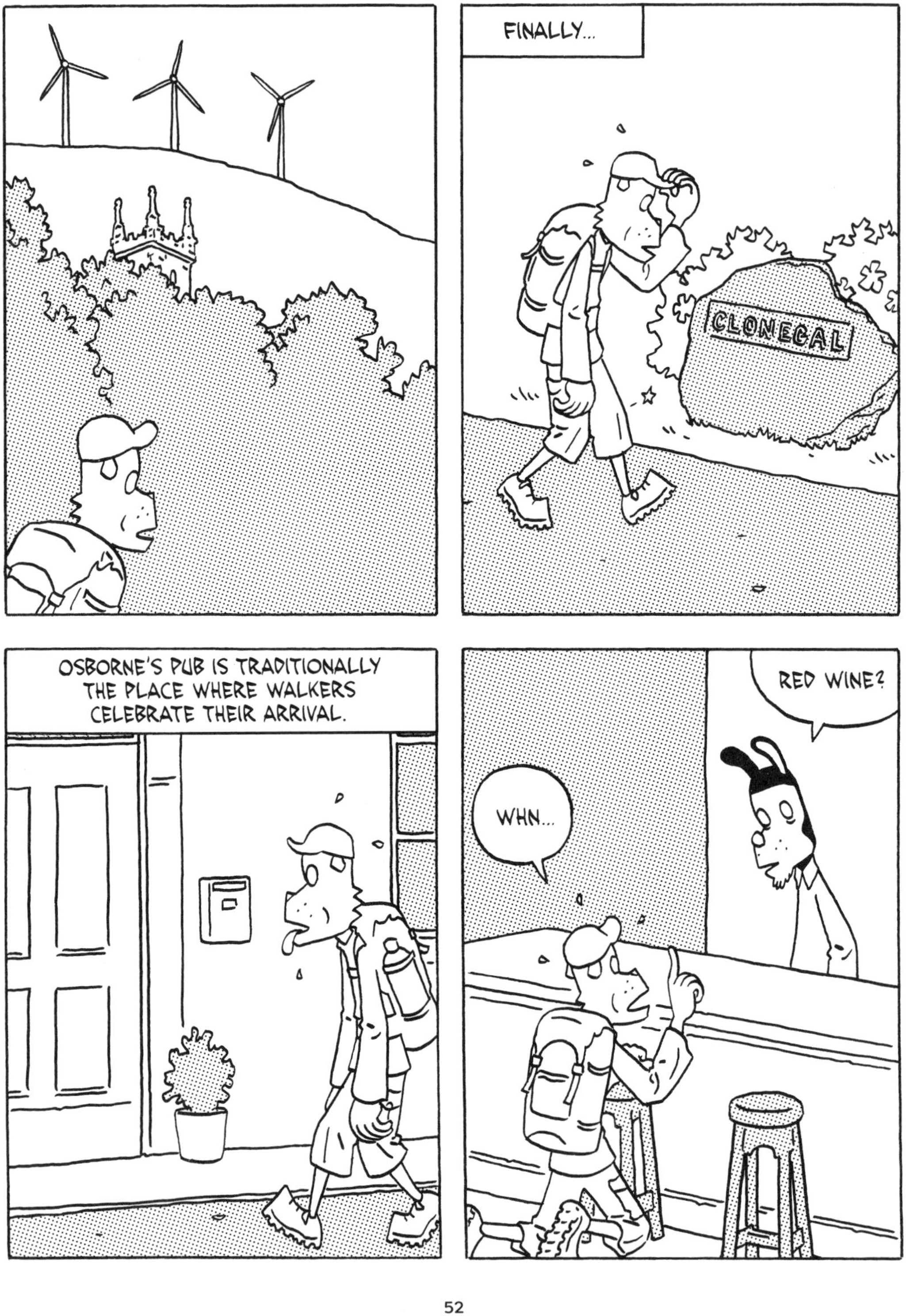
FINALLY...
CLONEGAL
OSBORNE'S PUB IS TRADITIONALLY THE PLACE WHERE WALKERS CELEBRATE THEIR ARRIVAL.
RED WINE?
WHN...

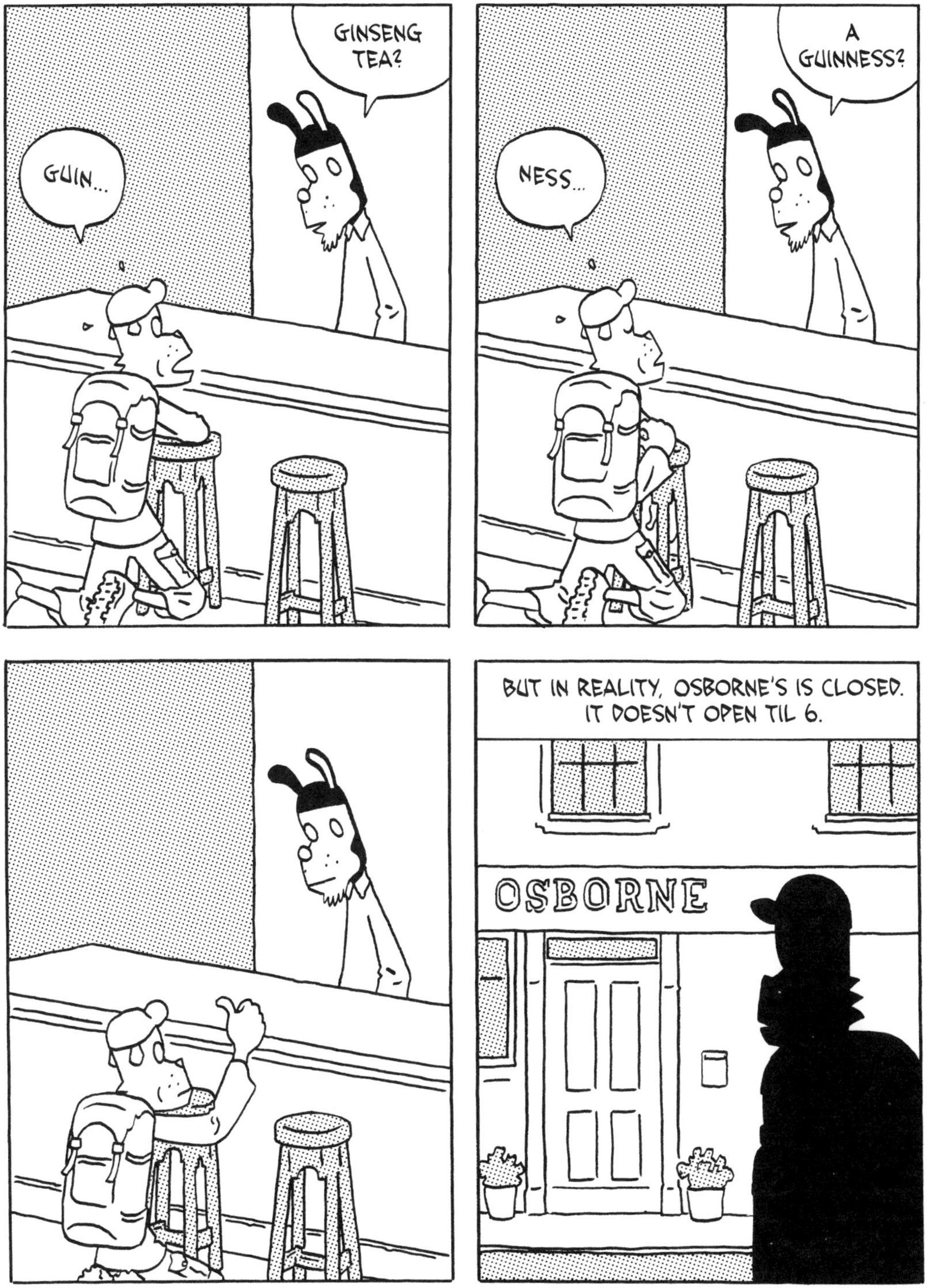
GINSENG TEA?
GUIN...
A GUINNESS?
NESS...
BUT IN REALITY, OSBORNE'S IS CLOSED. IT DOESN'T OPEN TIL 6.
OSBORNE

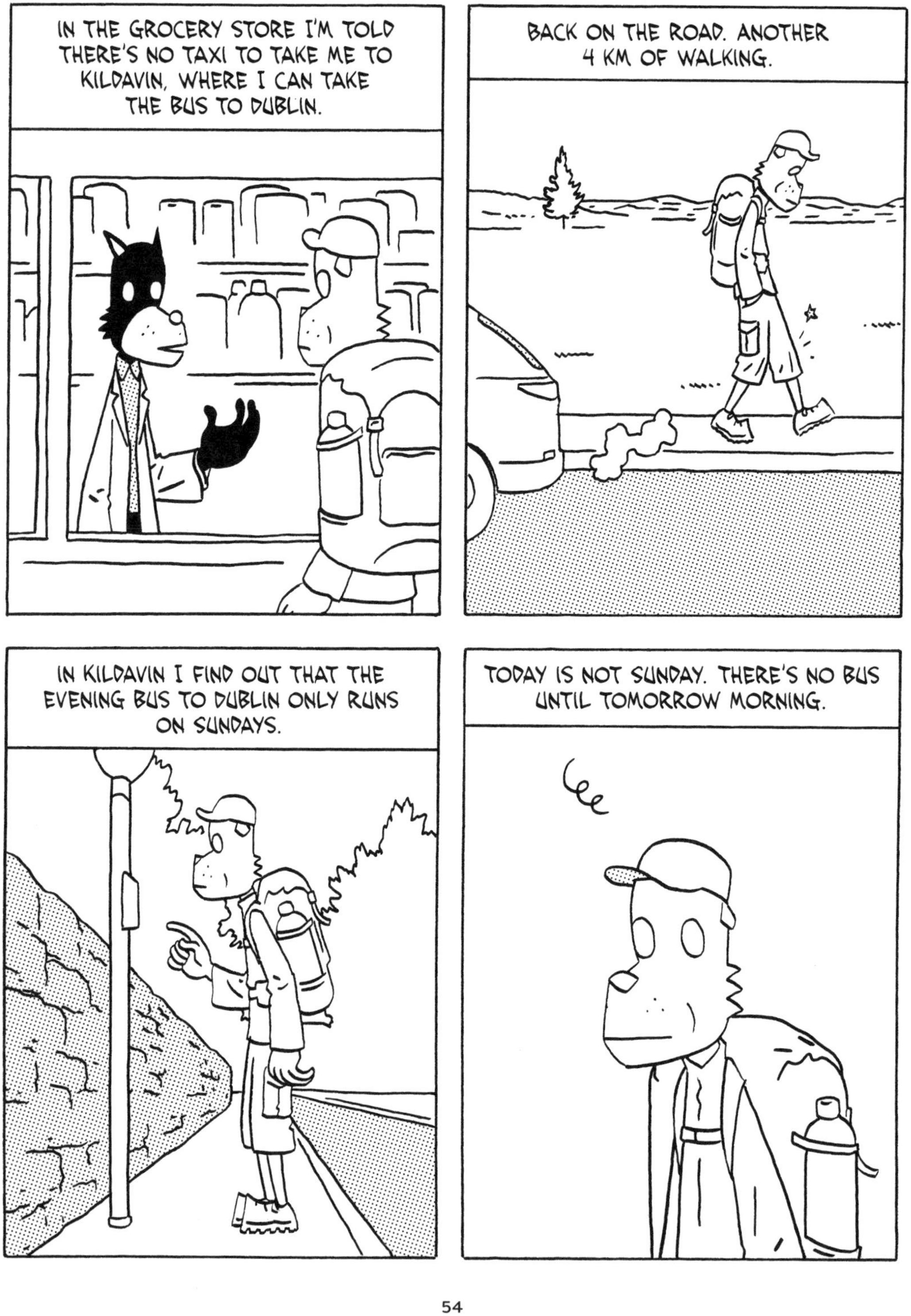
IN THE GROCERY STORE I'M TOLD THERE'S NO TAXI TO TAKE ME TO KILDAVIN, WHERE I CAN TAKE THE BUS TO DUBLIN.
BACK ON THE ROAD. ANOTHER 4 KM OF WALKING.
IN KILDAVIN I FIND OUT THAT THE EVENING BUS TO DUBLIN ONLY RUNS ON SUNDAYS.
TODAY IS NOT SUNDAY. THERE'S NO BUS UNTIL TOMORROW MORNING.

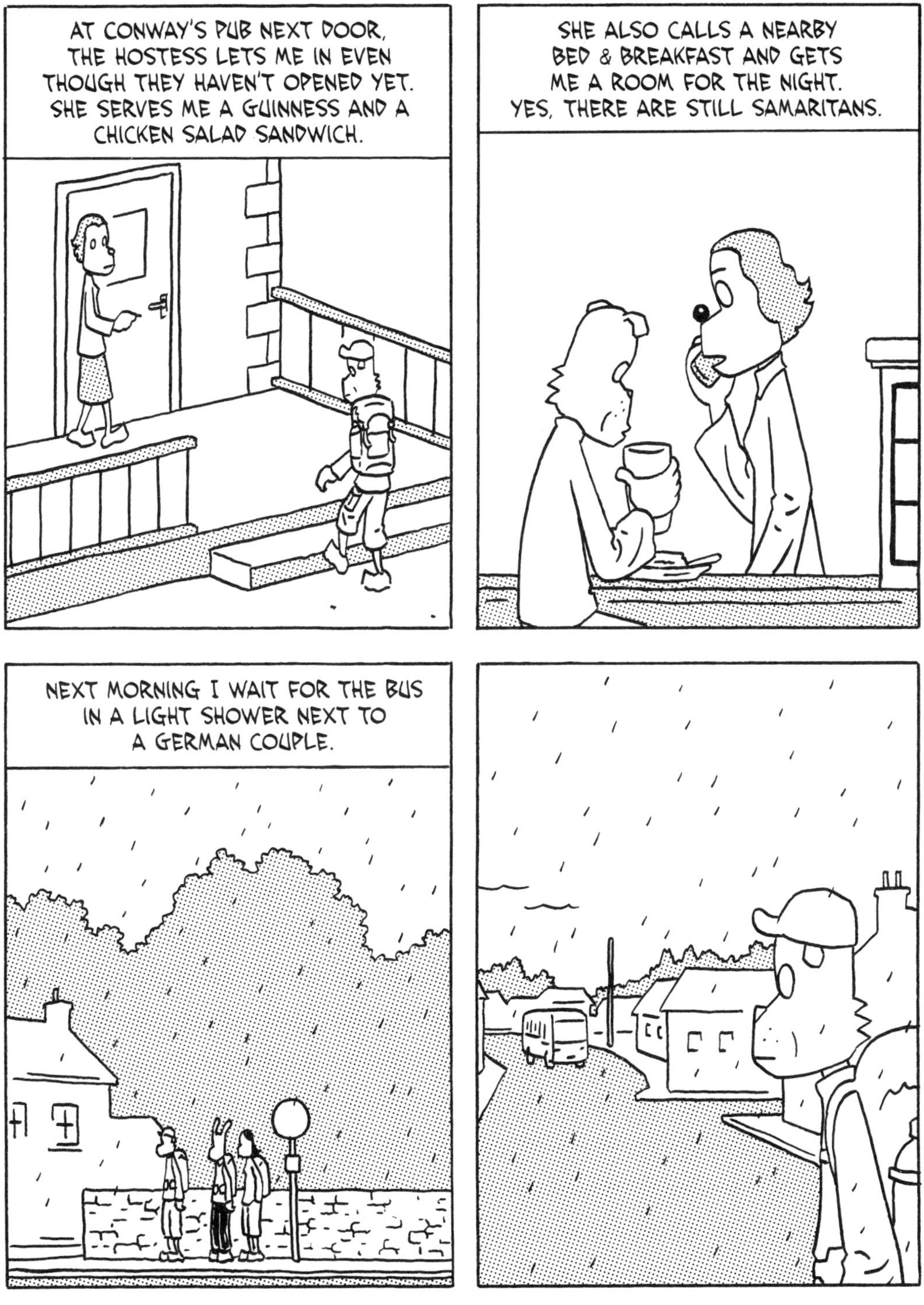
AT CONWAY'S PUB NEXT DOOR, THE HOSTESS LETS ME IN EVEN THOUGH THEY HAVEN'T OPENED YET. SHE SERVES ME A GUINNESS AND A CHICKEN SALAD SANDWICH.
SHE ALSO CALLS A NEARBY BED & BREAKFAST AND GETS ME A ROOM FOR THE NIGHT. YES, THERE ARE STILL SAMARITANS.
NEXT MORNING I WAIT FOR THE BUS IN A LIGHT SHOWER NEXT TO A GERMAN COUPLE.

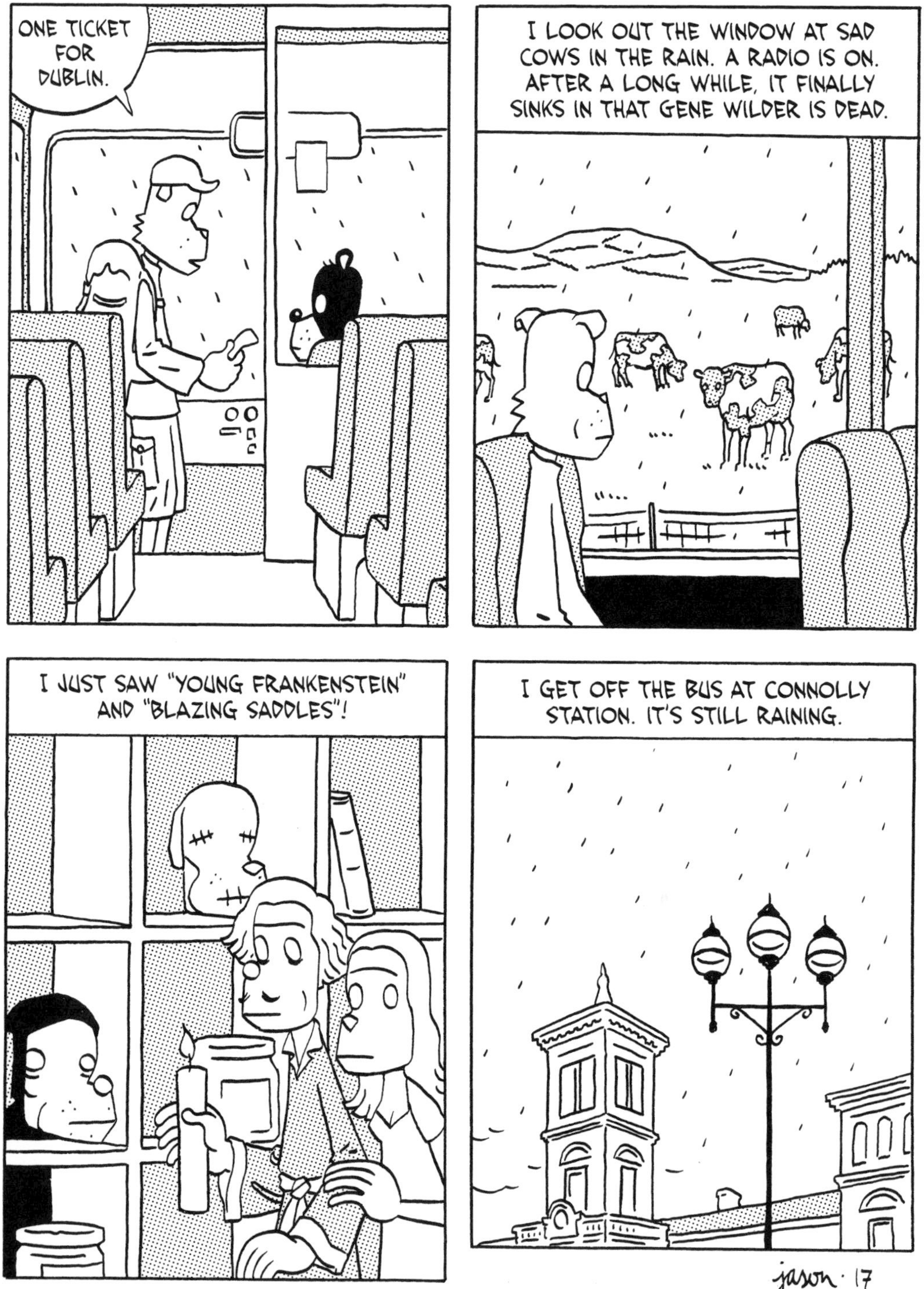
ONE TICKET FOR DUBLIN.
I LOOK OUT THE WINDOW AT SAD COWS IN THE RAIN. A RADIO IS ON. AFTER A LONG WHILE, IT FINALLY SINKS IN THAT GENE WILDER IS DEAD.
I JUST SAW "YOUNG FRANKENSTEIN" AND "BLAZING SADDLES"!
I GET OFF THE BUS AT CONNOLLY STATION. IT'S STILL RAINING.
jason · 17

L. Cohen: A Life

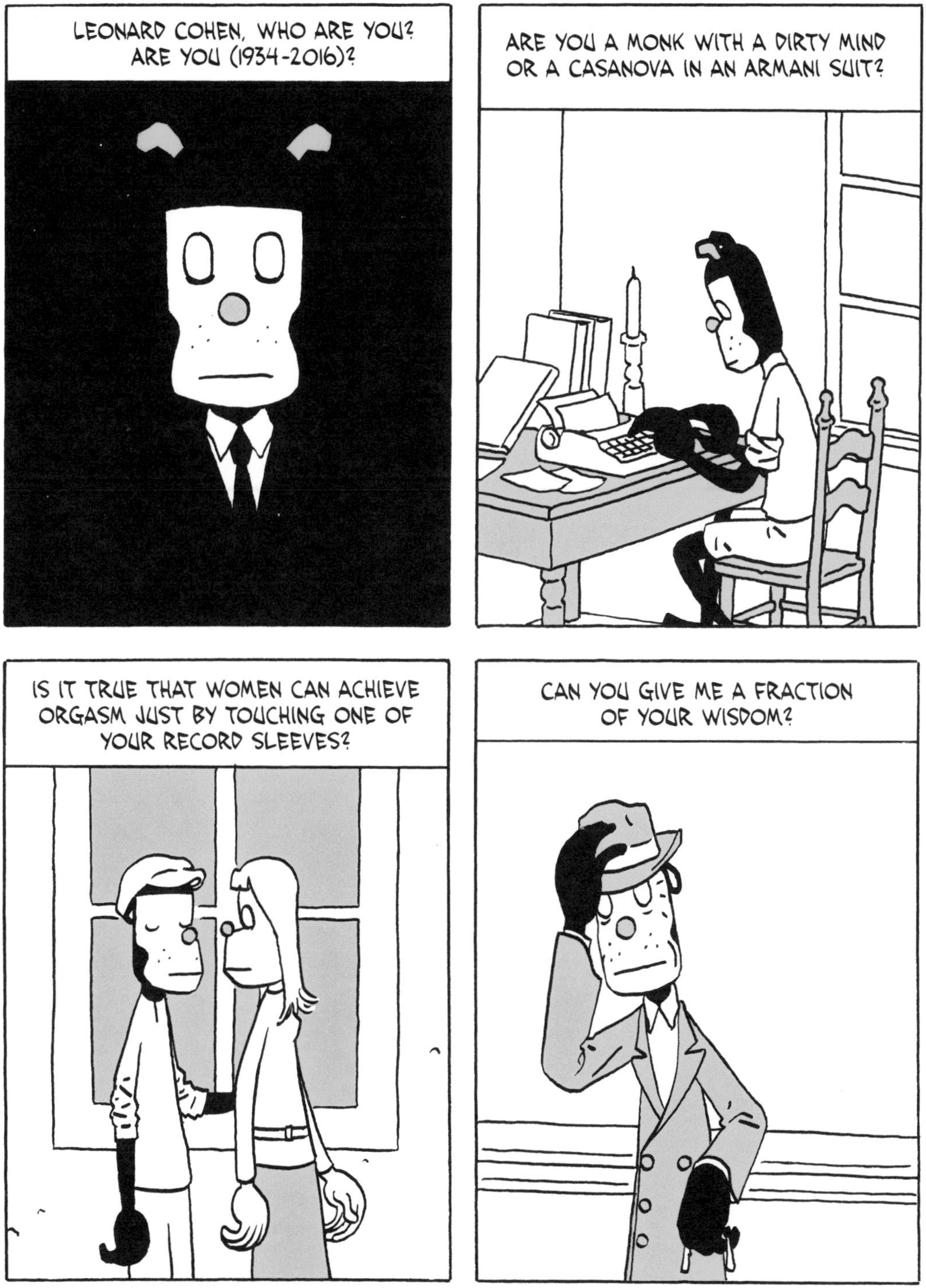
LEONARD COHEN, WHO ARE YOU? ARE YOU (1934-2016)?
ARE YOU A MONK WITH A DIRTY MIND OR A CASANOVA IN AN ARMANI SUIT?
IS IT TRUE THAT WOMEN CAN ACHIEVE ORGASM JUST BY TOUCHING ONE OF YOUR RECORD SLEEVES?
CAN YOU GIVE ME A FRACTION OF YOUR WISDOM?

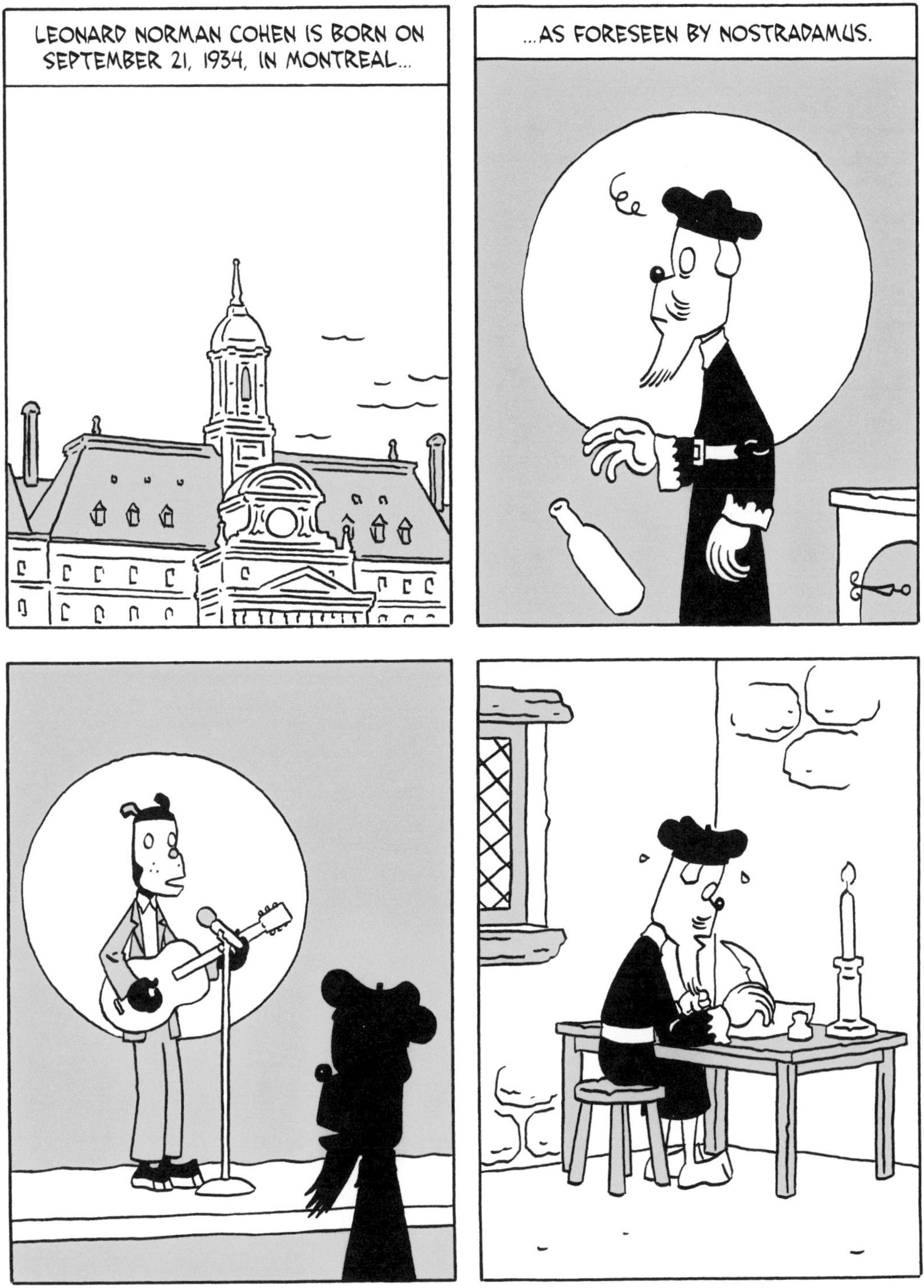
LEONARD NORMAN COHEN IS BORN ON SEPTEMBER 21, 1934, IN MONTREAL...
...AS FORESEEN BY NOSTRADAMUS.

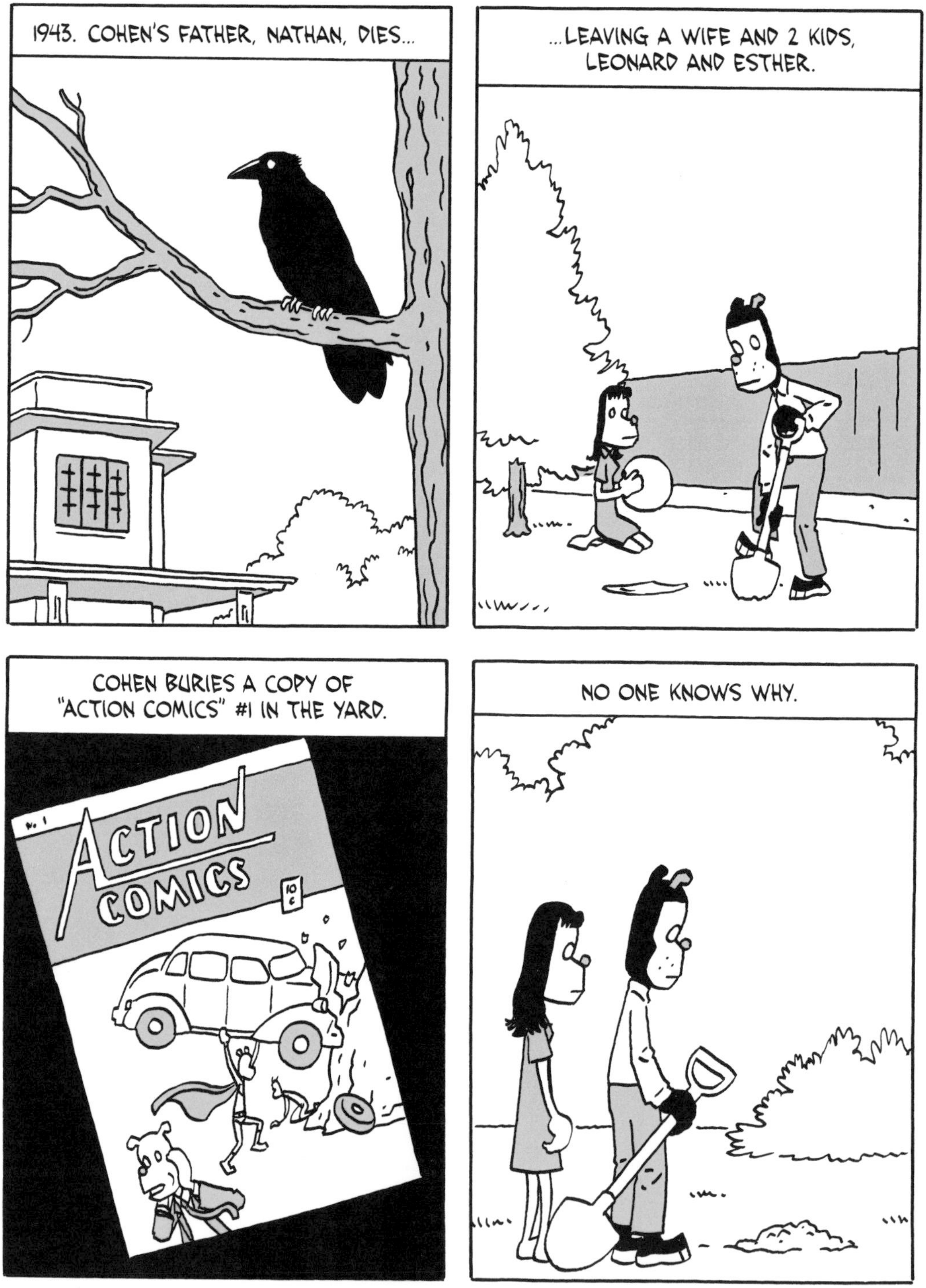
1943. COHEN'S FATHER, NATHAN, DIES...
...LEAVING A WIFE AND 2 KIDS, LEONARD AND ESTHER.
COHEN BURIES A COPY OF "ACTION COMICS" #1 IN THE YARD.
ACTION COMICS
10¢
NO ONE KNOWS WHY.

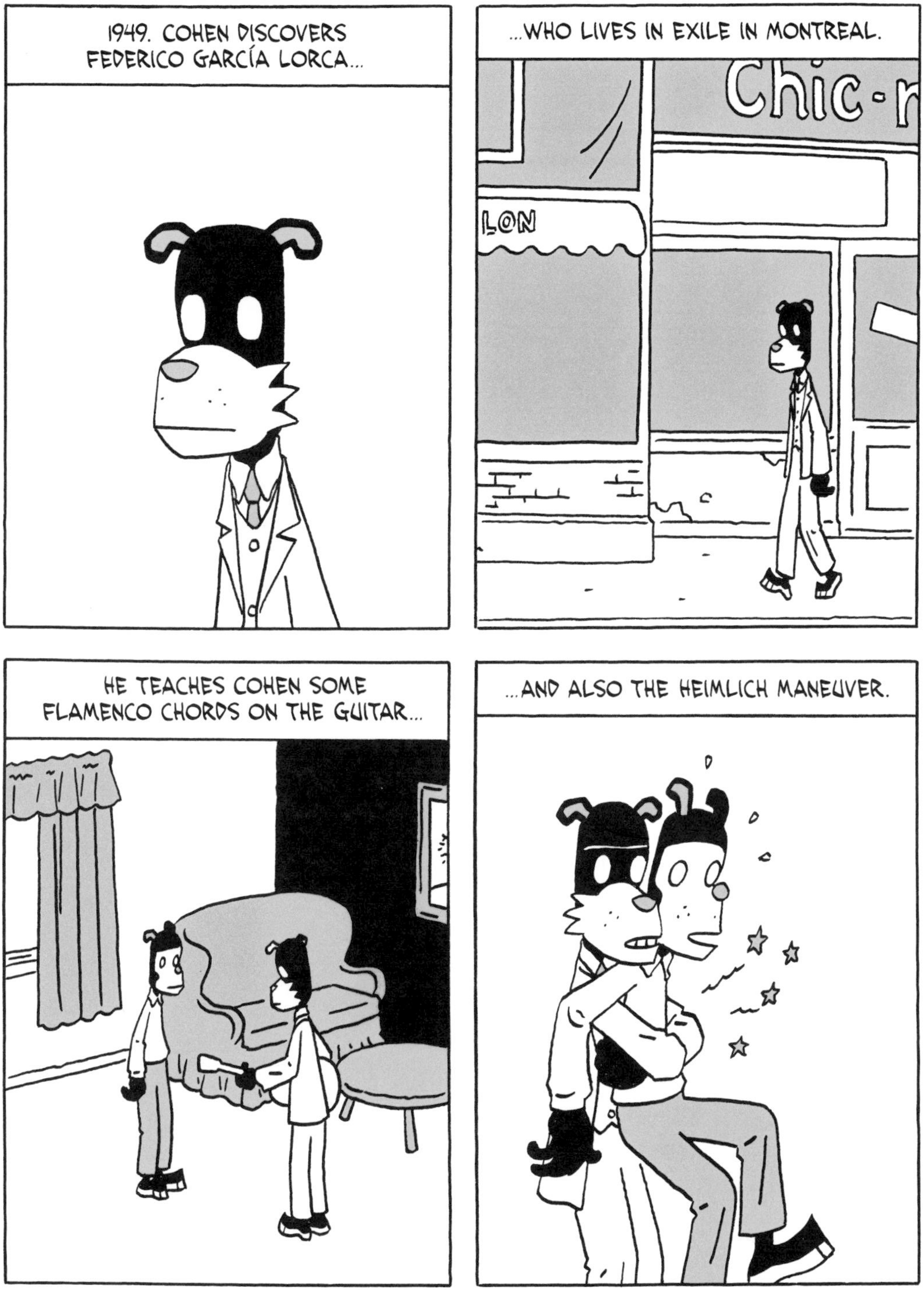
1949. COHEN DISCOVERS FEDERICO GARCÍA LORCA...
...WHO LIVES IN EXILE IN MONTREAL.
Chic-r
LON
HE TEACHES COHEN SOME FLAMENCO CHORDS ON THE GUITAR...
...AND ALSO THE HEIMLICH MANEUVER.

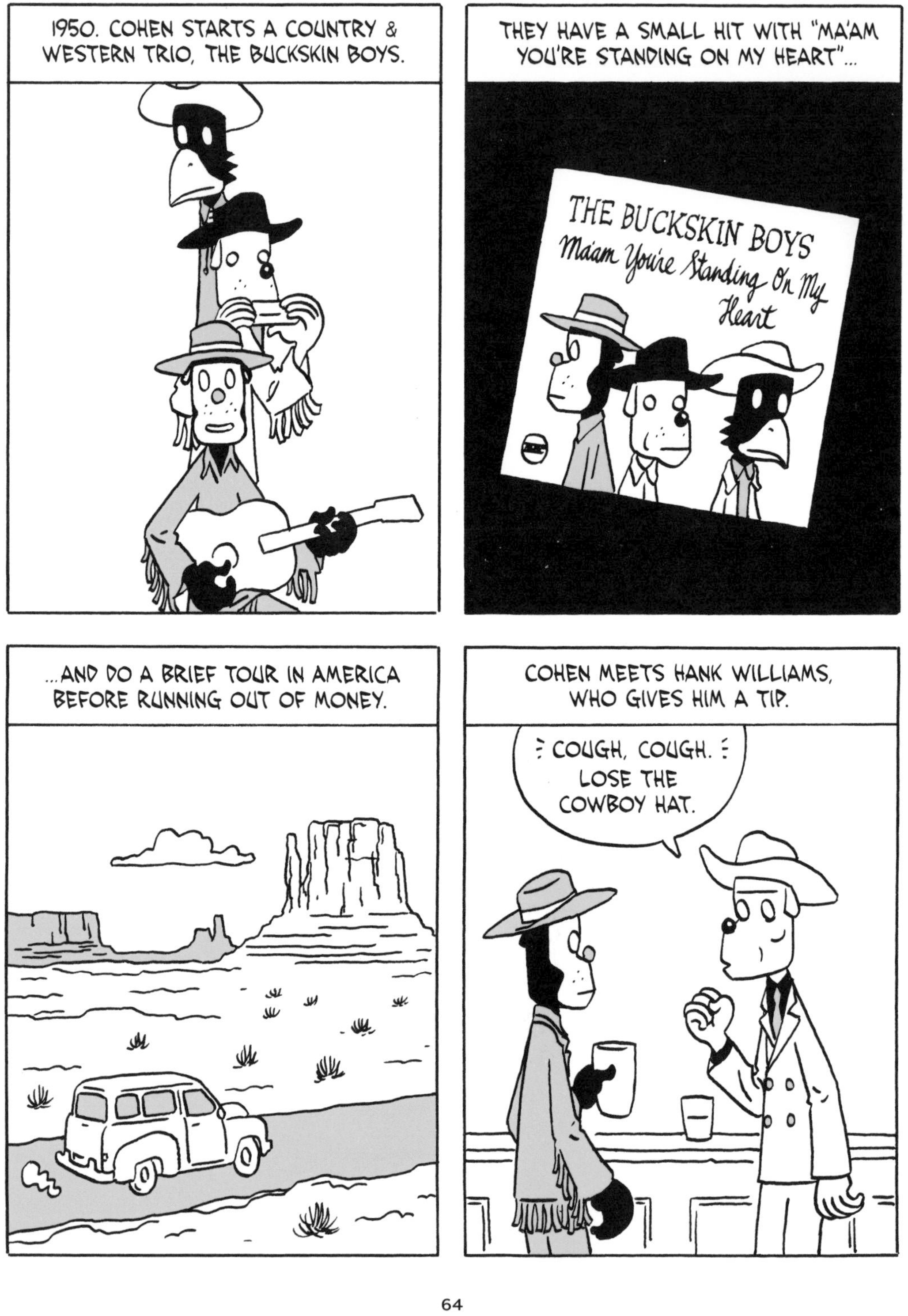
1950. COHEN STARTS A COUNTRY & WESTERN TRIO, THE BUCKSKIN BOYS.
THEY HAVE A SMALL HIT WITH "MA'AM YOU'RE STANDING ON MY HEART"...
THE BUCKSKIN BOYS
Ma'am You're Standing On My Heart
...AND DO A BRIEF TOUR IN AMERICA BEFORE RUNNING OUT OF MONEY.
COHEN MEETS HANK WILLIAMS, WHO GIVES HIM A TIP.
COUGH, COUGH. LOSE THE COWBOY HAT.

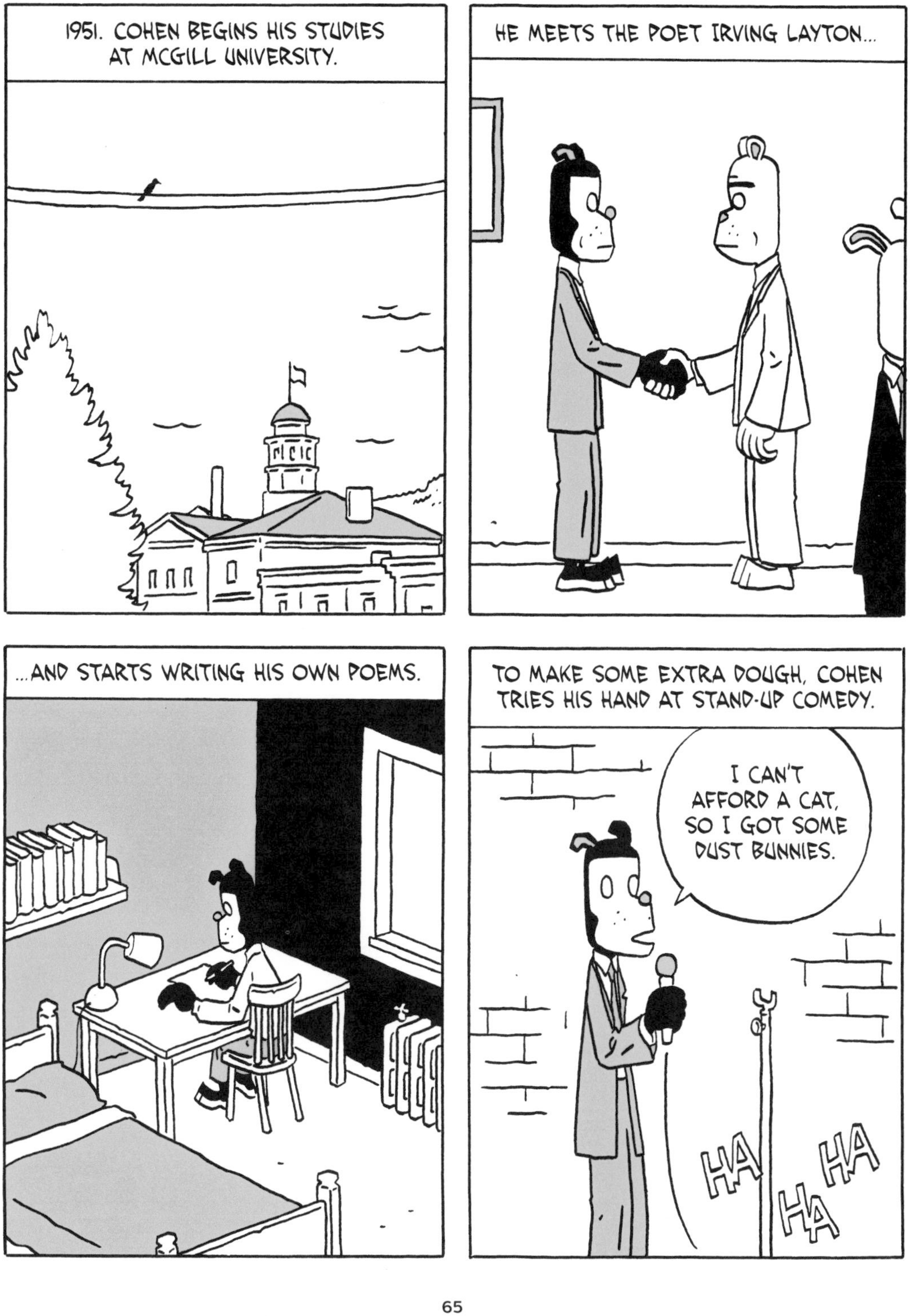
1951. COHEN BEGINS HIS STUDIES AT MCGILL UNIVERSITY.
HE MEETS THE POET IRVING LAYTON...
...AND STARTS WRITING HIS OWN POEMS.
TO MAKE SOME EXTRA DOUGH, COHEN TRIES HIS HAND AT STAND-UP COMEDY.
I CAN'T AFFORD A CAT, SO I GOT SOME DUST BUNNIES.
HA HA HA

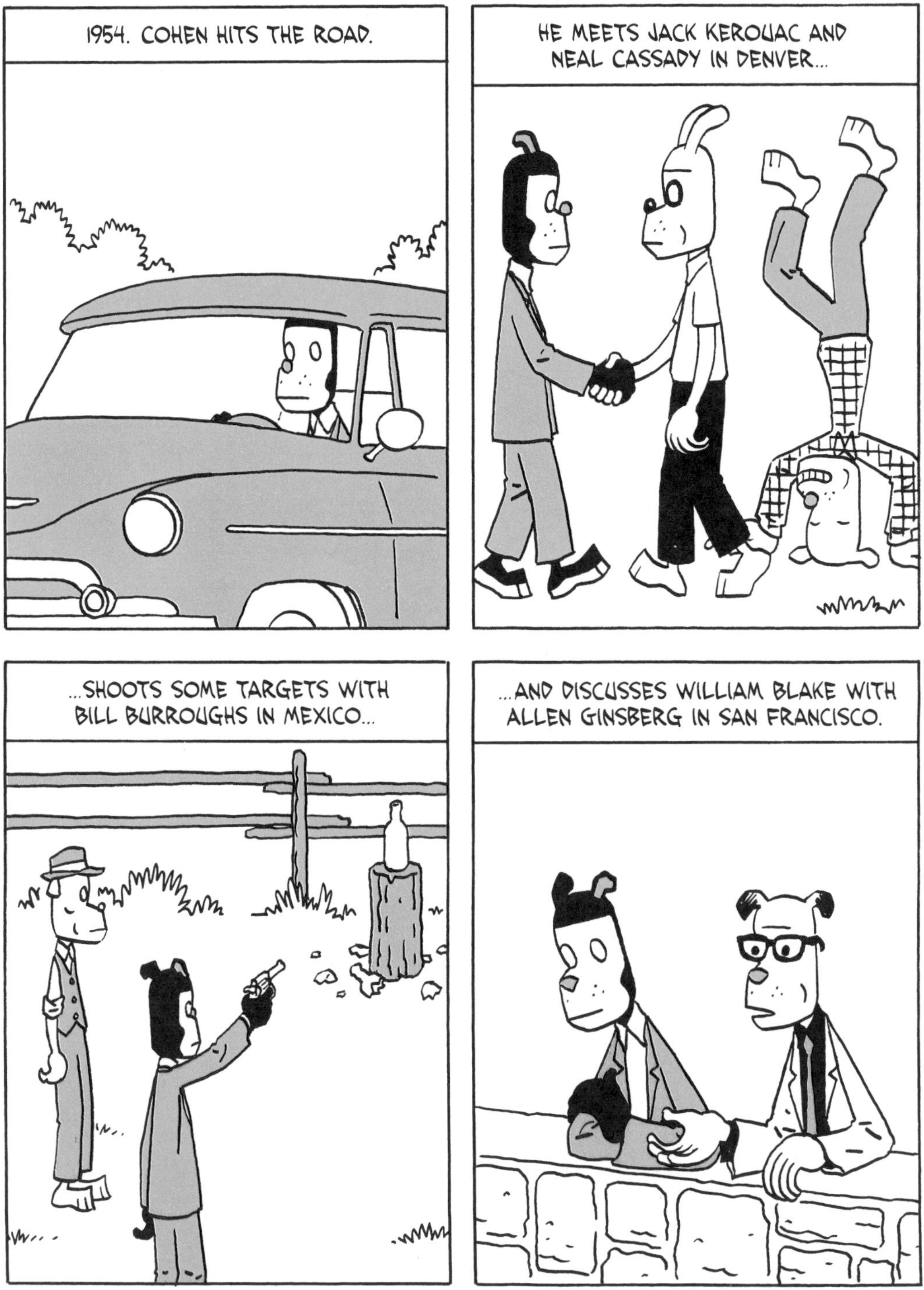
1954. COHEN HITS THE ROAD.
HE MEETS JACK KEROUAC AND NEAL CASSADY IN DENVER...
...SHOOTS SOME TARGETS WITH BILL BURROUGHS IN MEXICO...
...AND DISCUSSES WILLIAM BLAKE WITH ALLEN GINSBERG IN SAN FRANCISCO.

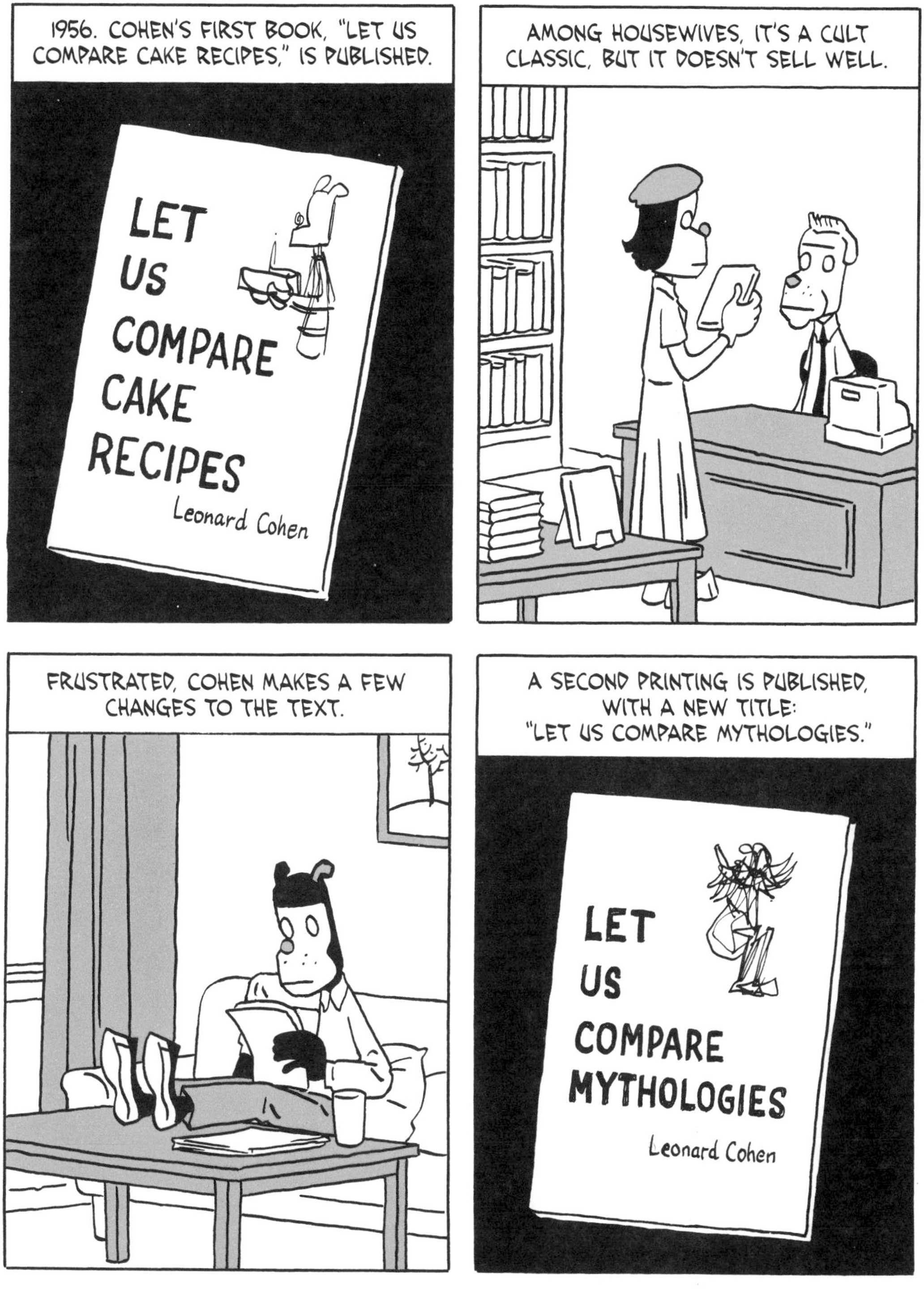
1956. COHEN'S FIRST BOOK, "LET US COMPARE CAKE RECIPES," IS PUBLISHED.
LET US COMPARE CAKE RECIPES
Leonard Cohen
AMONG HOUSEWIVES, IT'S A CULT CLASSIC, BUT IT DOESN'T SELL WELL.
FRUSTRATED, COHEN MAKES A FEW CHANGES TO THE TEXT.
A SECOND PRINTING IS PUBLISHED, WITH A NEW TITLE: "LET US COMPARE MYTHOLOGIES."
LET US COMPARE MYTHOLOGIES
Leonard Cohen

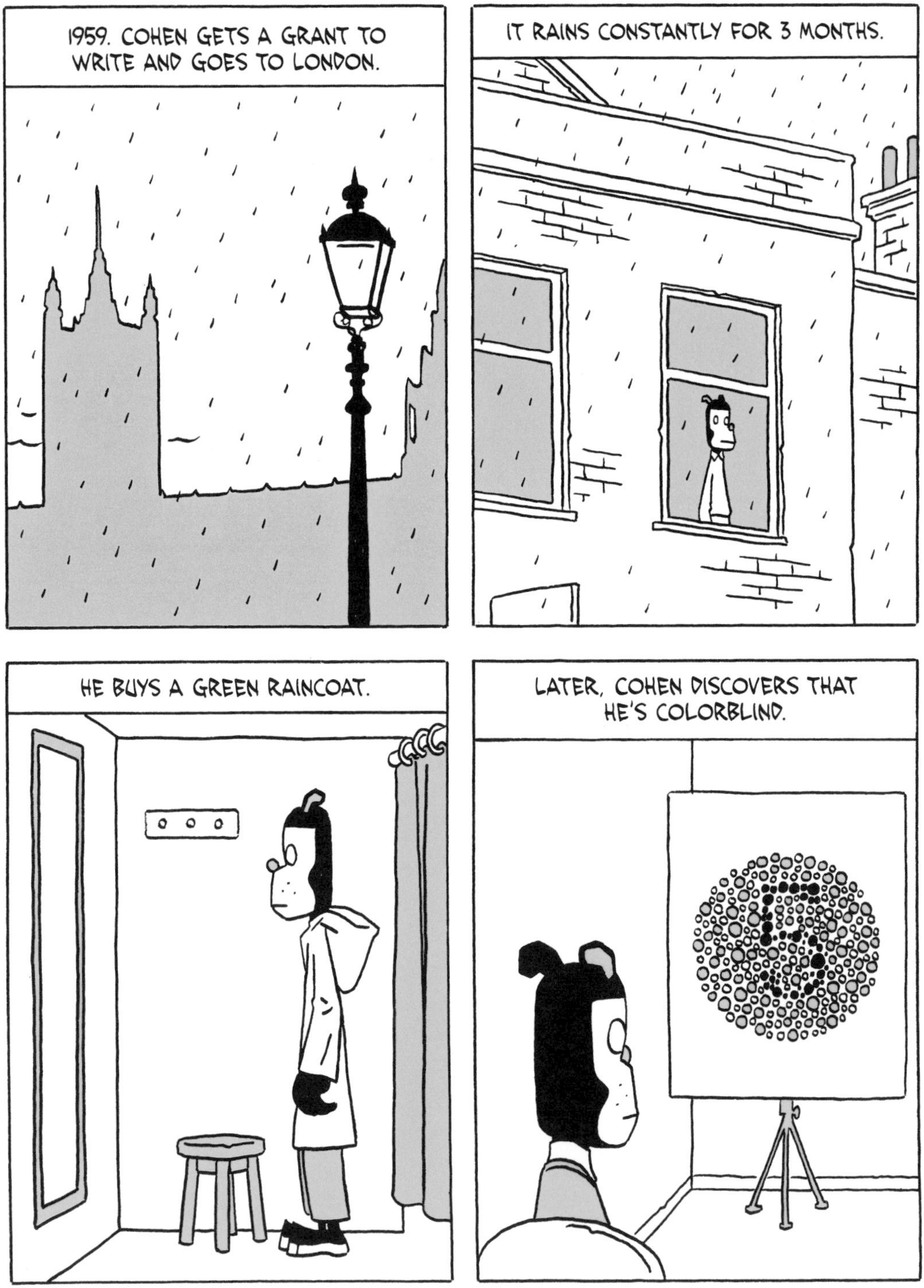
1959. COHEN GETS A GRANT TO WRITE AND GOES TO LONDON.
IT RAINS CONSTANTLY FOR 3 MONTHS.
HE BUYS A GREEN RAINCOAT.
LATER, COHEN DISCOVERS THAT HE'S COLORBLIND.

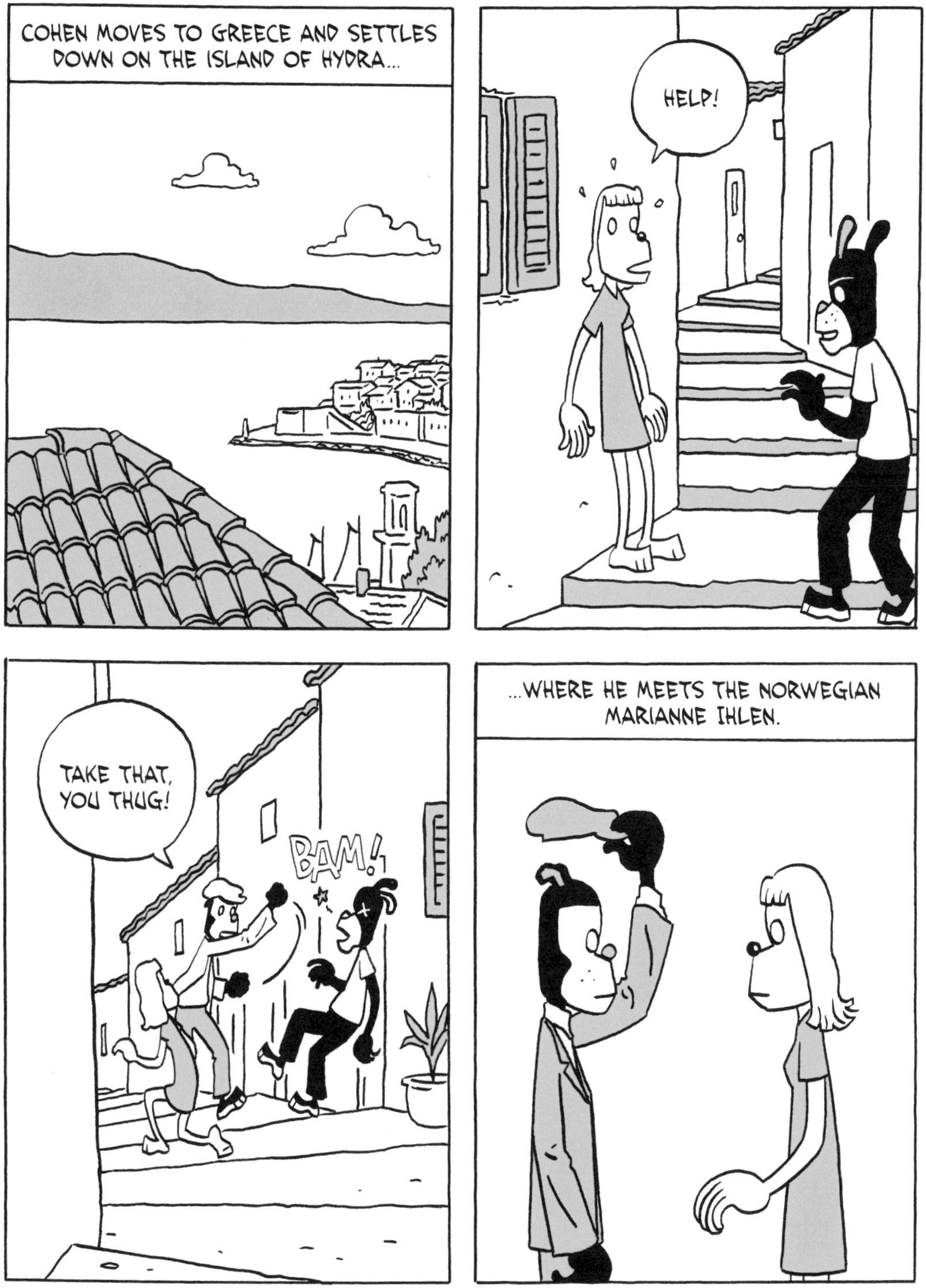
COHEN MOVES TO GREECE AND SETTLES DOWN ON THE ISLAND OF HYDRA...
HELP!
TAKE THAT, YOU THUG!
BAM!
...WHERE HE MEETS THE NORWEGIAN MARIANNE IHLEN.

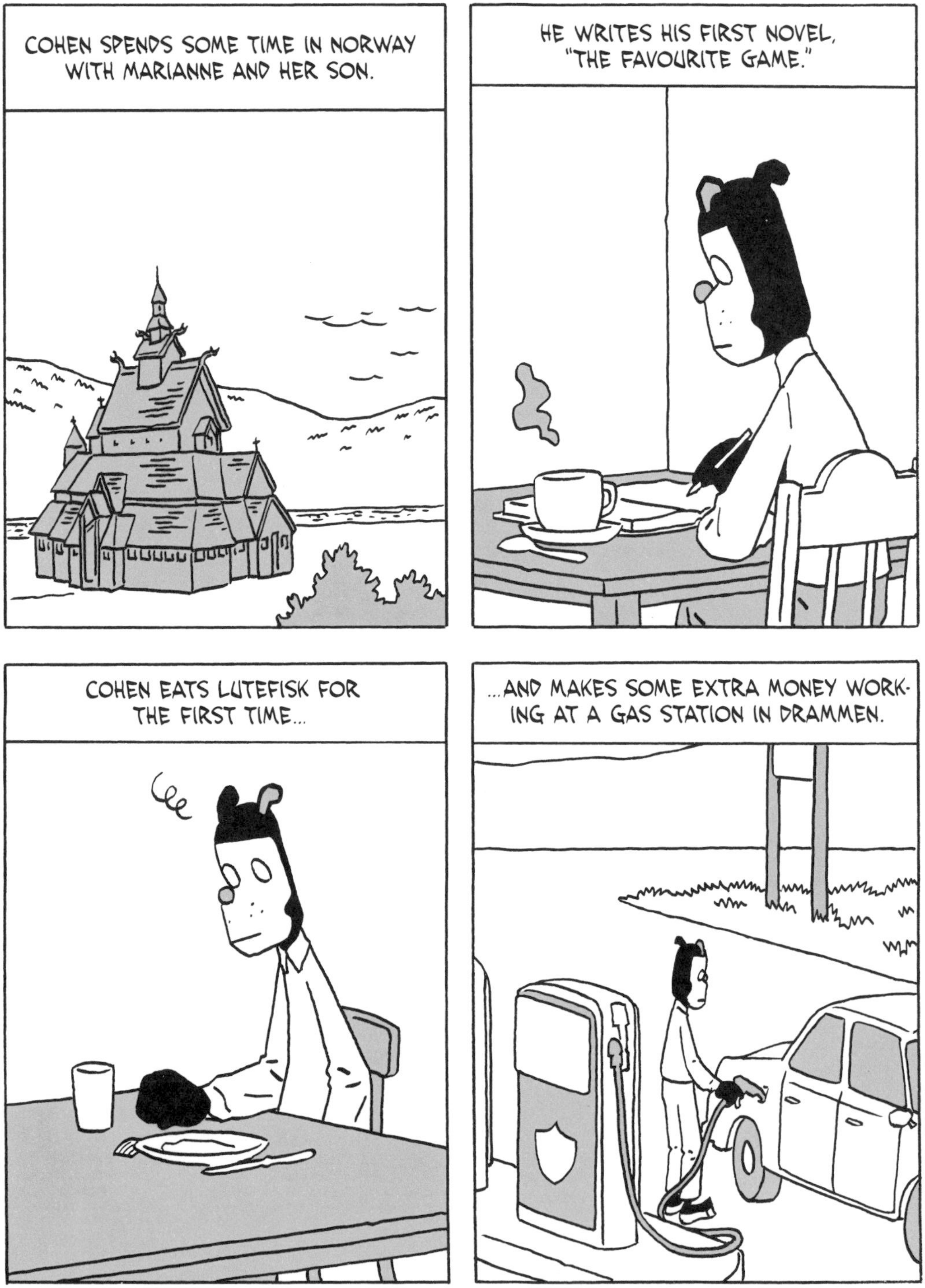
COHEN SPENDS SOME TIME IN NORWAY WITH MARIANNE AND HER SON.
HE WRITES HIS FIRST NOVEL, "THE FAVOURITE GAME."
COHEN EATS LUTEFISK FOR THE FIRST TIME...
...AND MAKES SOME EXTRA MONEY WORK-ING AT A GAS STATION IN DRAMMEN.

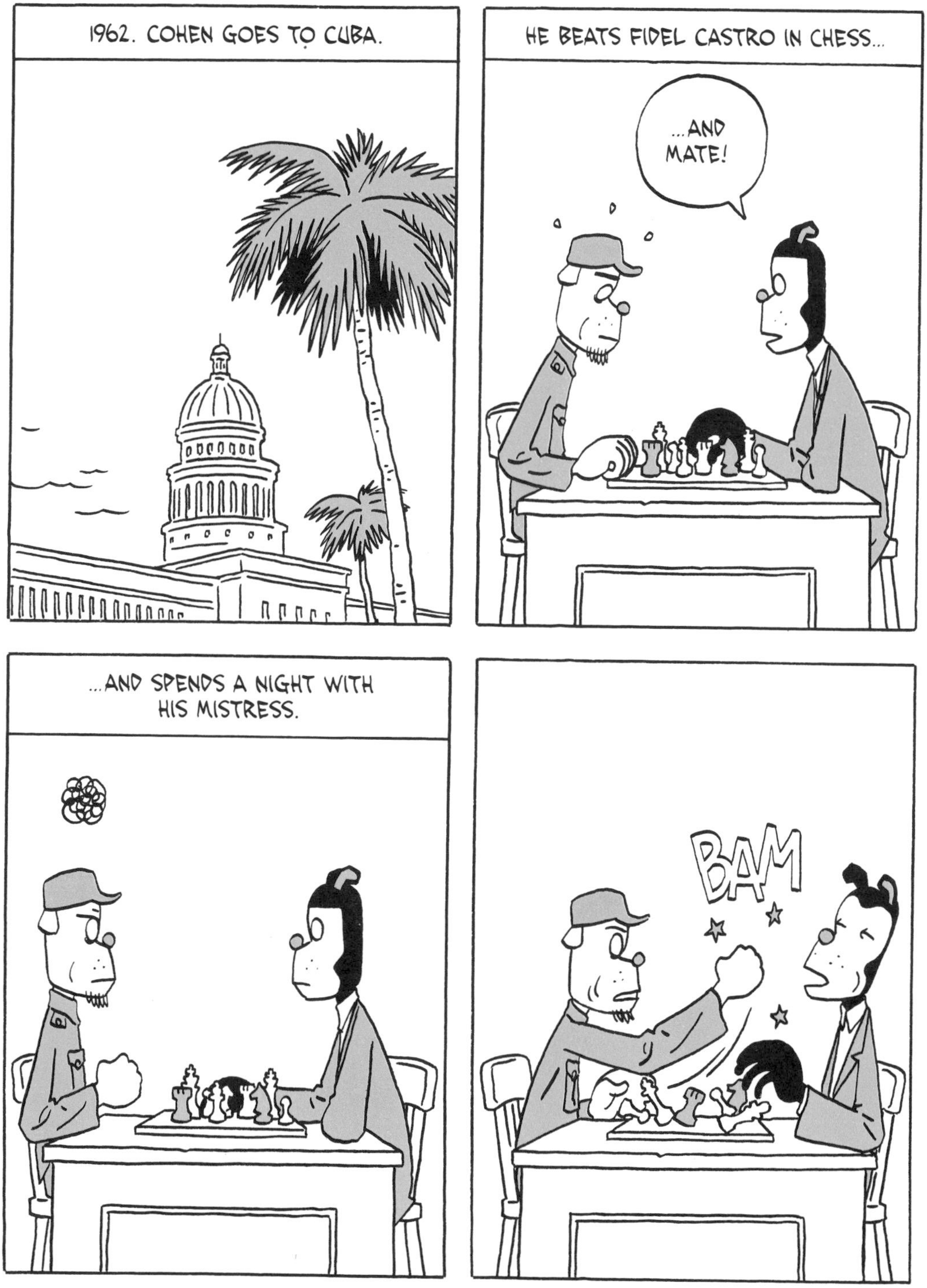
1962. COHEN GOES TO CUBA.
HE BEATS FIDEL CASTRO IN CHESS...
...AND MATE!
...AND SPENDS A NIGHT WITH HIS MISTRESS.
BAM

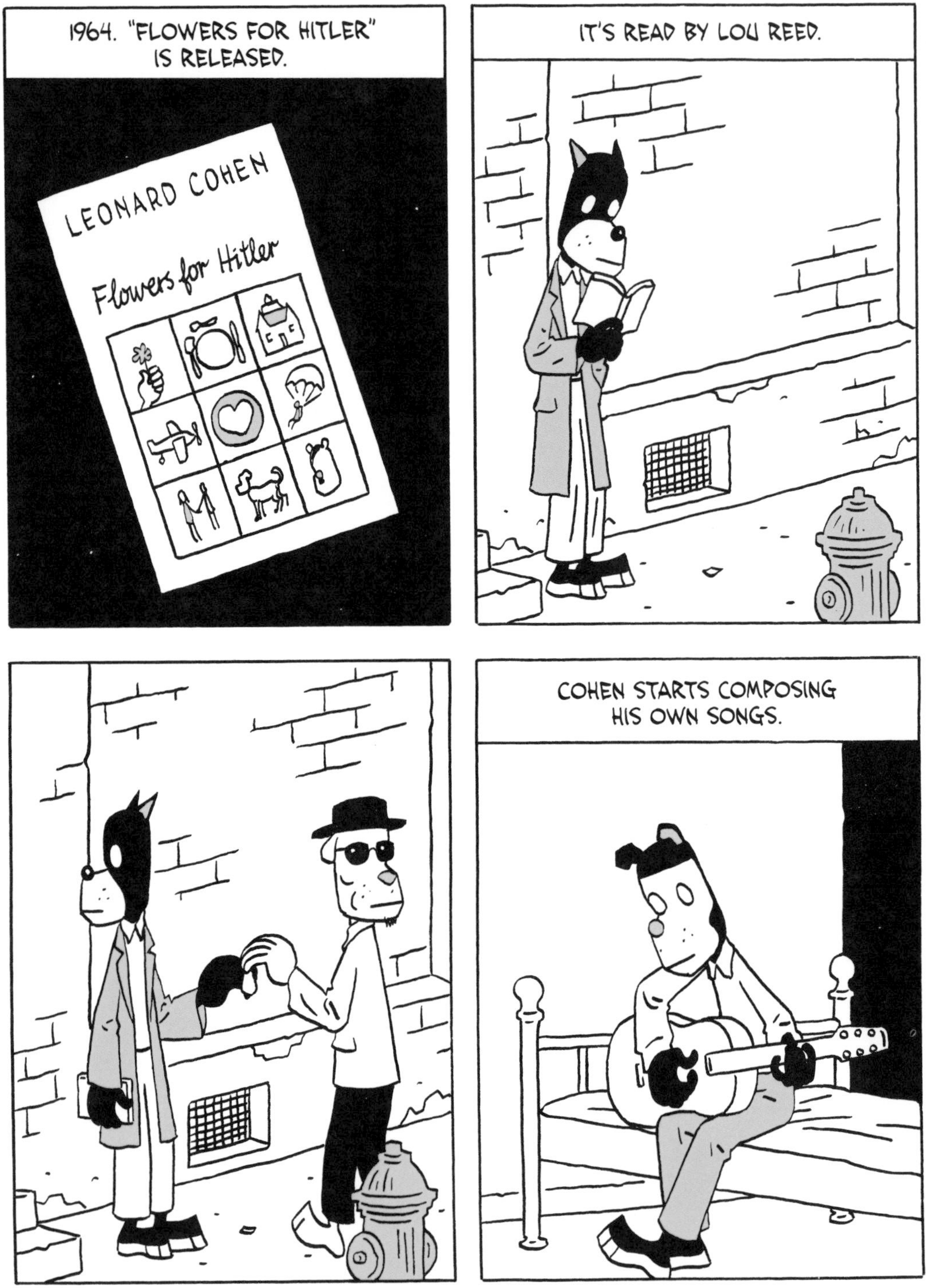
1964. "FLOWERS FOR HITLER" IS RELEASED.
LEONARD COHEN
Flowers for Hitler
IT'S READ BY LOU REED.
COHEN STARTS COMPOSING HIS OWN SONGS.

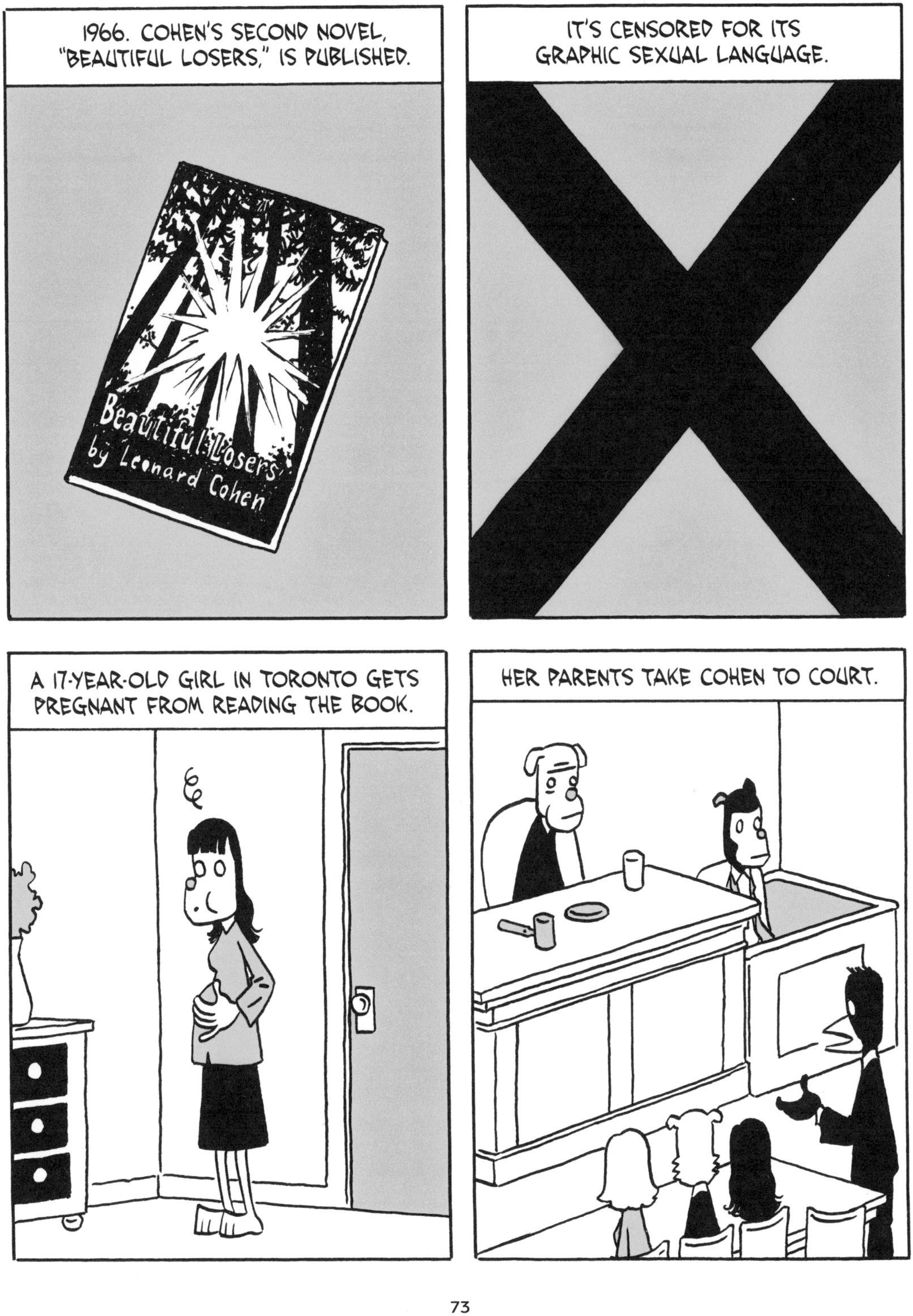
1966. COHEN'S SECOND NOVEL, "BEAUTIFUL LOSERS," IS PUBLISHED.
Beautiful Losers
by Leonard Cohen
IT'S CENSORED FOR ITS GRAPHIC SEXUAL LANGUAGE.
A 17-YEAR-OLD GIRL IN TORONTO GETS PREGNANT FROM READING THE BOOK.
HER PARENTS TAKE COHEN TO COURT.

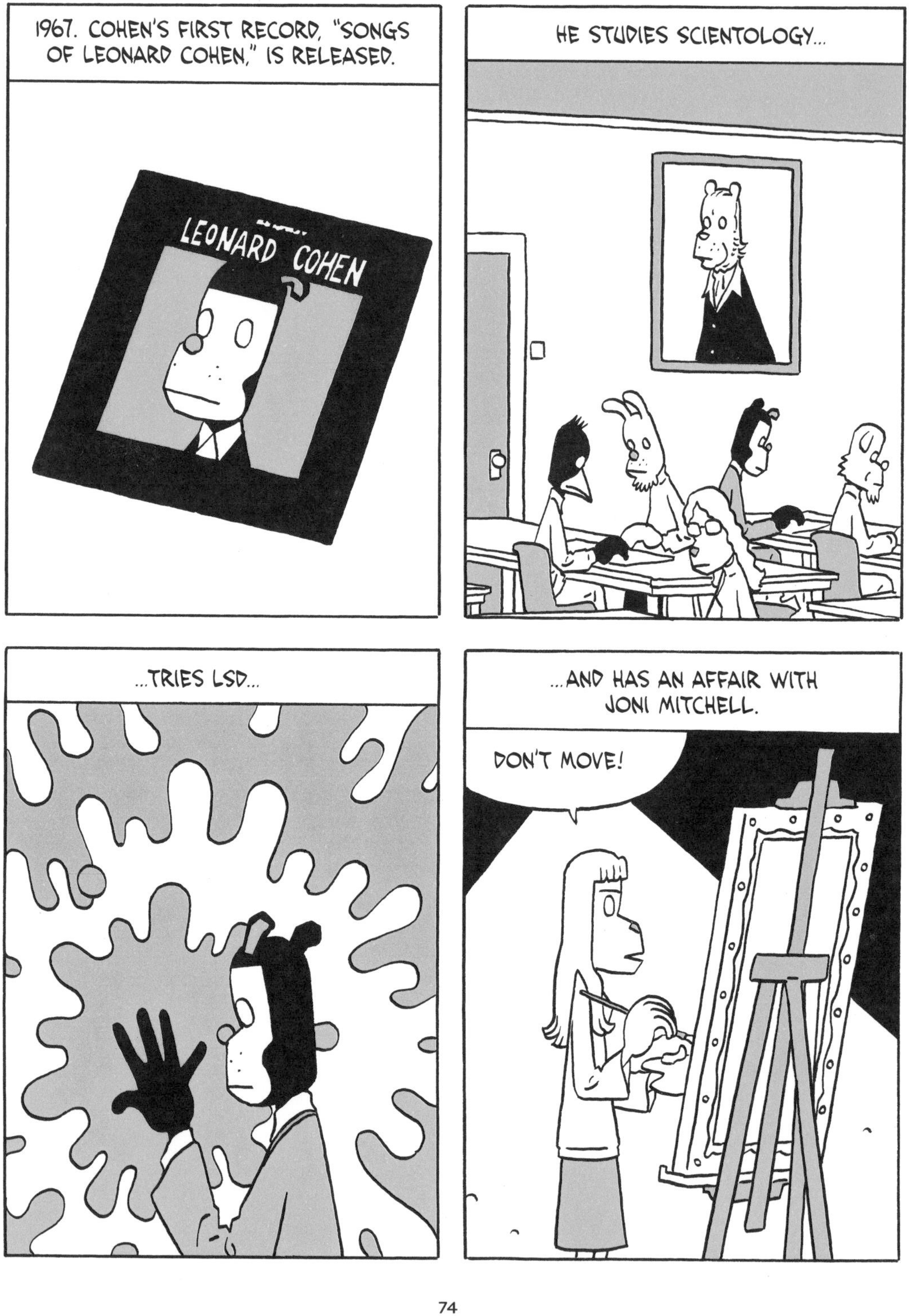
1967. COHEN'S FIRST RECORD, "SONGS OF LEONARD COHEN," IS RELEASED.
LEONARD COHEN
HE STUDIES SCIENTOLOGY...
...TRIES LSD...
...AND HAS AN AFFAIR WITH JONI MITCHELL.
DON'T MOVE!

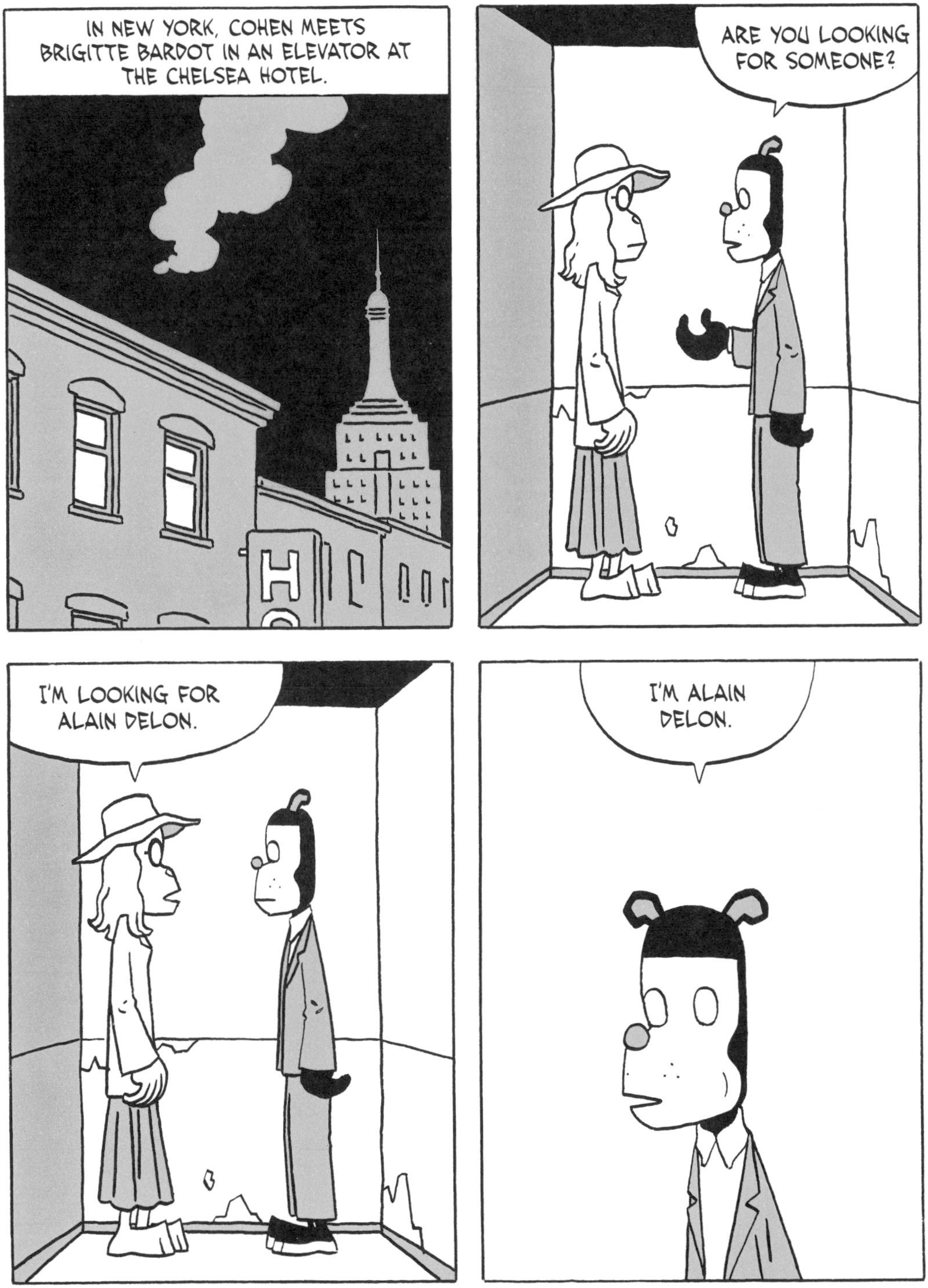
IN NEW YORK, COHEN MEETS BRIGITTE BARDOT IN AN ELEVATOR AT THE CHELSEA HOTEL.
H
ARE YOU LOOKING FOR SOMEONE?
I'M LOOKING FOR ALAIN DELON.
I'M ALAIN DELON.

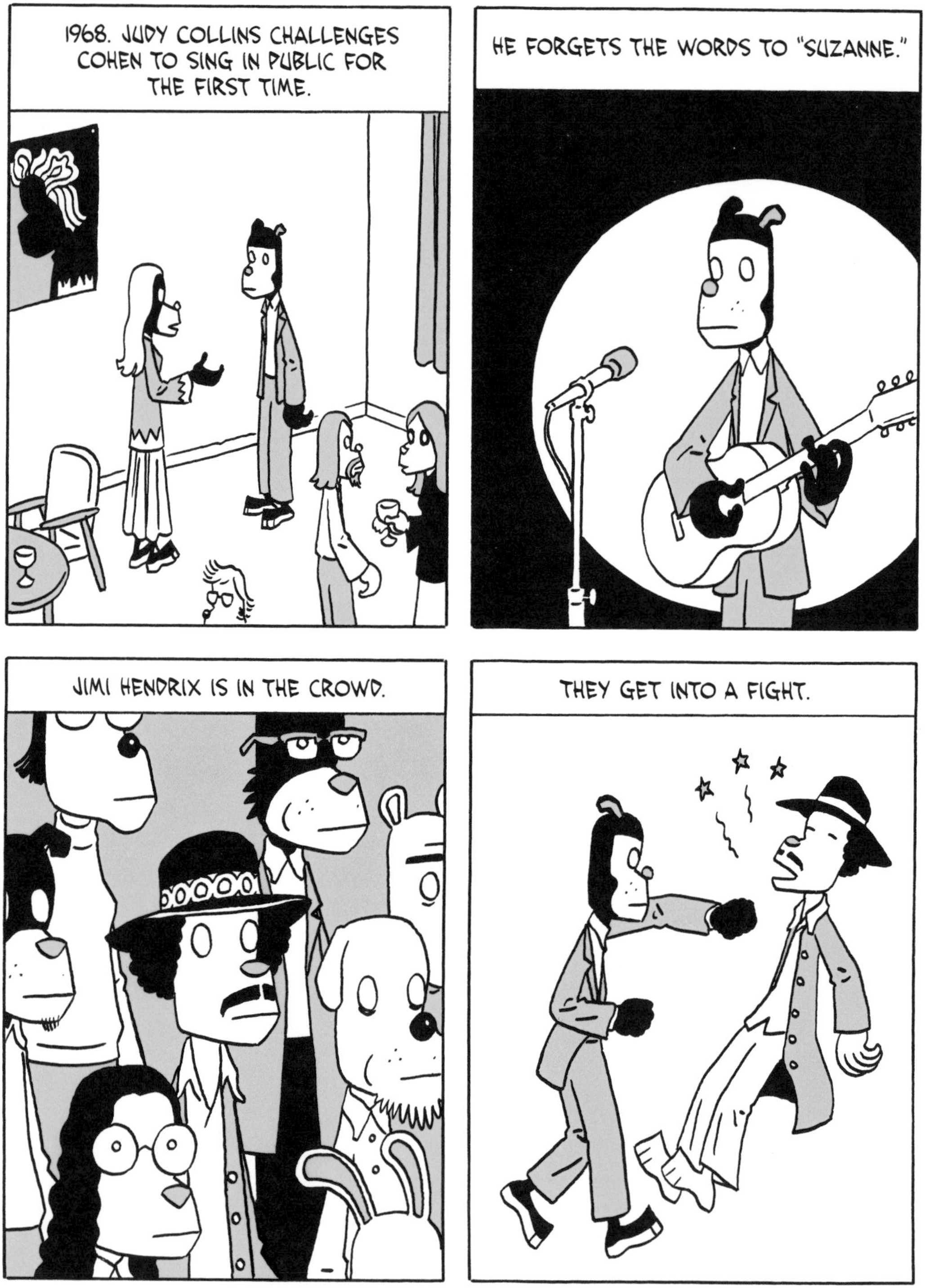
1968. JUDY COLLINS CHALLENGES COHEN TO SING IN PUBLIC FOR THE FIRST TIME.
HE FORGETS THE WORDS TO "SUZANNE."
JIMI HENDRIX IS IN THE CROWD.
THEY GET INTO A FIGHT.

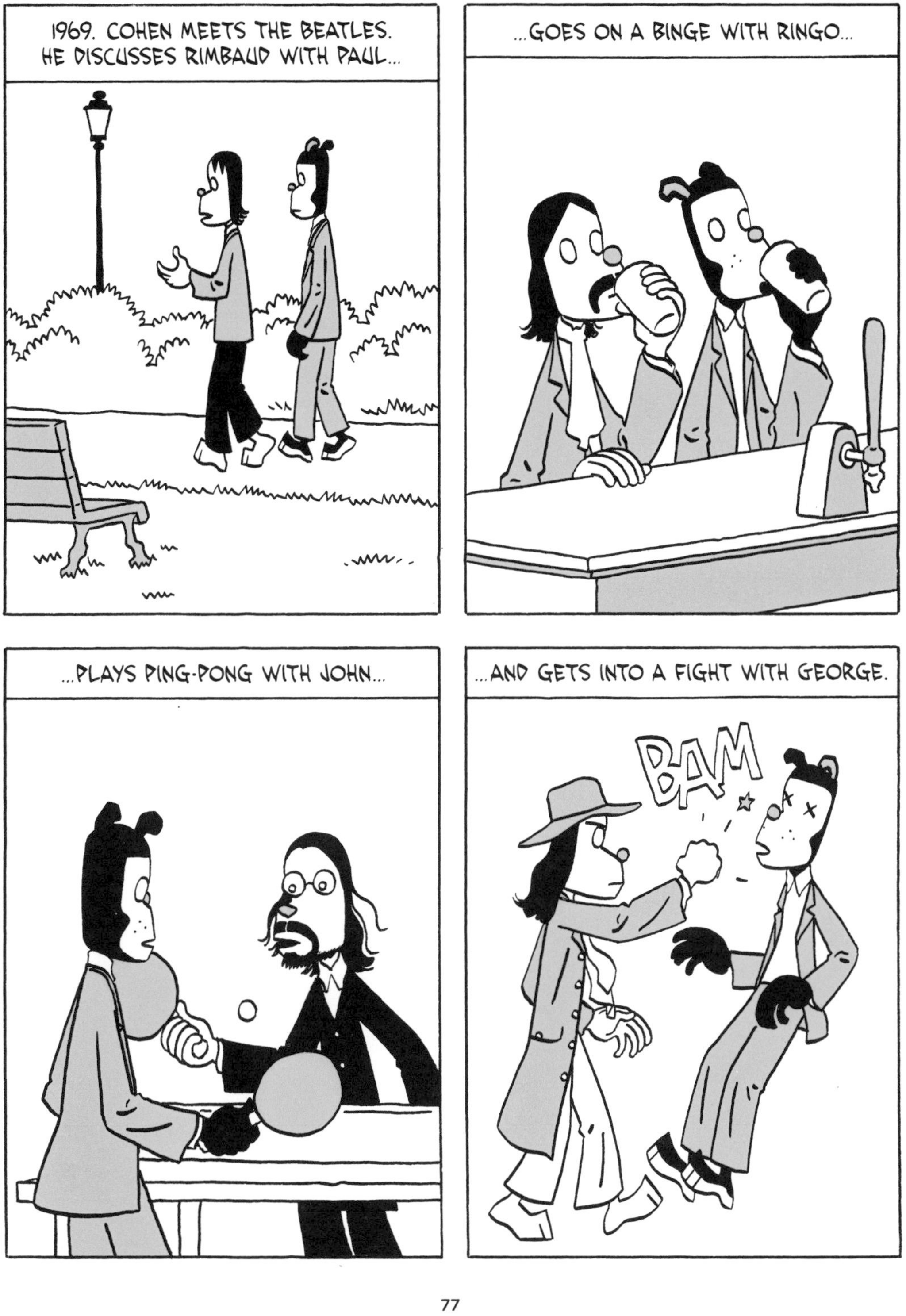
1969. COHEN MEETS THE BEATLES. HE DISCUSSES RIMBAUD WITH PAUL...
...GOES ON A BINGE WITH RINGO...
...PLAYS PING-PONG WITH JOHN...
...AND GETS INTO A FIGHT WITH GEORGE.
BAM

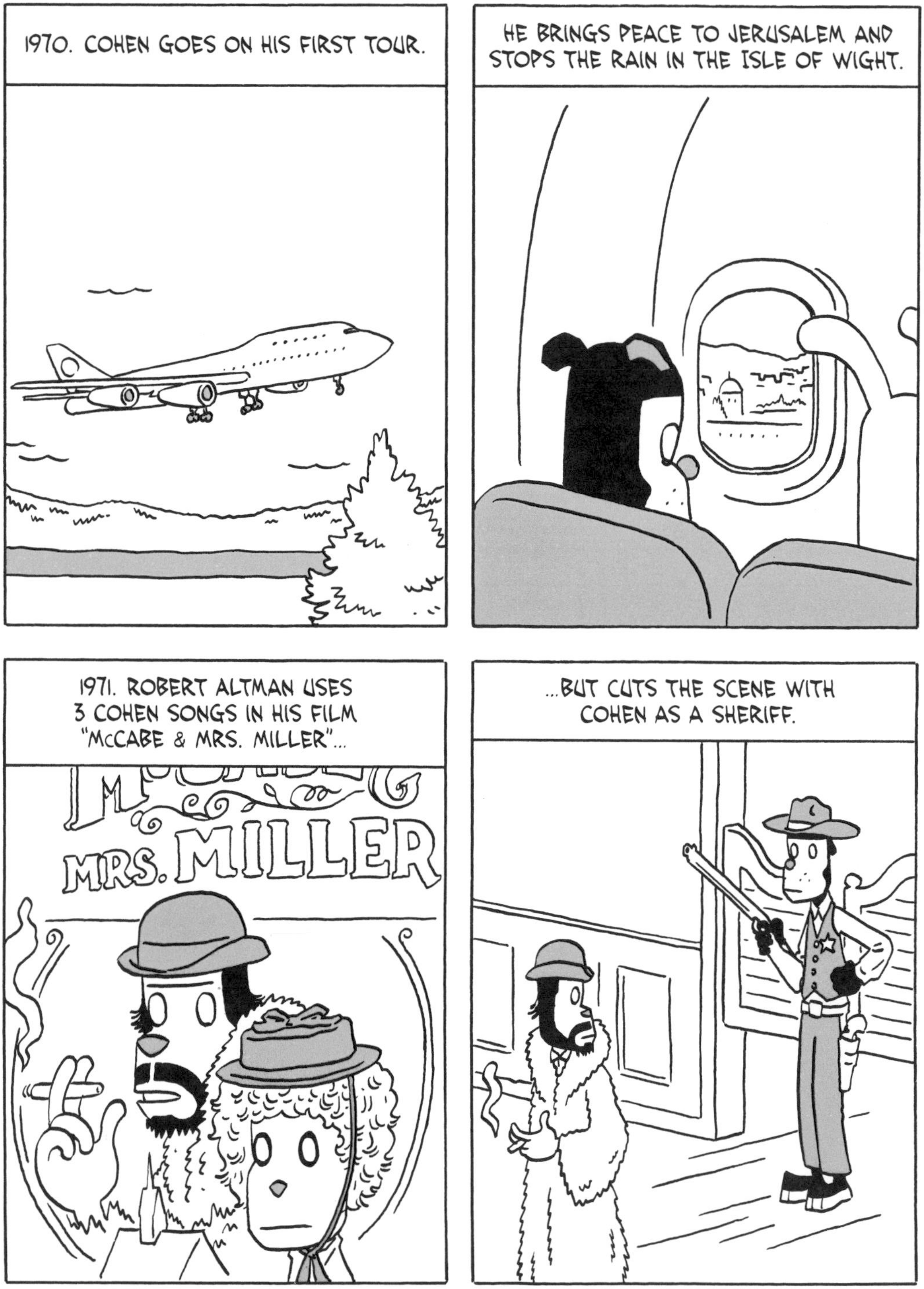
1970. COHEN GOES ON HIS FIRST TOUR.
HE BRINGS PEACE TO JERUSALEM AND STOPS THE RAIN IN THE ISLE OF WIGHT.
1971. ROBERT ALTMAN USES 3 COHEN SONGS IN HIS FILM "McCABE & MRS. MILLER"...
MRS. MILLER
...BUT CUTS THE SCENE WITH COHEN AS A SHERIFF.

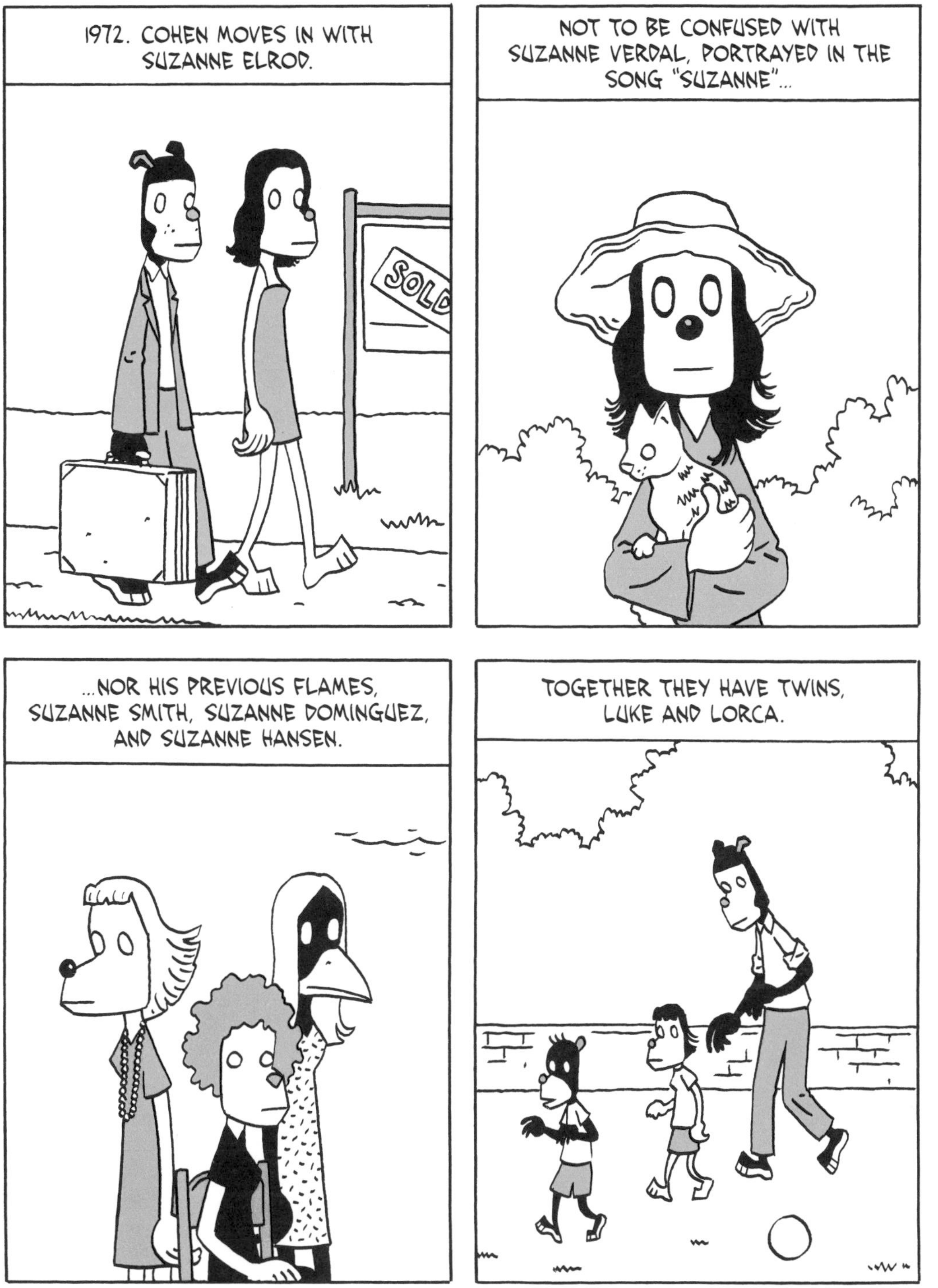
1972. COHEN MOVES IN WITH SUZANNE ELROD.
SOLD
NOT TO BE CONFUSED WITH SUZANNE VERDAL, PORTRAYED IN THE SONG "SUZANNE"...
...NOR HIS PREVIOUS FLAMES, SUZANNE SMITH, SUZANNE DOMINGUEZ, AND SUZANNE HANSEN.
TOGETHER THEY HAVE TWINS, LUKE AND LORCA.

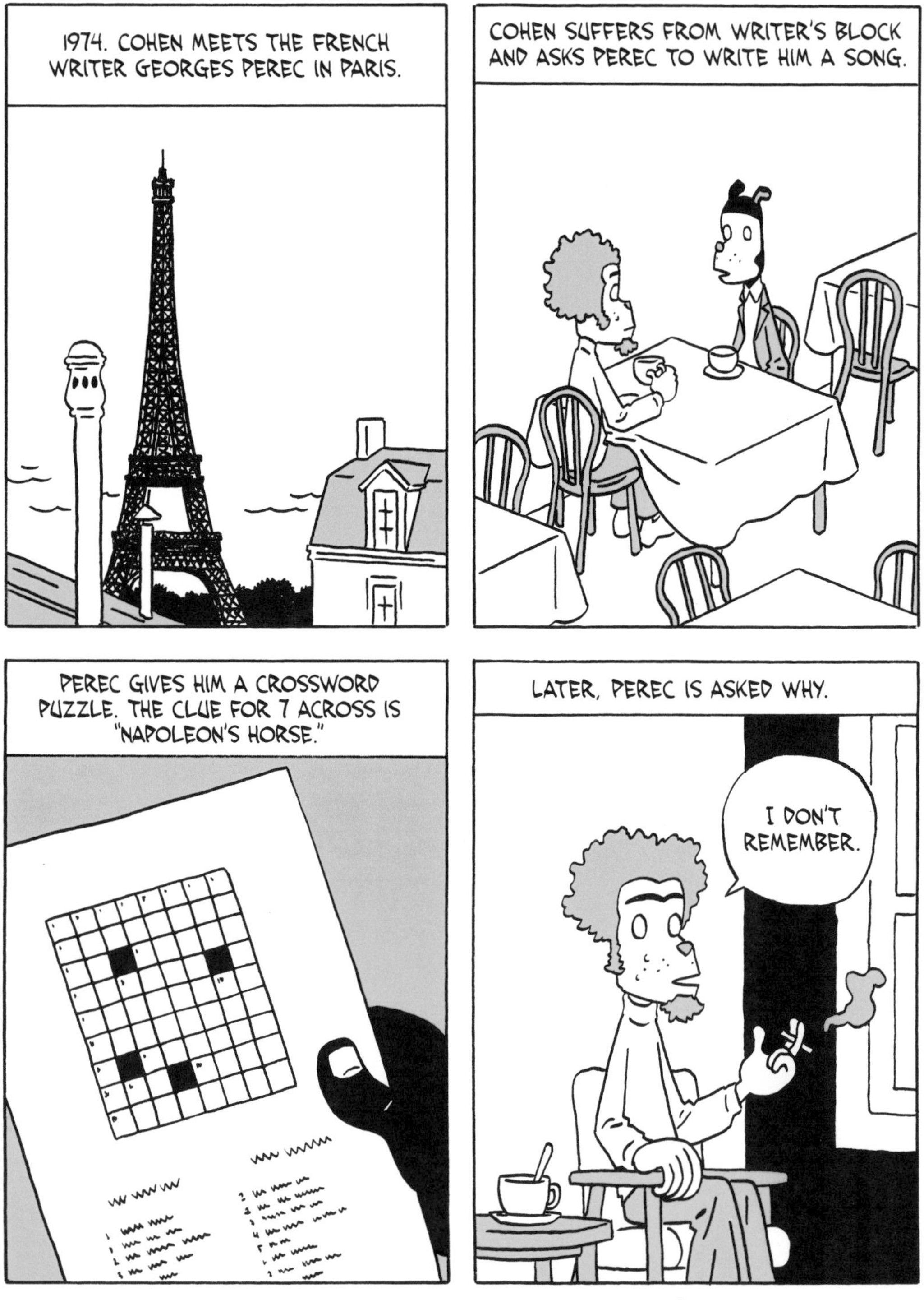

1974. COHEN MEETS THE FRENCH WRITER GEORGES PEREC IN PARIS.
COHEN SUFFERS FROM WRITER'S BLOCK AND ASKS PEREC TO WRITE HIM A SONG.
PEREC GIVES HIM A CROSSWORD PUZZLE. THE CLUE FOR 7 ACROSS IS "NAPOLEON'S HORSE."
LATER, PEREC IS ASKED WHY.
I DON'T REMEMBER.

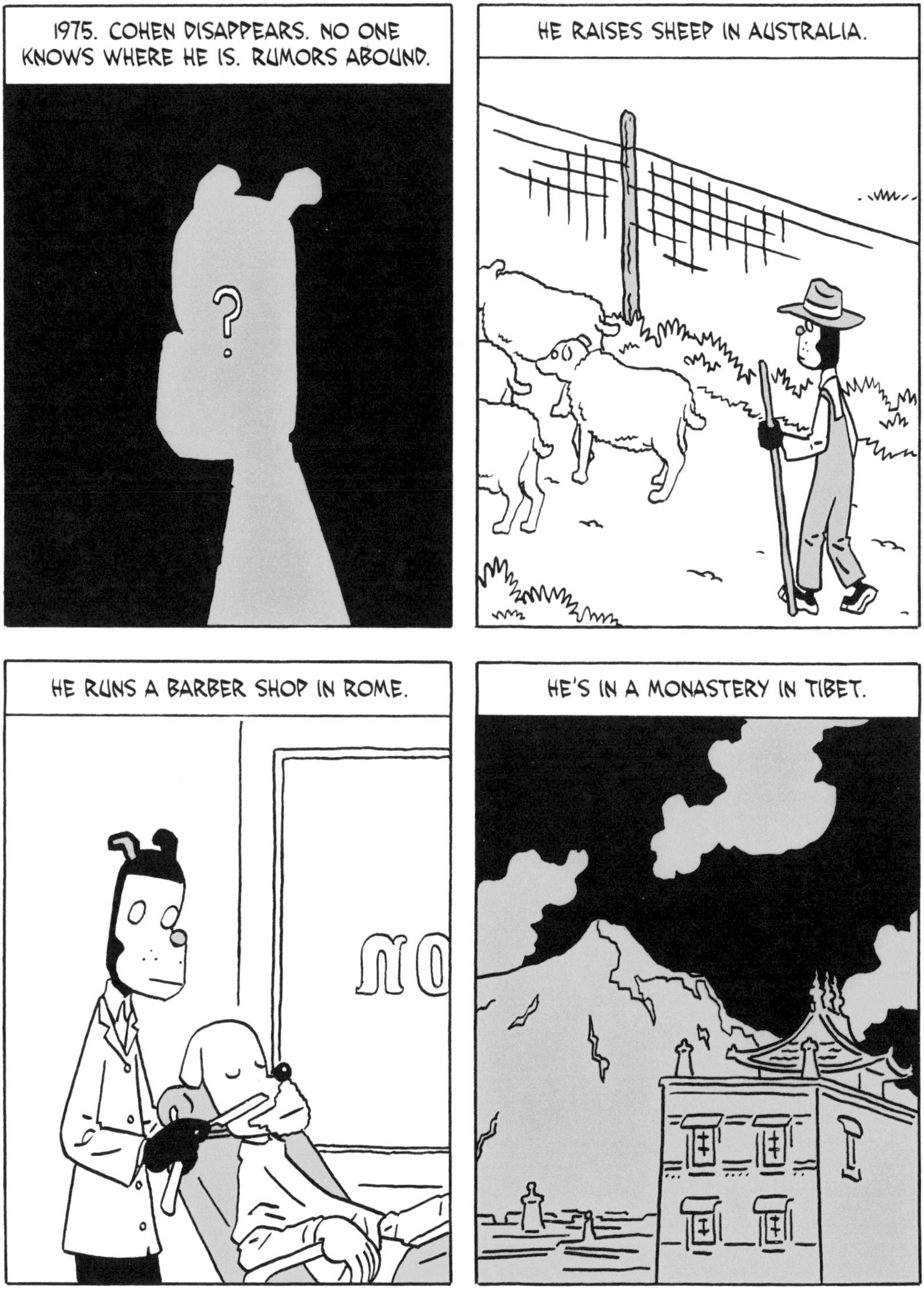
1975. COHEN DISAPPEARS. NO ONE KNOWS WHERE HE IS. RUMORS ABOUND.
HE RAISES SHEEP IN AUSTRALIA.
HE RUNS A BARBER SHOP IN ROME.
HE'S IN A MONASTERY IN TIBET.

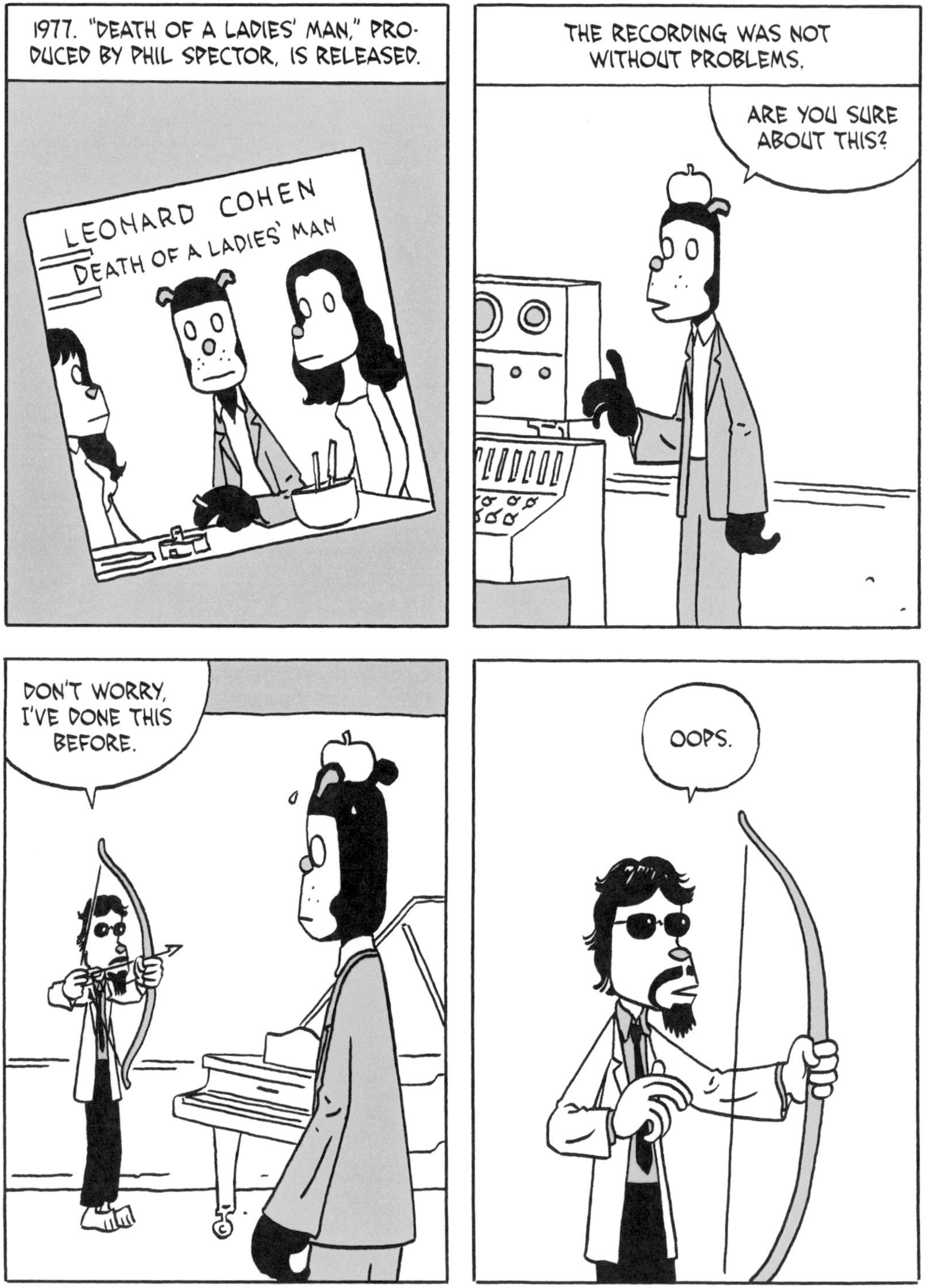
1977. "DEATH OF A LADIES' MAN," PRODUCED BY PHIL SPECTOR, IS RELEASED.
LEONARD COHEN
DEATH OF A LADIES' MAN
THE RECORDING WAS NOT WITHOUT PROBLEMS.
ARE YOU SURE ABOUT THIS?
DON'T WORRY, I'VE DONE THIS BEFORE.
OOPS.

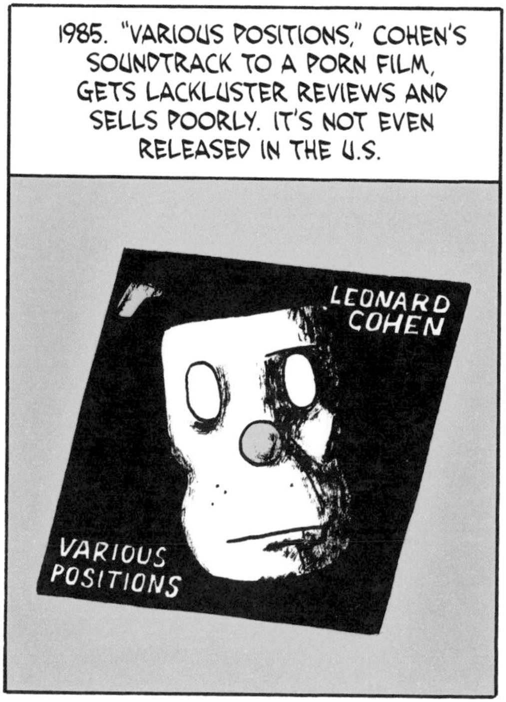
1985. "VARIOUS POSITIONS," COHEN'S SOUNDTRACK TO A PORN FILM, GETS LACKLUSTER REVIEWS AND SELLS POORLY. IT'S NOT EVEN RELEASED IN THE U.S.
LEONARD COHEN
VARIOUS POSITIONS

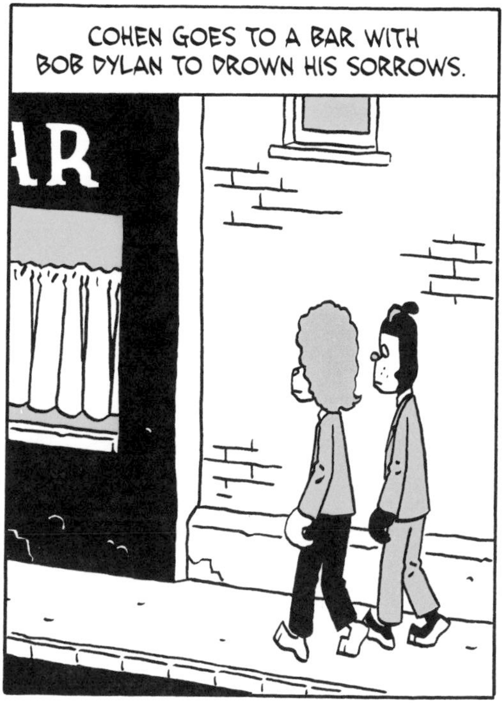
COHEN GOES TO A BAR WITH BOB DYLAN TO DROWN HIS SORROWS.
AR

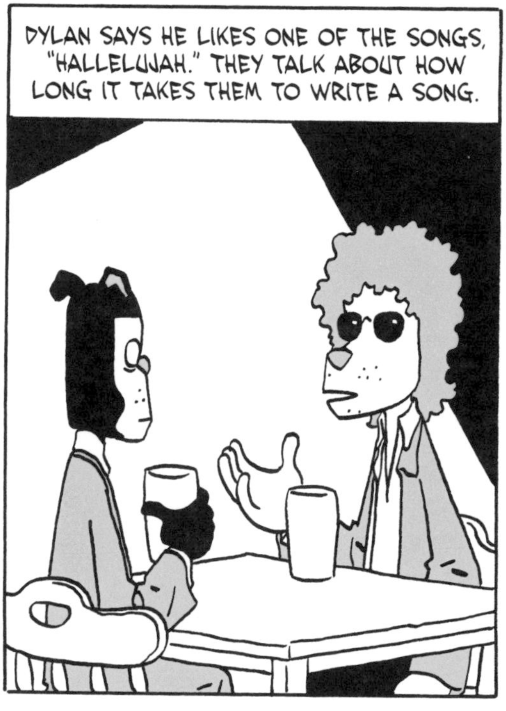
DYLAN SAYS HE LIKES ONE OF THE SONGS, "HALLELUJAH." THEY TALK ABOUT HOW LONG IT TAKES THEM TO WRITE A SONG.

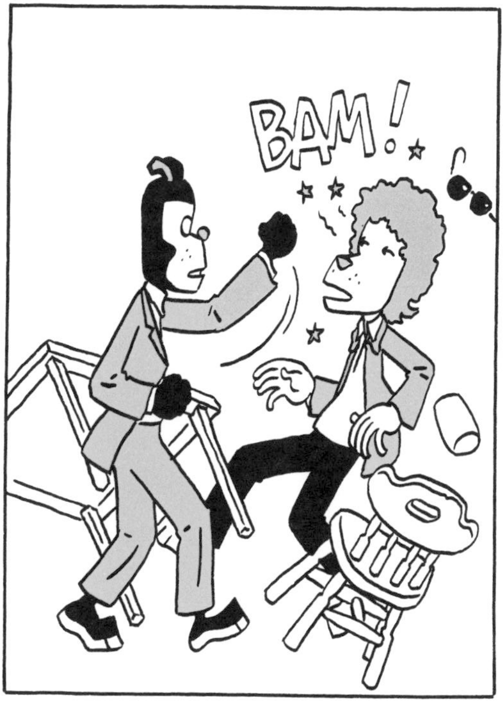
BAM!

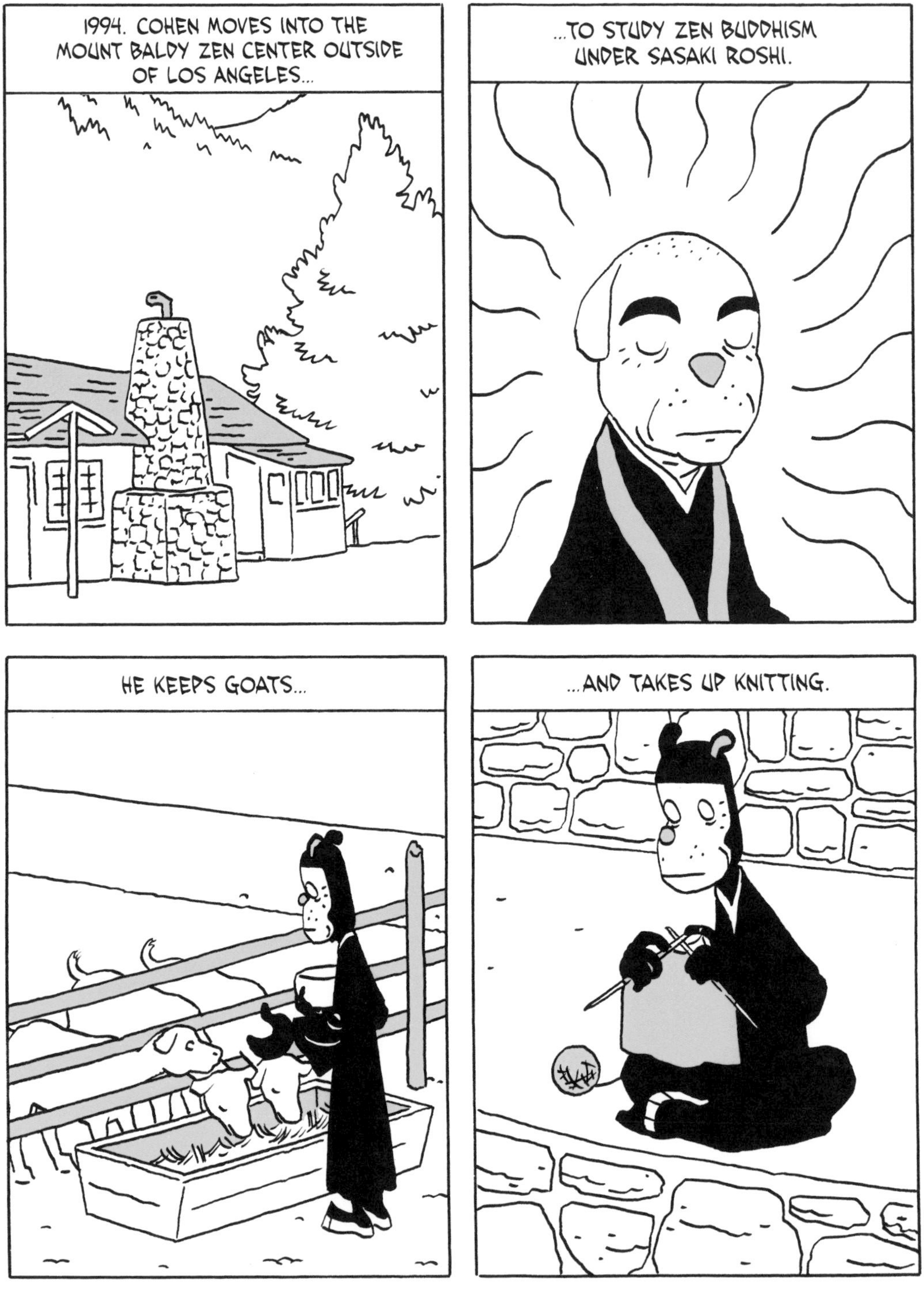

1994. COHEN MOVES INTO THE MOUNT BALDY ZEN CENTER OUTSIDE OF LOS ANGELES...
...TO STUDY ZEN BUDDHISM UNDER SASAKI ROSHI.
HE KEEPS GOATS...
...AND TAKES UP KNITTING.

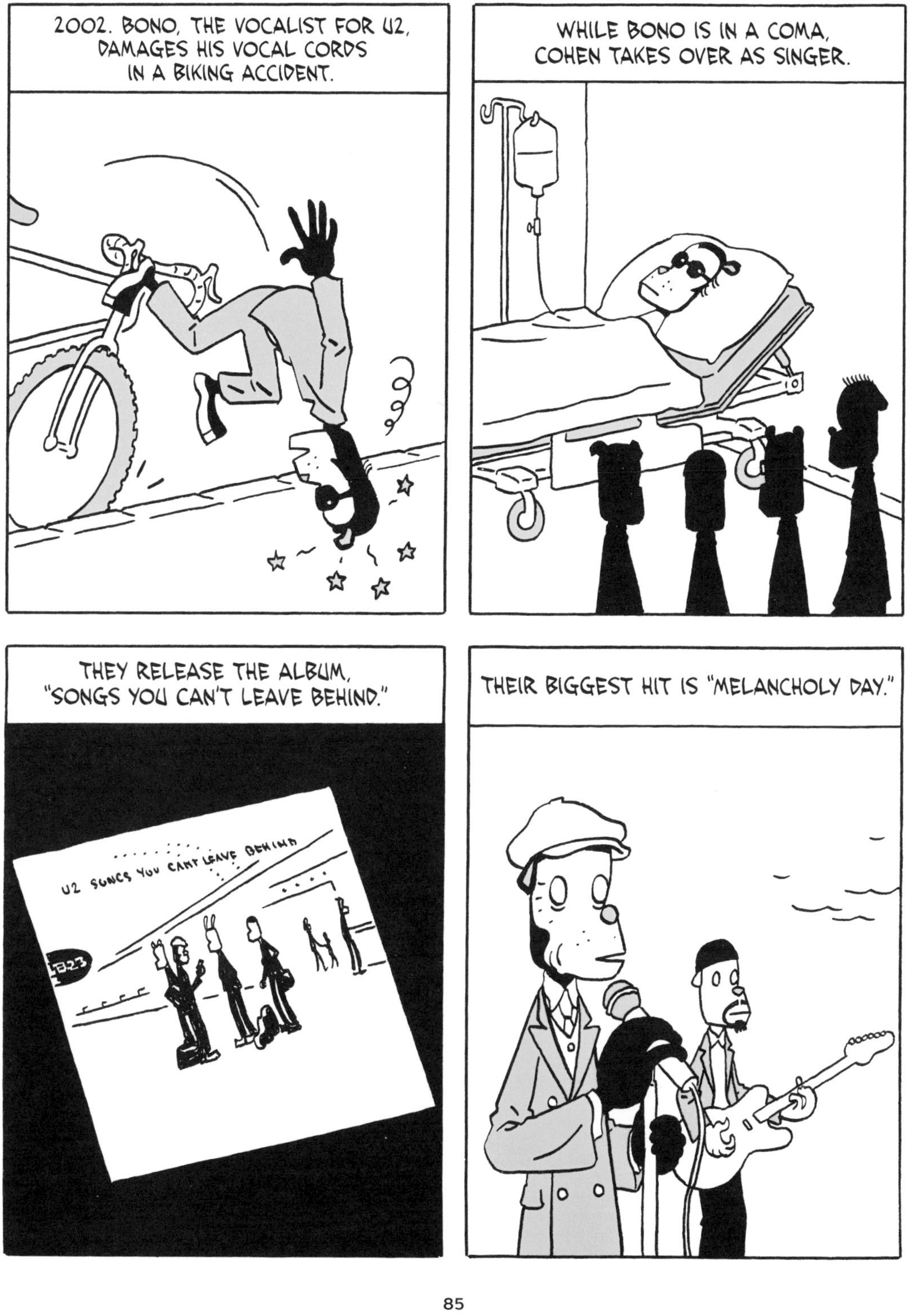
2002. BONO, THE VOCALIST FOR U2, DAMAGES HIS VOCAL CORDS IN A BIKING ACCIDENT.
WHILE BONO IS IN A COMA, COHEN TAKES OVER AS SINGER.
THEY RELEASE THE ALBUM, "SONGS YOU CAN'T LEAVE BEHIND."
U2 SONGS YOU CANT LEAVE BEHIND
THEIR BIGGEST HIT IS "MELANCHOLY DAY."

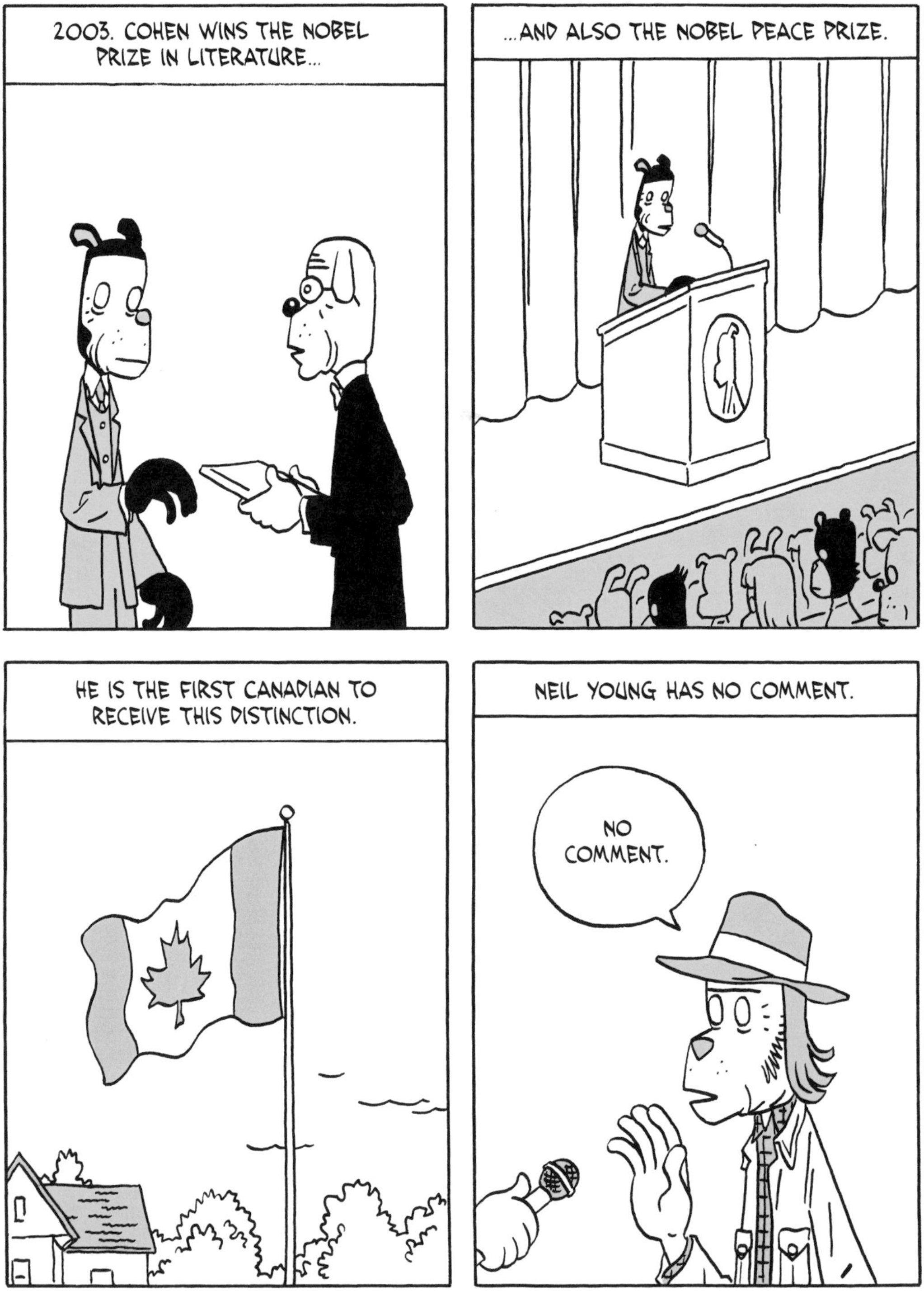
2003. COHEN WINS THE NOBEL PRIZE IN LITERATURE...
...AND ALSO THE NOBEL PEACE PRIZE.
HE IS THE FIRST CANADIAN TO RECEIVE THIS DISTINCTION.
NEIL YOUNG HAS NO COMMENT.
NO COMMENT.

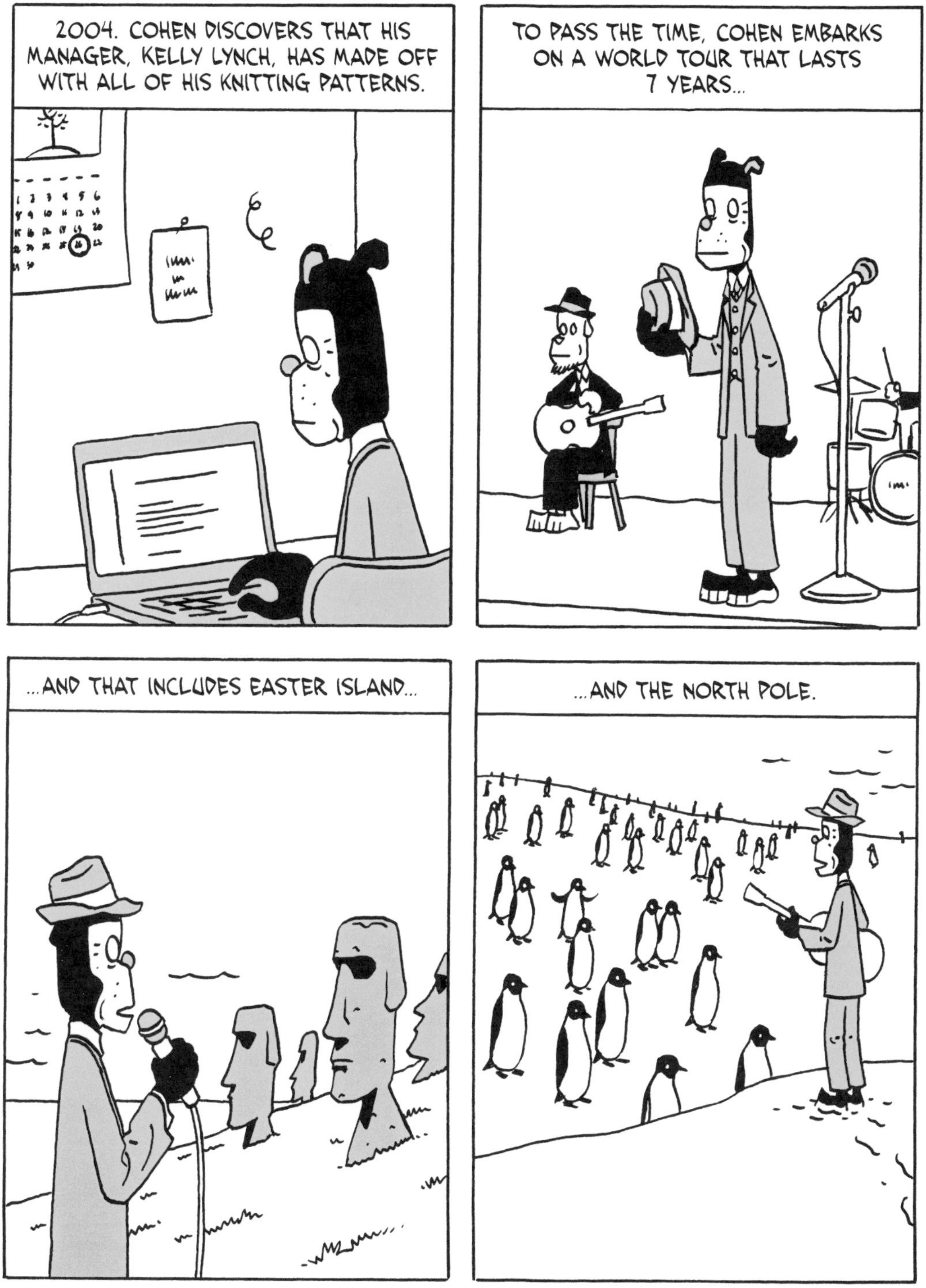
2004. COHEN DISCOVERS THAT HIS MANAGER, KELLY LYNCH, HAS MADE OFF WITH ALL OF HIS KNITTING PATTERNS.
TO PASS THE TIME, COHEN EMBARKS ON A WORLD TOUR THAT LASTS 7 YEARS...
...AND THAT INCLUDES EASTER ISLAND...
...AND THE NORTH POLE.

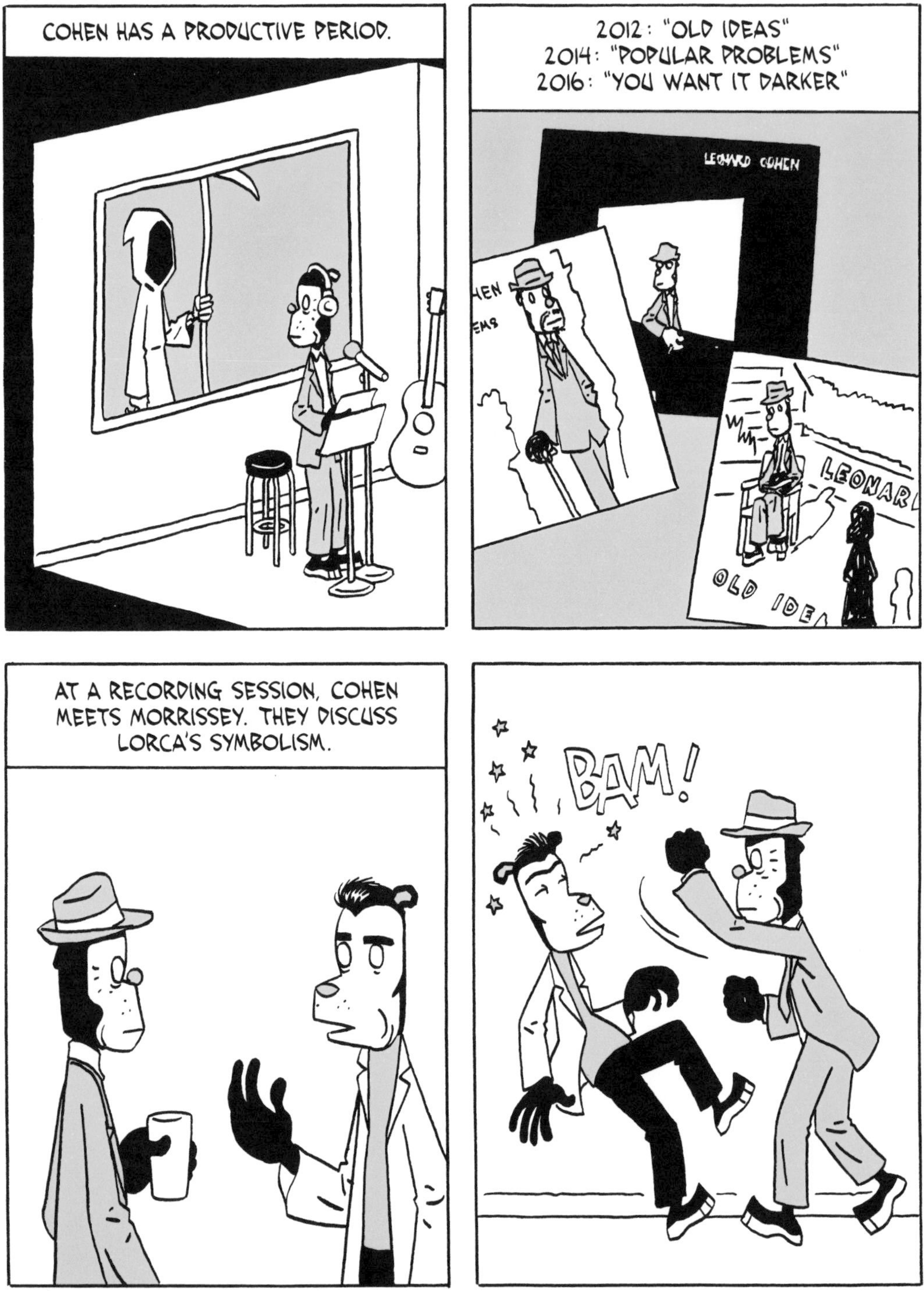
COHEN HAS A PRODUCTIVE PERIOD.
2012: "OLD IDEAS"
2014: "POPULAR PROBLEMS"
2016: "YOU WANT IT DARKER"
LEONARD COHEN
AT A RECORDING SESSION, COHEN MEETS MORRISSEY. THEY DISCUSS LORCA'S SYMBOLISM.
BAM!

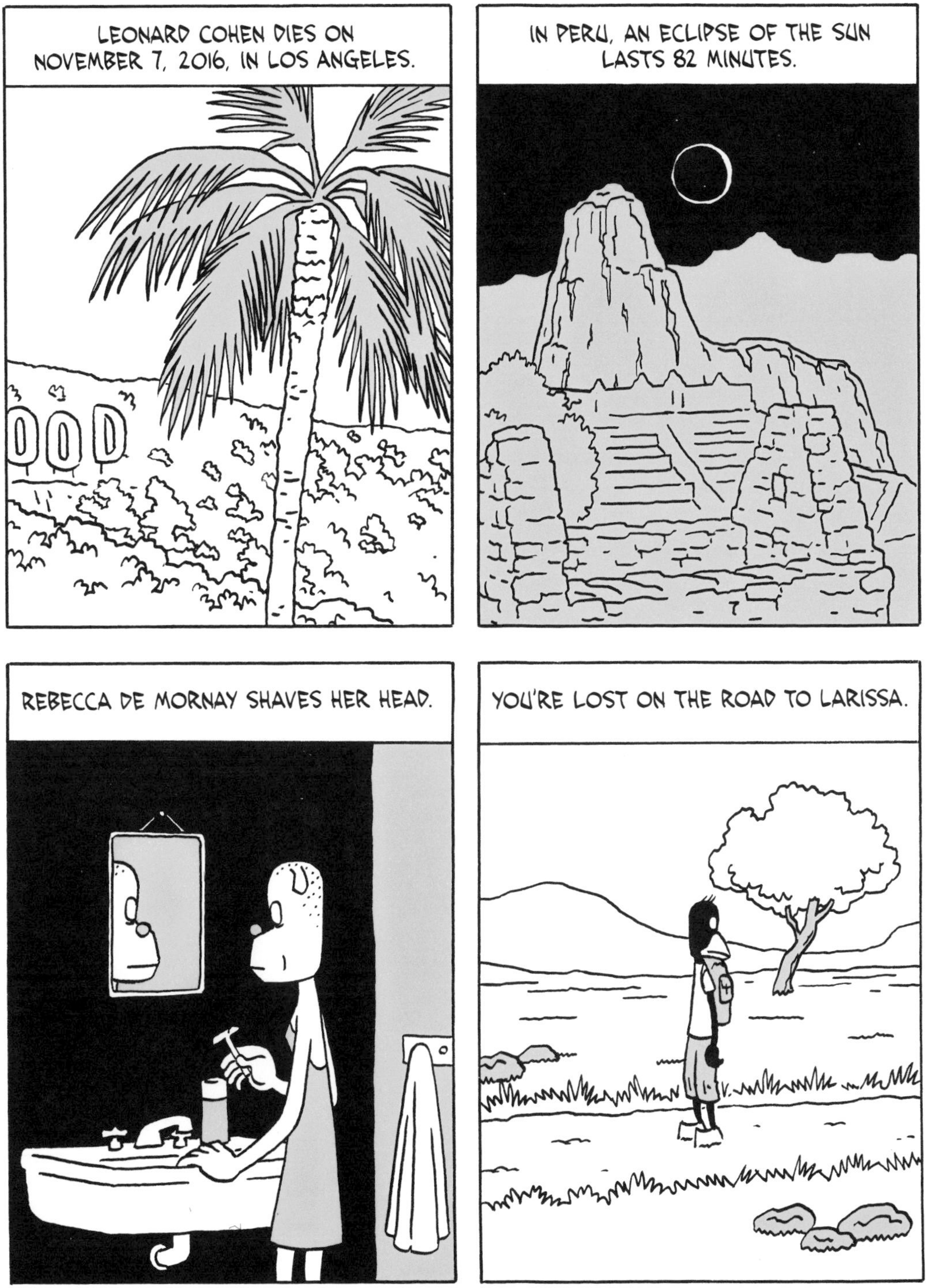
LEONARD COHEN DIES ON NOVEMBER 7, 2016, IN LOS ANGELES.
IN PERU, AN ECLIPSE OF THE SUN LASTS 82 MINUTES.
REBECCA DE MORNAY SHAVES HER HEAD.
YOU'RE LOST ON THE ROAD TO LARISSA.

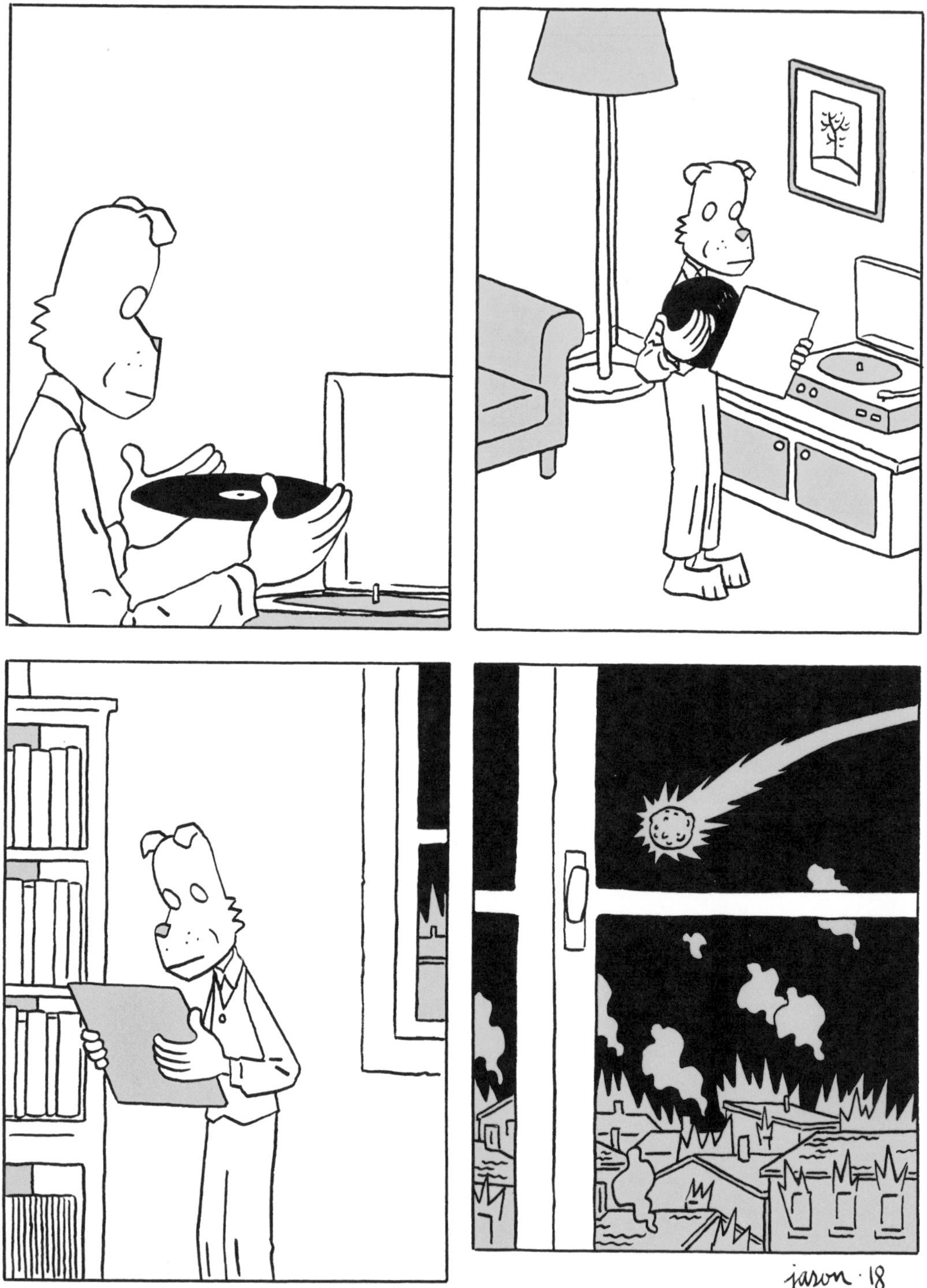
jason · 18

The Diamonds

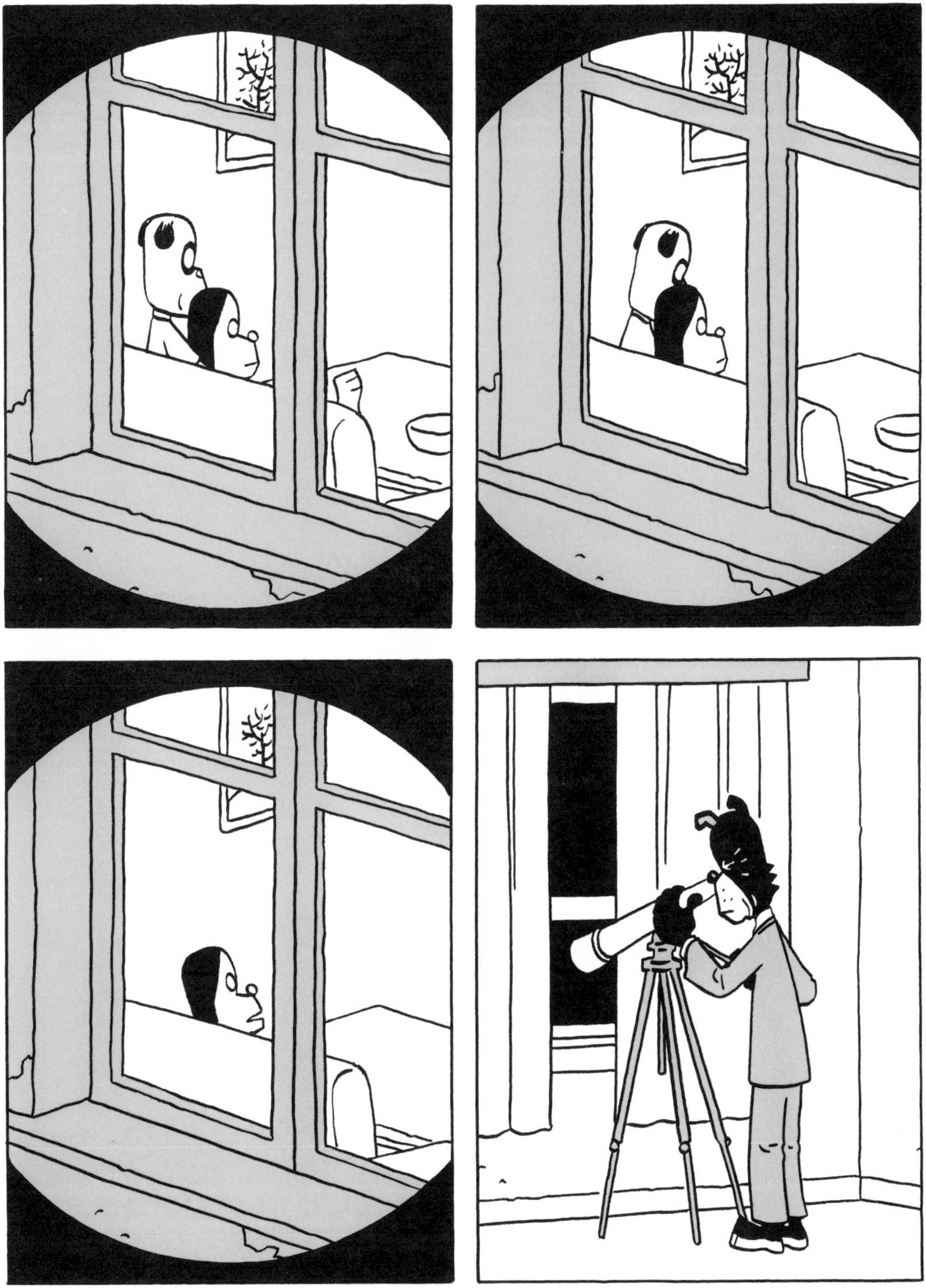

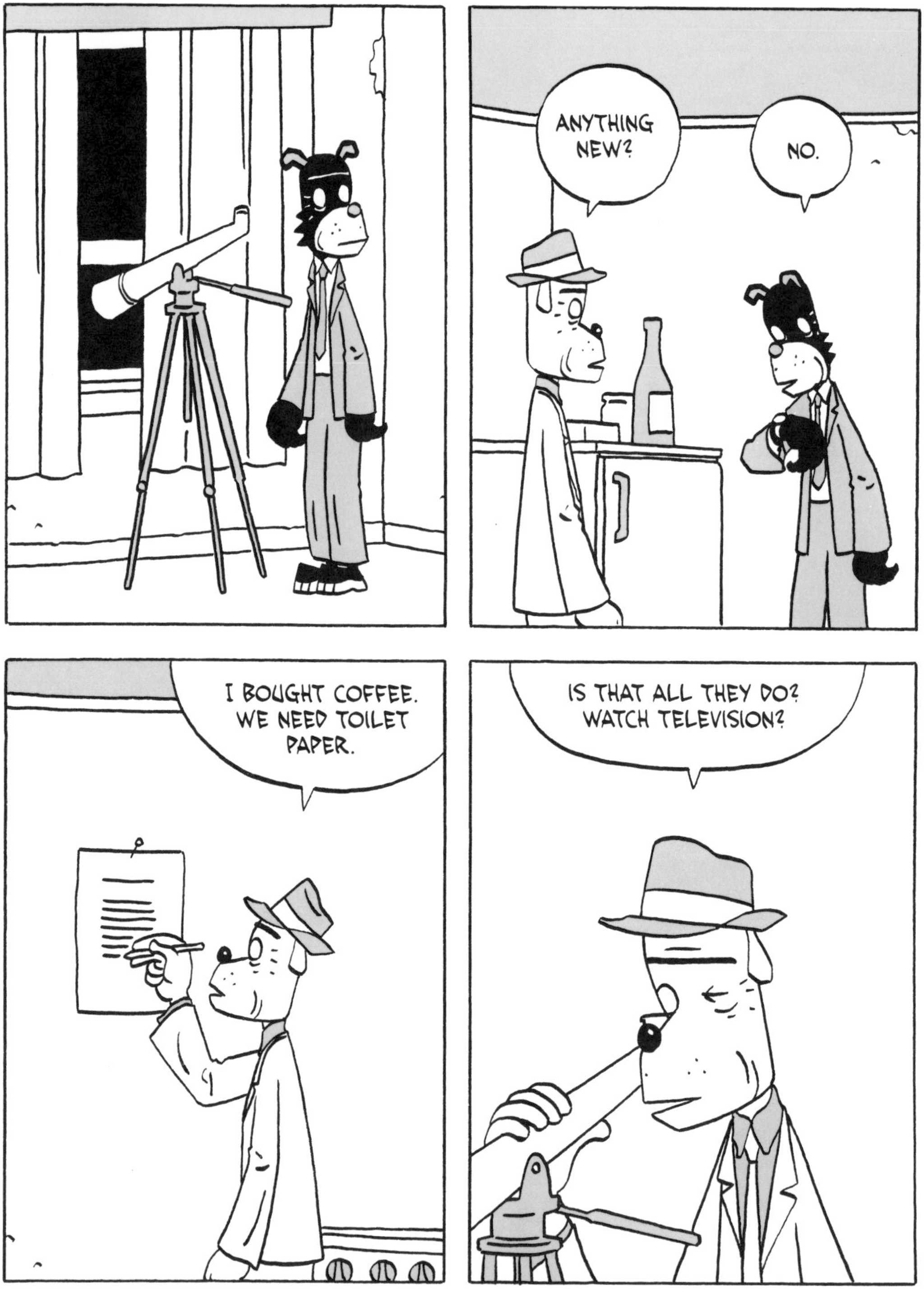
ANYTHING NEW?
NO.
I BOUGHT COFFEE. WE NEED TOILET PAPER.
IS THAT ALL THEY DO? WATCH TELEVISION?

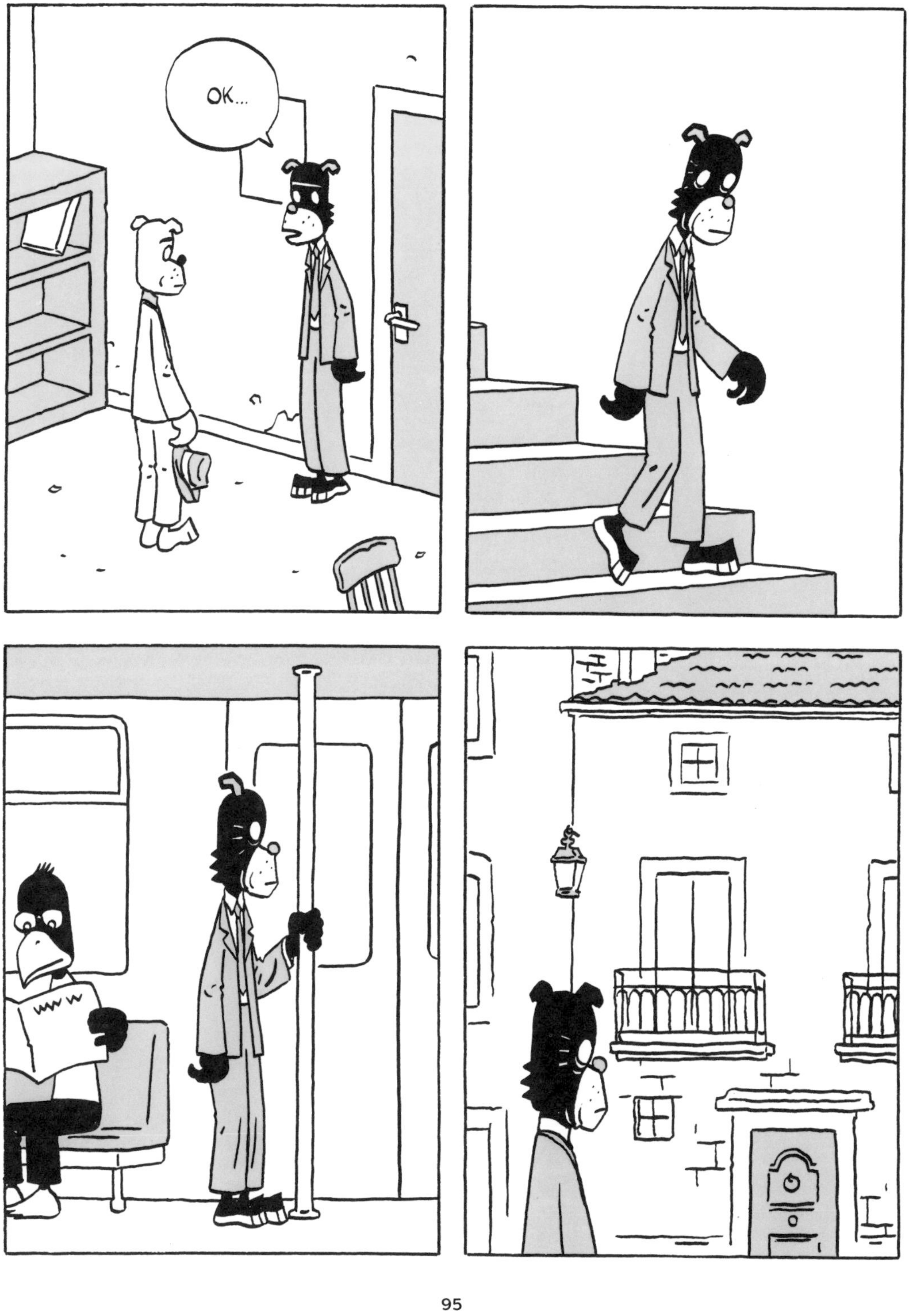
OK...

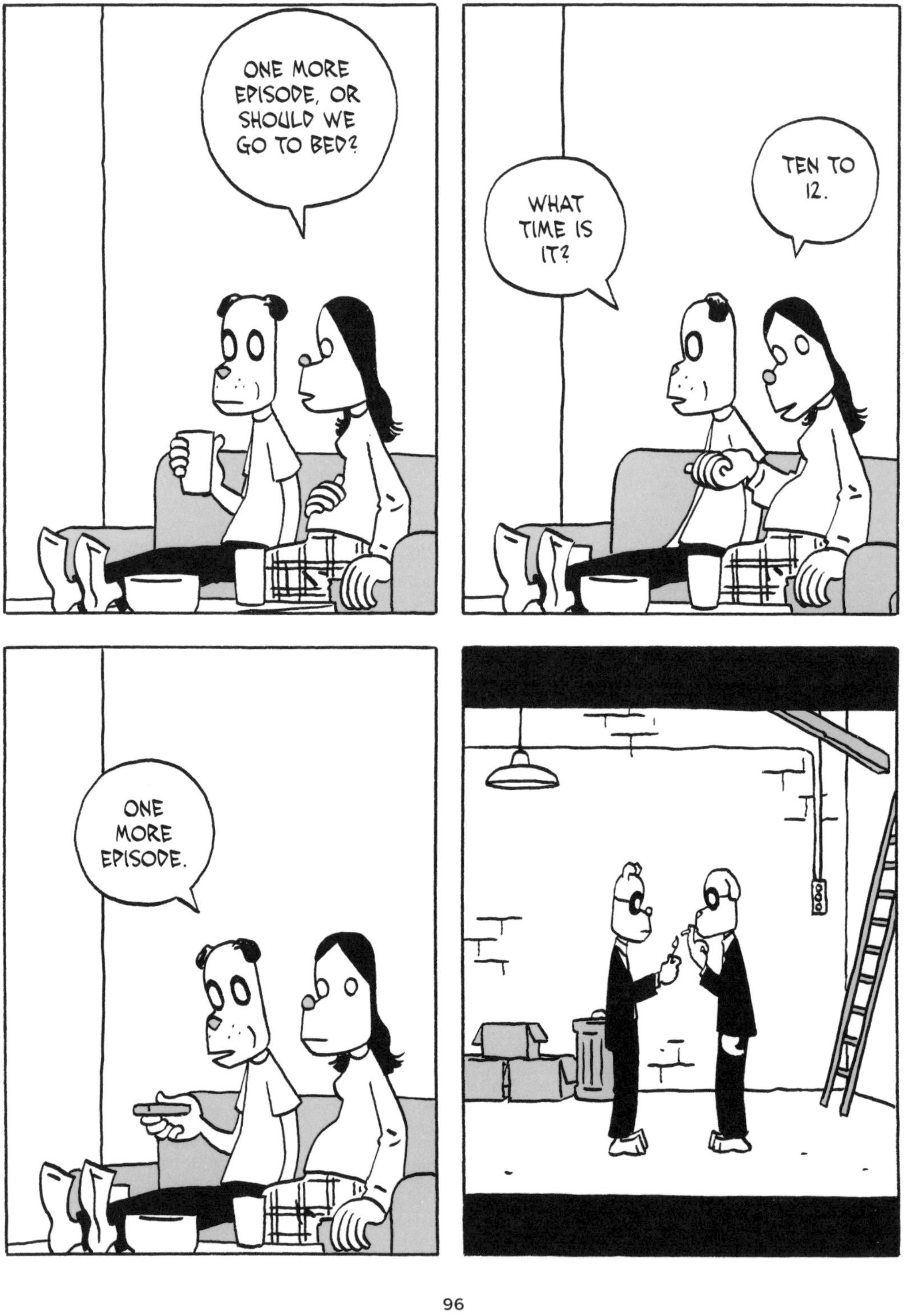
ONE MORE EPISODE, OR SHOULD WE GO TO BED?
WHAT TIME IS IT?
TEN TO 12.
ONE MORE EPISODE.

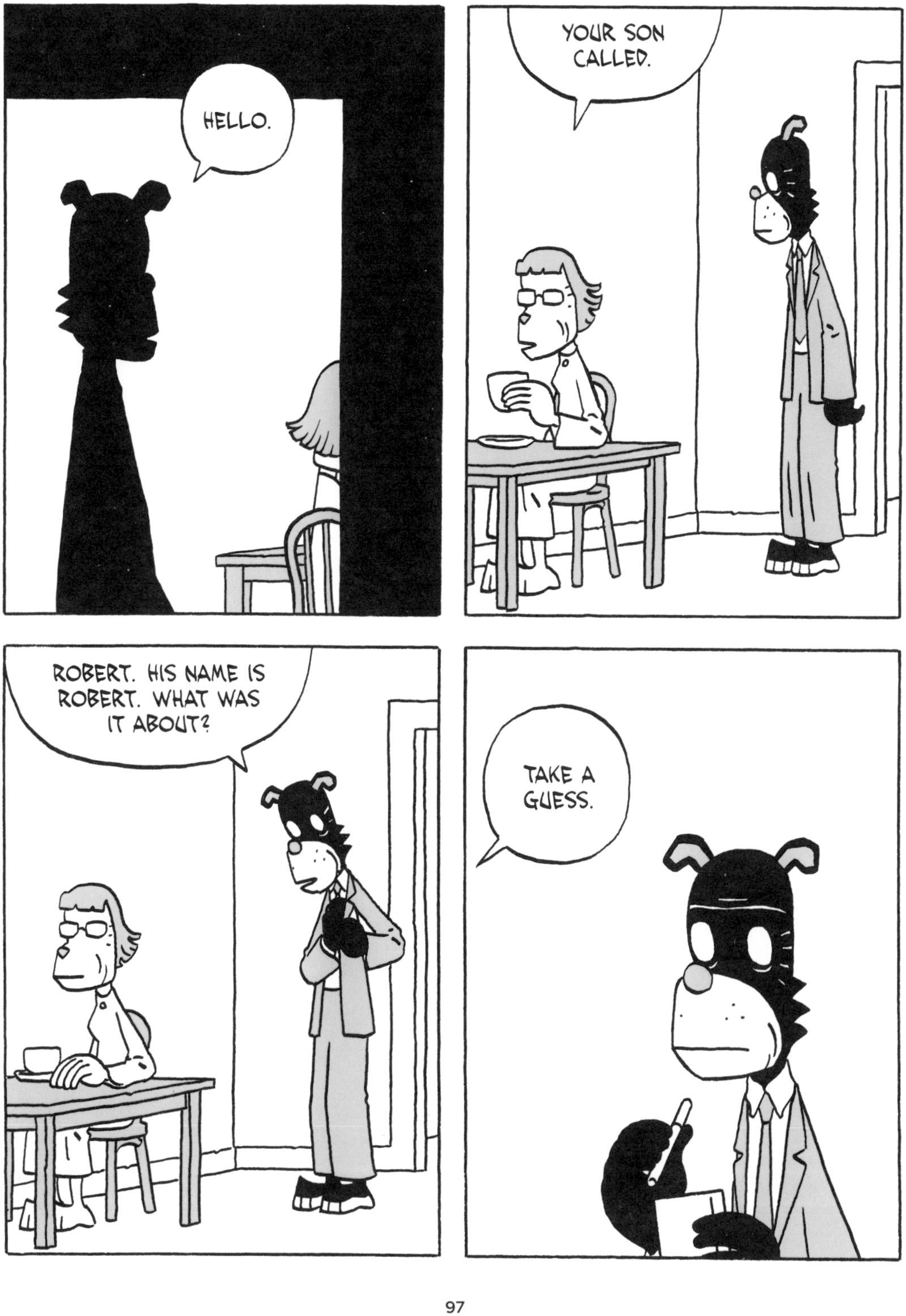
HELLO.
YOUR SON CALLED.
ROBERT. HIS NAME IS ROBERT. WHAT WAS IT ABOUT?
TAKE A GUESS.

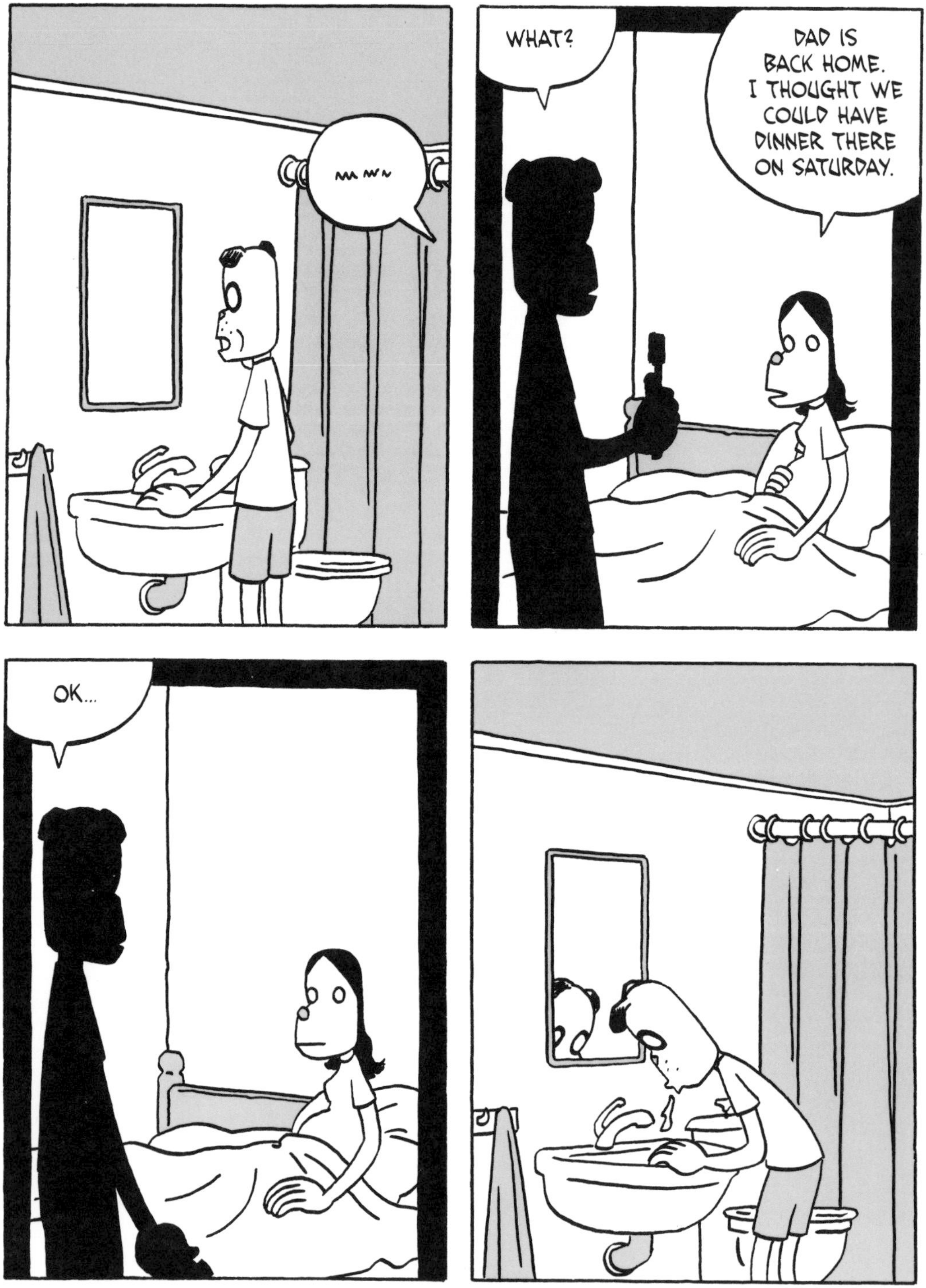
WHAT?
DAD IS BACK HOME. I THOUGHT WE COULD HAVE DINNER THERE ON SATURDAY.
OK...

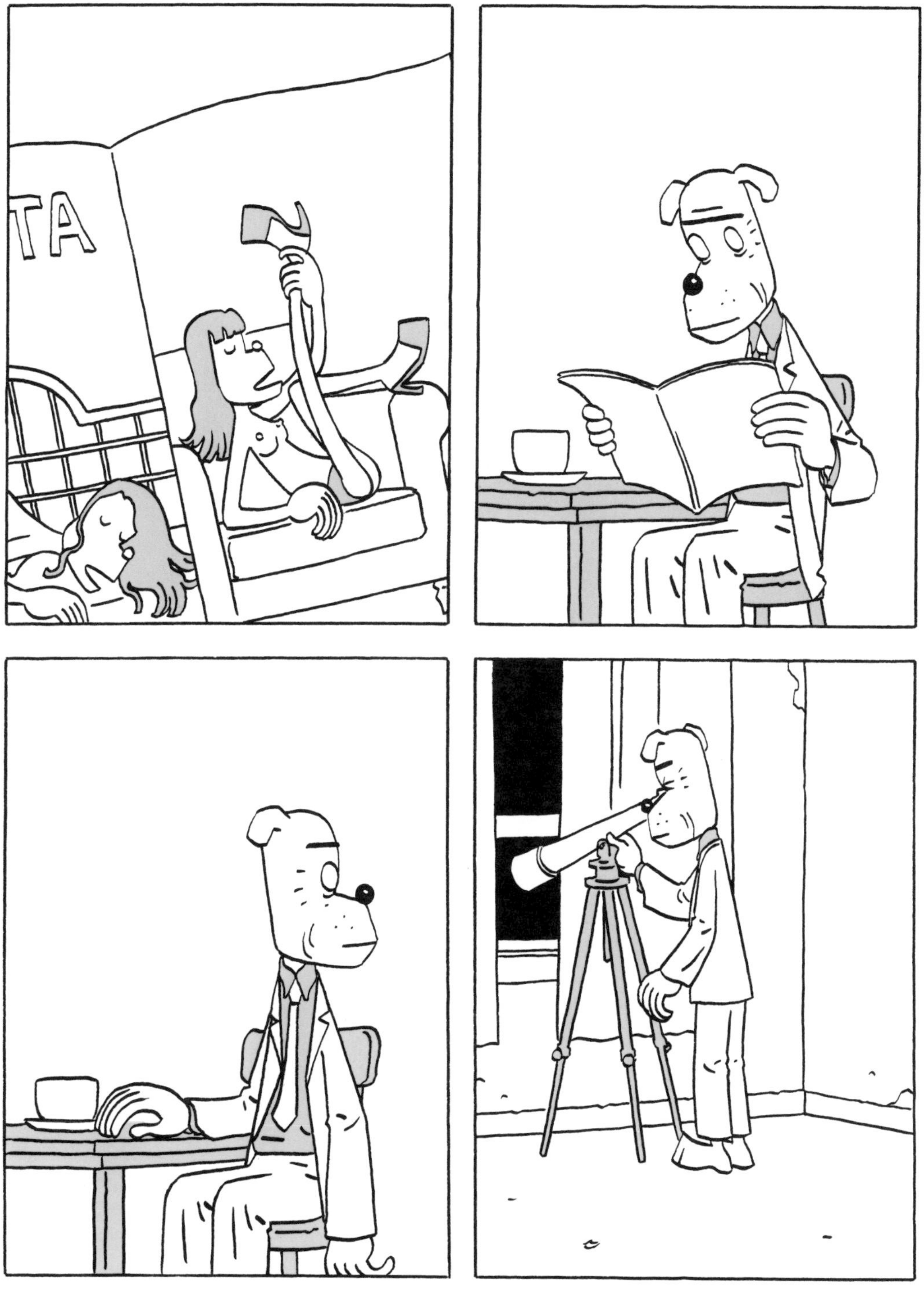
TA

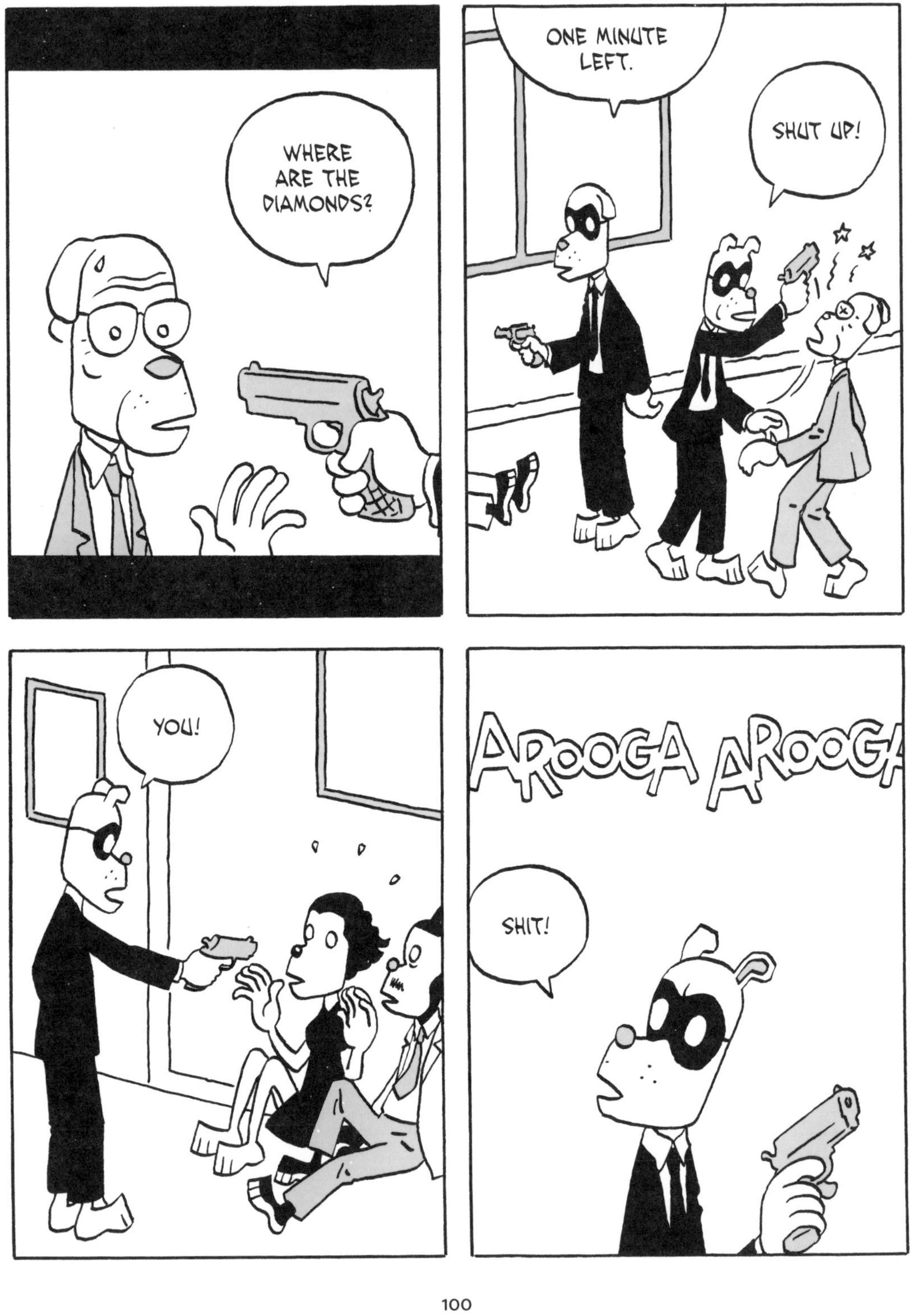
WHERE ARE THE DIAMONDS?
ONE MINUTE LEFT.
SHUT UP!
YOU!
AROOGA AROOGA
SHIT!

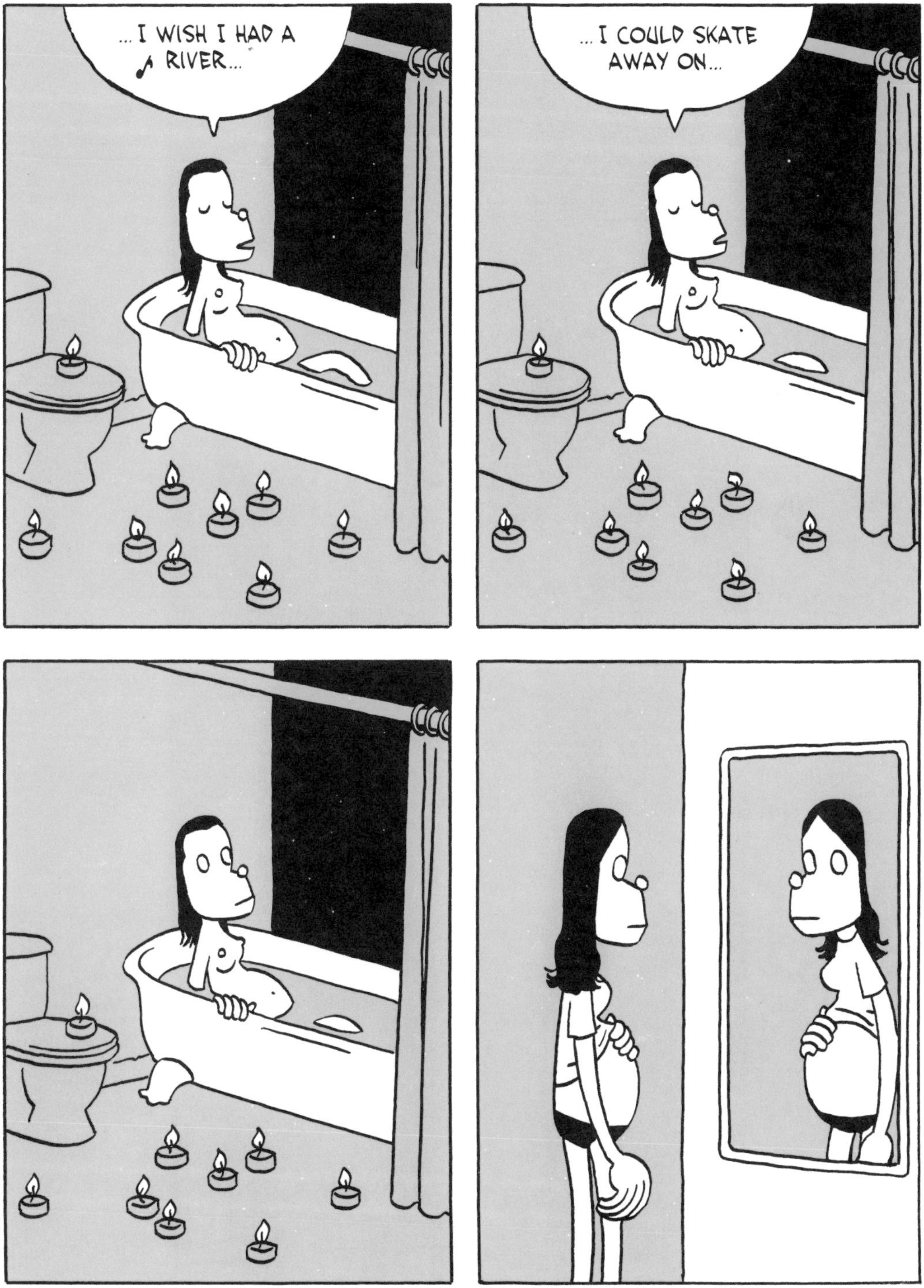
... I WISH I HAD A RIVER...
... I COULD SKATE AWAY ON...

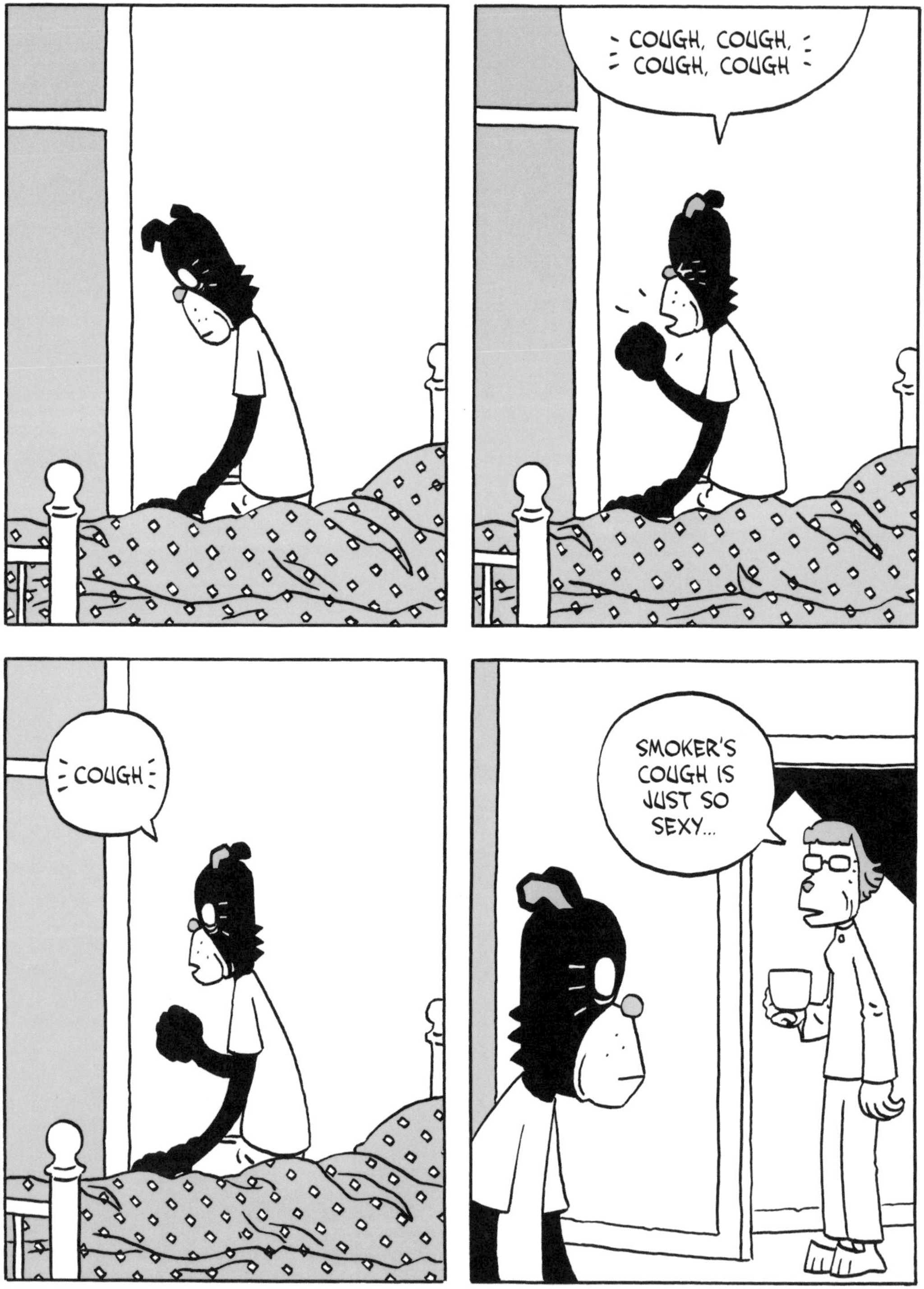
COUGH, COUGH,
COUGH, COUGH
COUGH
SMOKER'S COUGH IS JUST SO SEXY...

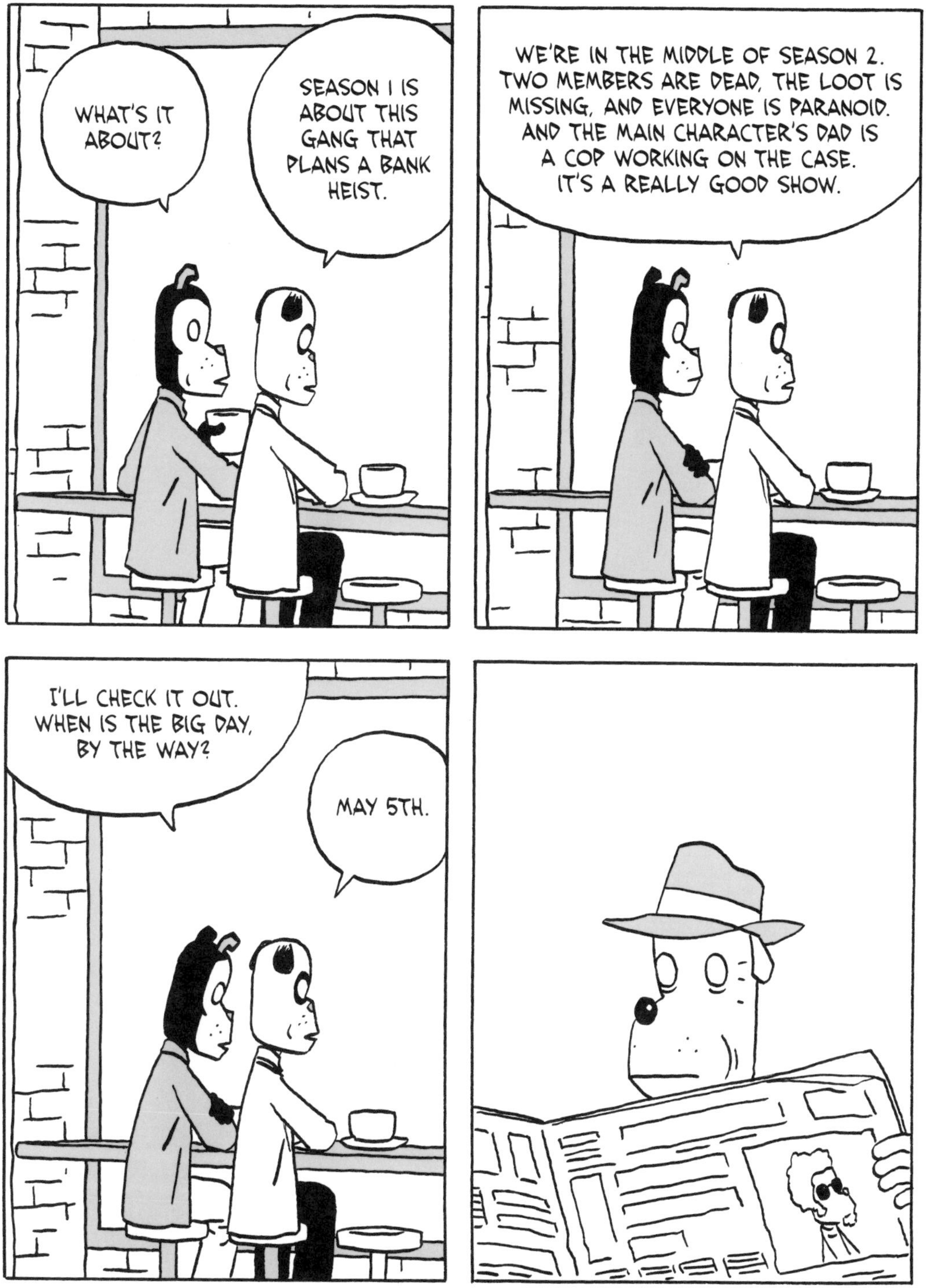
WHAT'S IT ABOUT?
SEASON 1 IS ABOUT THIS GANG THAT PLANS A BANK HEIST.
WE'RE IN THE MIDDLE OF SEASON 2. TWO MEMBERS ARE DEAD, THE LOOT IS MISSING, AND EVERYONE IS PARANOID. AND THE MAIN CHARACTER'S DAD IS A COP WORKING ON THE CASE. IT'S A REALLY GOOD SHOW.
I'LL CHECK IT OUT. WHEN IS THE BIG DAY, BY THE WAY?
MAY 5TH.

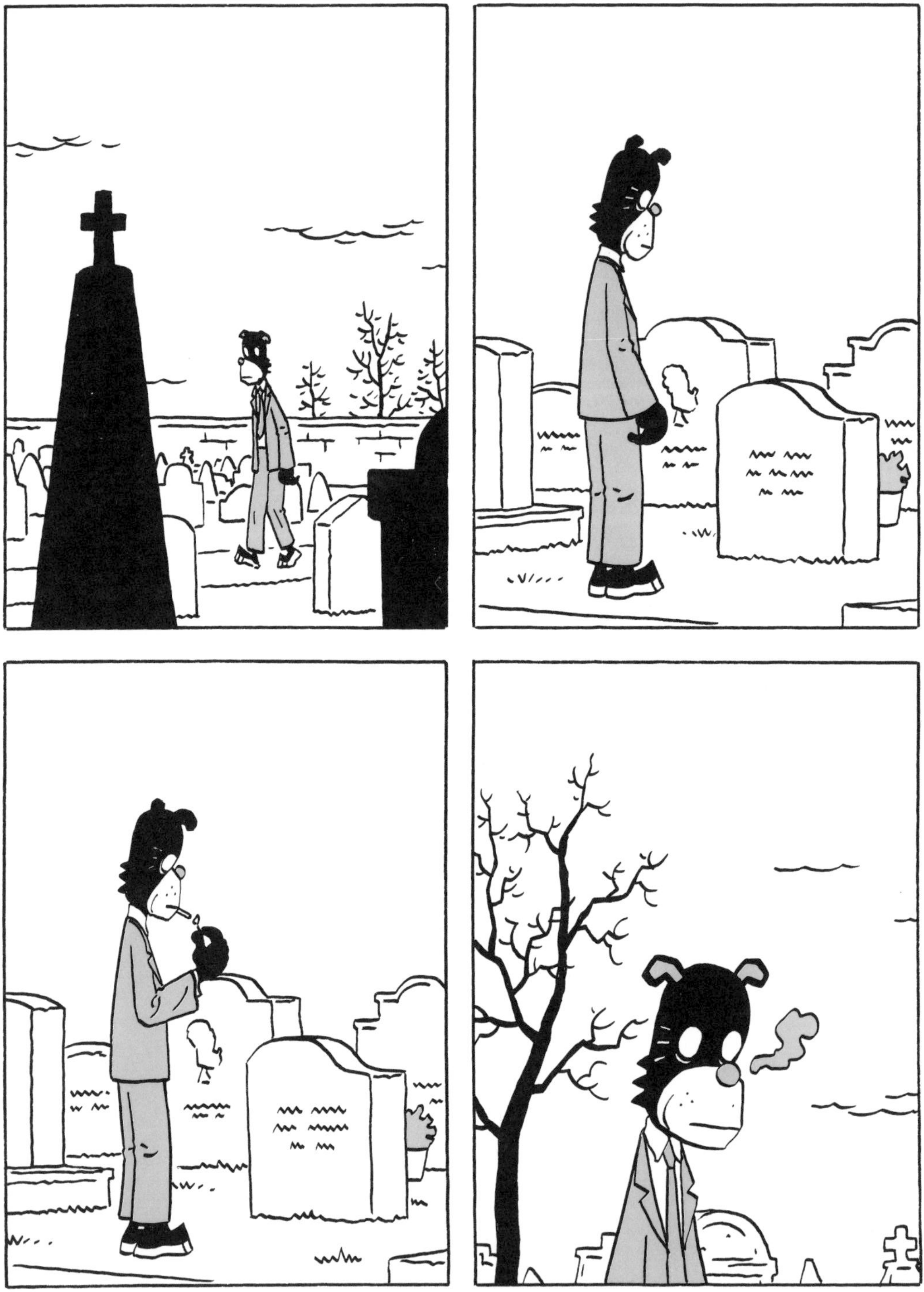

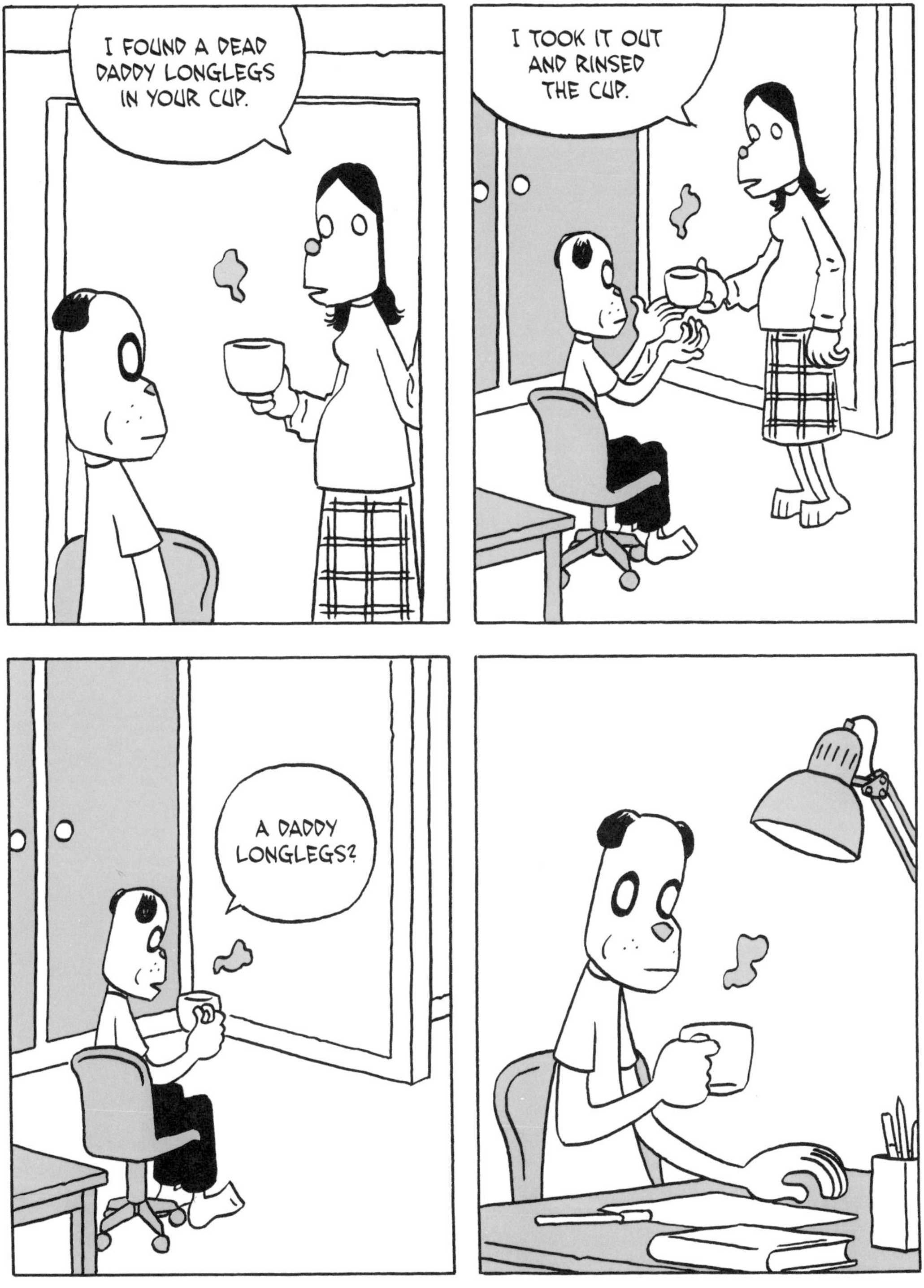
I FOUND A DEAD DADDY LONGLEGS IN YOUR CUP.
I TOOK IT OUT AND RINSED THE CUP.
A DADDY LONGLEGS?

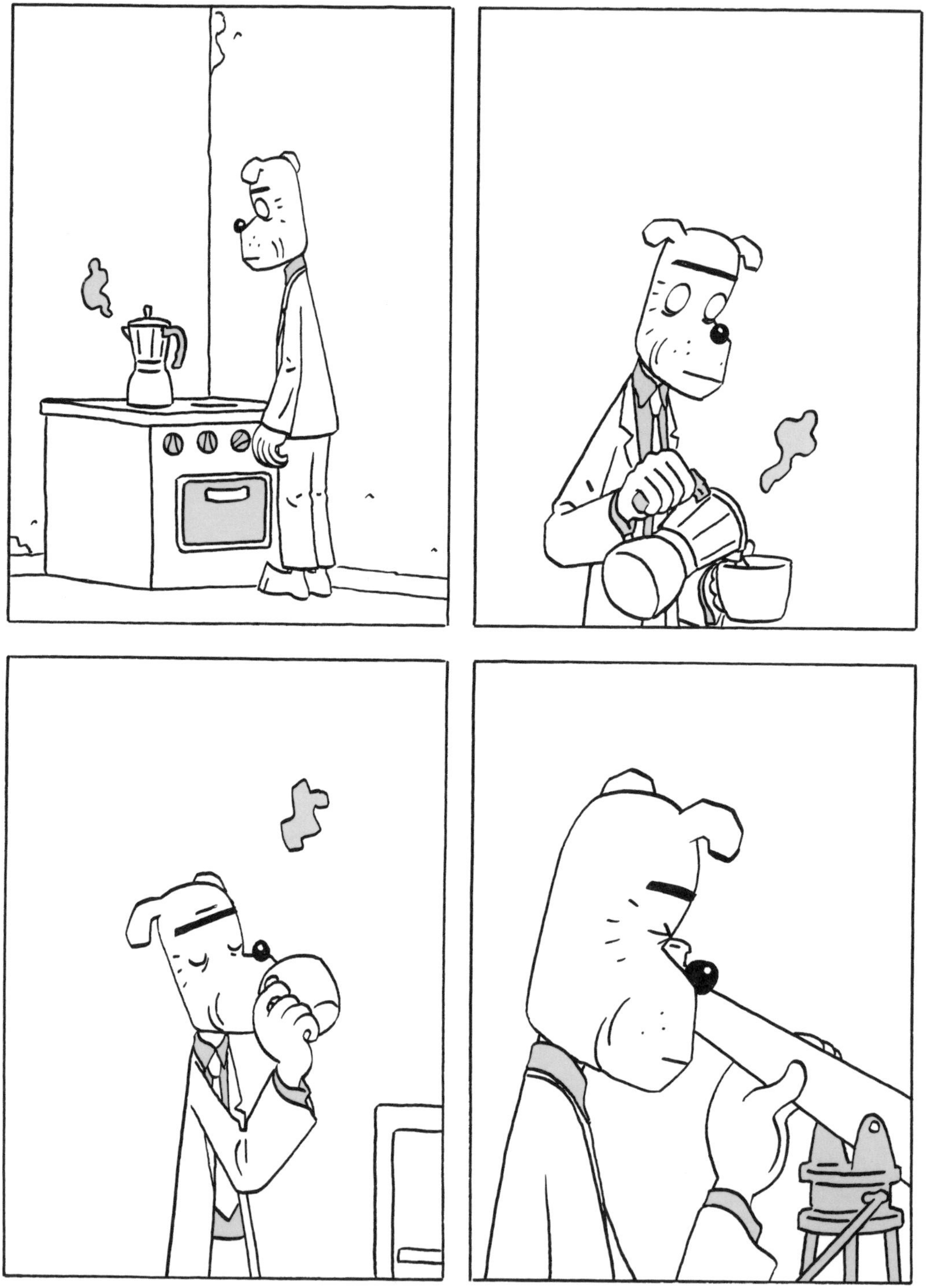

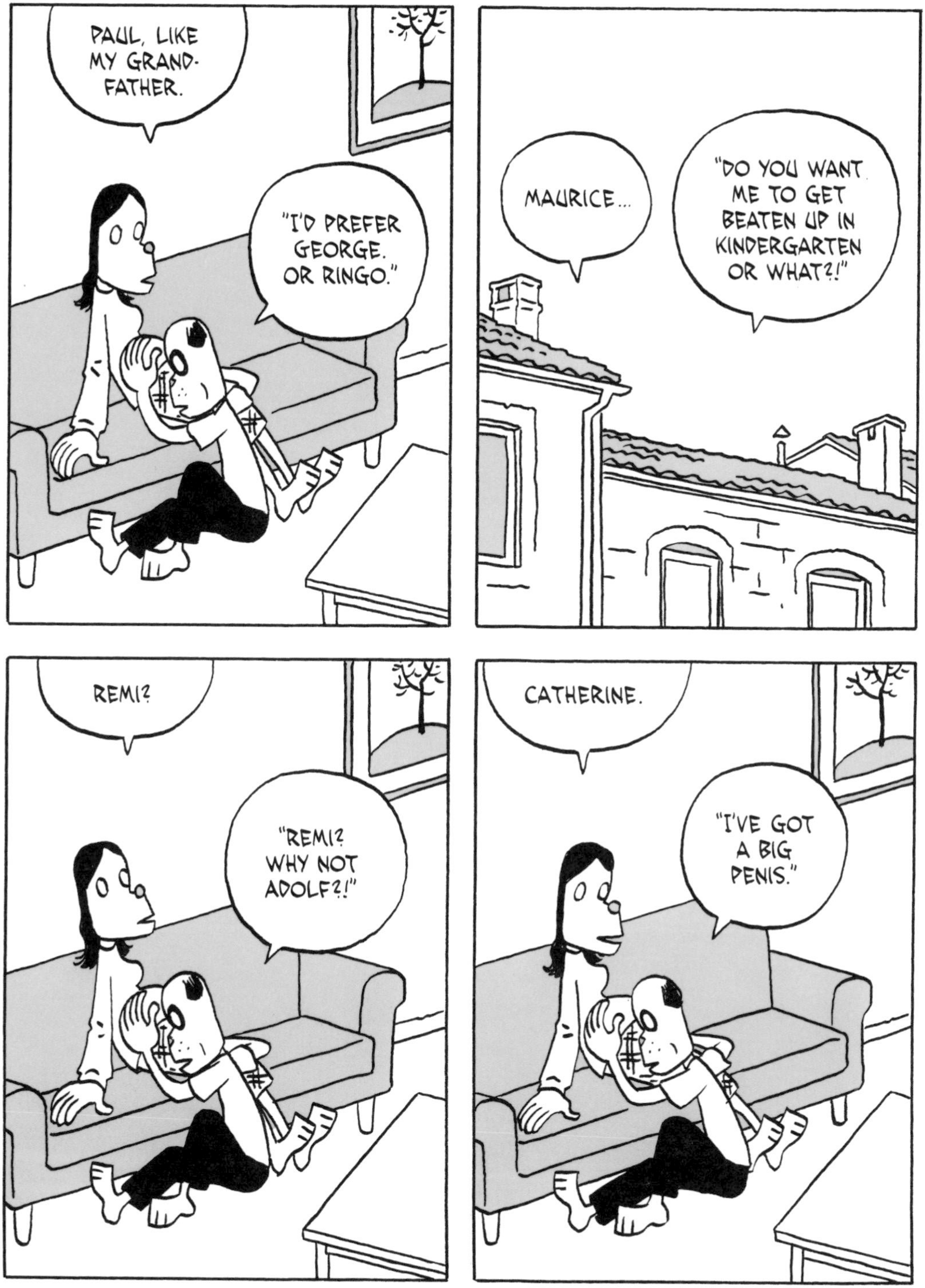
PAUL, LIKE MY GRAND-FATHER.
"I'D PREFER GEORGE. OR RINGO."
MAURICE...
"DO YOU WANT ME TO GET BEATEN UP IN KINDERGARTEN OR WHAT?!"
REMI?
"REMI? WHY NOT ADOLF?!"
CATHERINE.
"I'VE GOT A BIG PENIS."

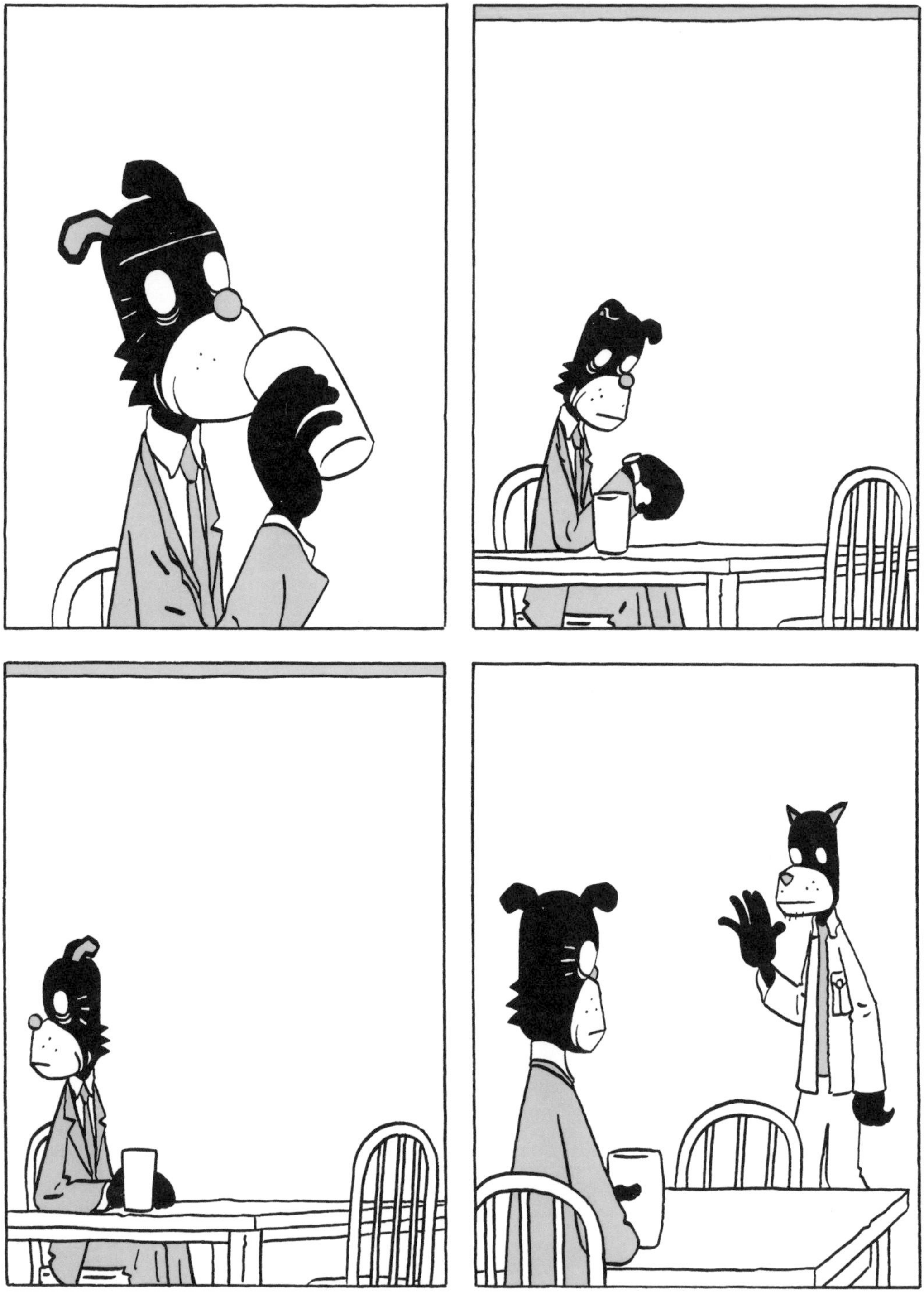

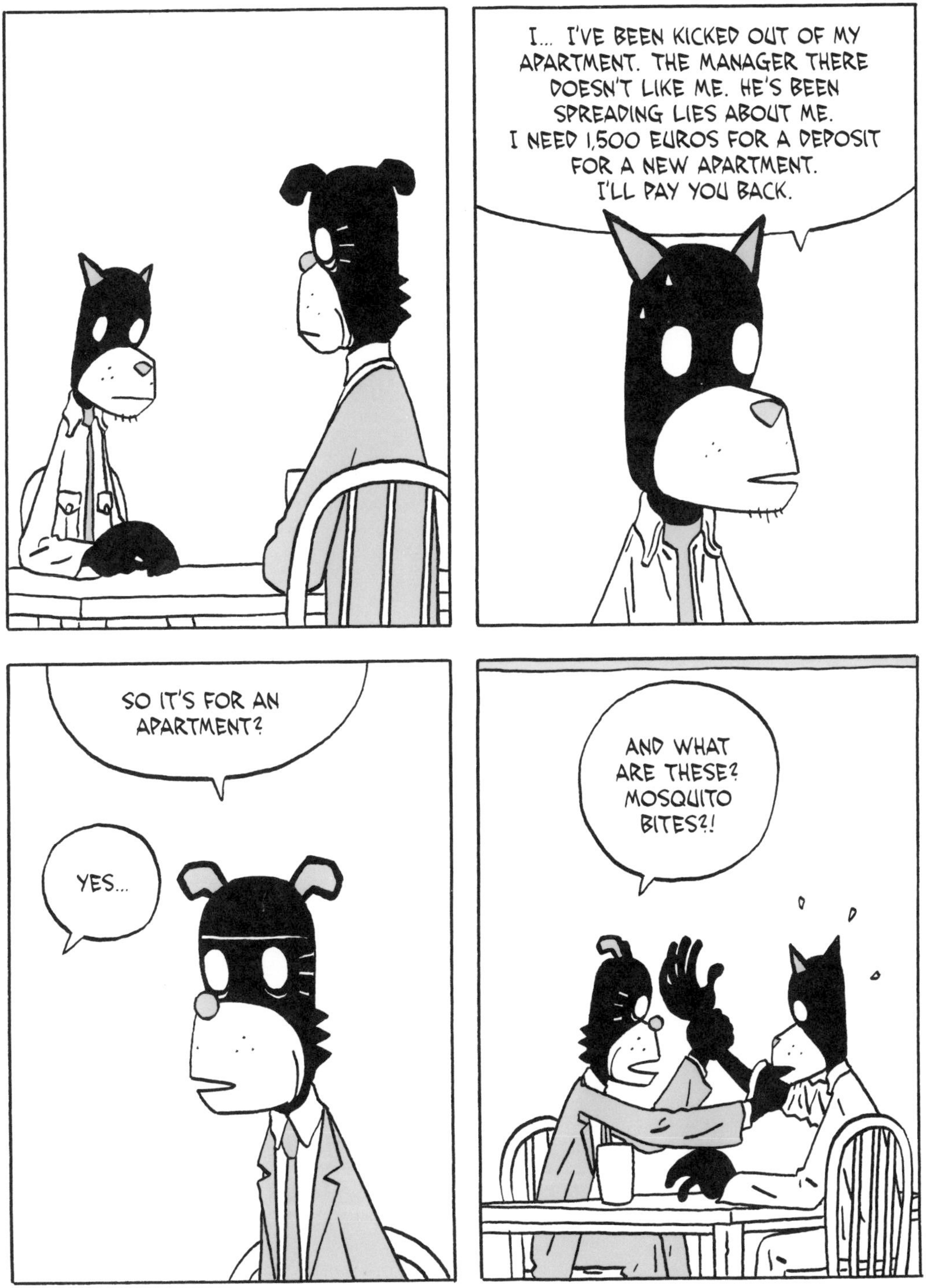
I... I'VE BEEN KICKED OUT OF MY APARTMENT. THE MANAGER THERE DOESN'T LIKE ME. HE'S BEEN SPREADING LIES ABOUT ME. I NEED 1,500 EUROS FOR A DEPOSIT FOR A NEW APARTMENT. I'LL PAY YOU BACK.
SO IT'S FOR AN APARTMENT?
YES...
AND WHAT ARE THESE? MOSQUITO BITES?!

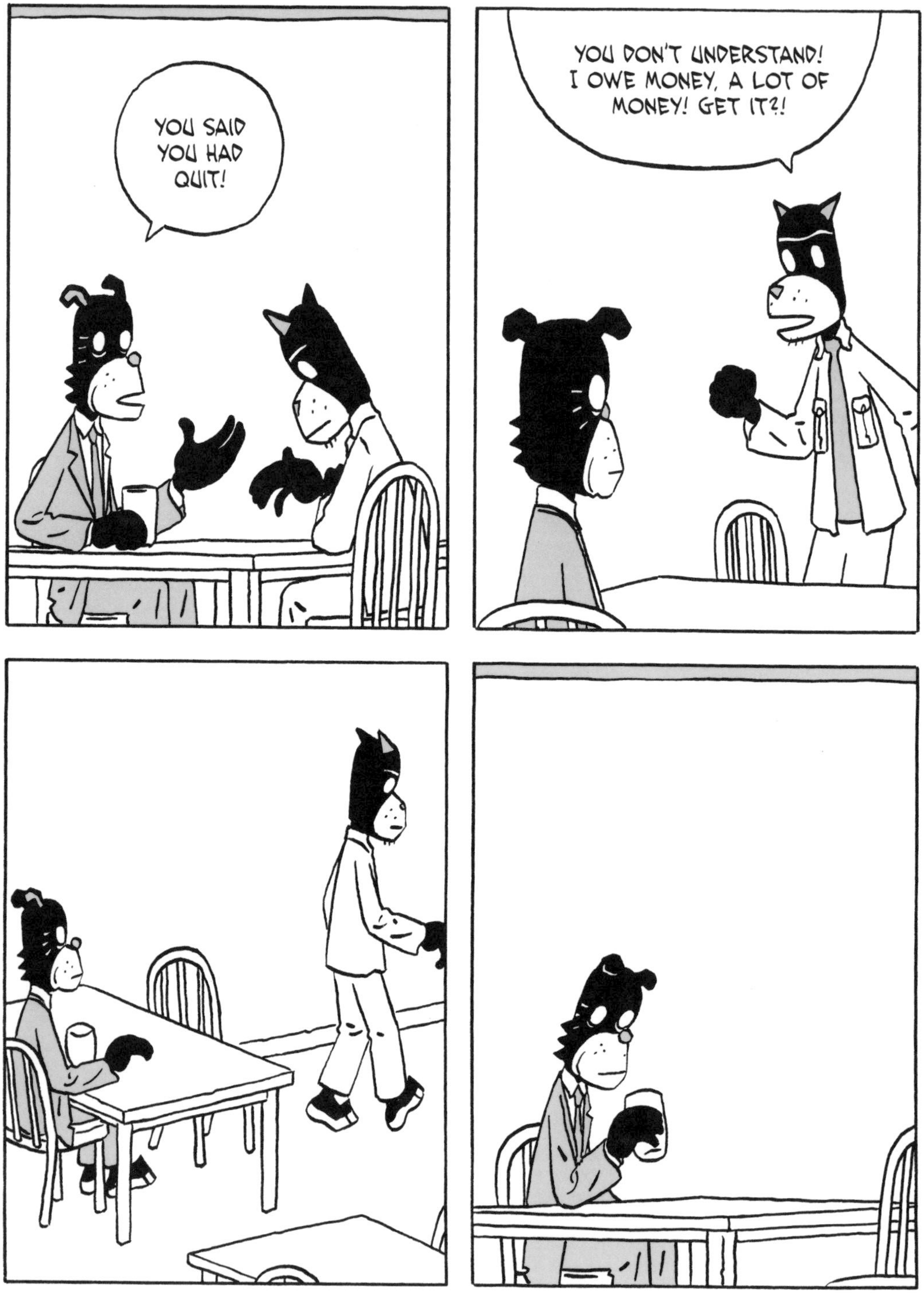
YOU SAID YOU HAD QUIT!
YOU DON'T UNDERSTAND! I OWE MONEY, A LOT OF MONEY! GET IT?!

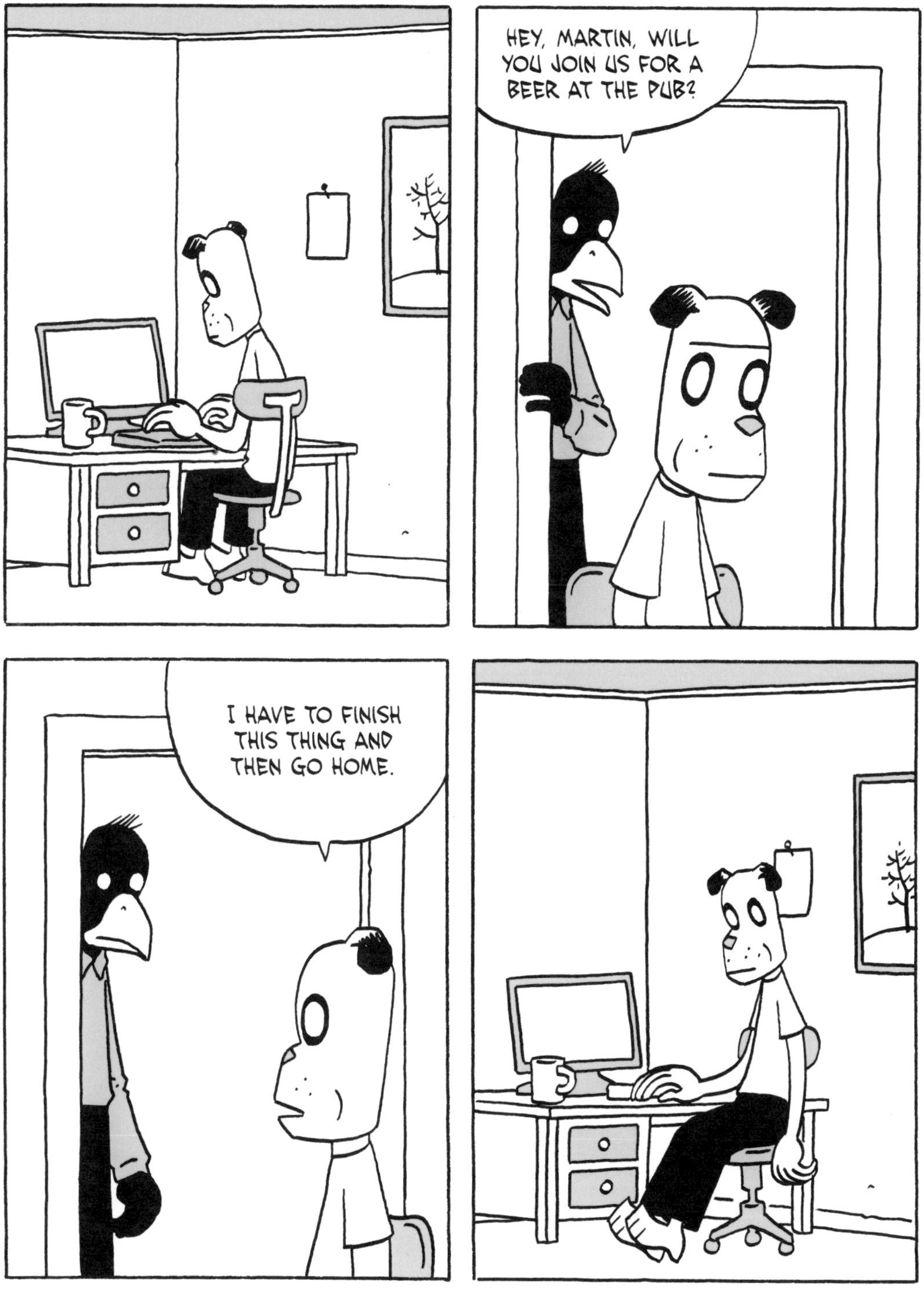
HEY, MARTIN, WILL YOU JOIN US FOR A BEER AT THE PUB?
I HAVE TO FINISH THIS THING AND THEN GO HOME.

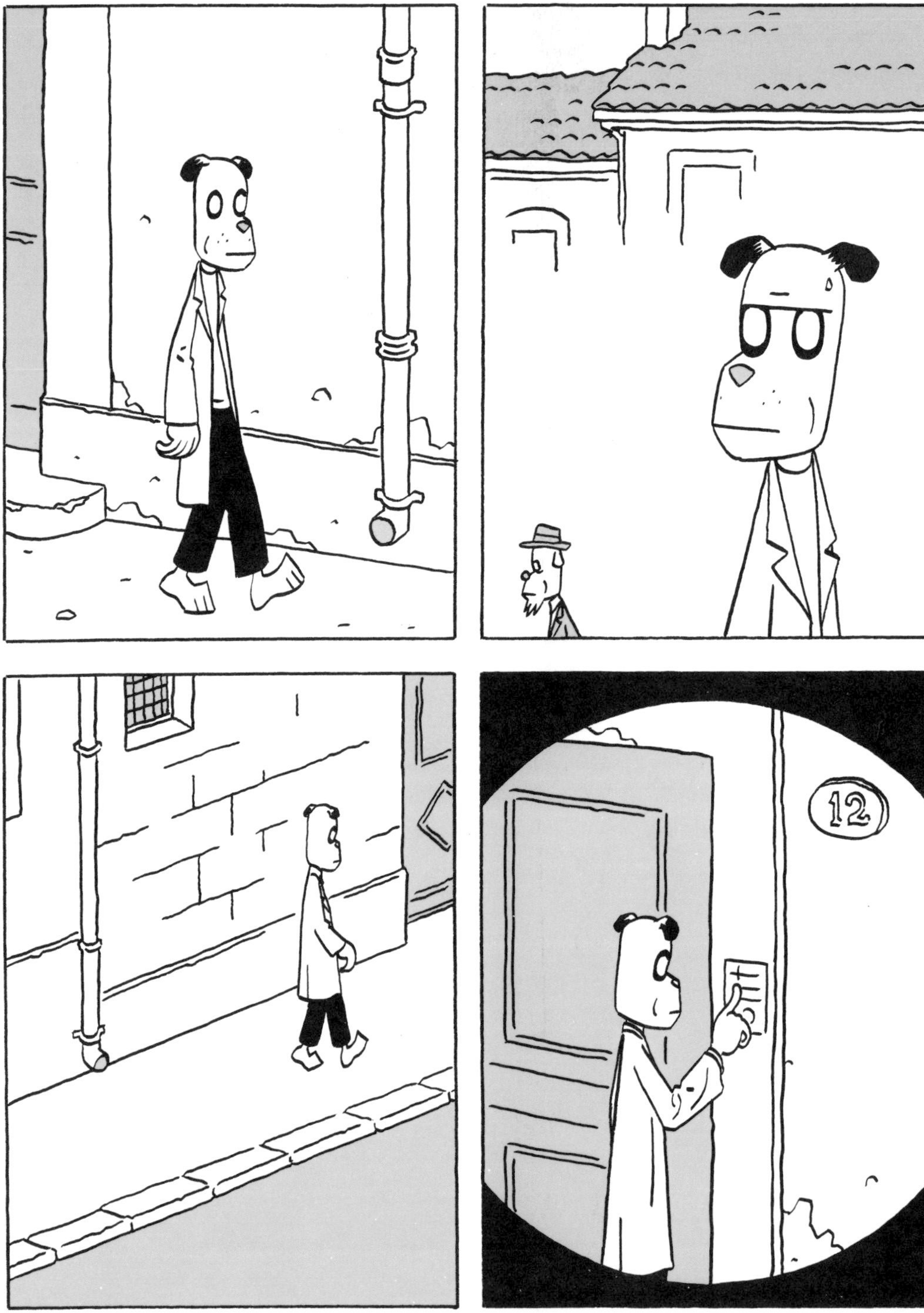
12

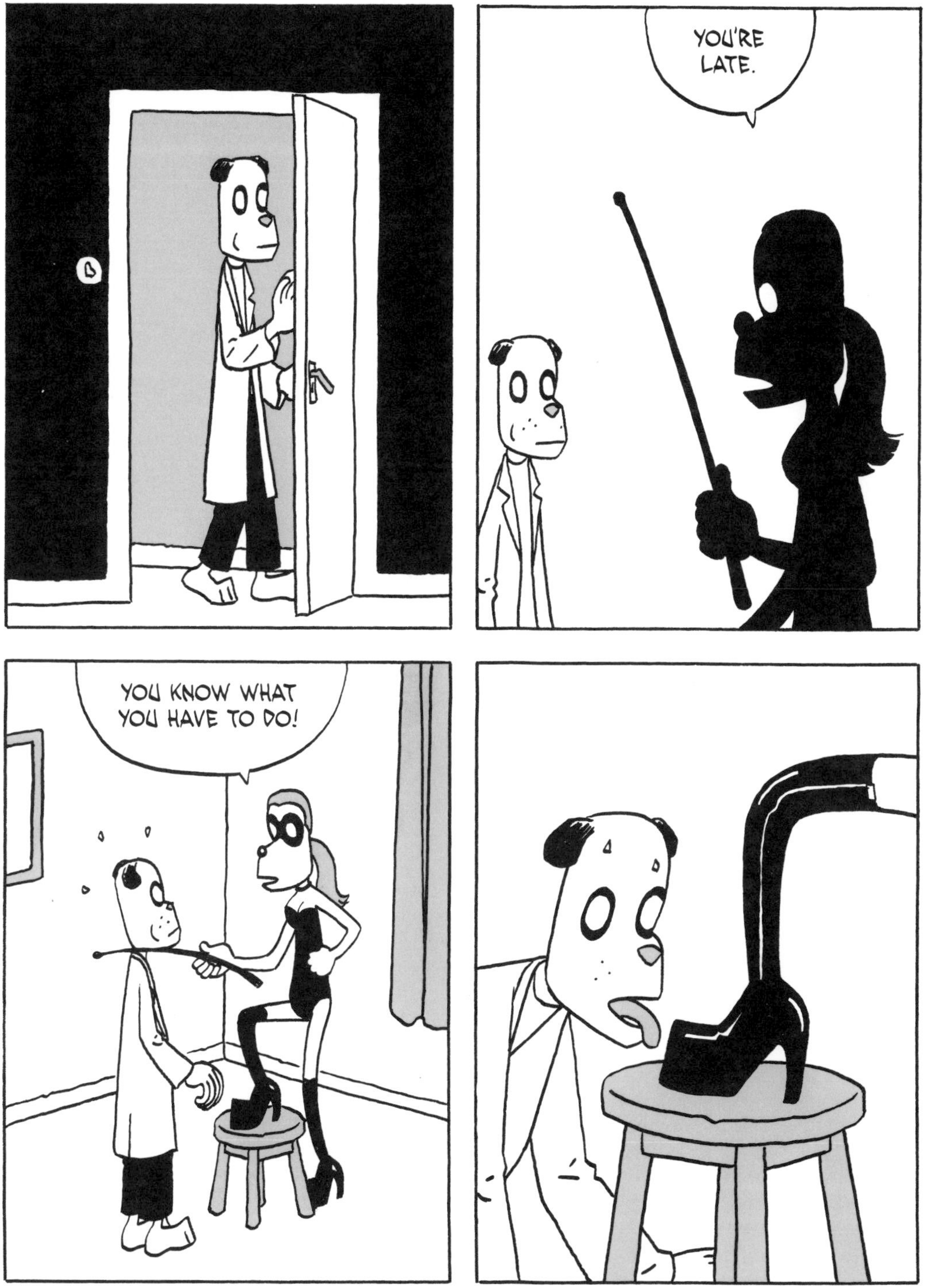
YOU'RE LATE.
YOU KNOW WHAT YOU HAVE TO DO!

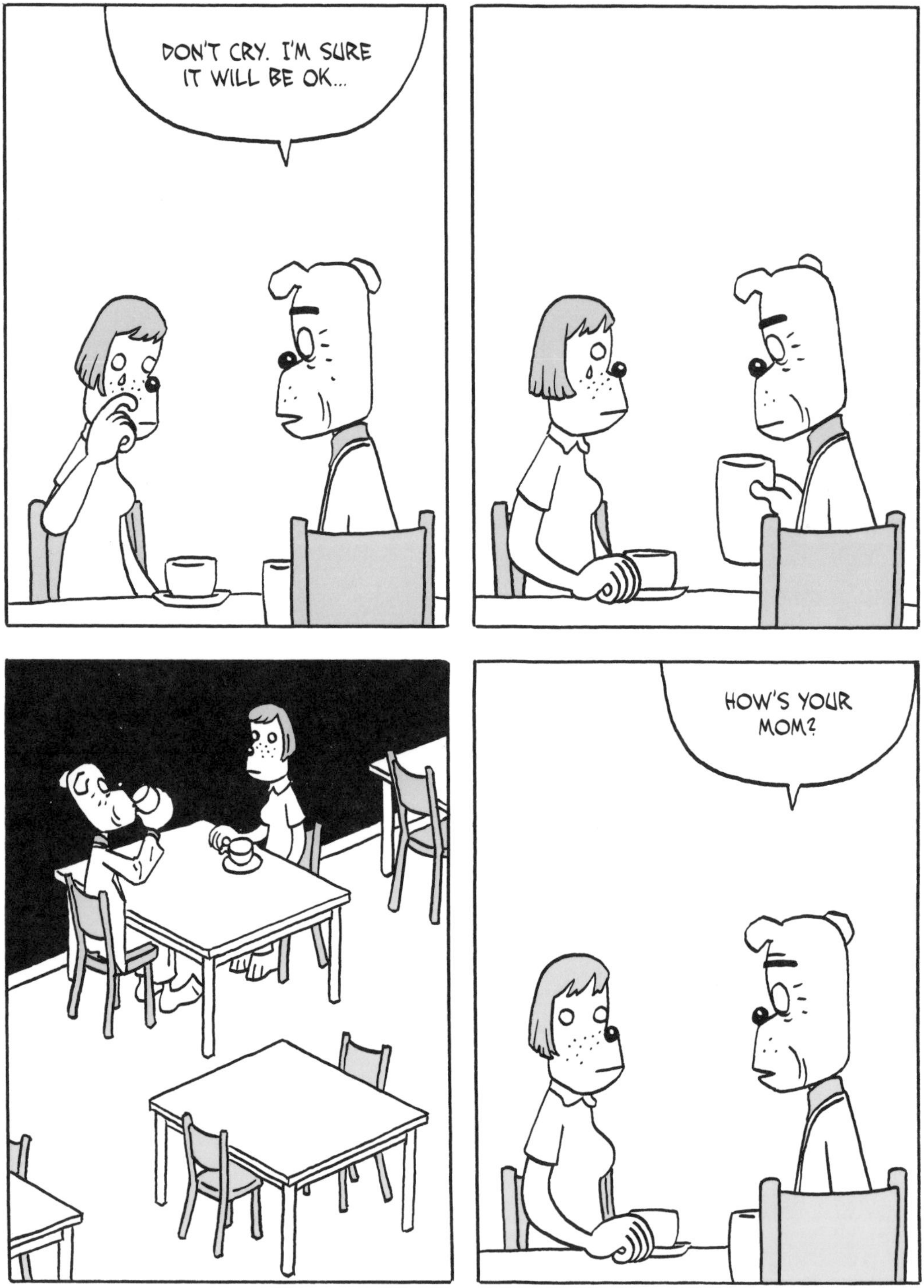
DON'T CRY. I'M SURE IT WILL BE OK...
HOW'S YOUR MOM?

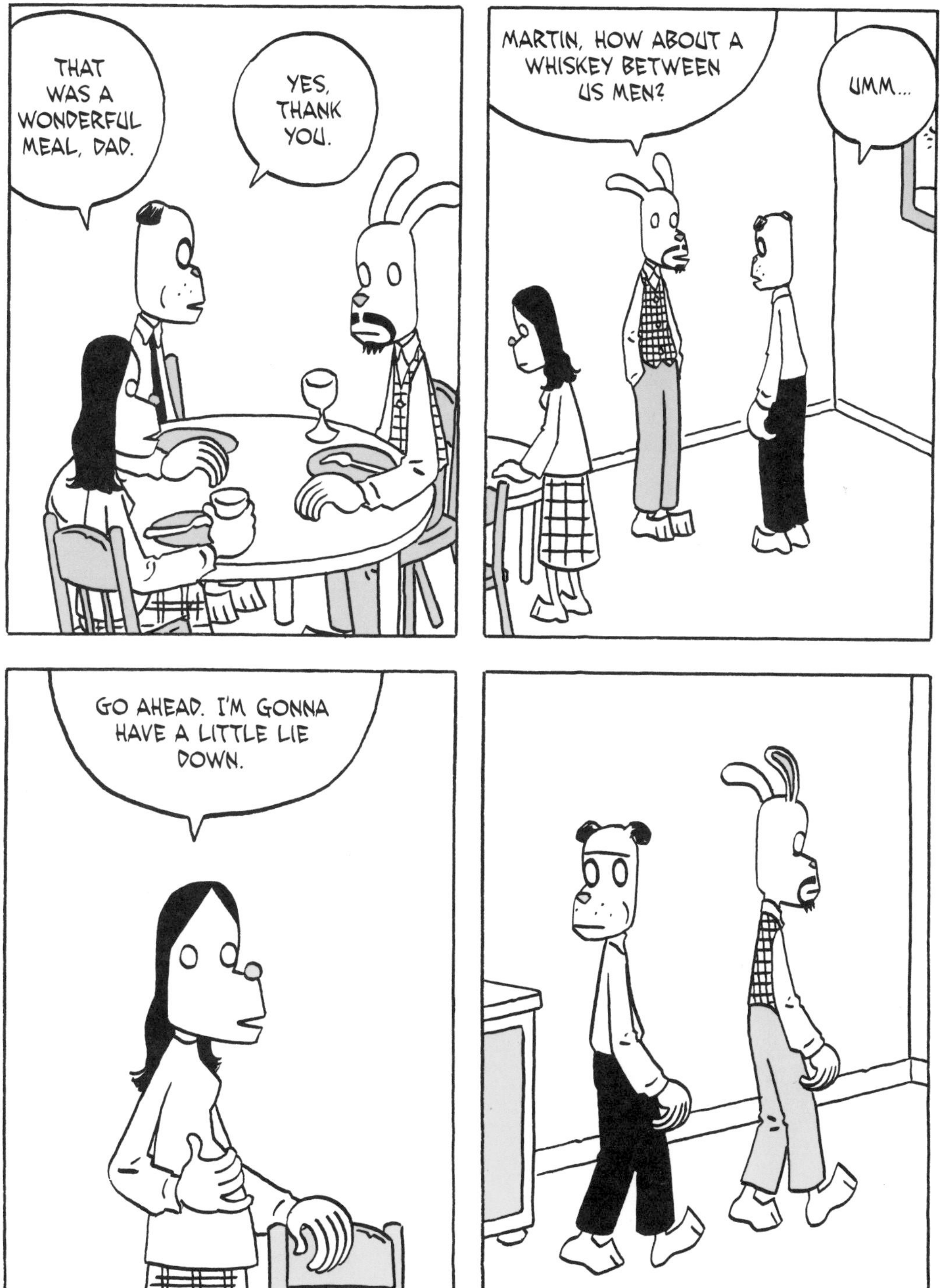
THAT WAS A WONDERFUL MEAL, DAD.
YES, THANK YOU.
MARTIN, HOW ABOUT A WHISKEY BETWEEN US MEN?
UMM...
GO AHEAD. I'M GONNA HAVE A LITTLE LIE DOWN.

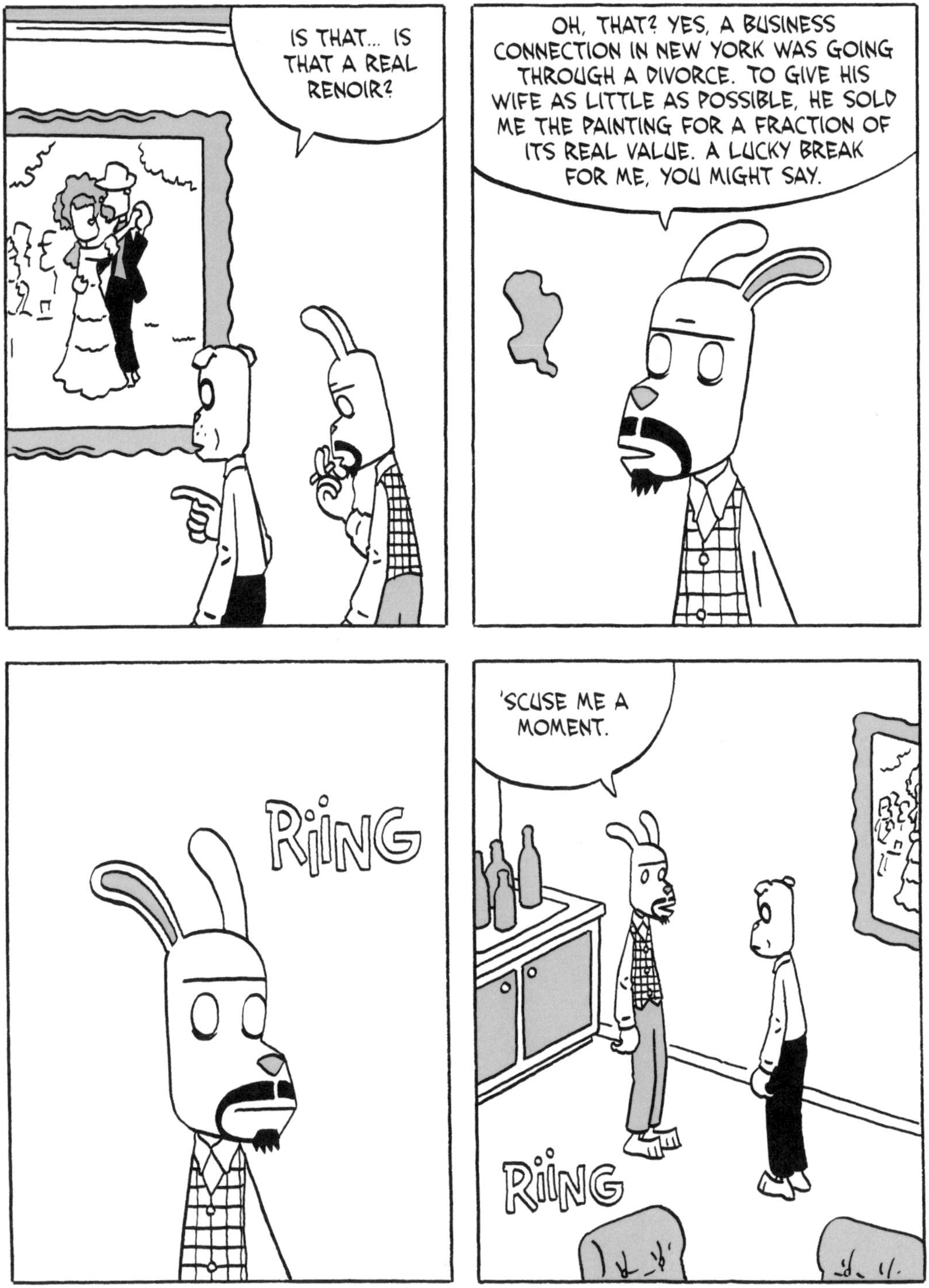
IS THAT... IS THAT A REAL RENOIR?
OH, THAT? YES, A BUSINESS CONNECTION IN NEW YORK WAS GOING THROUGH A DIVORCE. TO GIVE HIS WIFE AS LITTLE AS POSSIBLE, HE SOLD ME THE PAINTING FOR A FRACTION OF ITS REAL VALUE. A LUCKY BREAK FOR ME, YOU MIGHT SAY.
RING
'SCUSE ME A MOMENT.
RING

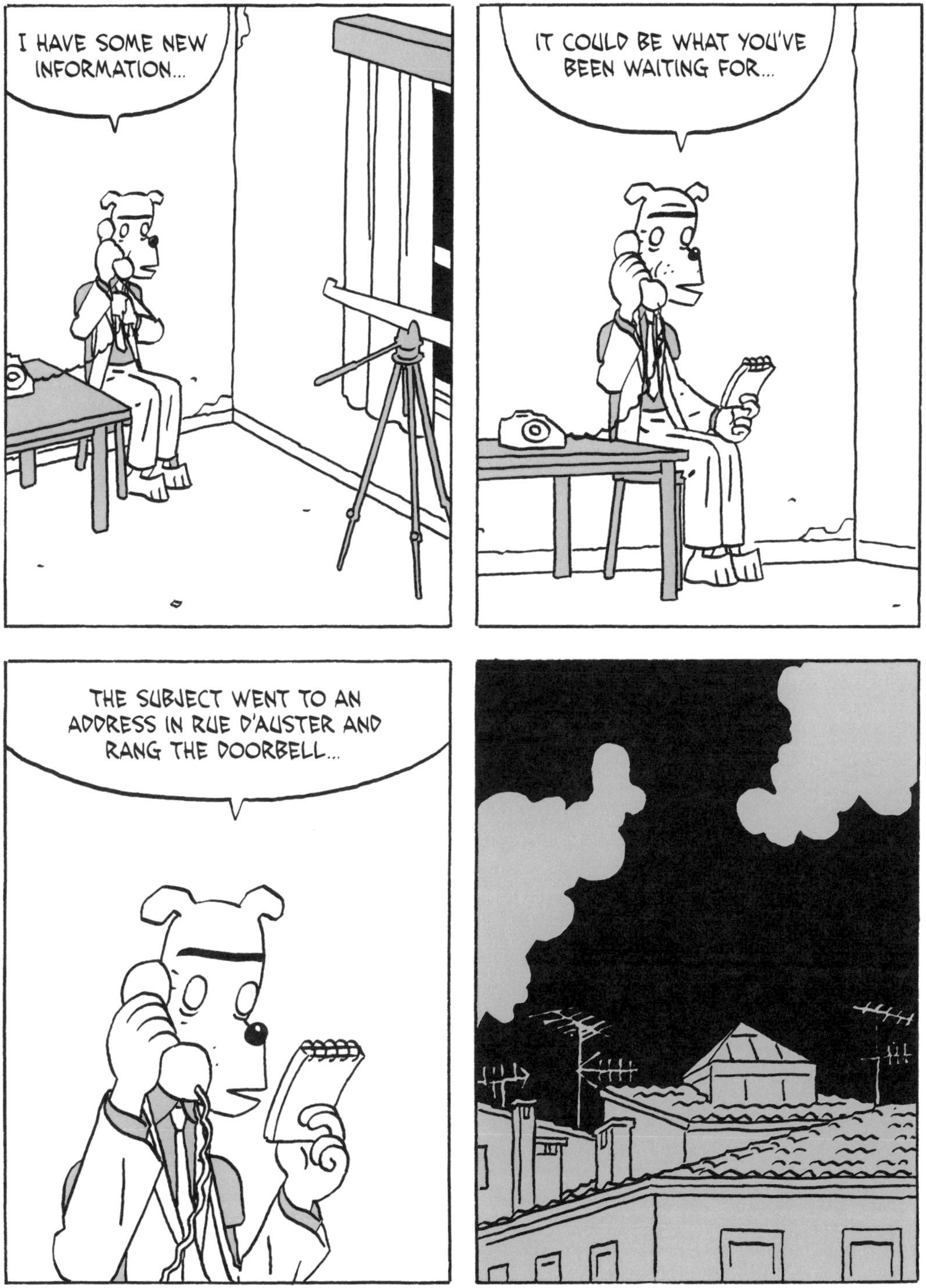
I HAVE SOME NEW INFORMATION...
IT COULD BE WHAT YOU'VE BEEN WAITING FOR...
THE SUBJECT WENT TO AN ADDRESS IN RUE D'AUSTER AND RANG THE DOORBELL...

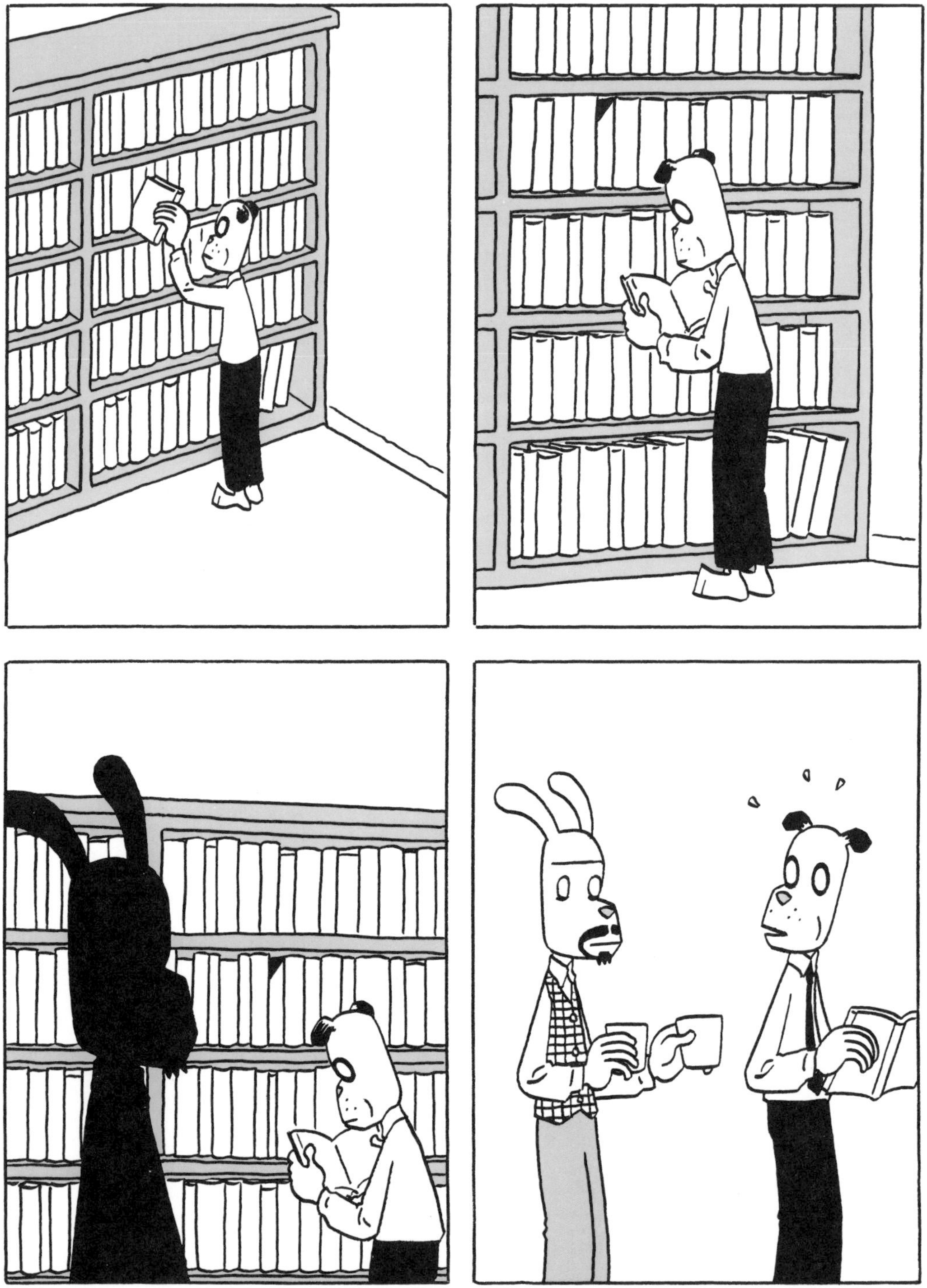

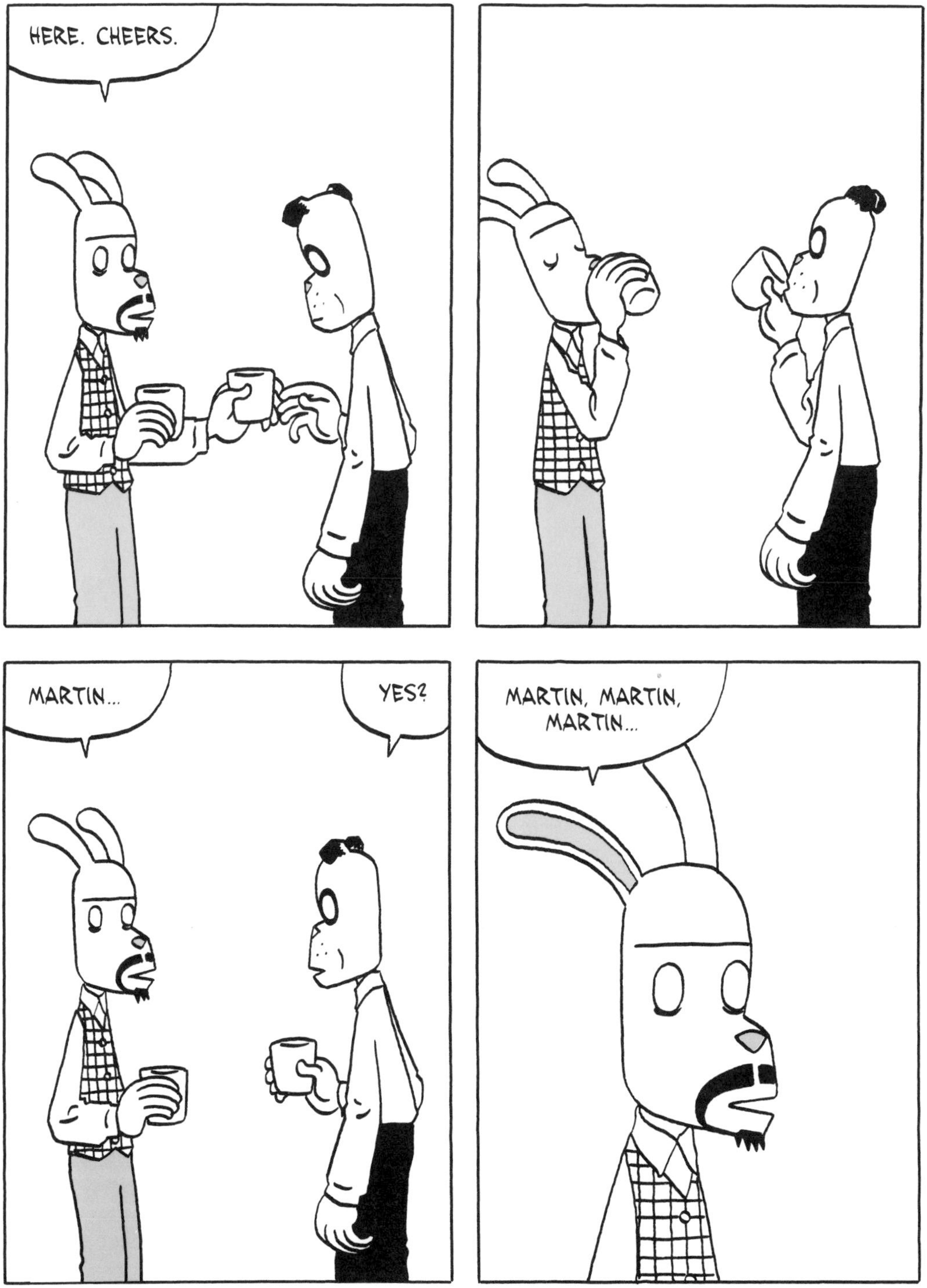
HERE. CHEERS.
MARTIN...
YES?
MARTIN, MARTIN, MARTIN...

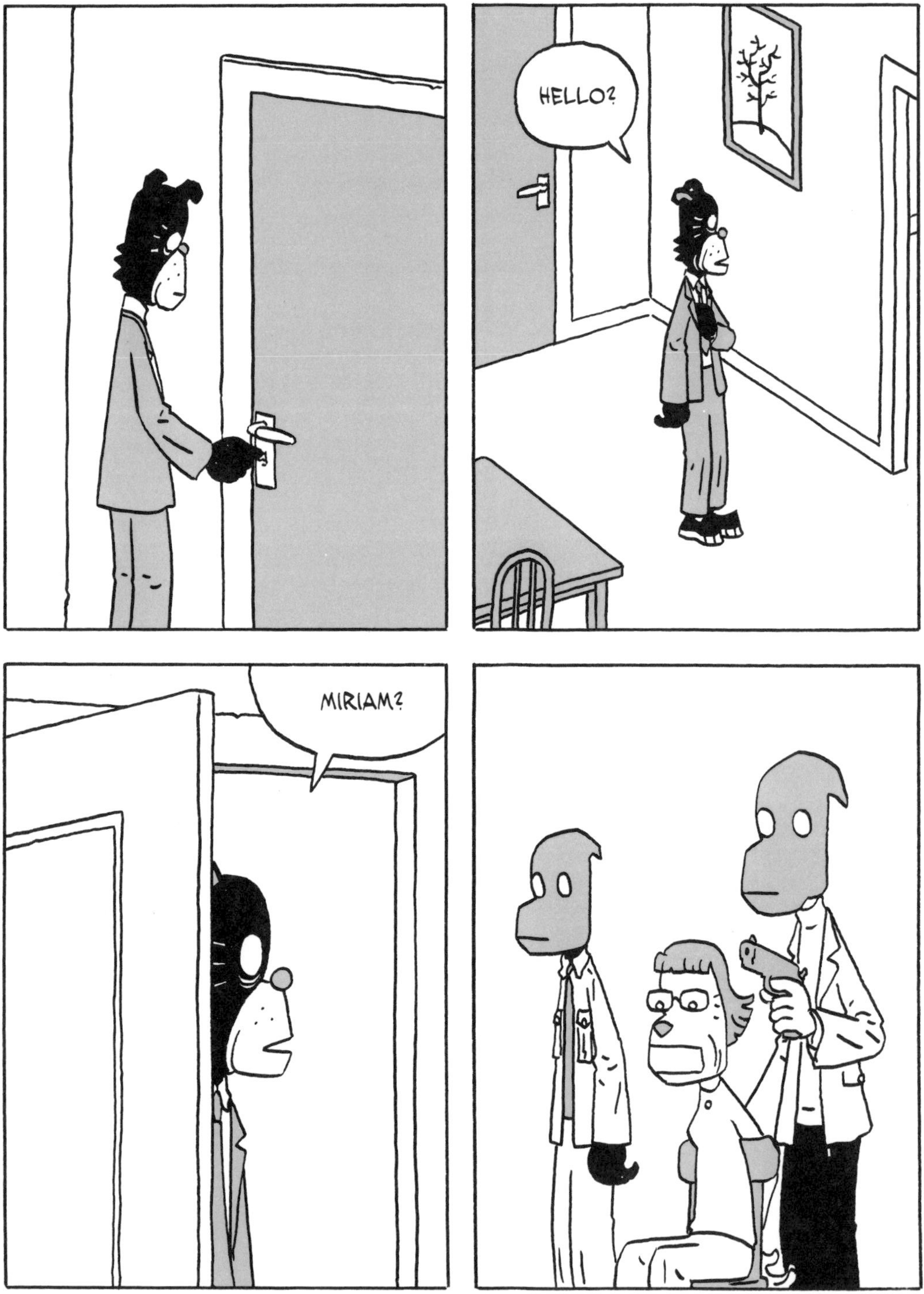
HELLO?
MIRIAM?

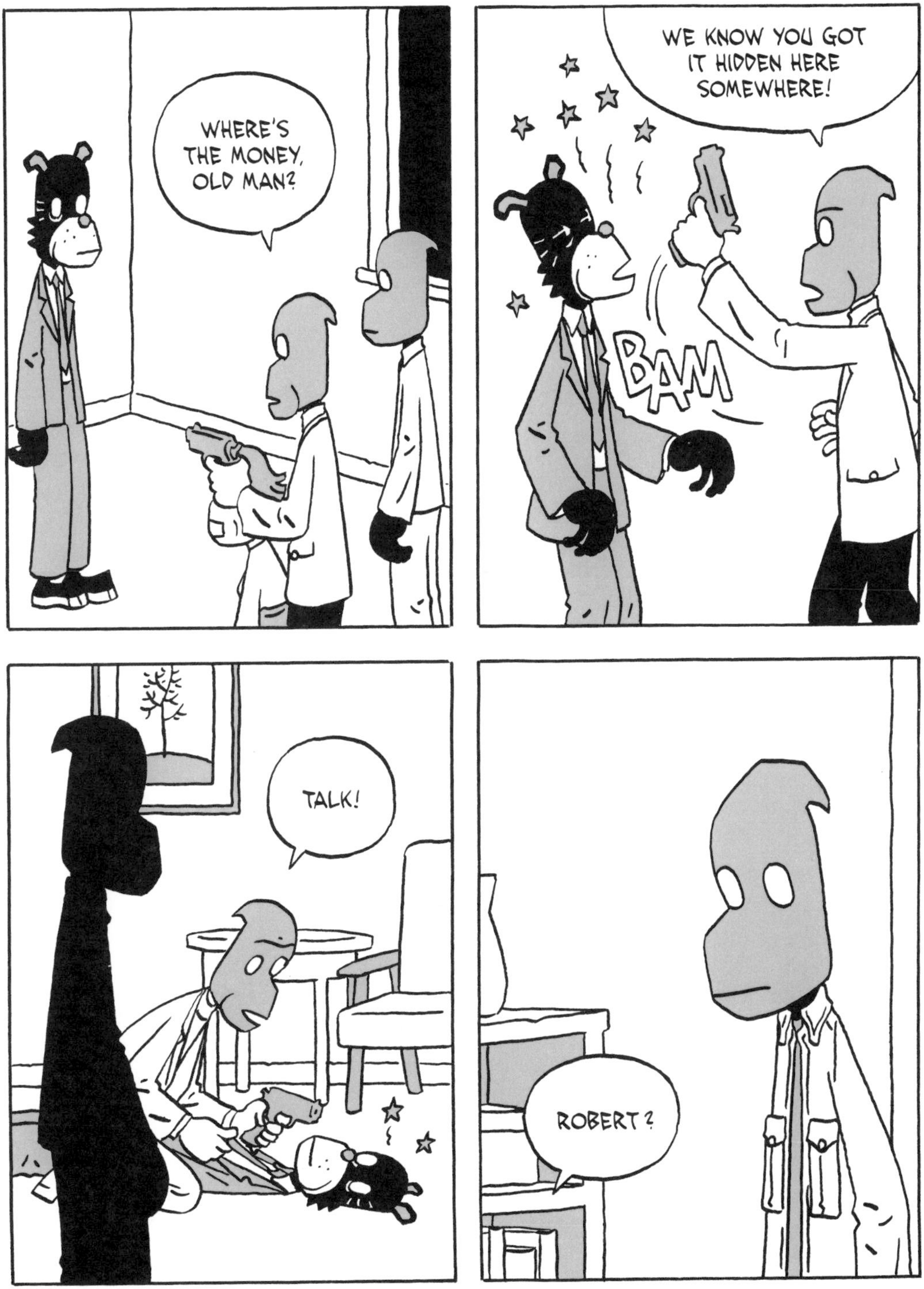
WHERE'S THE MONEY, OLD MAN?
WE KNOW YOU GOT IT HIDDEN HERE SOMEWHERE!
BAM
TALK!
ROBERT?

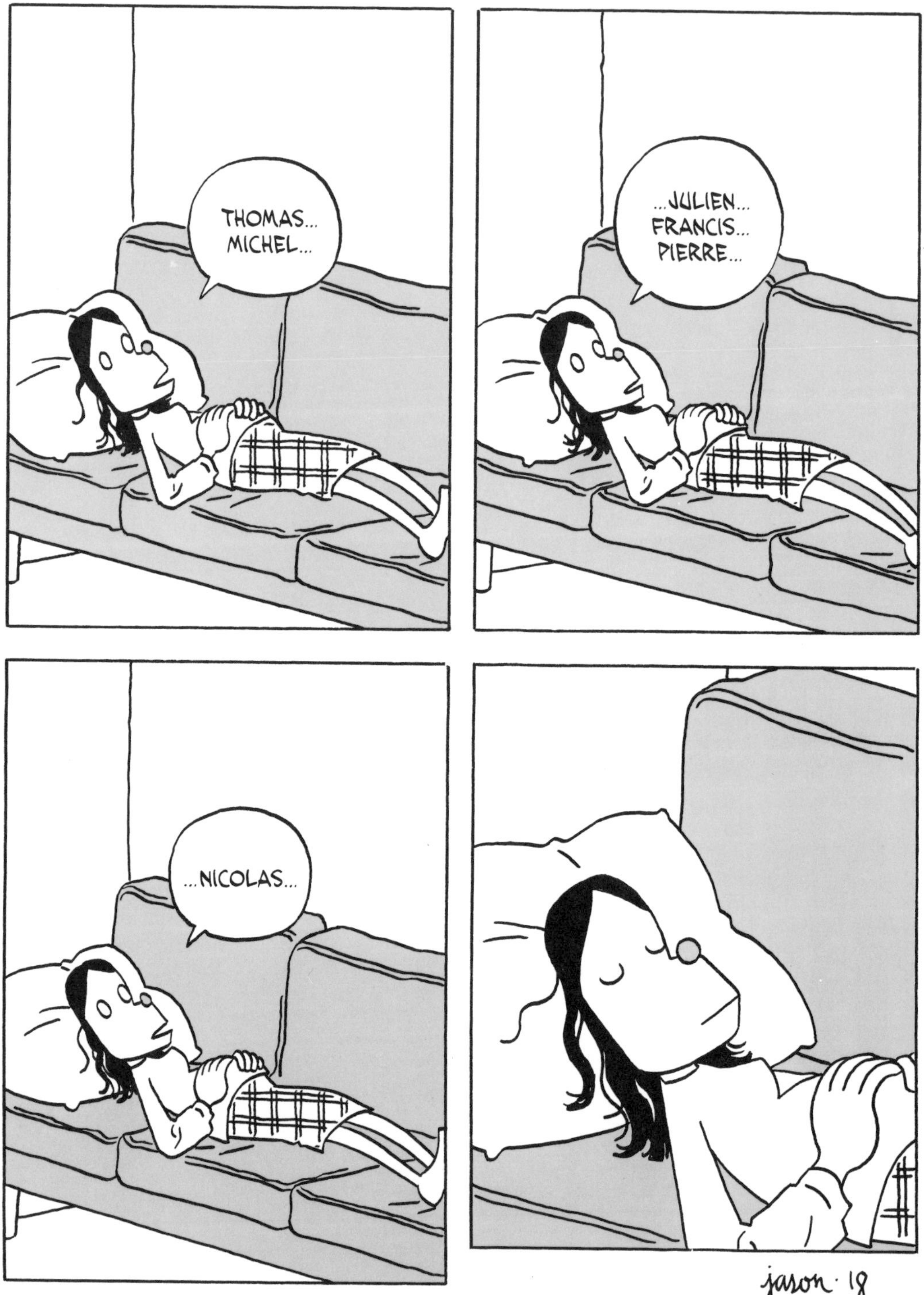
THOMAS...
MICHEL...
...JULIEN...
FRANCIS...
PIERRE...
...NICOLAS...
jason · 18

O Josephine!

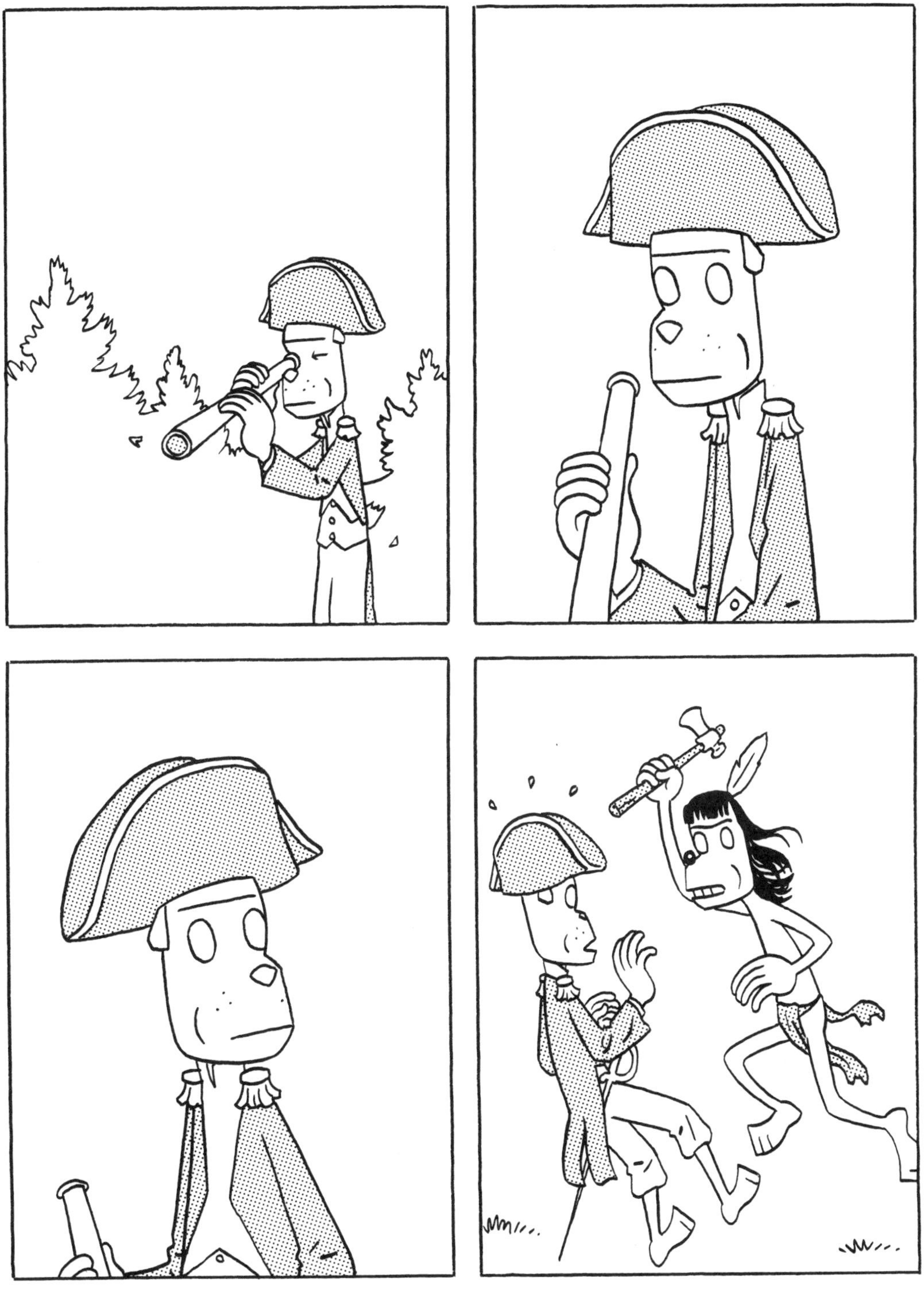

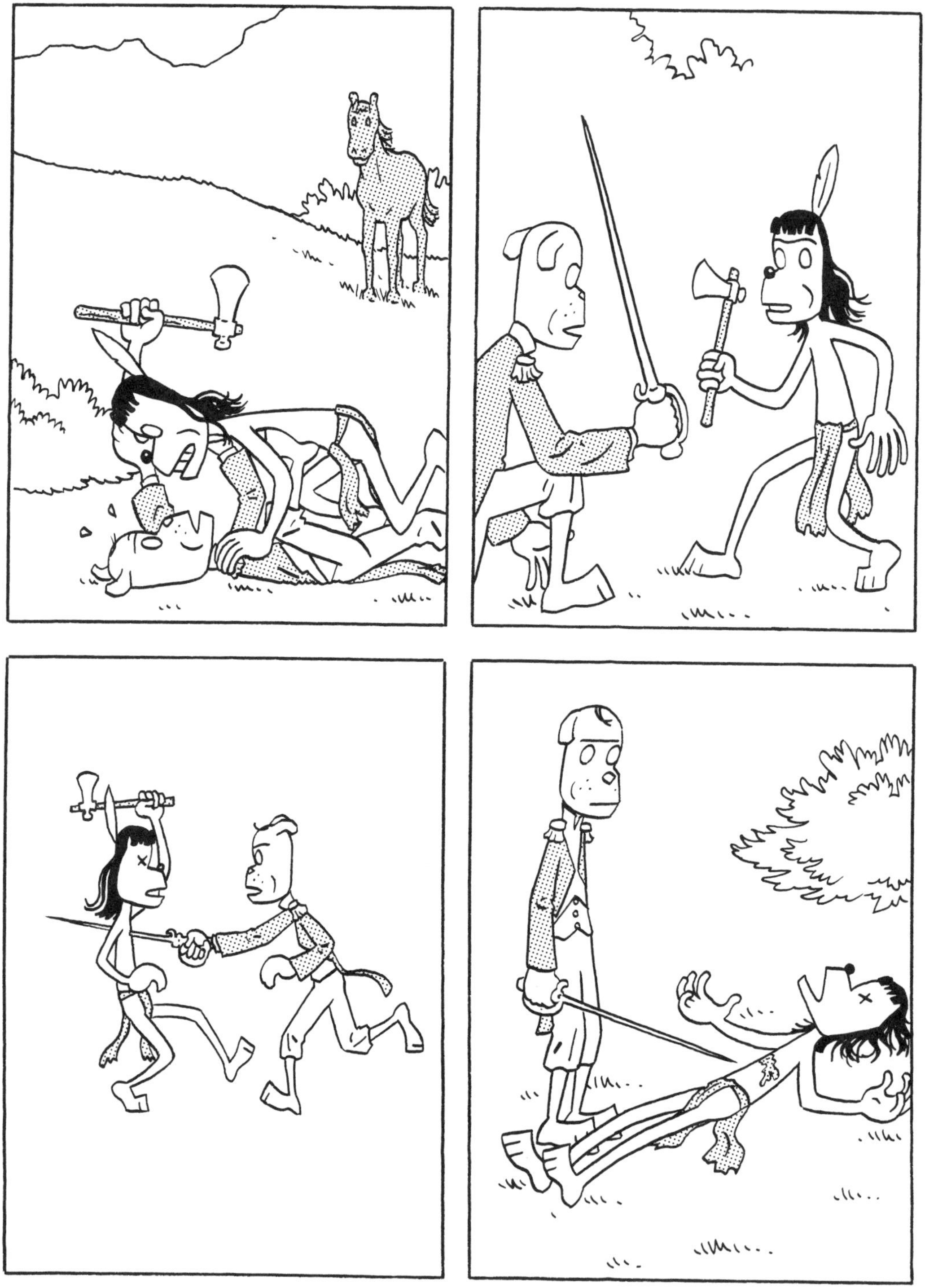

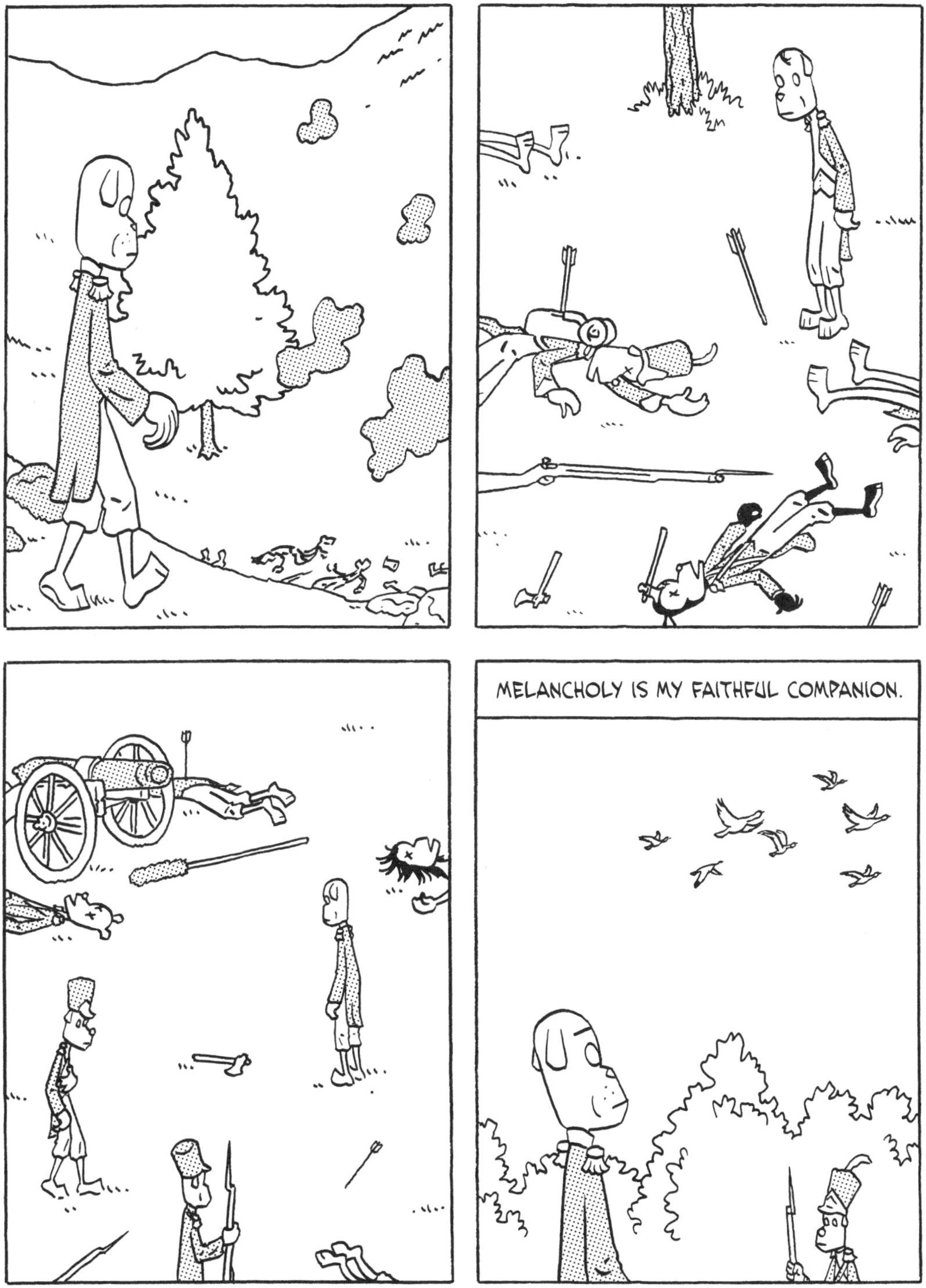
MELANCHOLY IS MY FAITHFUL COMPANION.

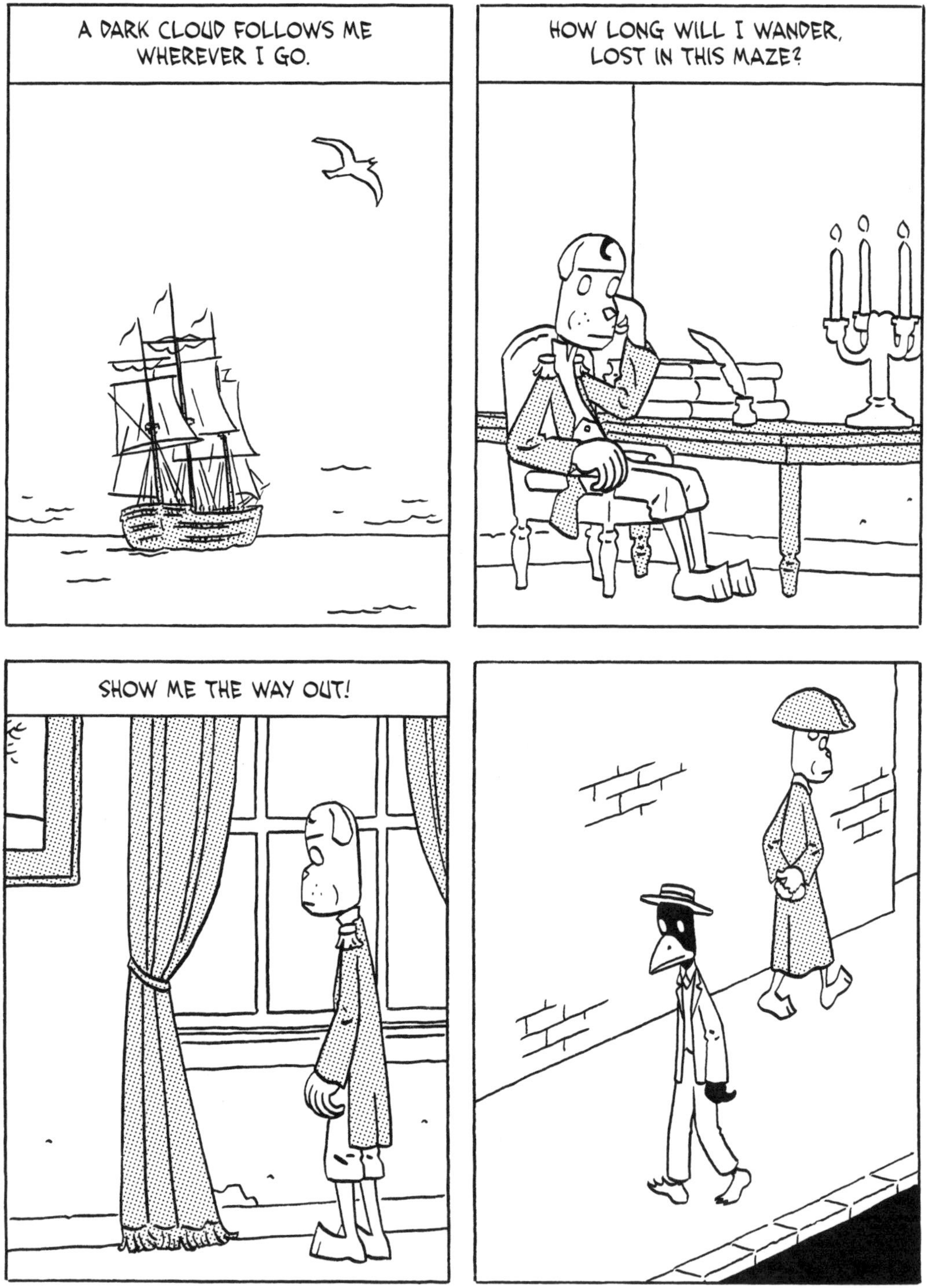

A DARK CLOUD FOLLOWS ME WHEREVER I GO.
HOW LONG WILL I WANDER, LOST IN THIS MAZE?
SHOW ME THE WAY OUT!

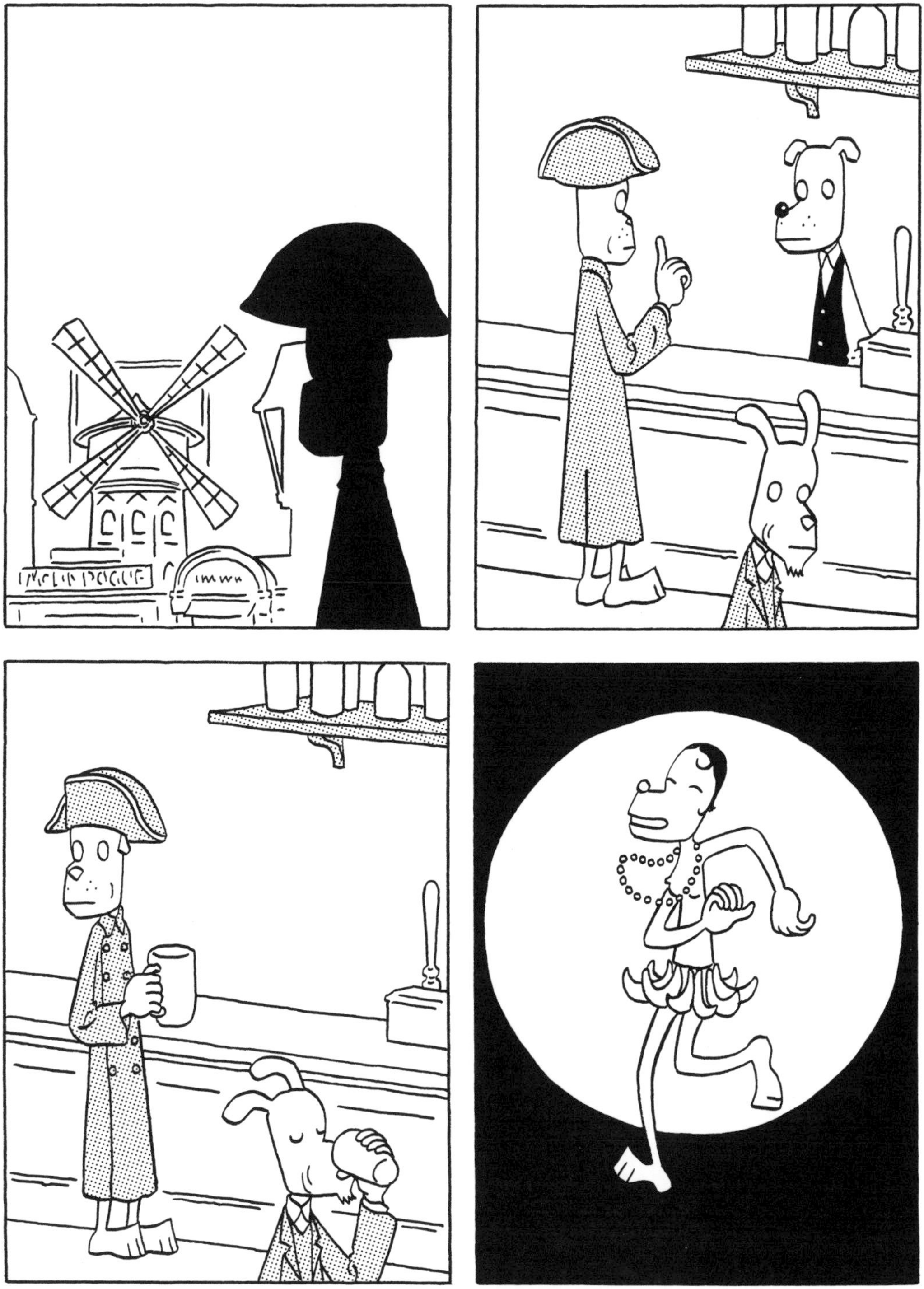

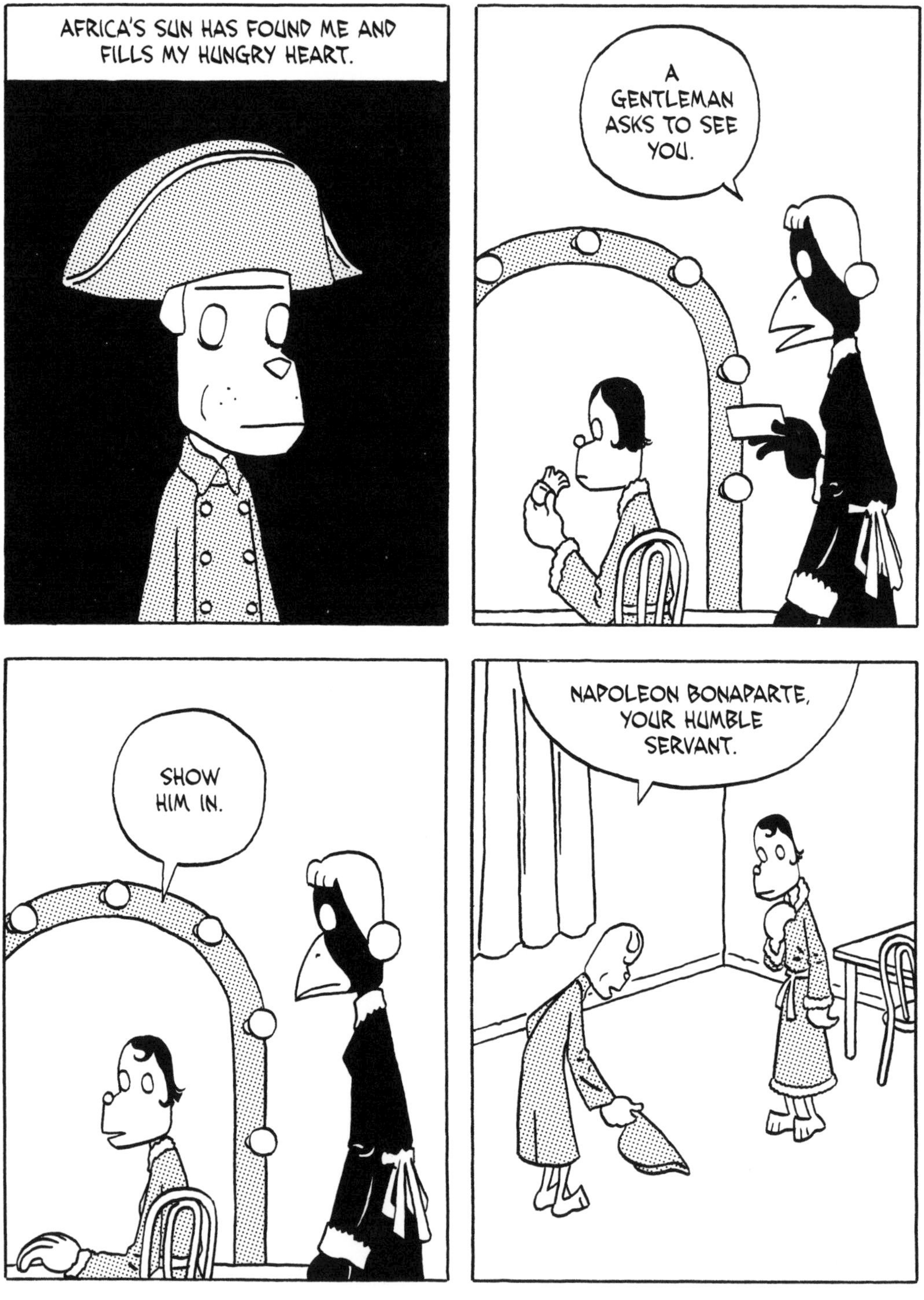
AFRICA'S SUN HAS FOUND ME AND FILLS MY HUNGRY HEART.
A GENTLEMAN ASKS TO SEE YOU.
SHOW HIM IN.
NAPOLEON BONAPARTE, YOUR HUMBLE SERVANT.

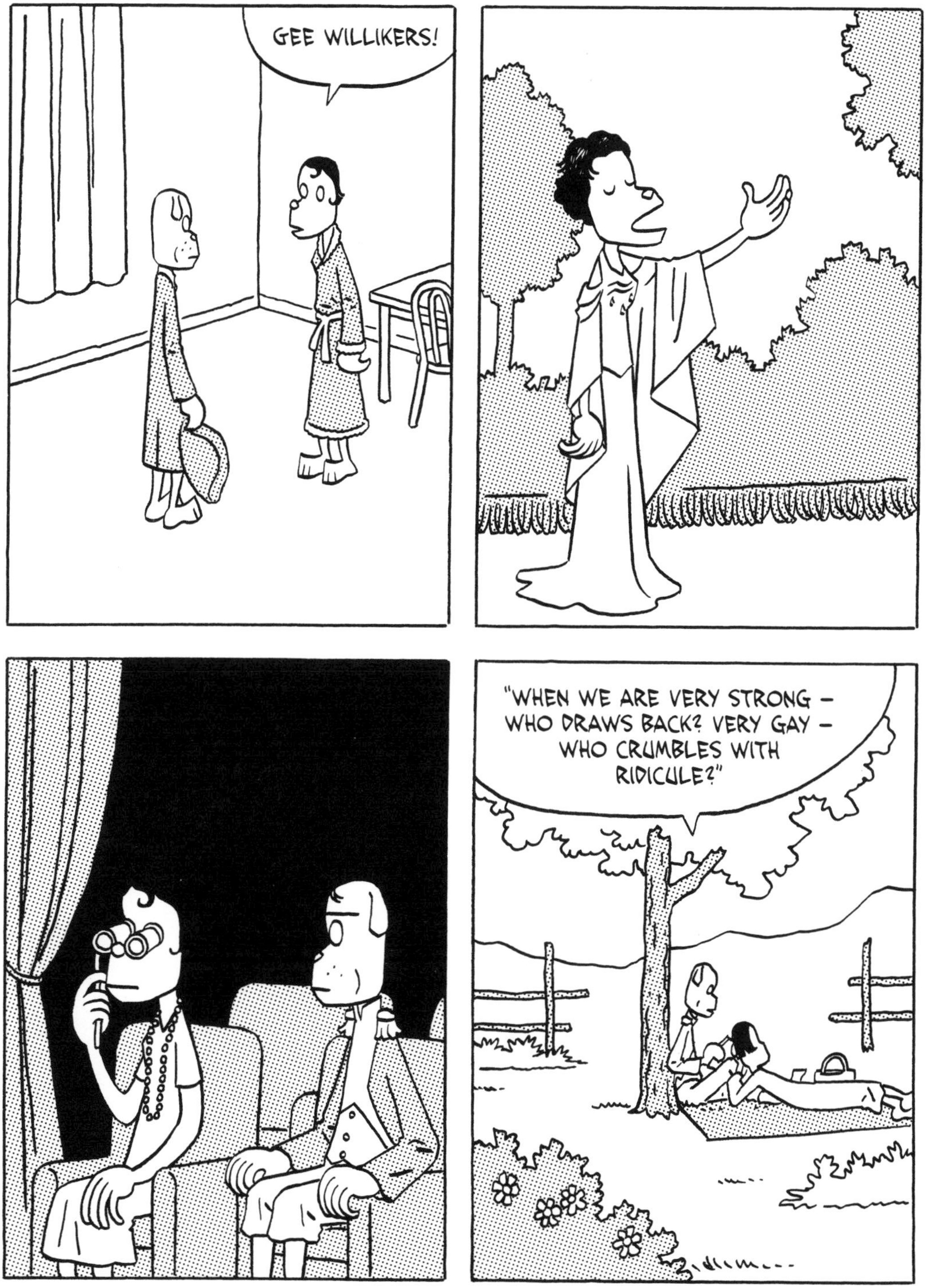
GEE WILLIKERS!
"WHEN WE ARE VERY STRONG – WHO DRAWS BACK? VERY GAY – WHO CRUMBLES WITH RIDICULE?"

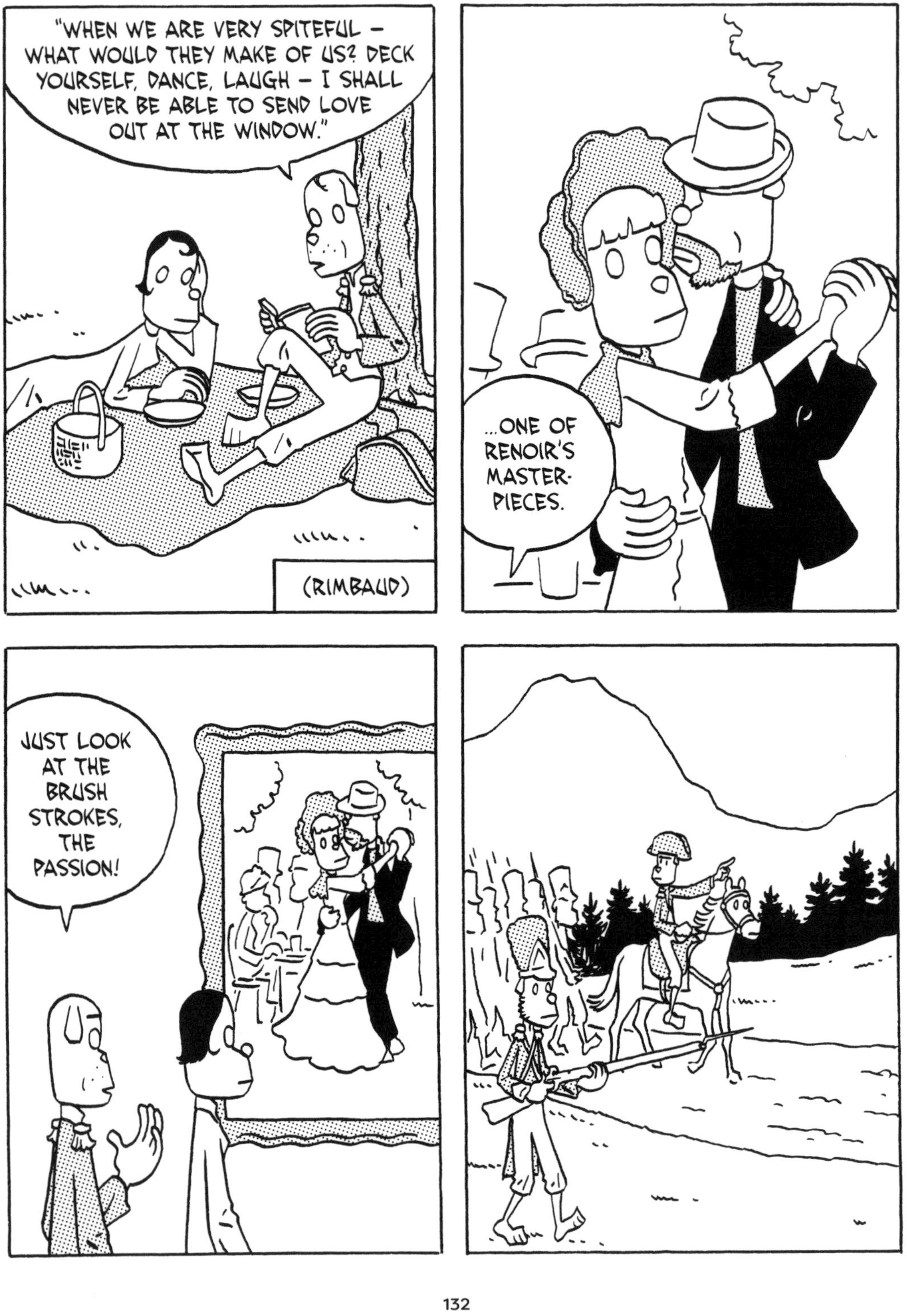
"WHEN WE ARE VERY SPITEFUL – WHAT WOULD THEY MAKE OF US? DECK YOURSELF, DANCE, LAUGH – I SHALL NEVER BE ABLE TO SEND LOVE OUT AT THE WINDOW."
(RIMBAUD)
...ONE OF RENOIR'S MASTER-PIECES.
JUST LOOK AT THE BRUSH STROKES, THE PASSION!

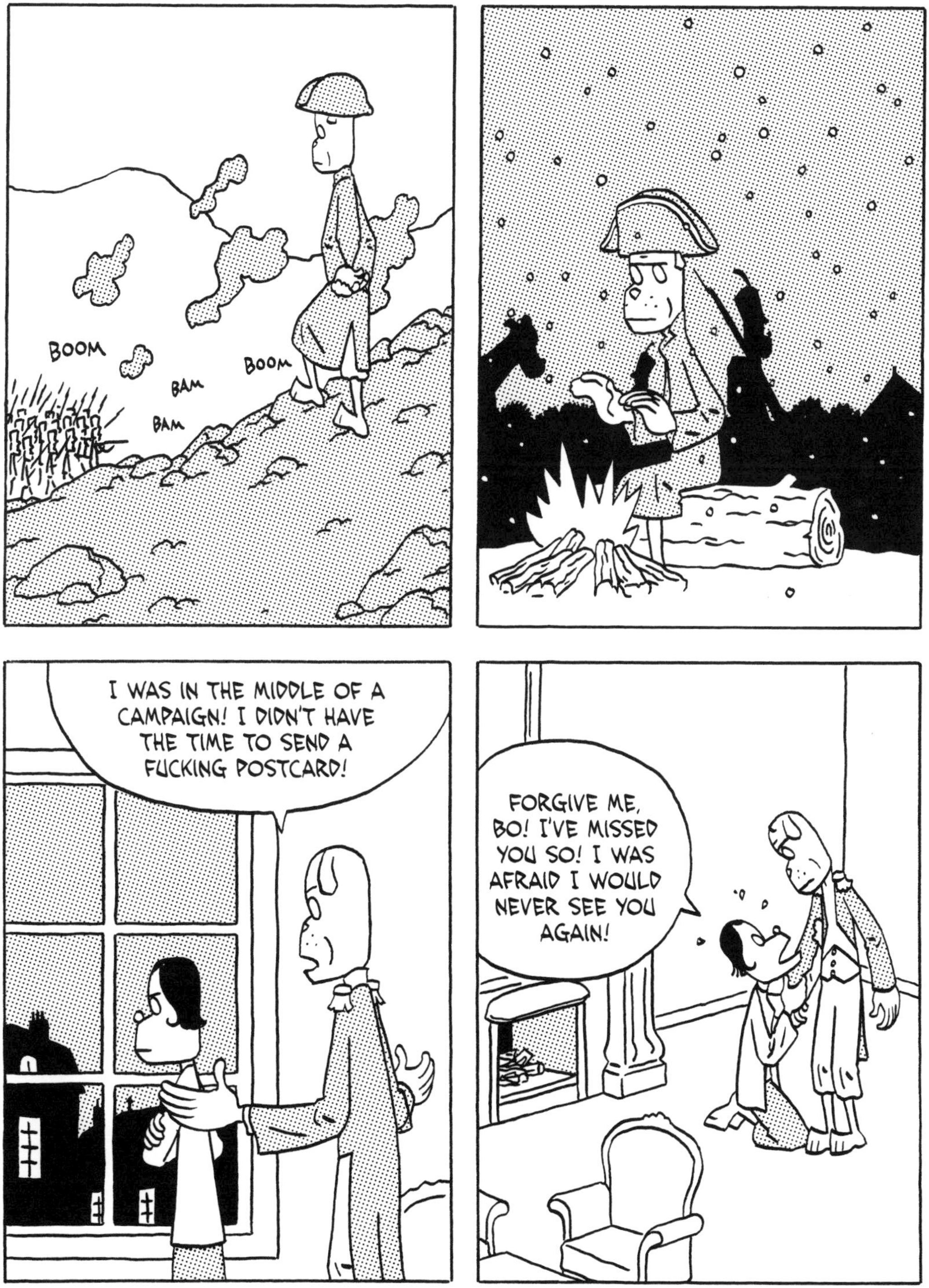
BOOM
BAM
BAM
BOOM
I WAS IN THE MIDDLE OF A CAMPAIGN! I DIDN'T HAVE THE TIME TO SEND A FUCKING POSTCARD!
FORGIVE ME, BO! I'VE MISSED YOU SO! I WAS AFRAID I WOULD NEVER SEE YOU AGAIN!

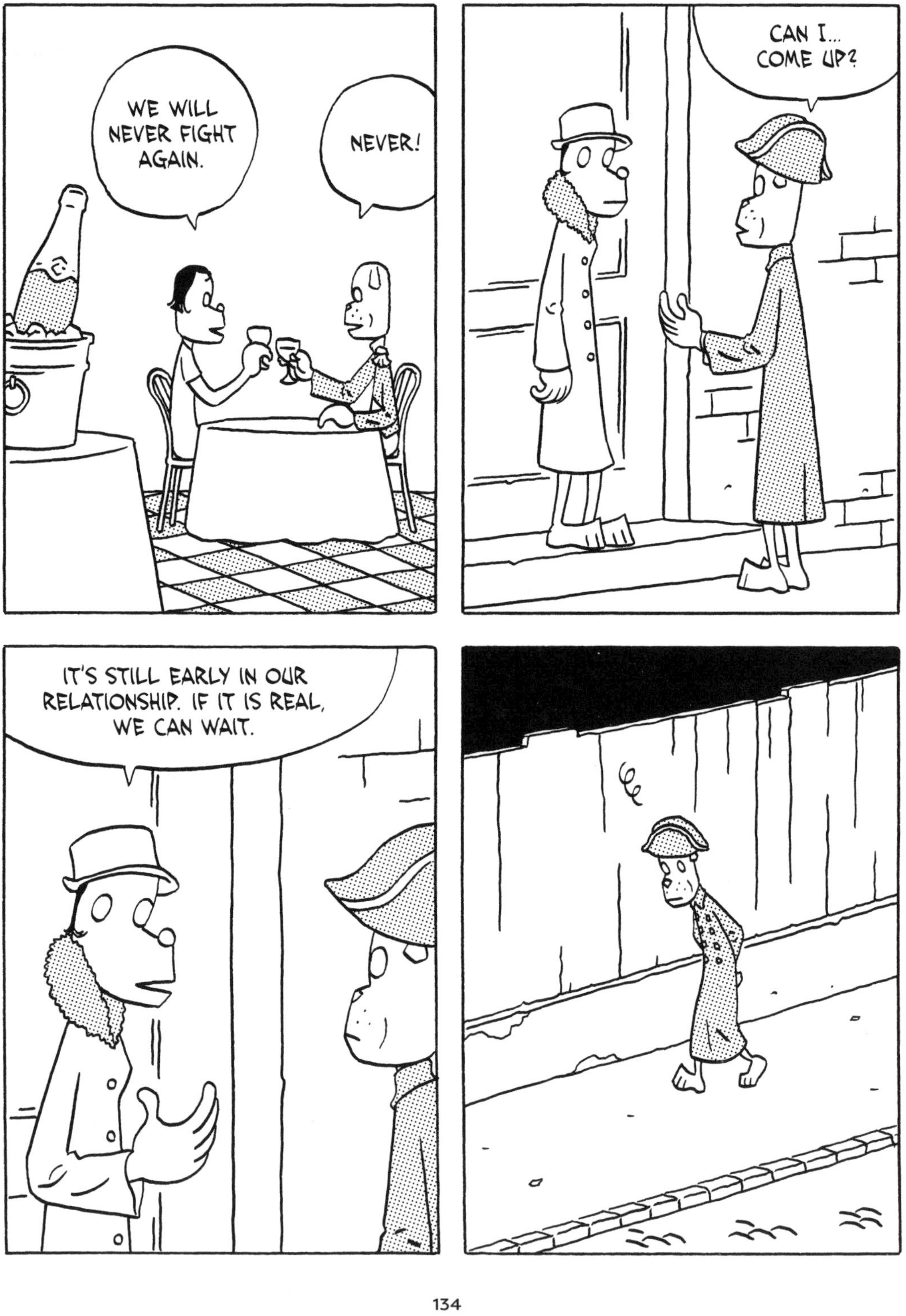
WE WILL NEVER FIGHT AGAIN.
NEVER!
CAN I... COME UP?
IT'S STILL EARLY IN OUR RELATIONSHIP. IF IT IS REAL, WE CAN WAIT.

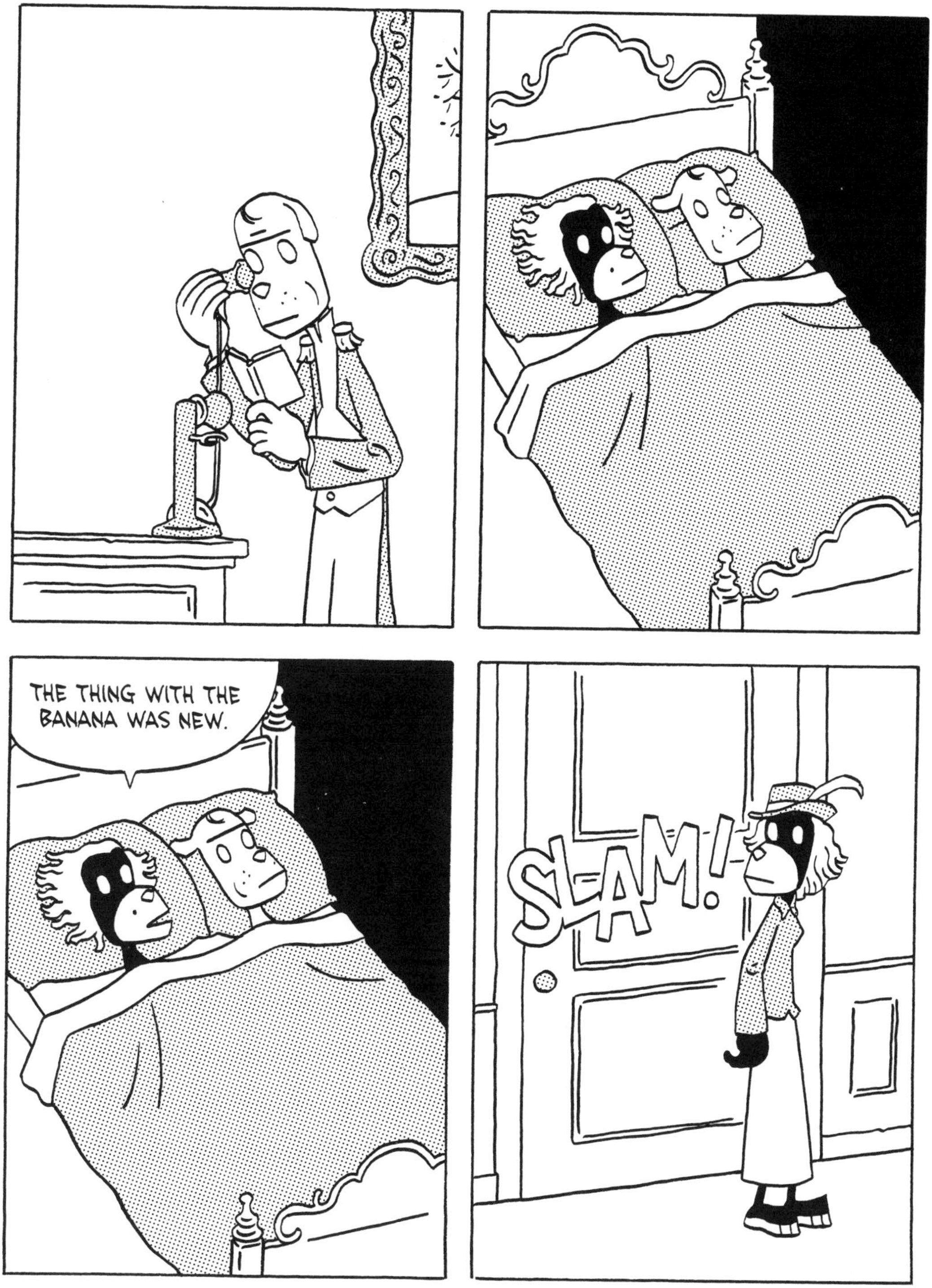
THE THING WITH THE BANANA WAS NEW.
SLAM!

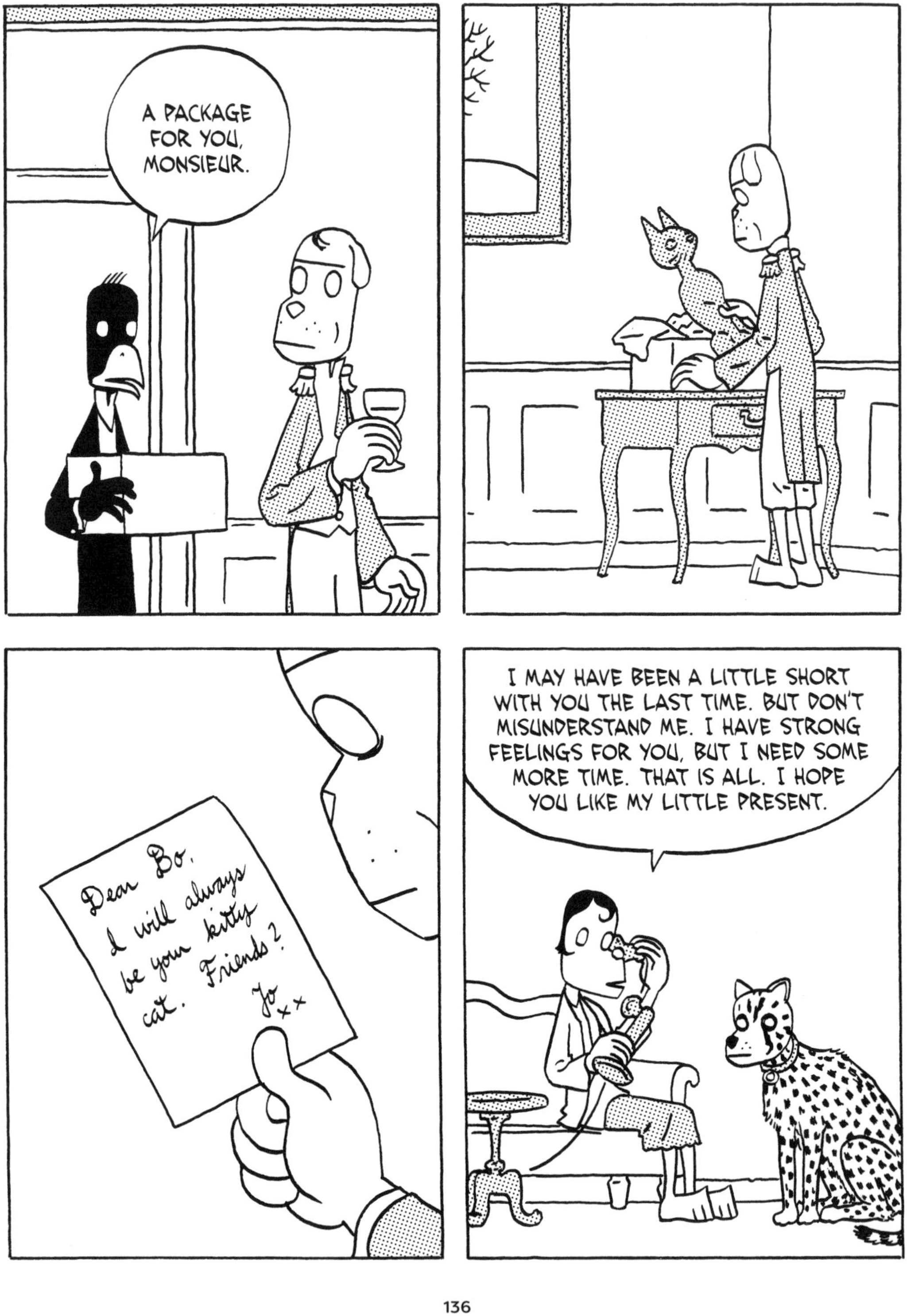
A PACKAGE FOR YOU, MONSIEUR.
Dear Bo,
I will always
be your kitty
cat. Friends?
Jo xx
I MAY HAVE BEEN A LITTLE SHORT WITH YOU THE LAST TIME. BUT DON'T MISUNDERSTAND ME. I HAVE STRONG FEELINGS FOR YOU, BUT I NEED SOME MORE TIME. THAT IS ALL. I HOPE YOU LIKE MY LITTLE PRESENT.

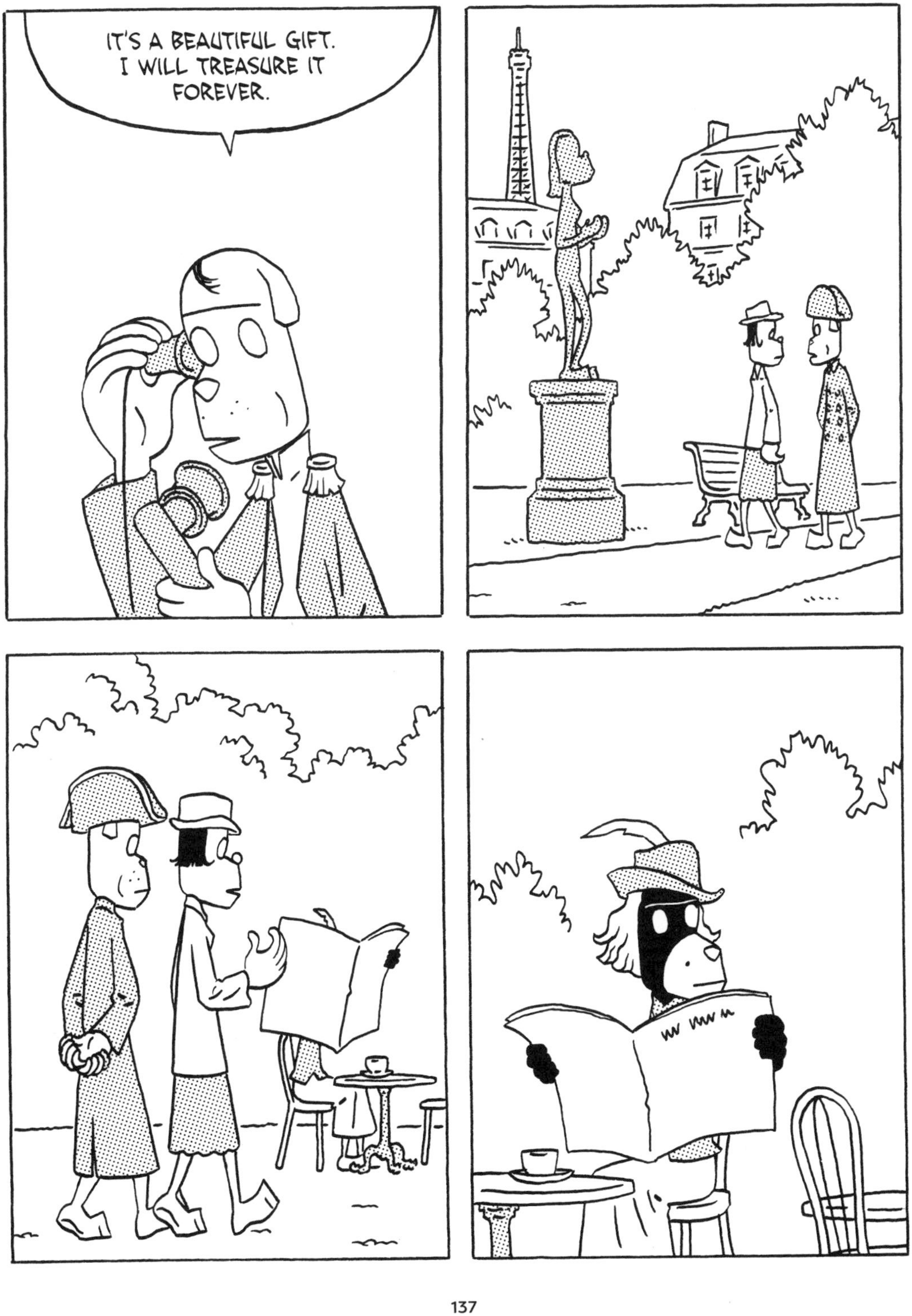
IT'S A BEAUTIFUL GIFT. I WILL TREASURE IT FOREVER.

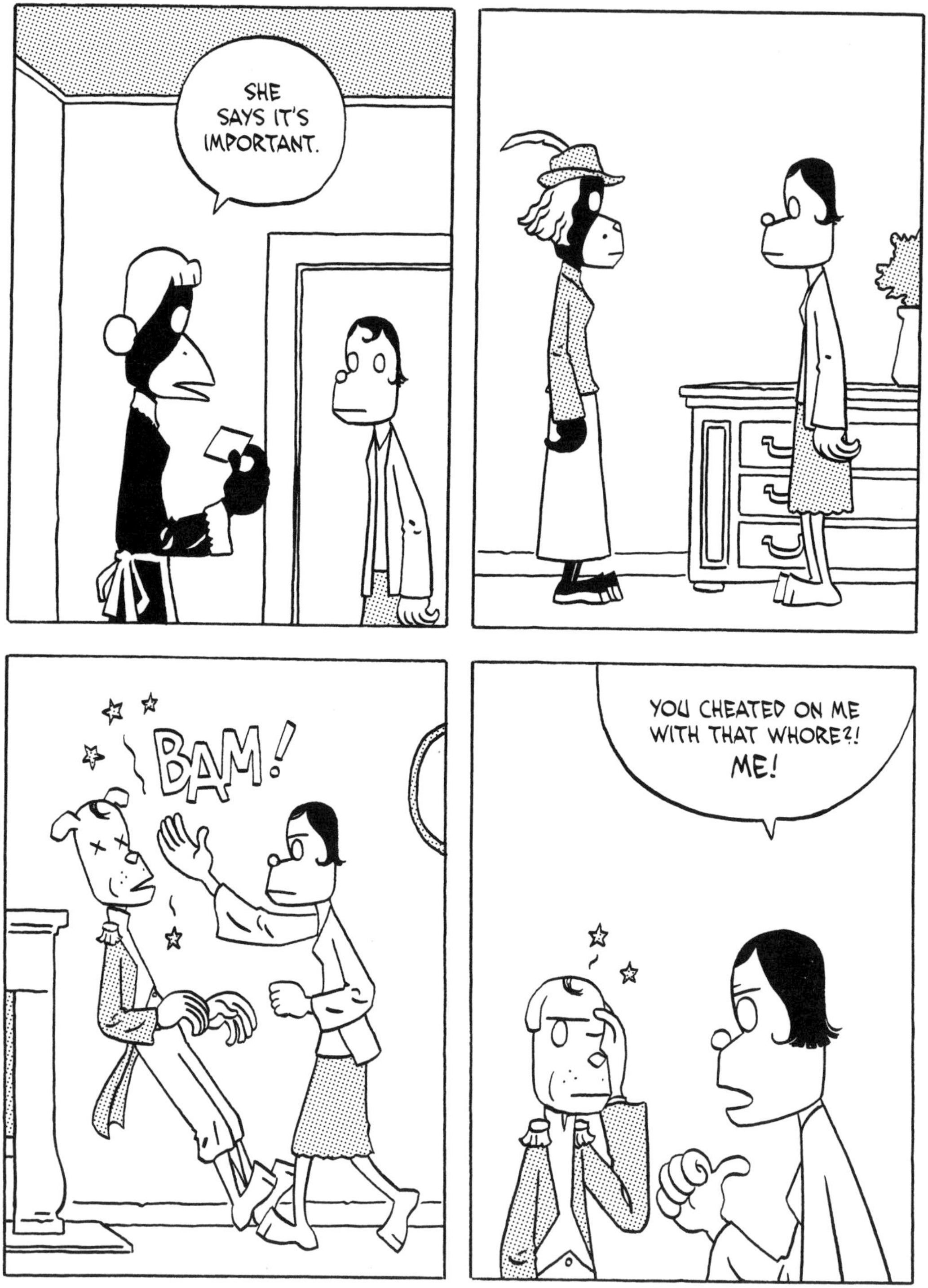
SHE SAYS IT'S IMPORTANT.
BAM!
YOU CHEATED ON ME WITH THAT WHORE?! ME!

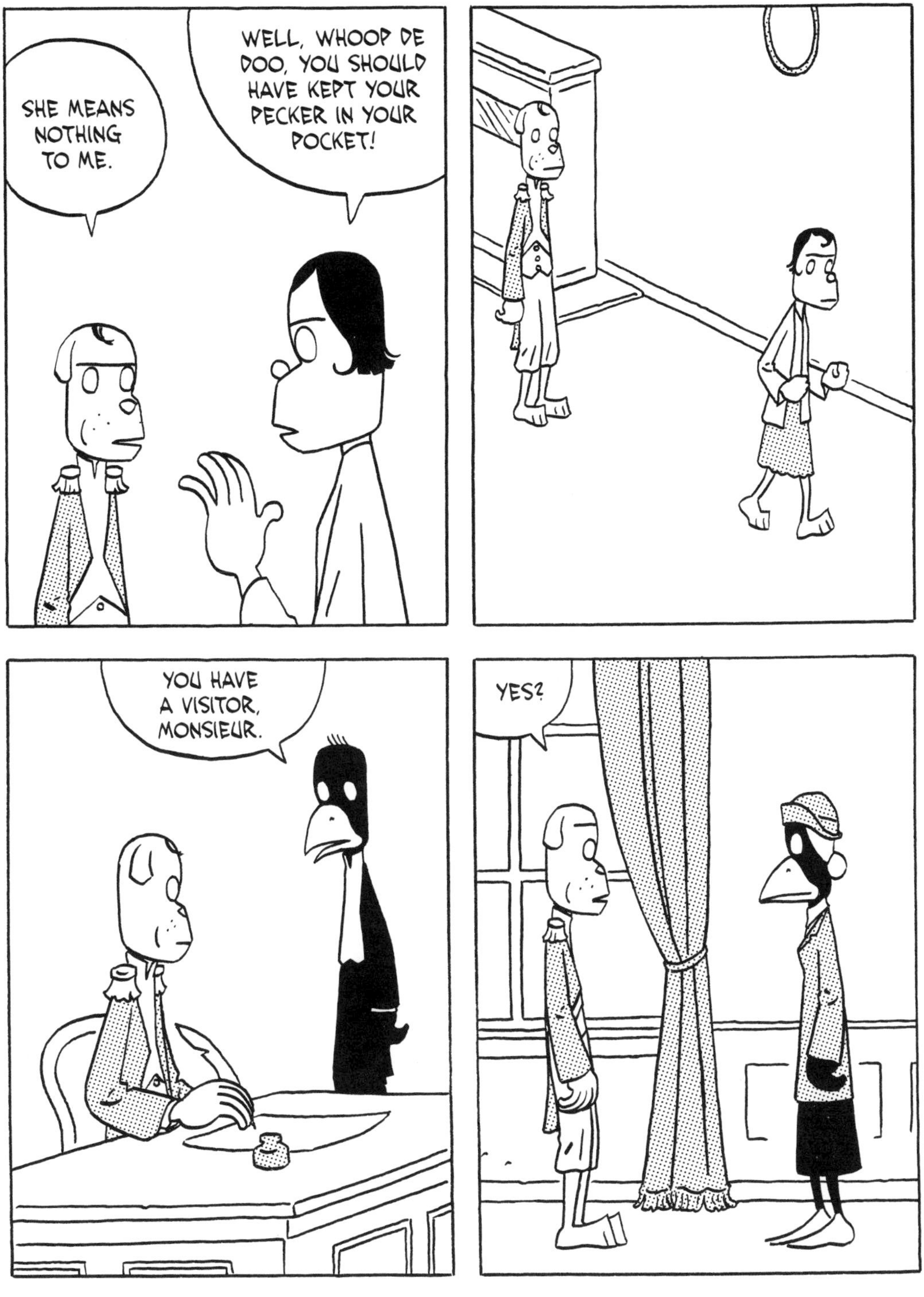
SHE MEANS NOTHING TO ME.
WELL, WHOOP DE DOO, YOU SHOULD HAVE KEPT YOUR PECKER IN YOUR POCKET!
YOU HAVE A VISITOR, MONSIEUR.
YES?

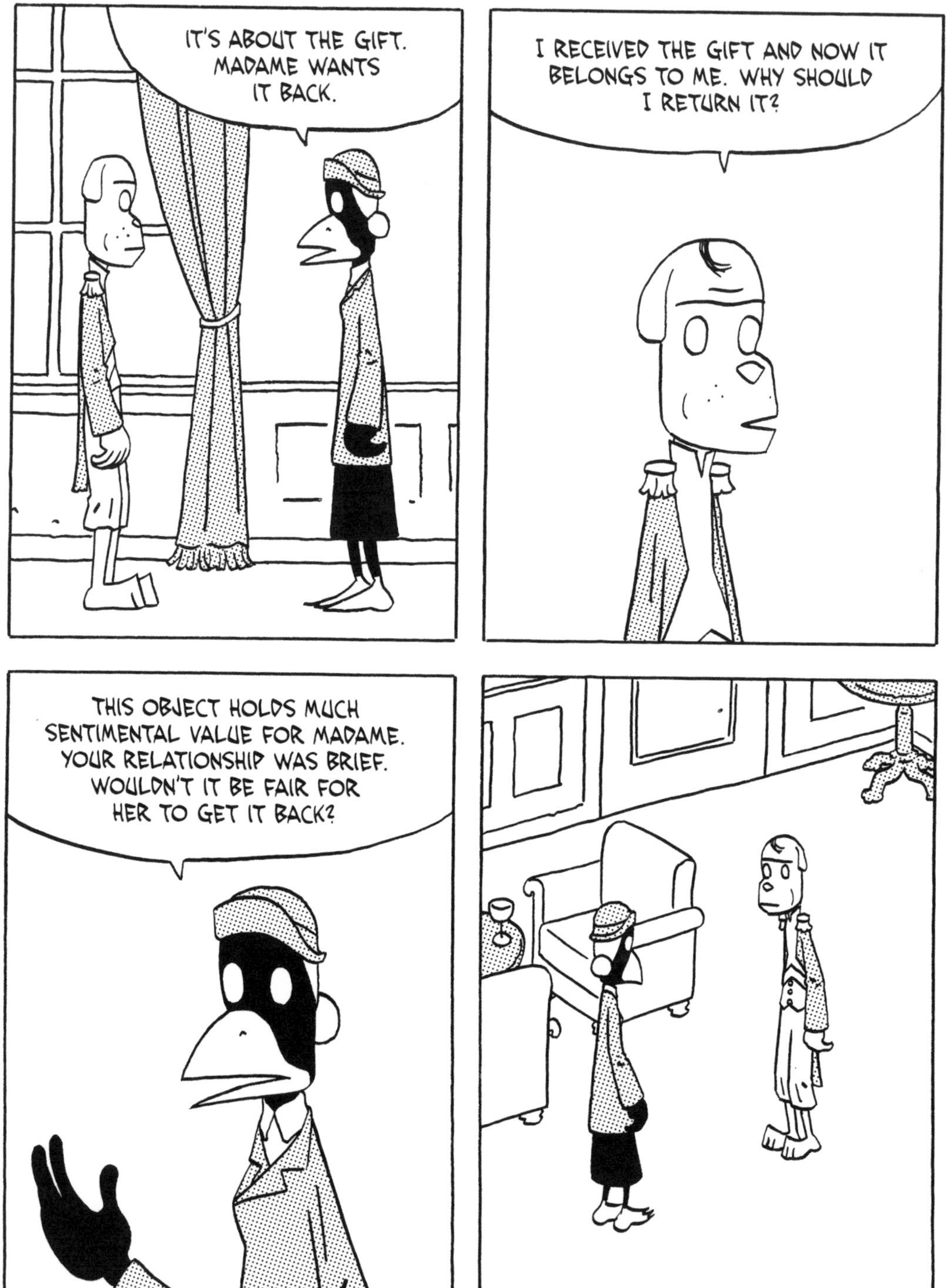
IT'S ABOUT THE GIFT. MADAME WANTS IT BACK.
I RECEIVED THE GIFT AND NOW IT BELONGS TO ME. WHY SHOULD I RETURN IT?
THIS OBJECT HOLDS MUCH SENTIMENTAL VALUE FOR MADAME. YOUR RELATIONSHIP WAS BRIEF. WOULDN'T IT BE FAIR FOR HER TO GET IT BACK?

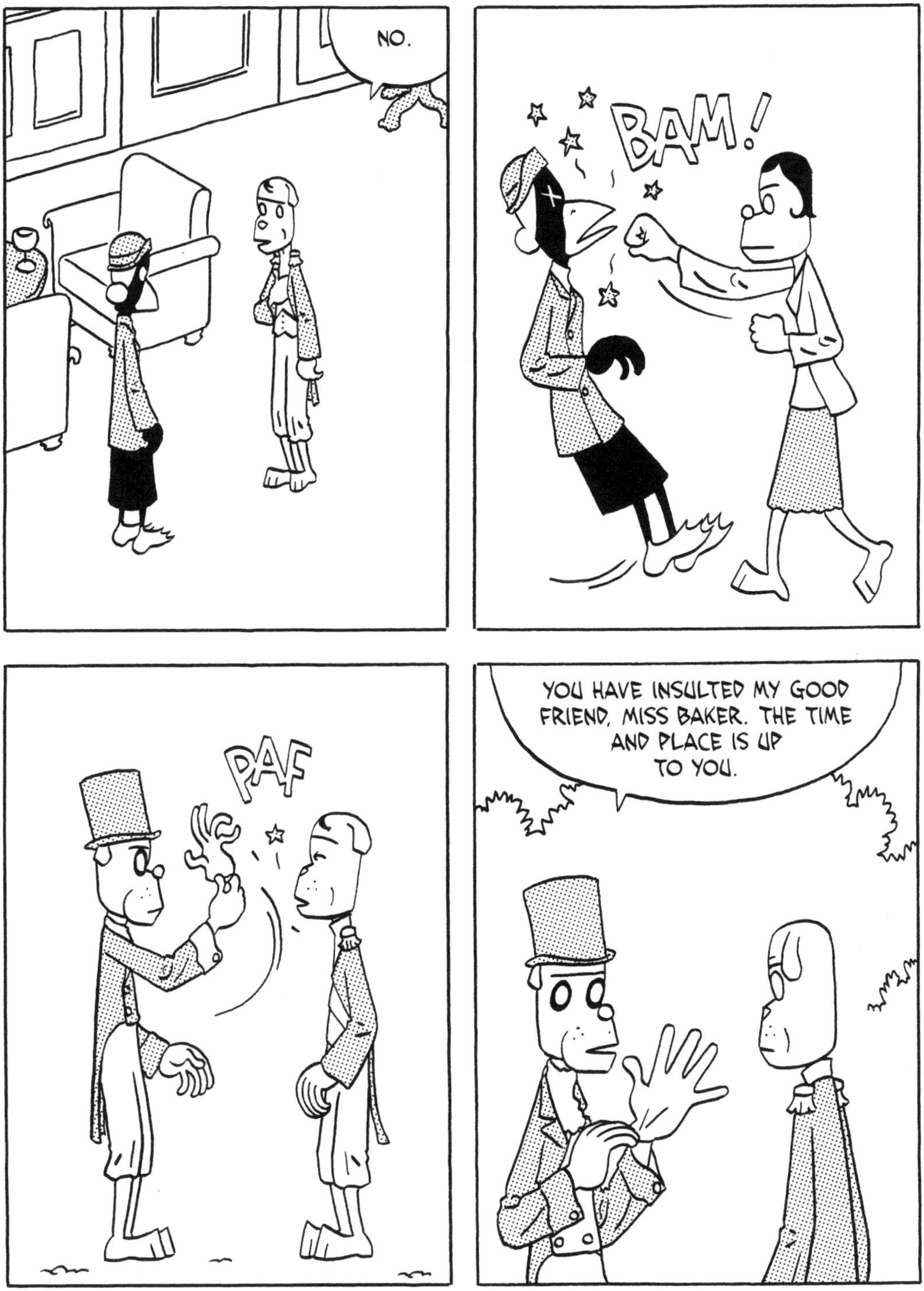
NO.
BAM!
PAF
YOU HAVE INSULTED MY GOOD FRIEND, MISS BAKER. THE TIME AND PLACE IS UP TO YOU.

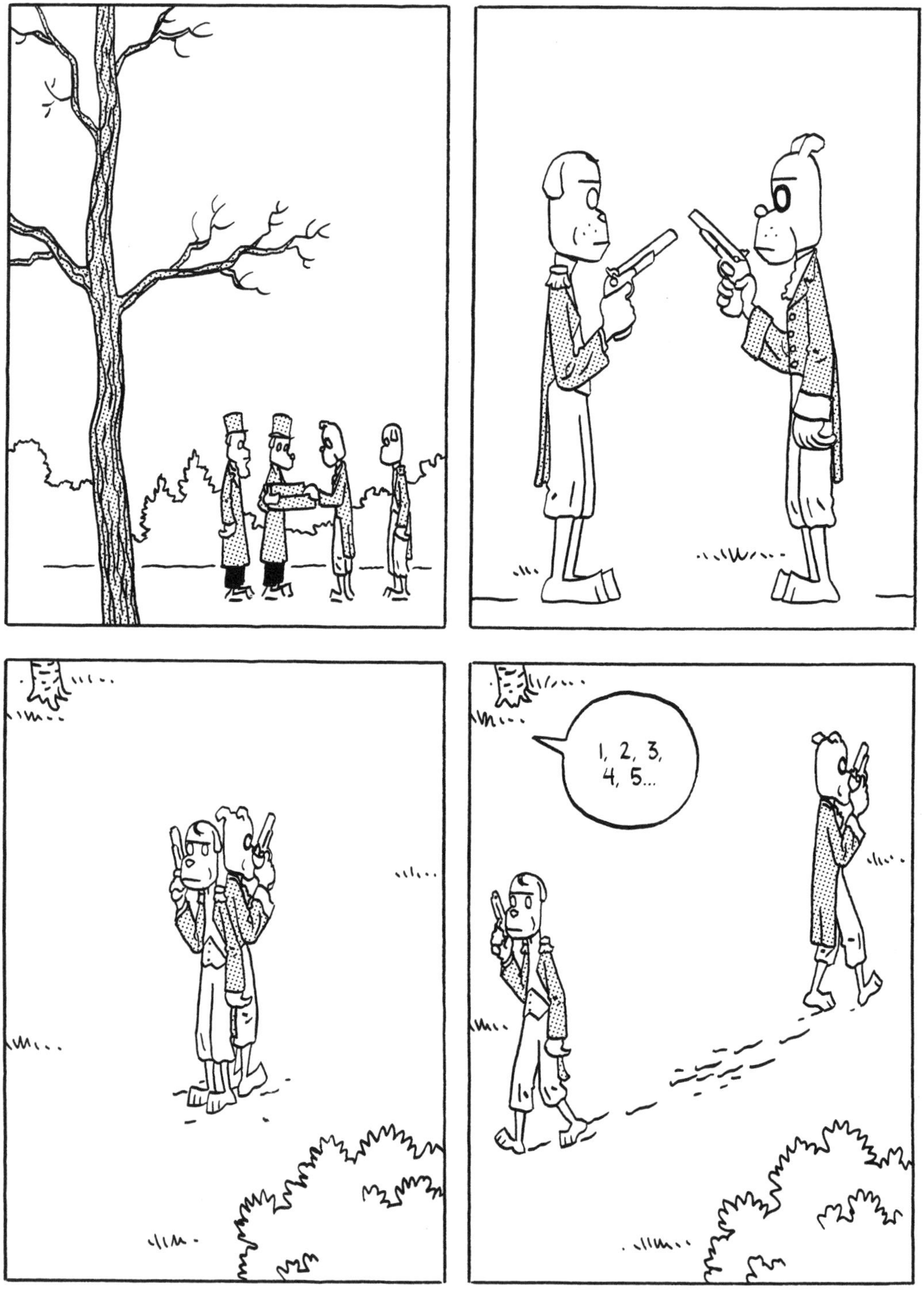
1, 2, 3,
4, 5...

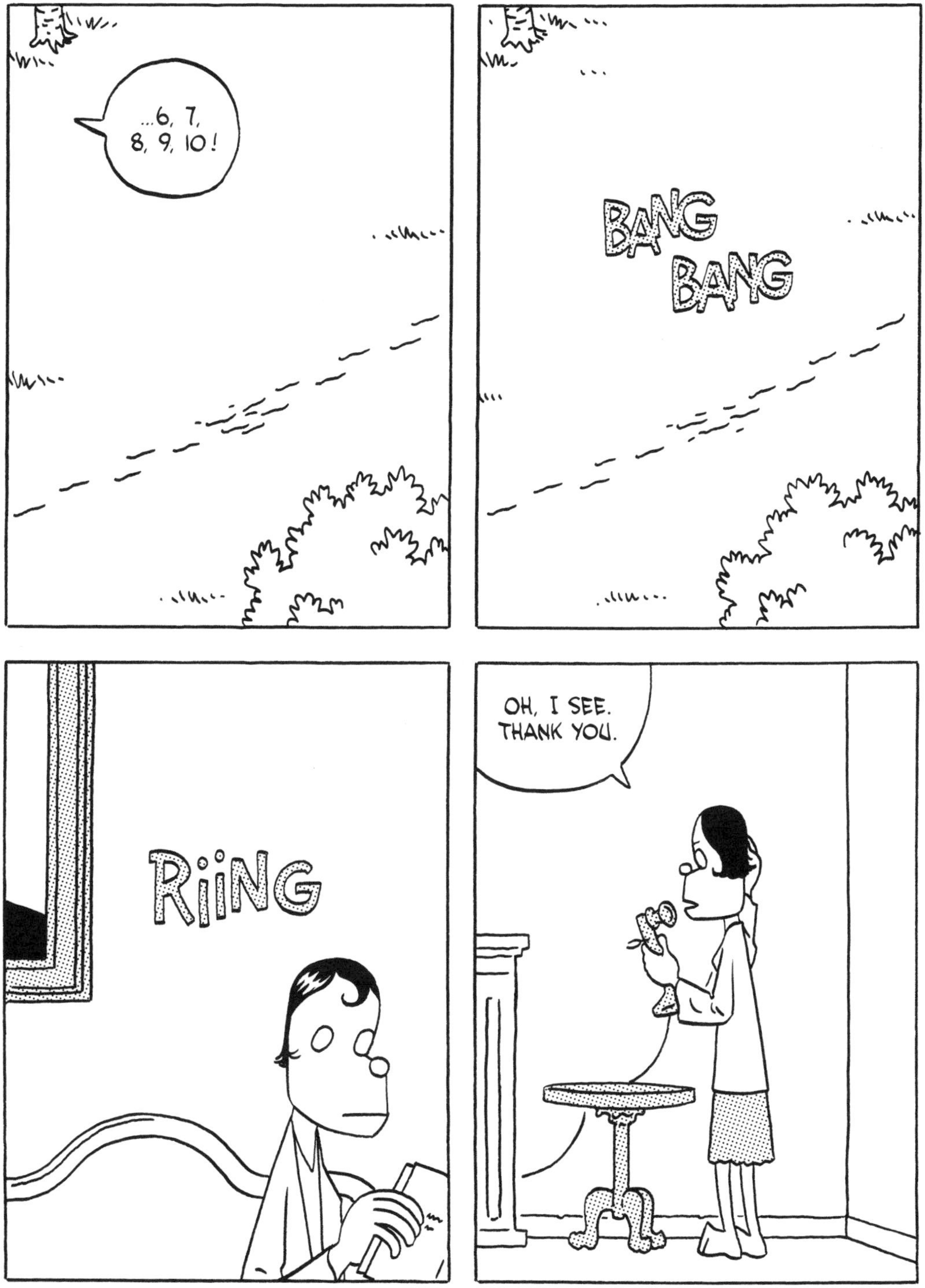
...6, 7, 8, 9, 10!
BANG BANG
RiiNG
OH, I SEE. THANK YOU.

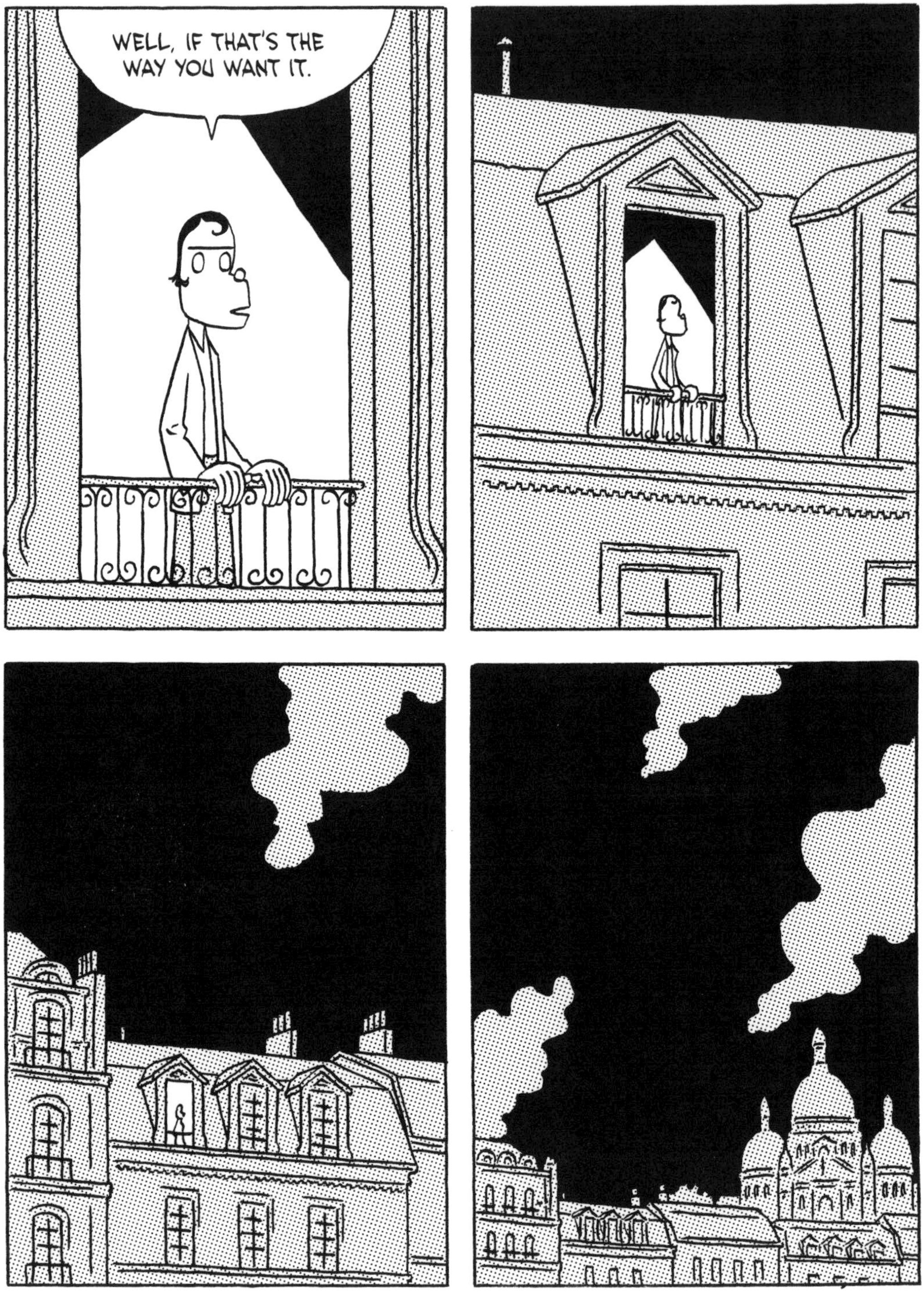
WELL, IF THAT'S THE WAY YOU WANT IT.

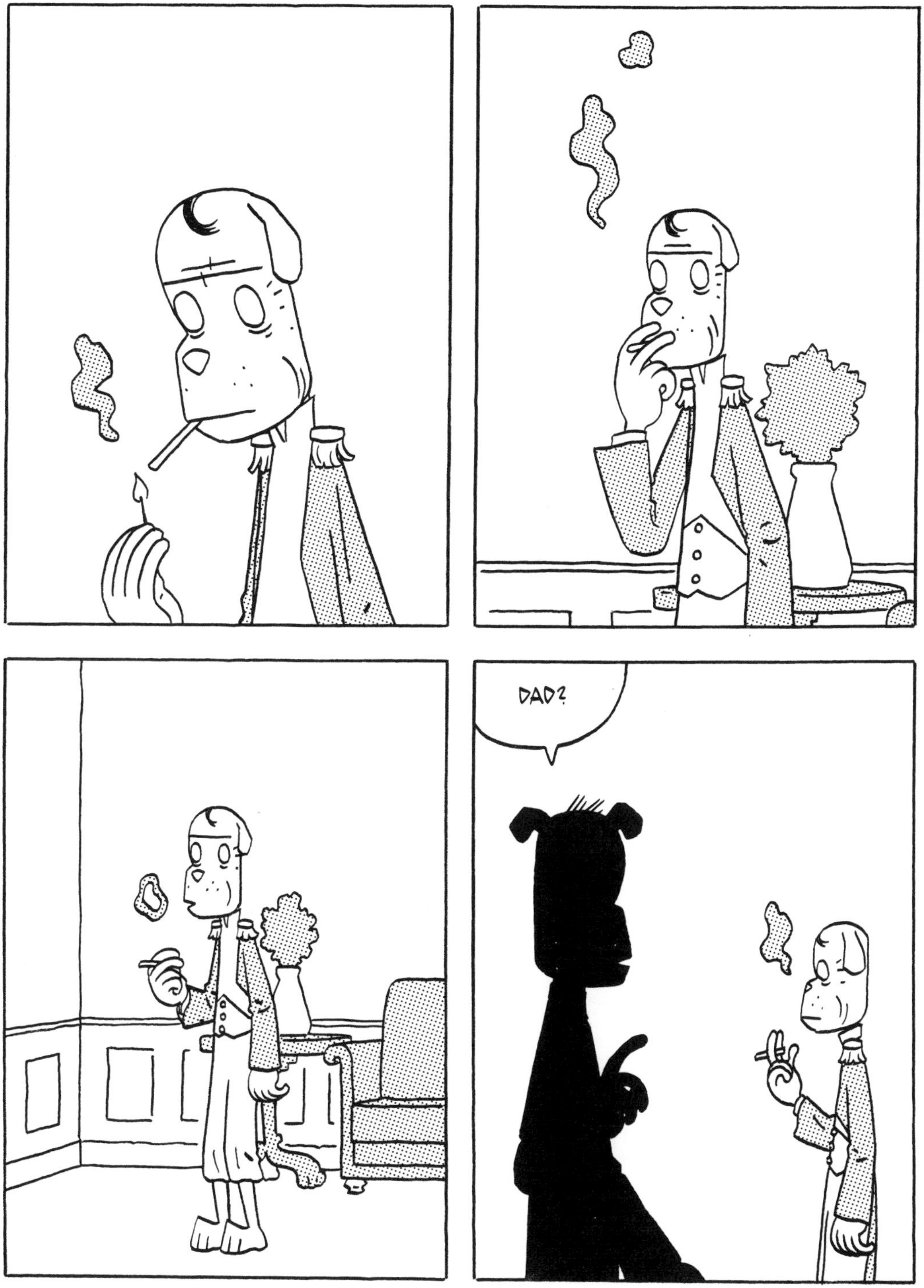
DAD?

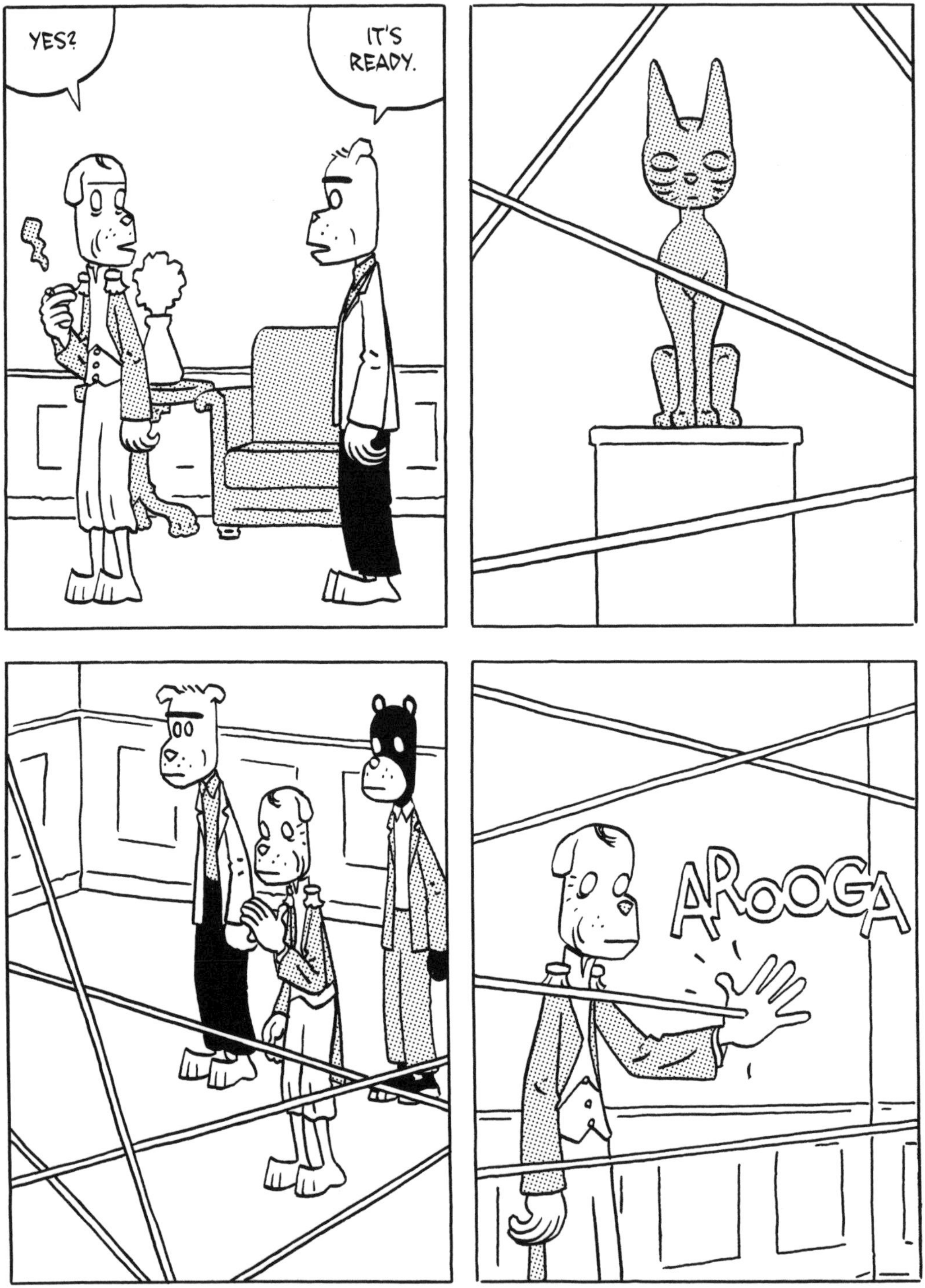
YES?
IT'S READY.
AROOGA

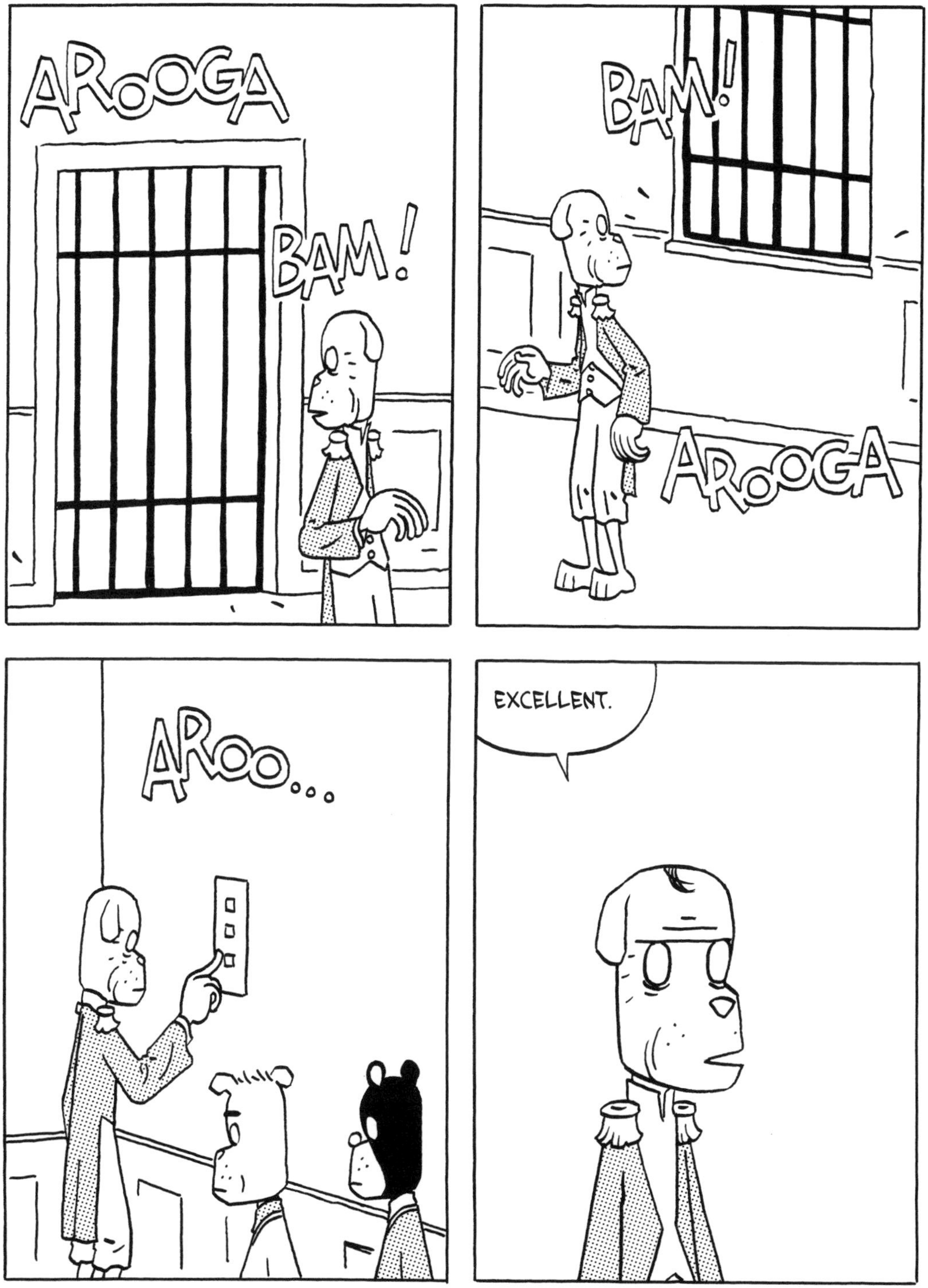
AROOGA
BAM!
BAM!
AROOGA
AROO...
EXCELLENT.

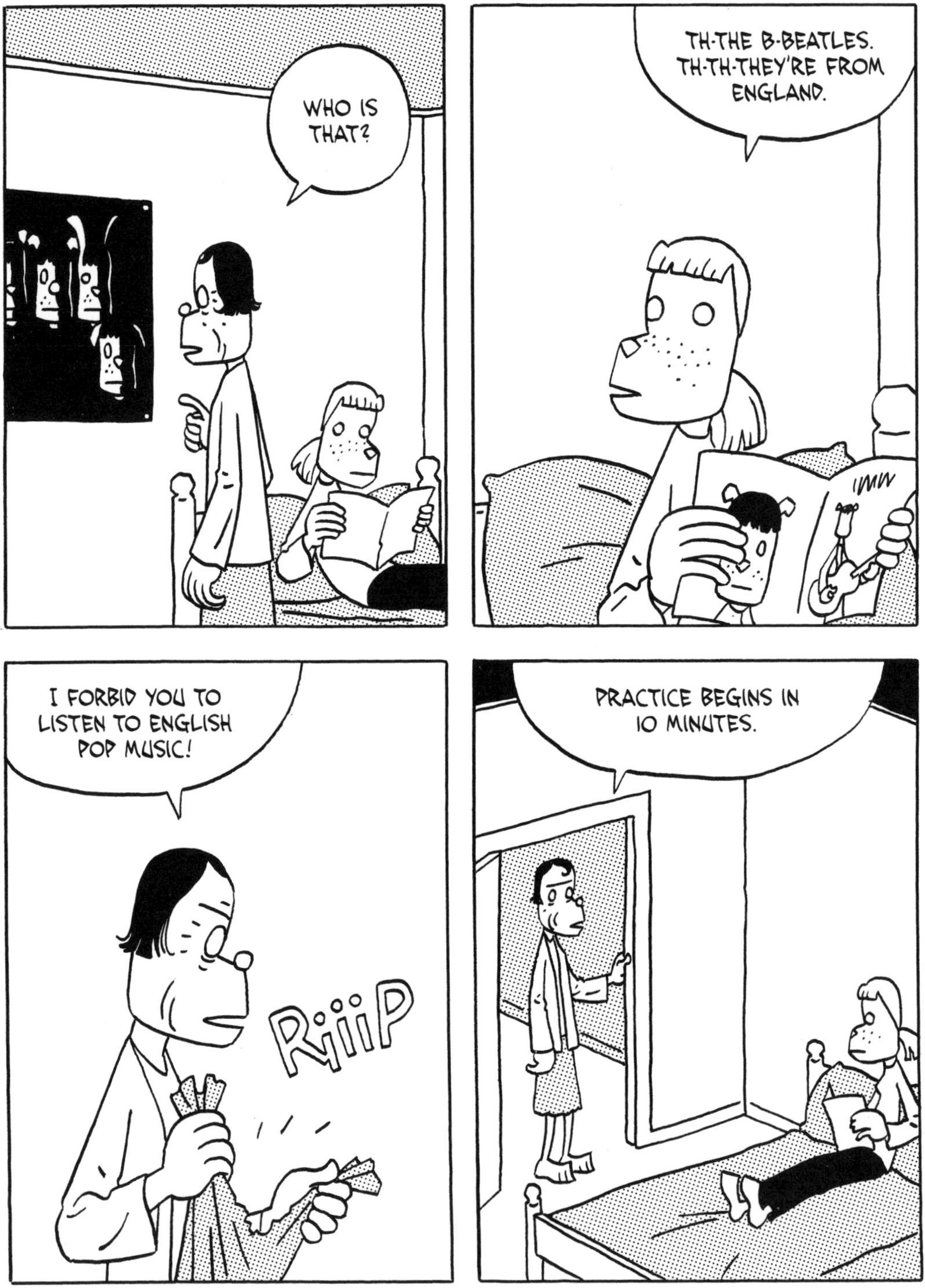
WHO IS THAT?
TH-THE B-BEATLES. TH-TH-THEY'RE FROM ENGLAND.
I FORBID YOU TO LISTEN TO ENGLISH POP MUSIC!
RiiiP
PRACTICE BEGINS IN 10 MINUTES.

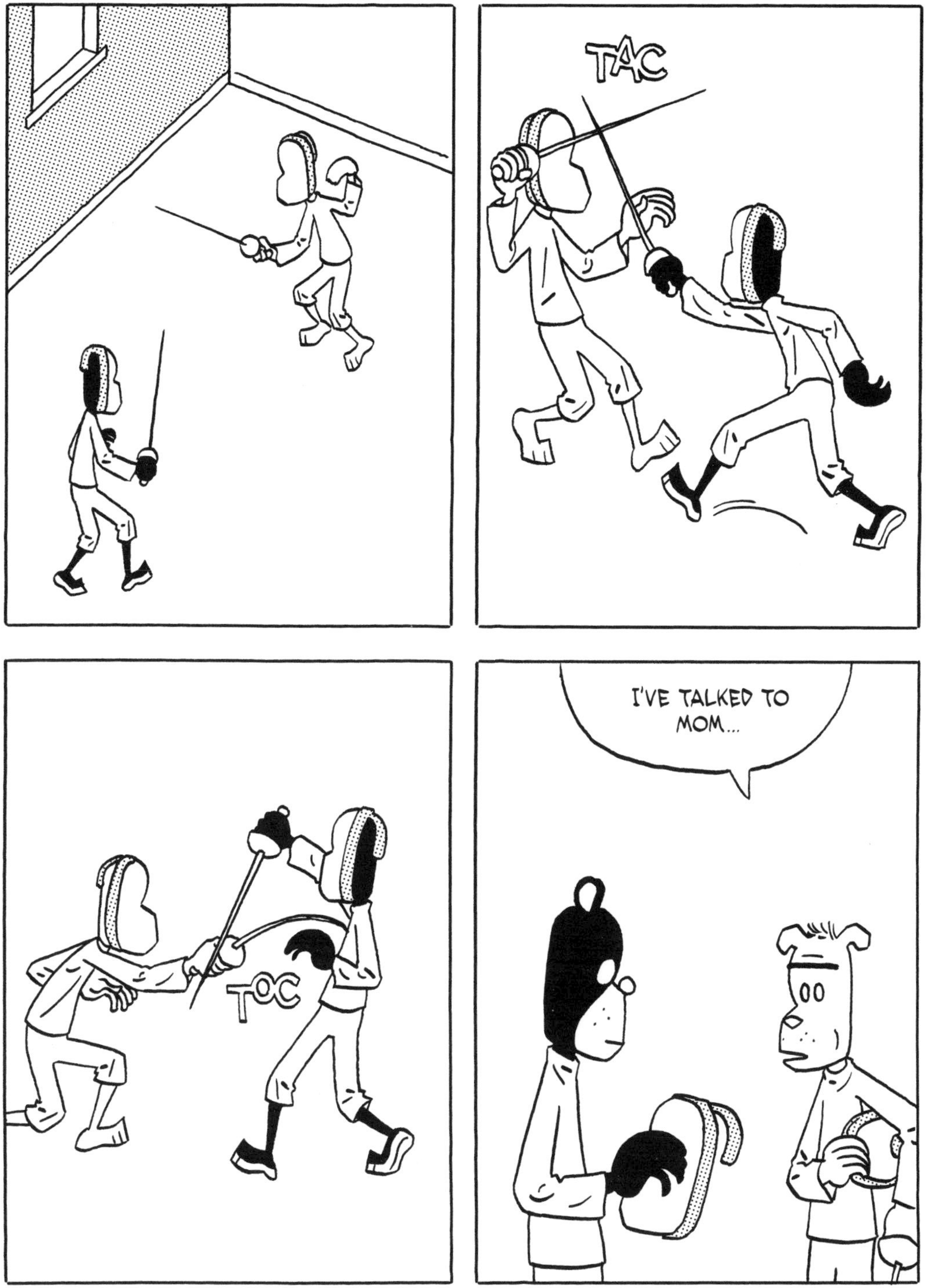
TAC
TOC
I'VE TALKED TO MOM...

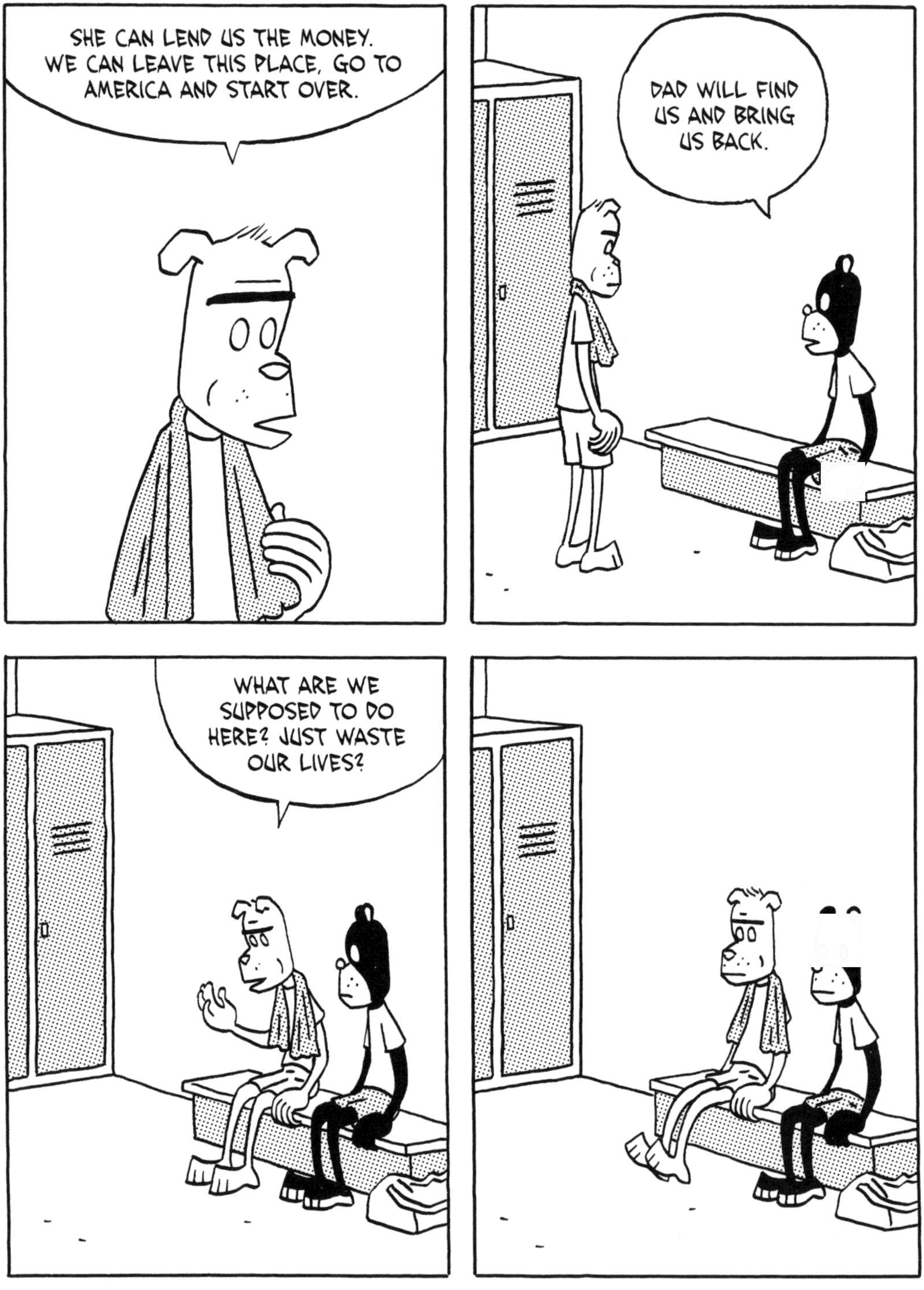
SHE CAN LEND US THE MONEY. WE CAN LEAVE THIS PLACE, GO TO AMERICA AND START OVER.
DAD WILL FIND US AND BRING US BACK.
WHAT ARE WE SUPPOSED TO DO HERE? JUST WASTE OUR LIVES?

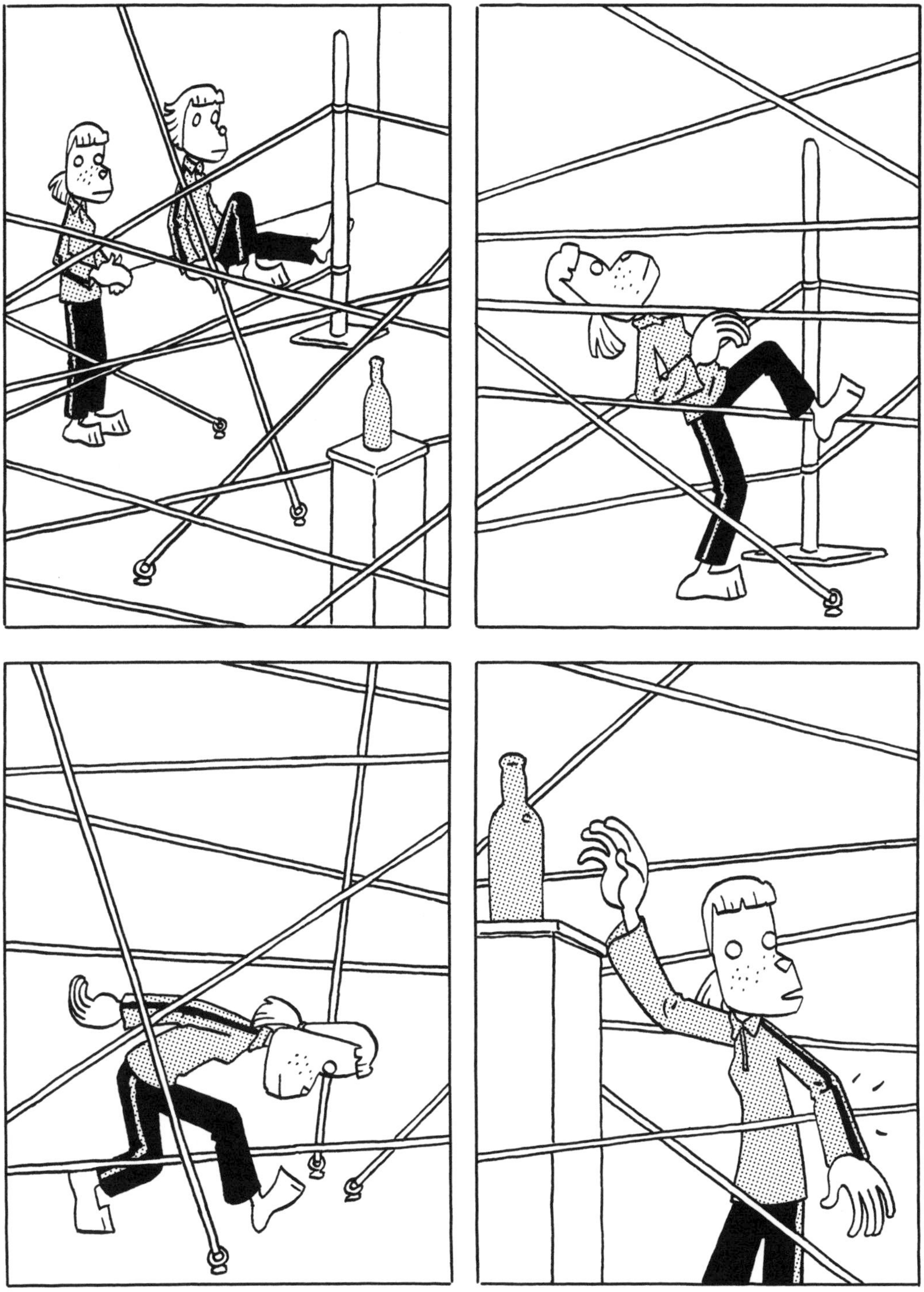

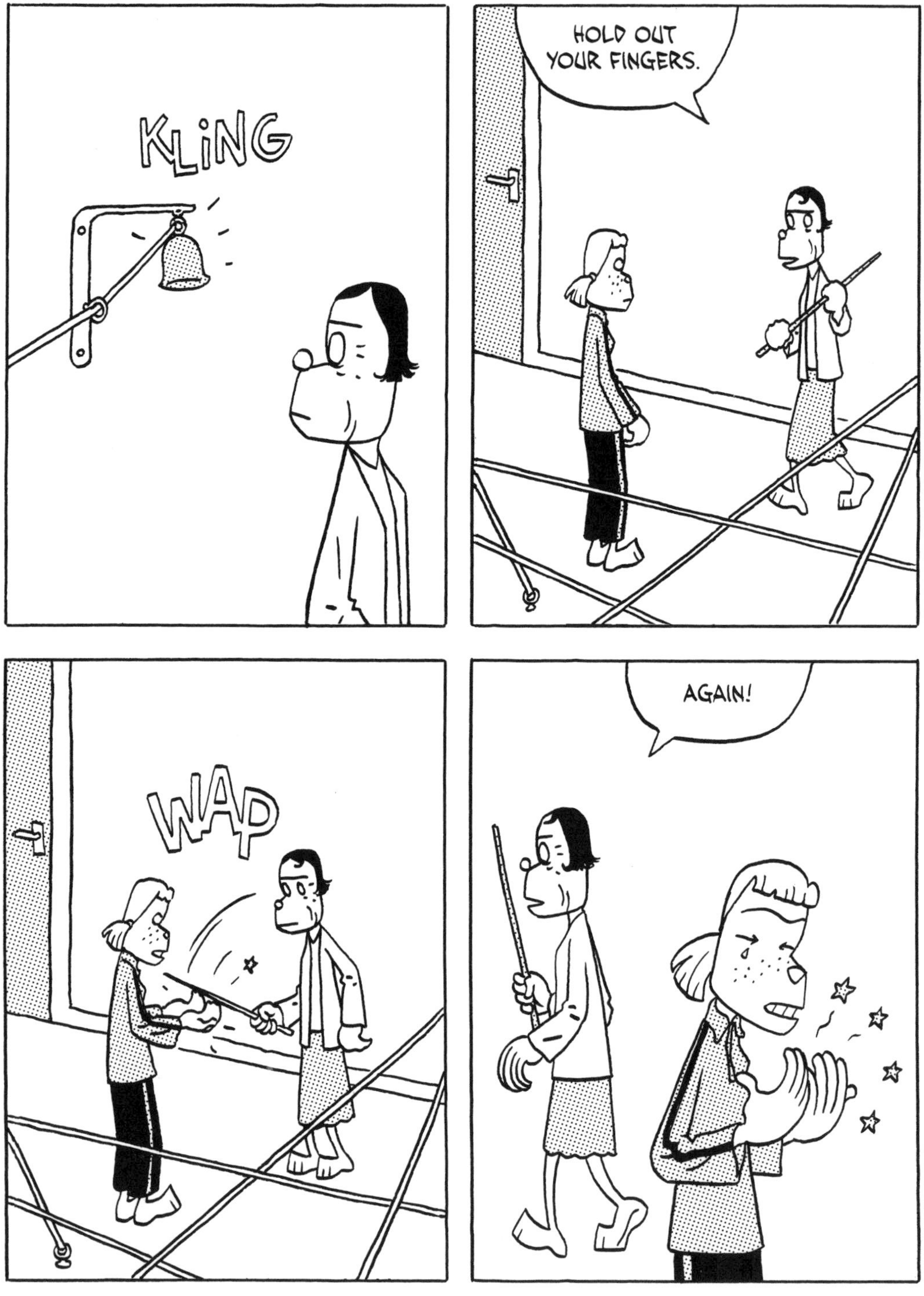
KLING
HOLD OUT YOUR FINGERS.
WAP
AGAIN!

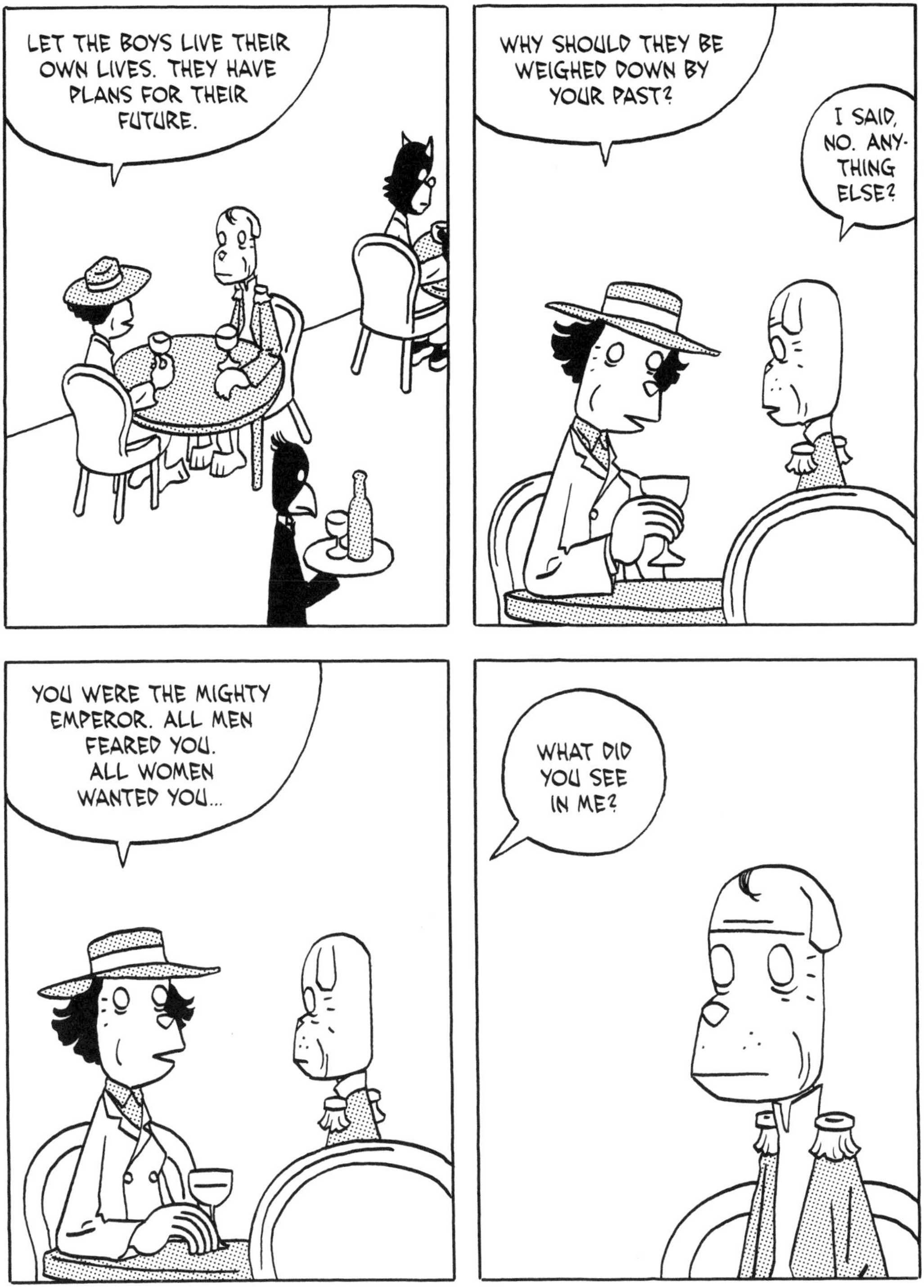
LET THE BOYS LIVE THEIR OWN LIVES. THEY HAVE PLANS FOR THEIR FUTURE.
WHY SHOULD THEY BE WEIGHED DOWN BY YOUR PAST?
I SAID, NO. ANYTHING ELSE?
YOU WERE THE MIGHTY EMPEROR. ALL MEN FEARED YOU. ALL WOMEN WANTED YOU...
WHAT DID YOU SEE IN ME?

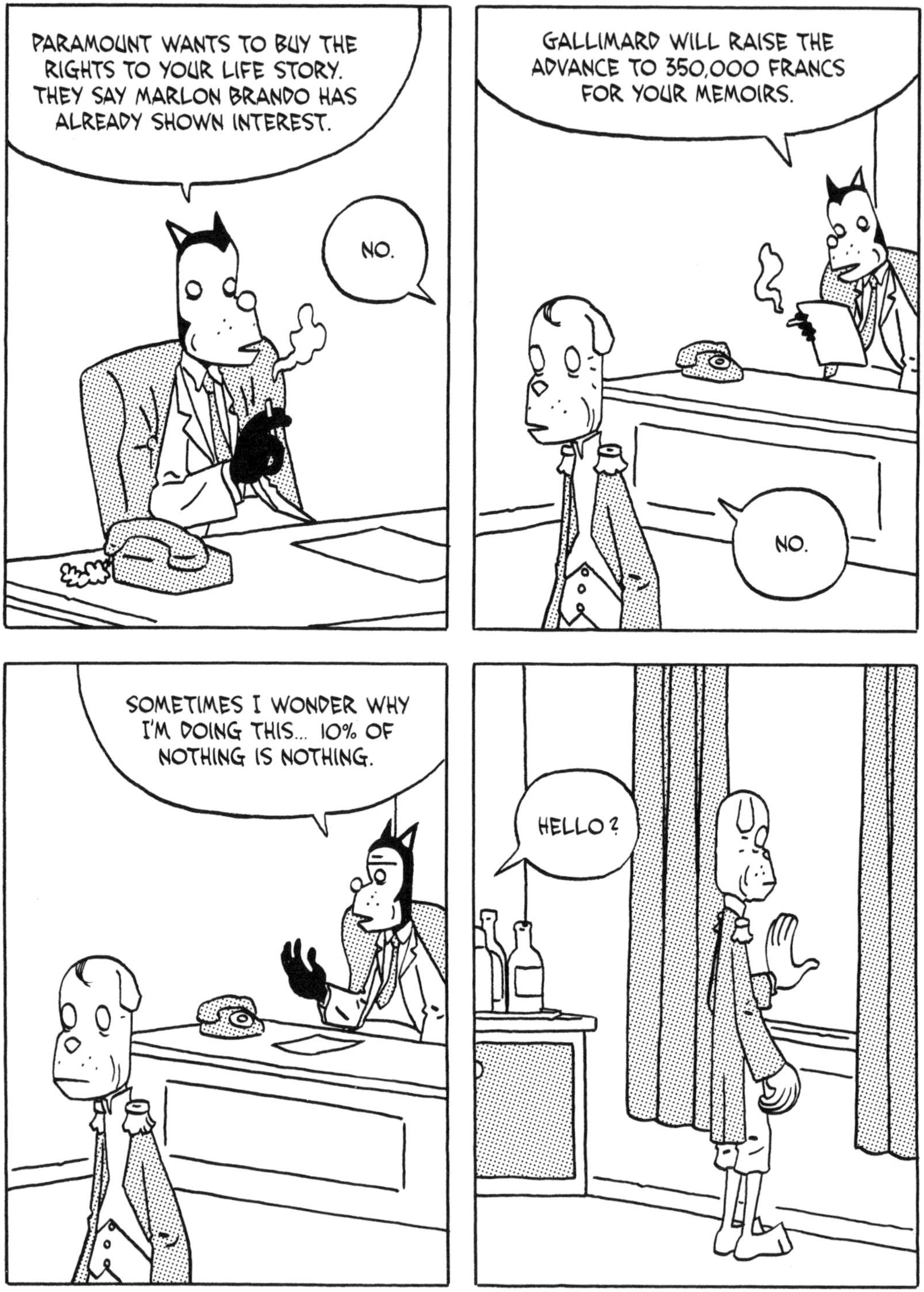
PARAMOUNT WANTS TO BUY THE RIGHTS TO YOUR LIFE STORY. THEY SAY MARLON BRANDO HAS ALREADY SHOWN INTEREST.
NO.
GALLIMARD WILL RAISE THE ADVANCE TO 350,000 FRANCS FOR YOUR MEMOIRS.
NO.
SOMETIMES I WONDER WHY I'M DOING THIS... 10% OF NOTHING IS NOTHING.
HELLO?

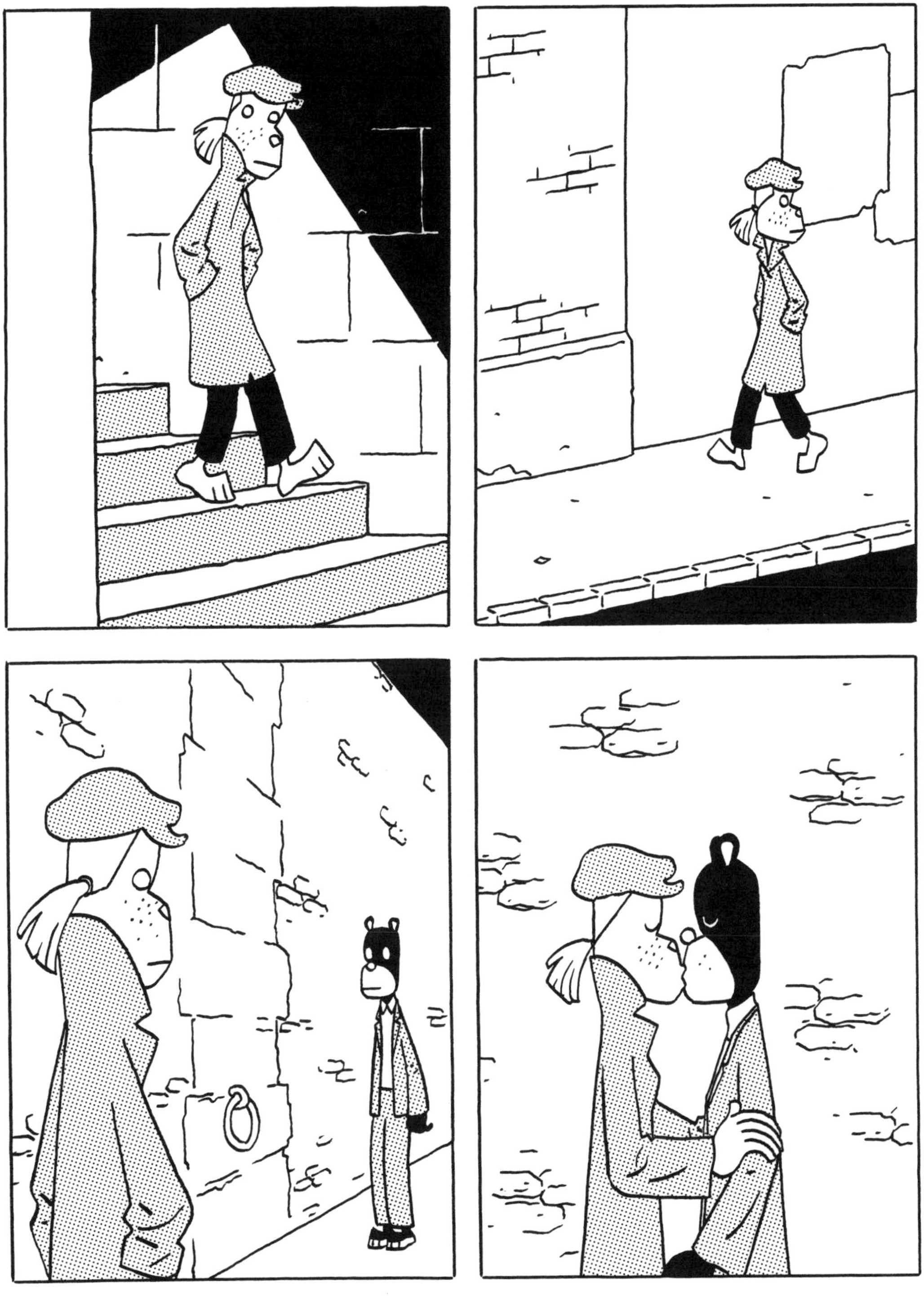

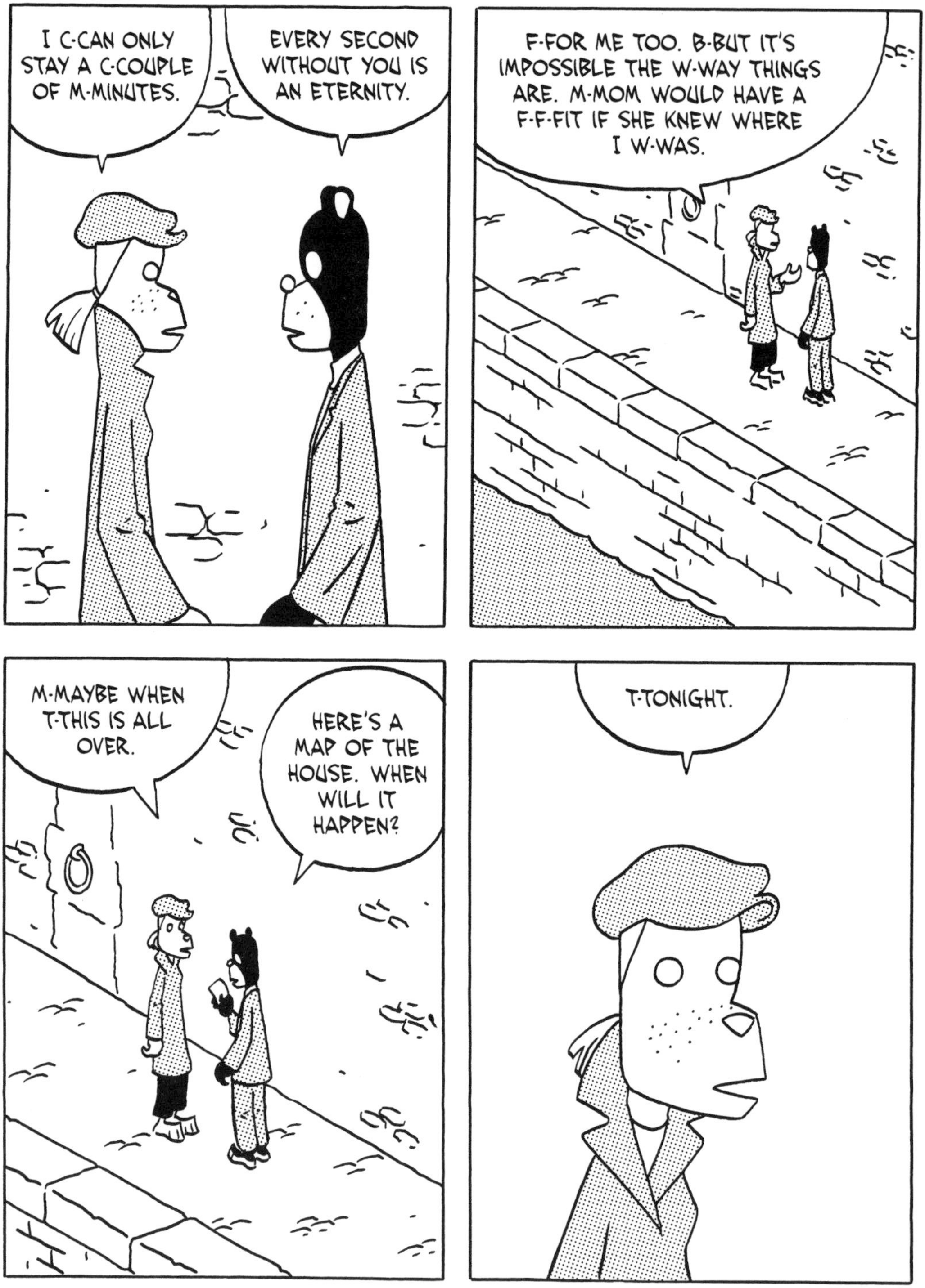
I C-CAN ONLY STAY A C-COUPLE OF M-MINUTES.
EVERY SECOND WITHOUT YOU IS AN ETERNITY.
F-FOR ME TOO. B-BUT IT'S IMPOSSIBLE THE W-WAY THINGS ARE. M-MOM WOULD HAVE A F-F-FIT IF SHE KNEW WHERE I W-WAS.
M-MAYBE WHEN T-THIS IS ALL OVER.
HERE'S A MAP OF THE HOUSE. WHEN WILL IT HAPPEN?
T-TONIGHT.

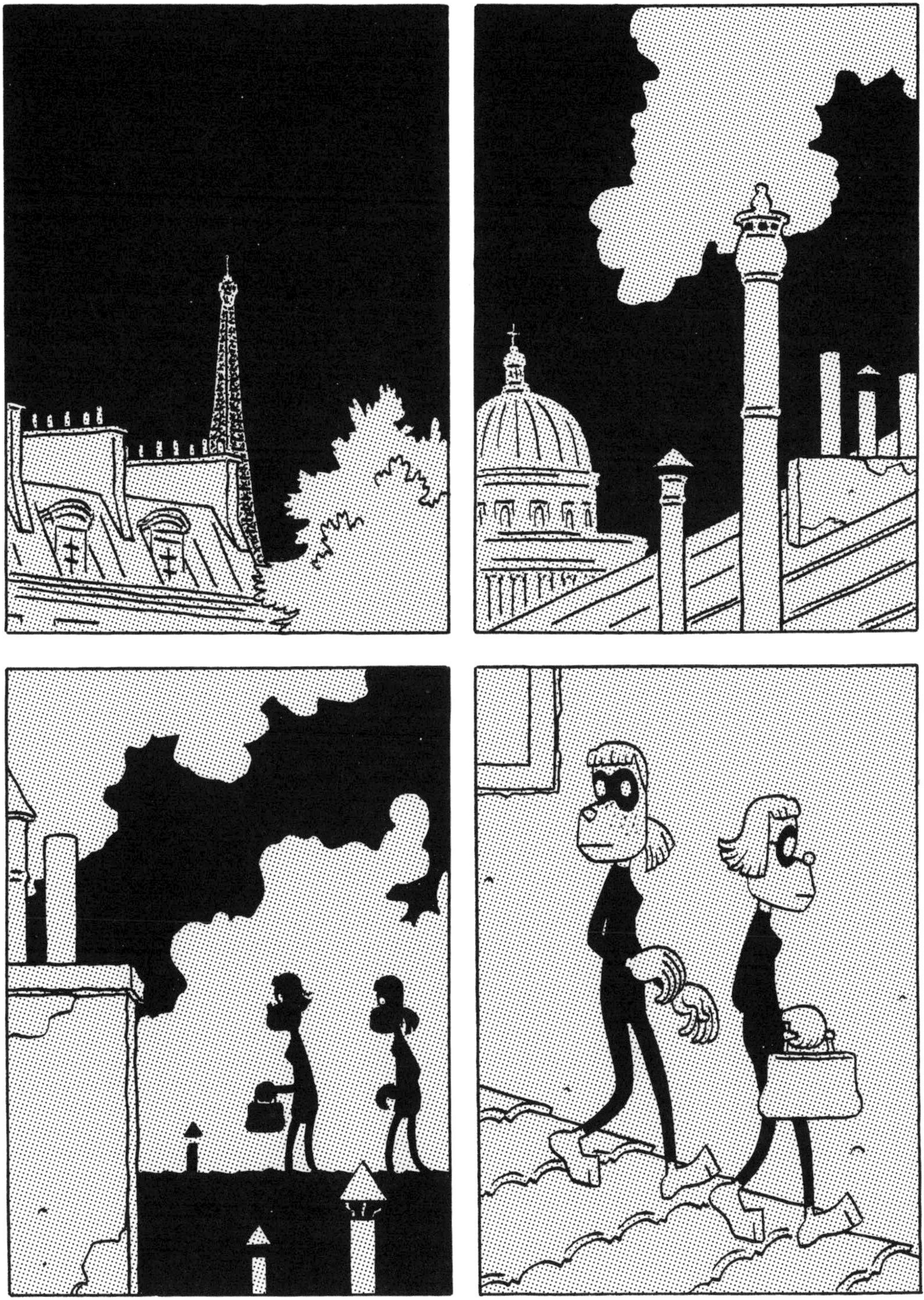

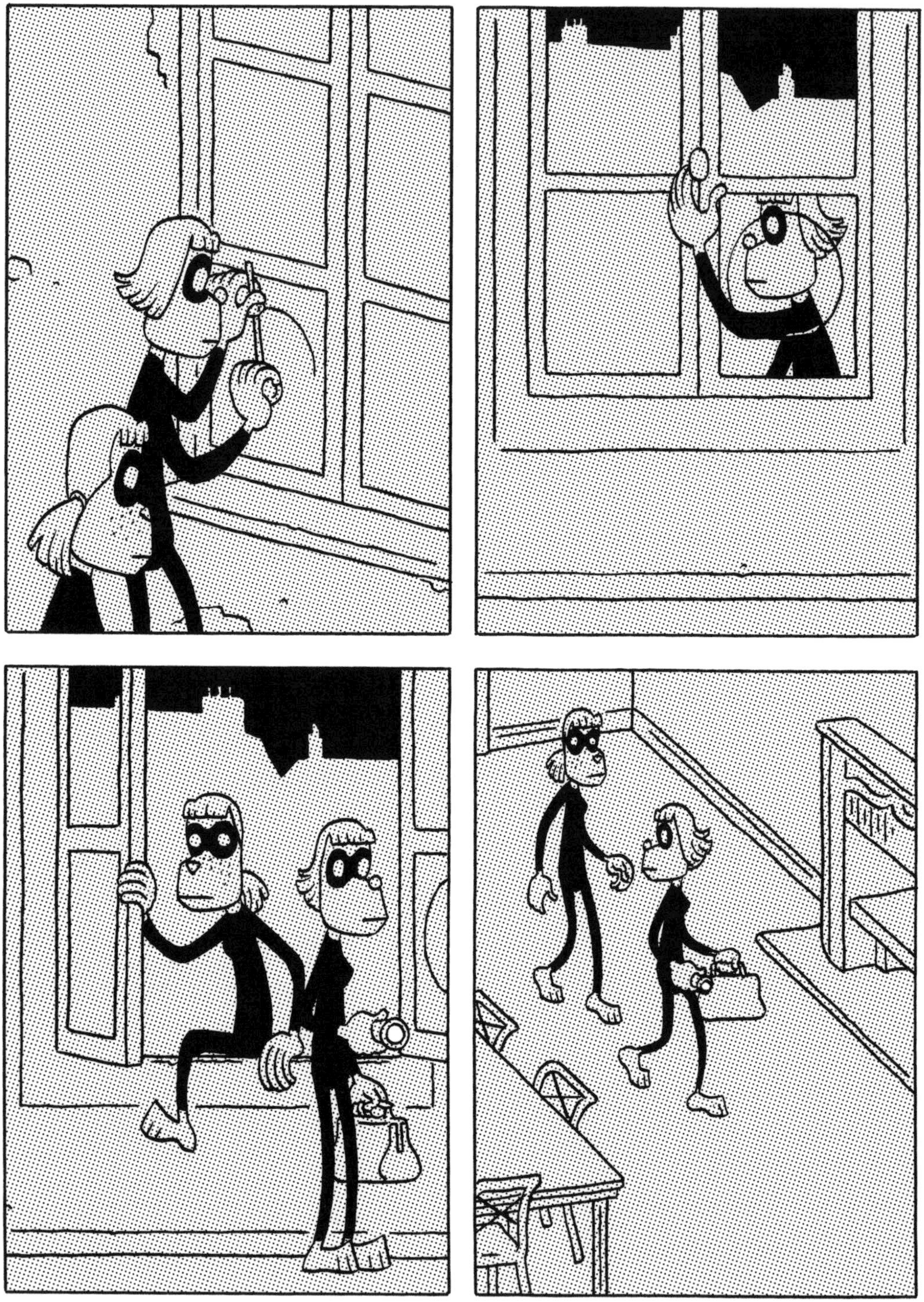

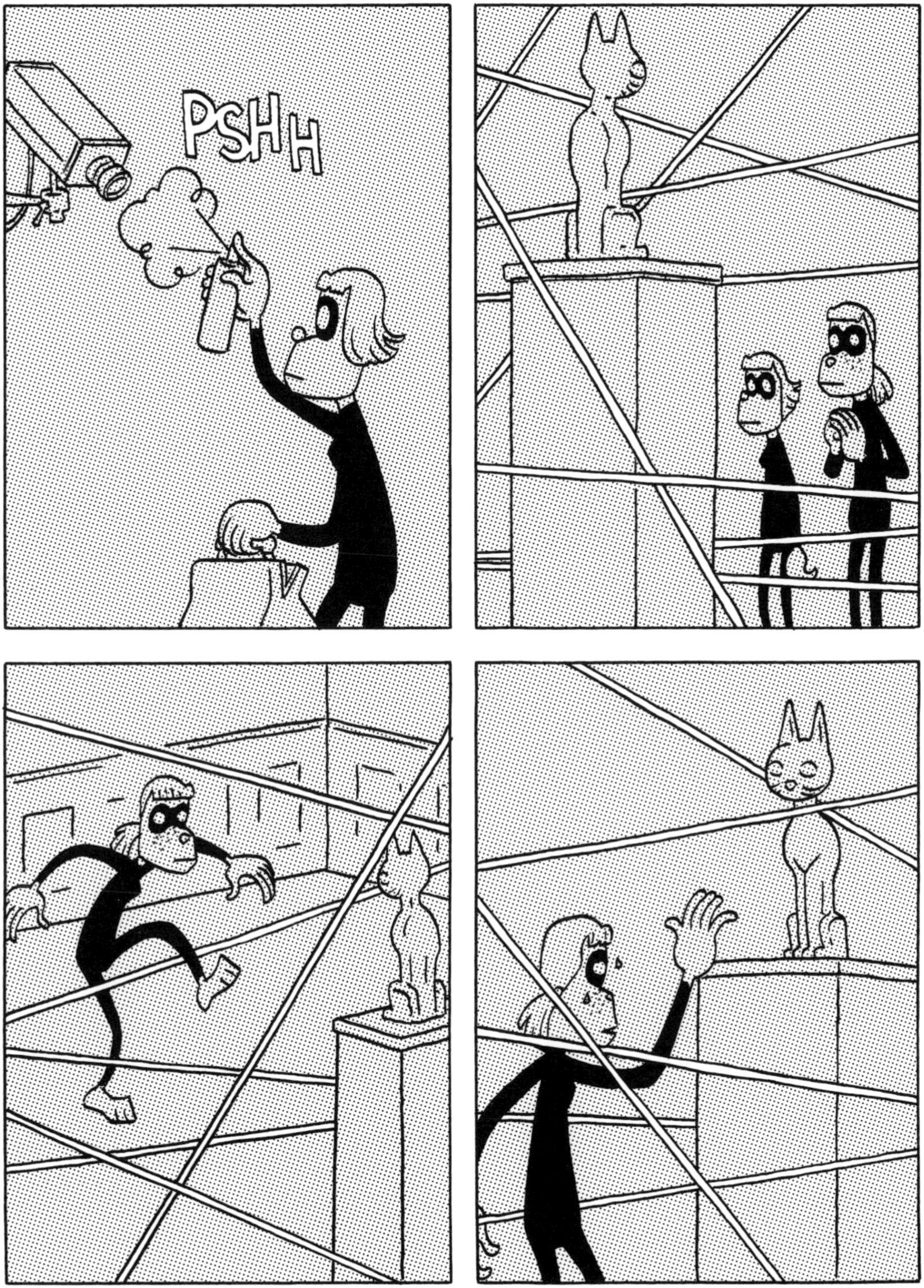
PSHH

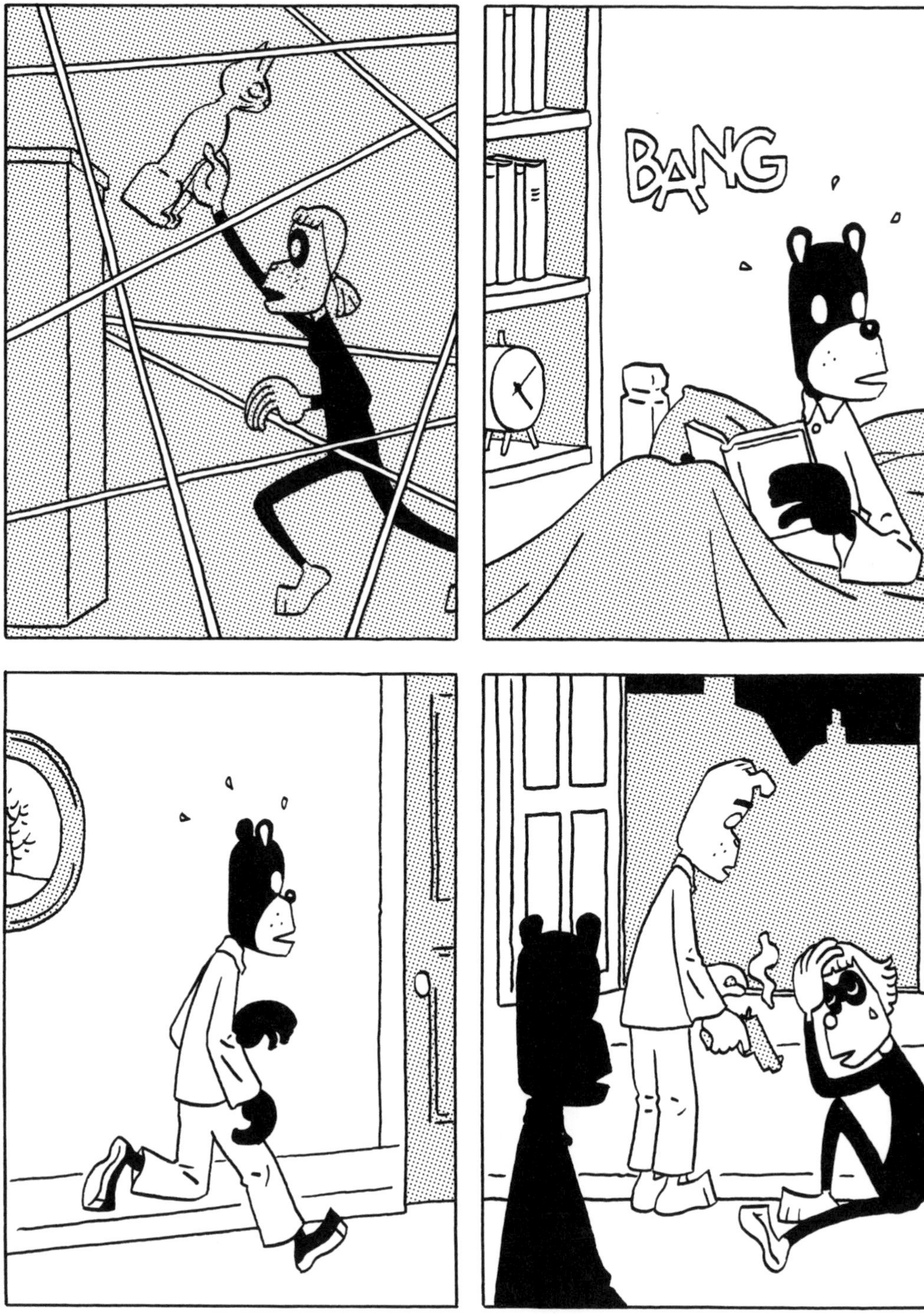
BANG

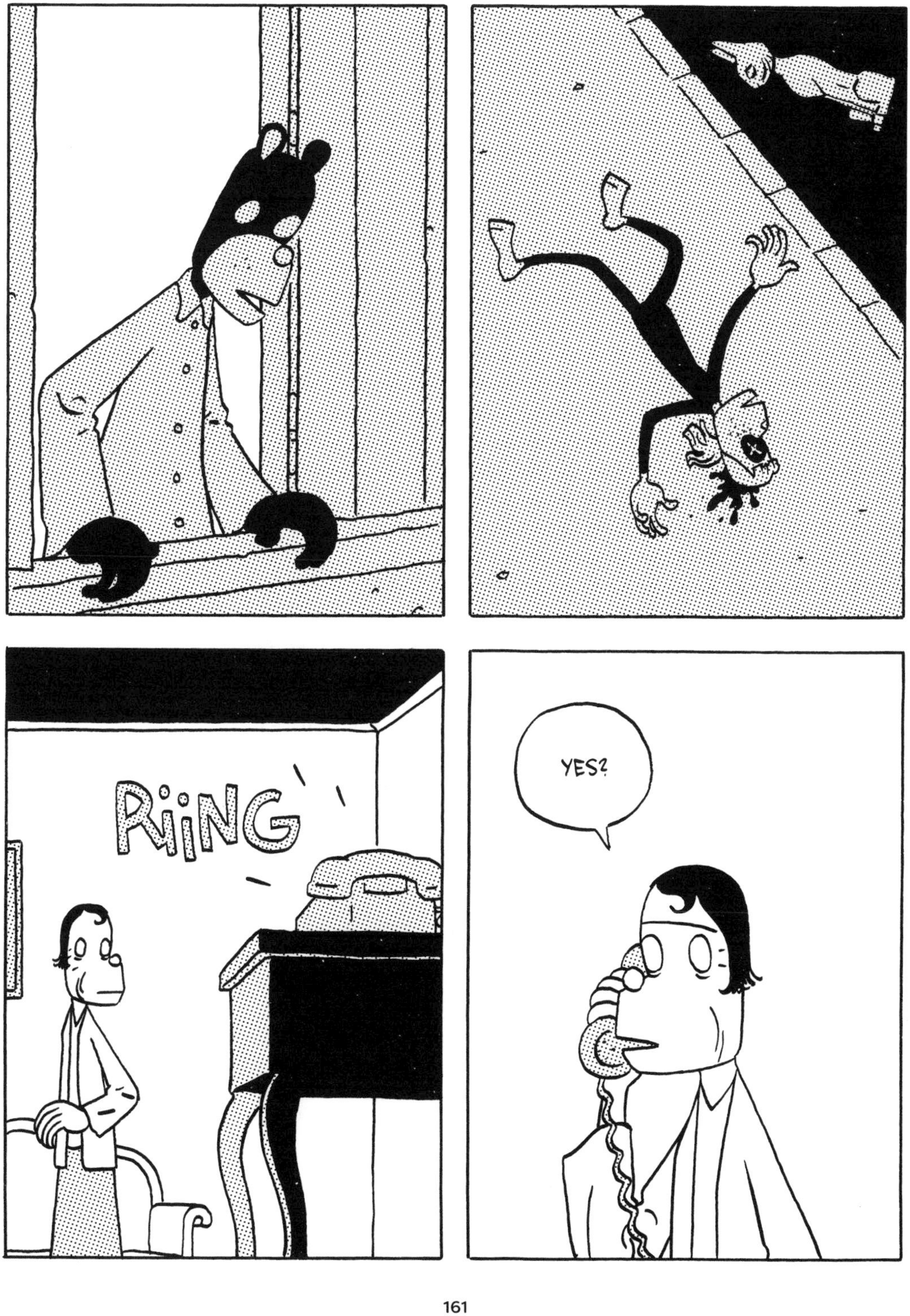
RiiNG
YES?

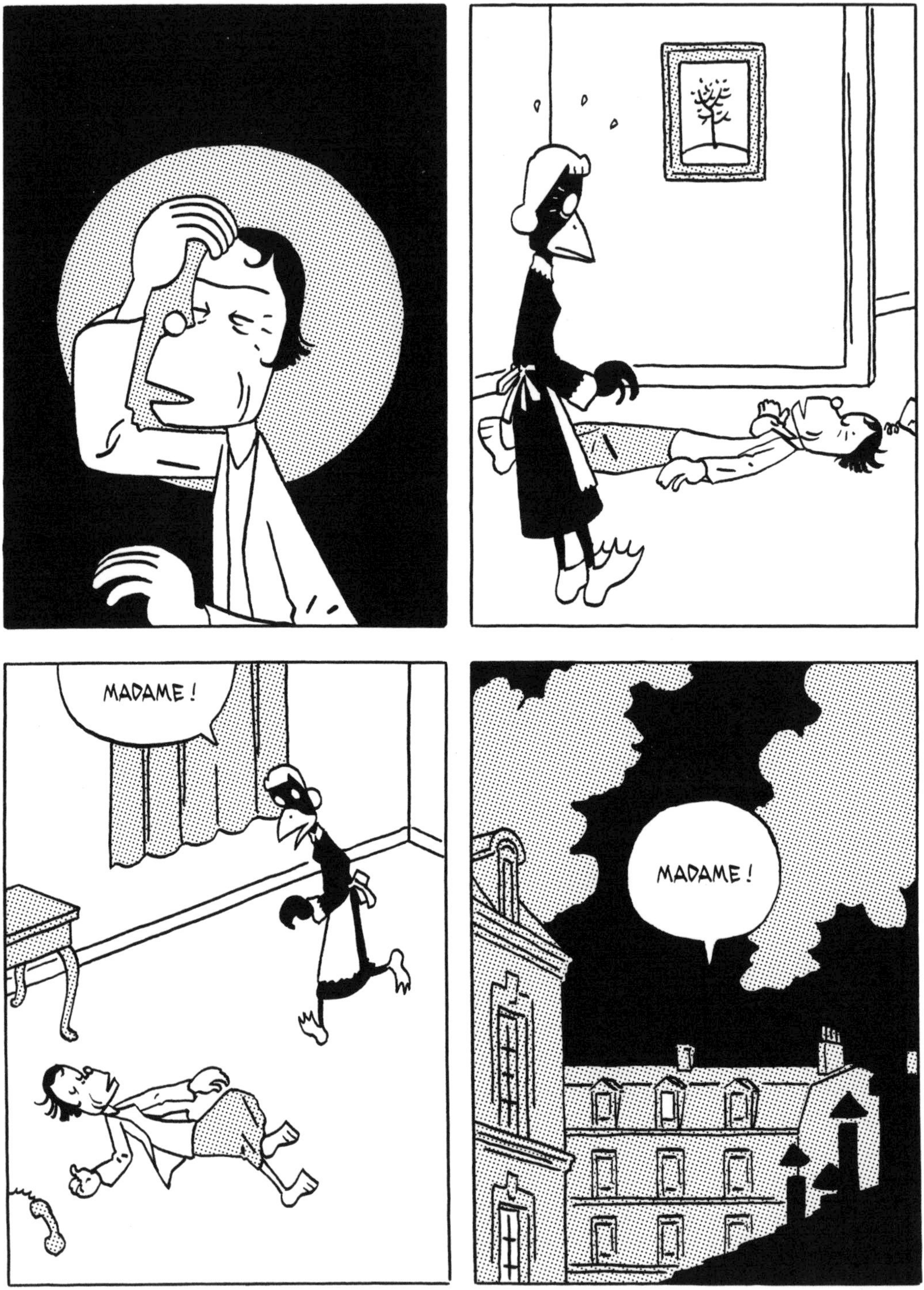
MADAME!
MADAME!

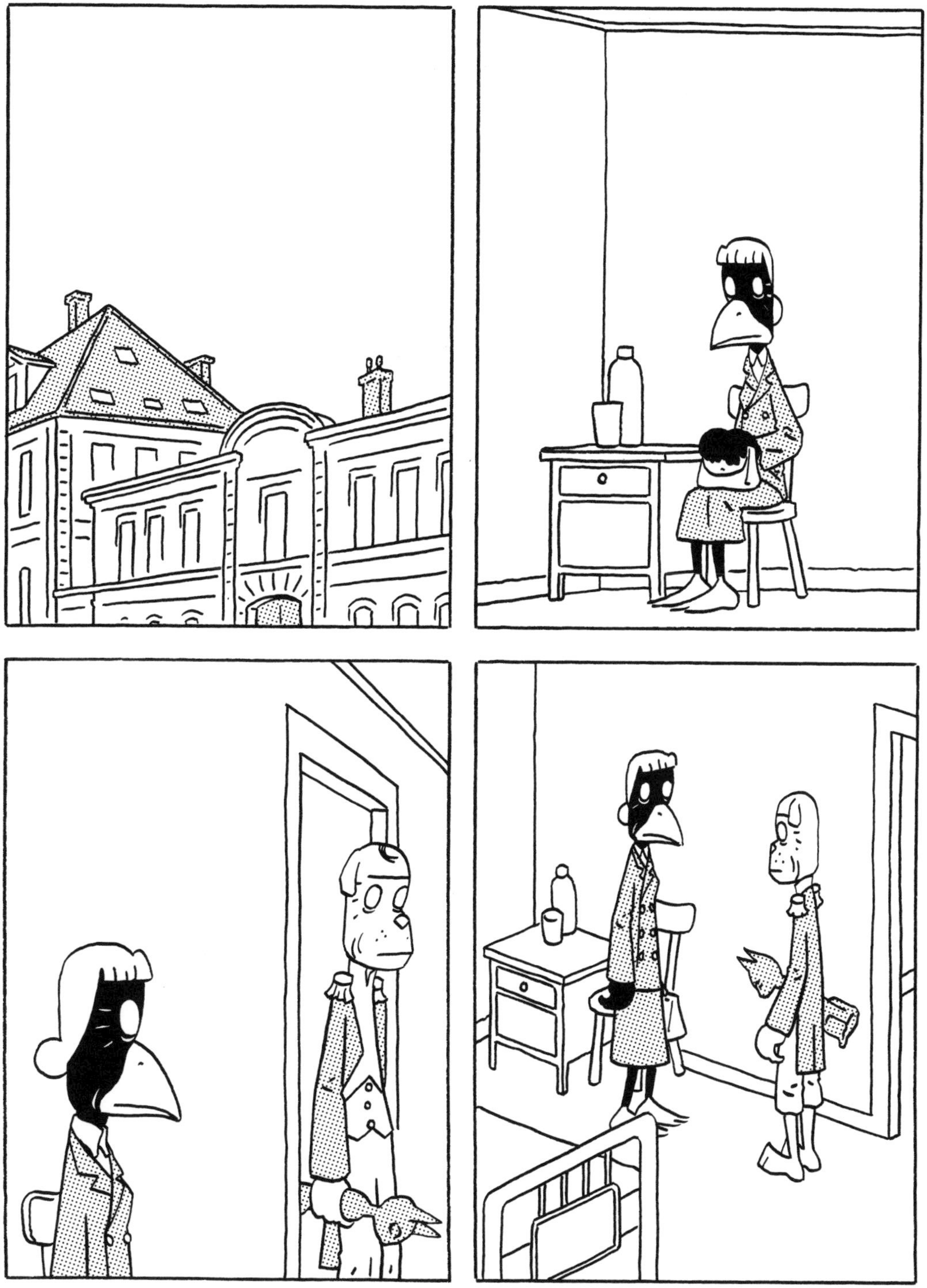

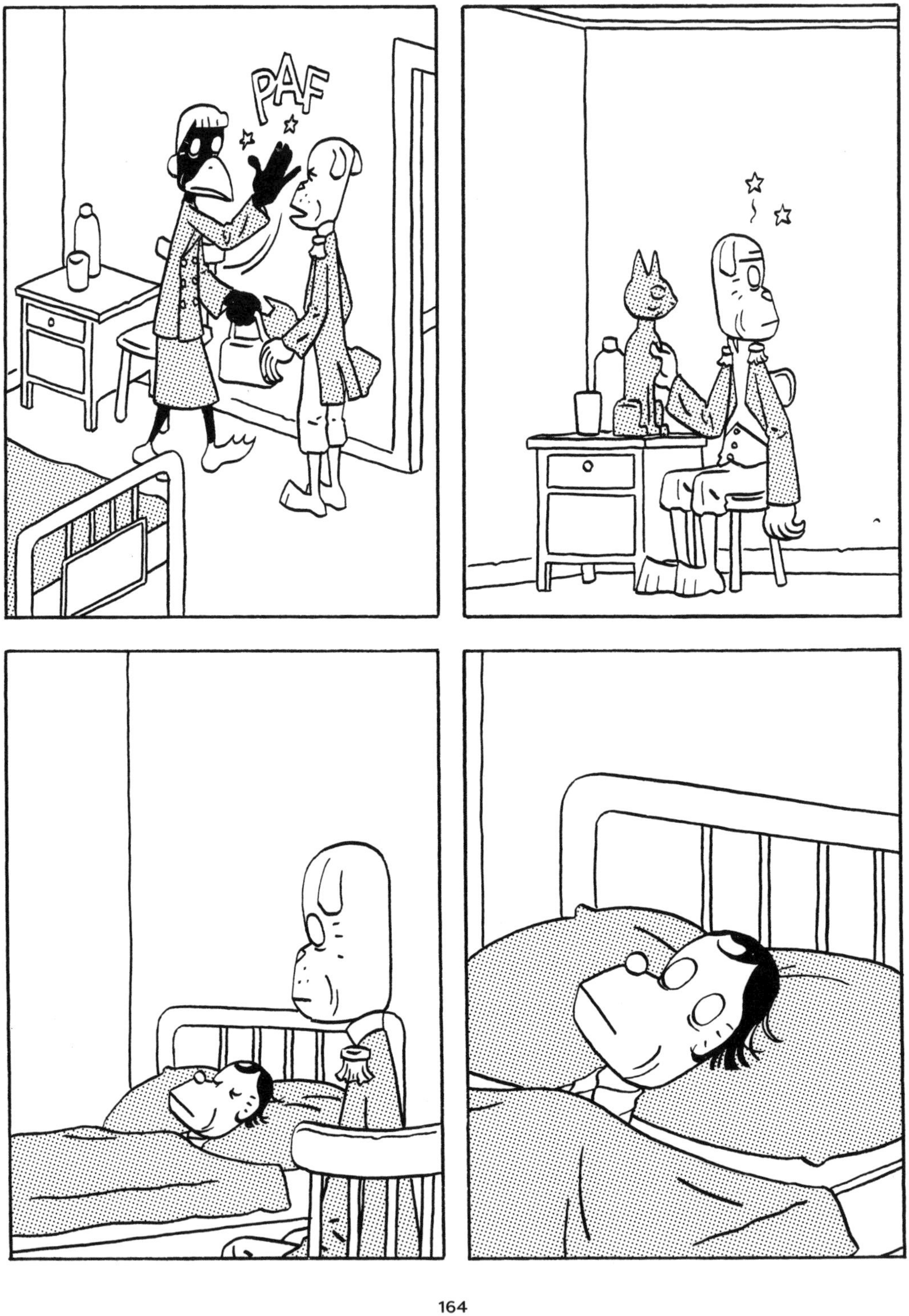
PAF

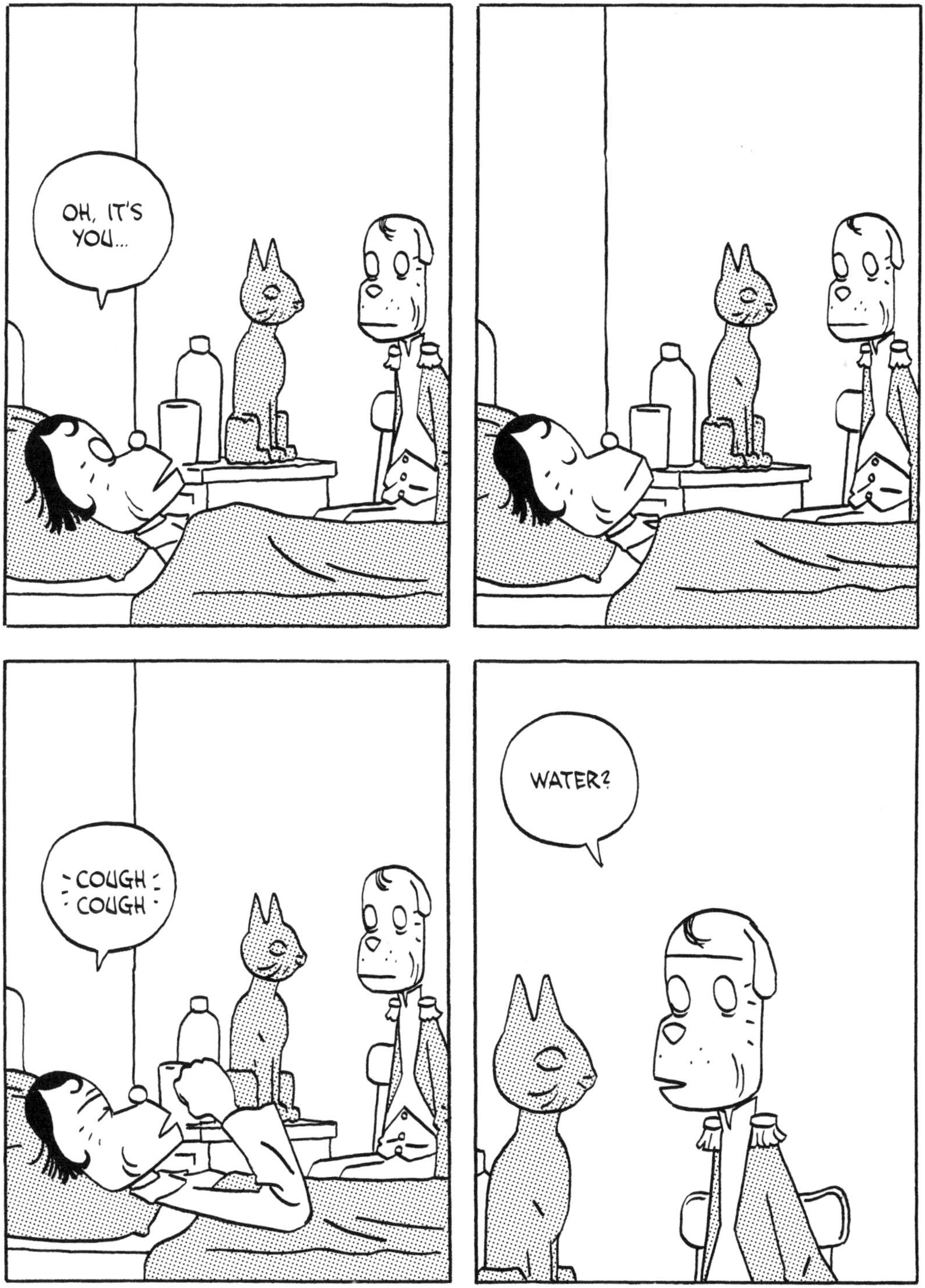
OH, IT'S YOU...
COUGH COUGH
WATER?

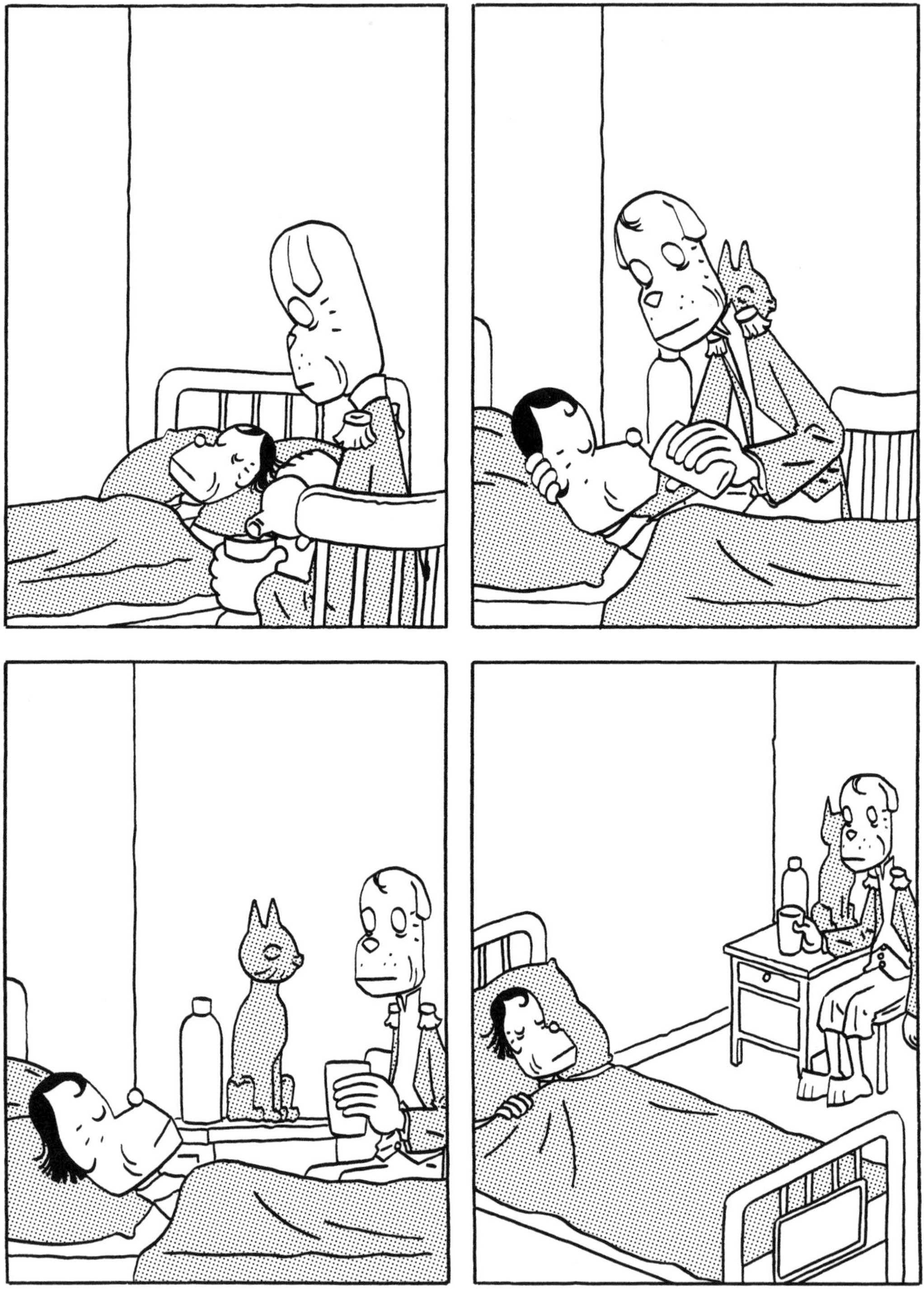

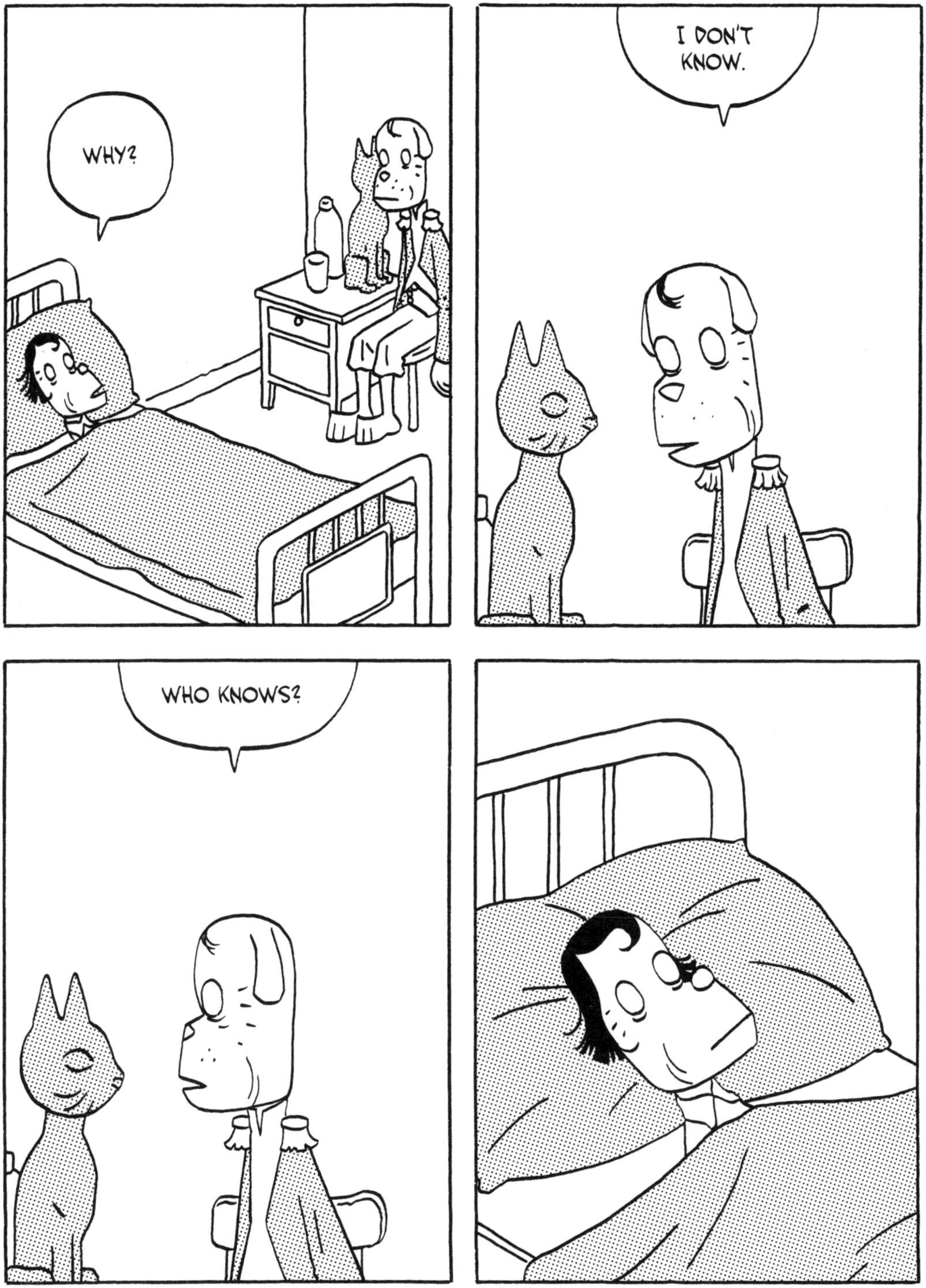
WHY?
I DON'T KNOW.
WHO KNOWS?

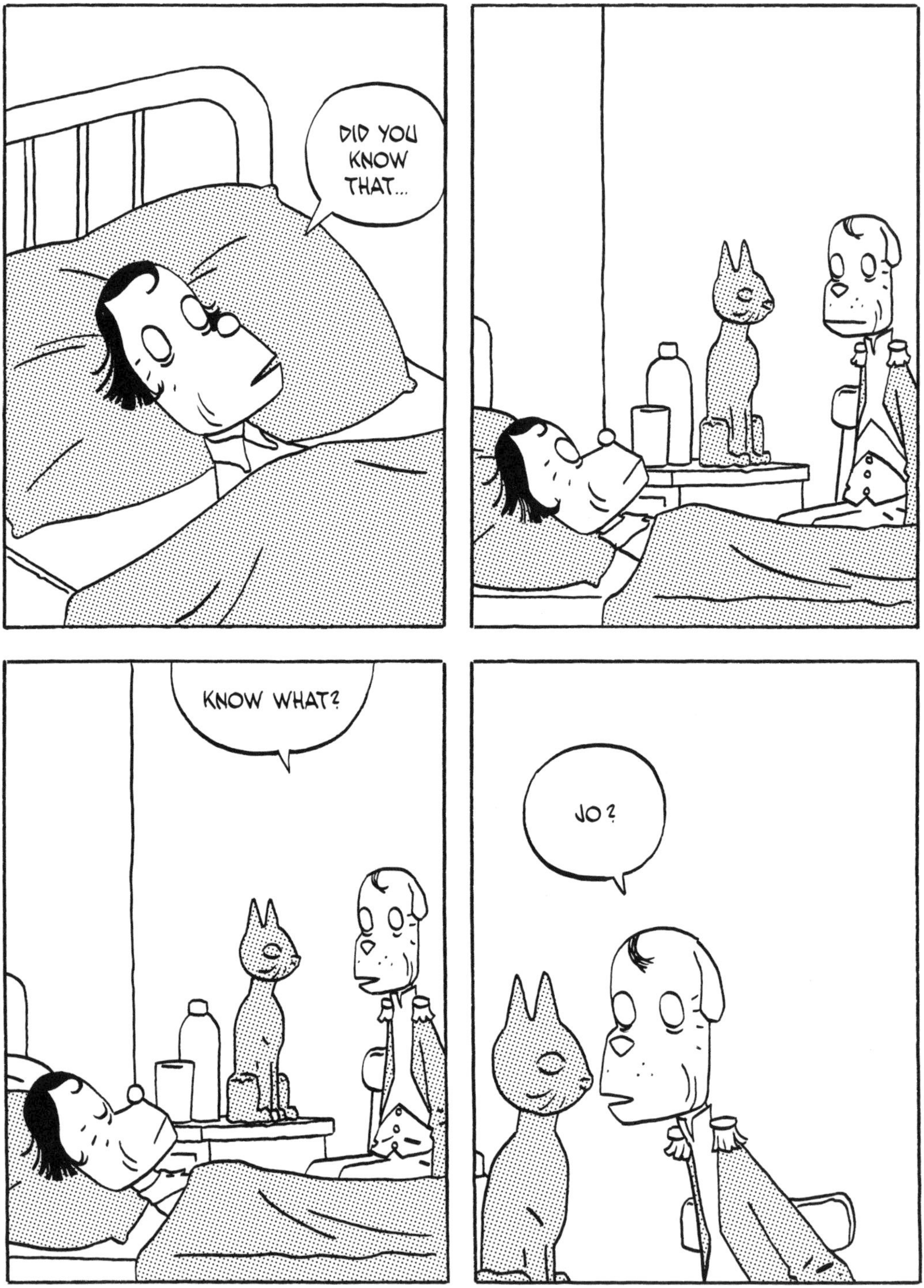
DID YOU KNOW THAT...
KNOW WHAT?
JO?

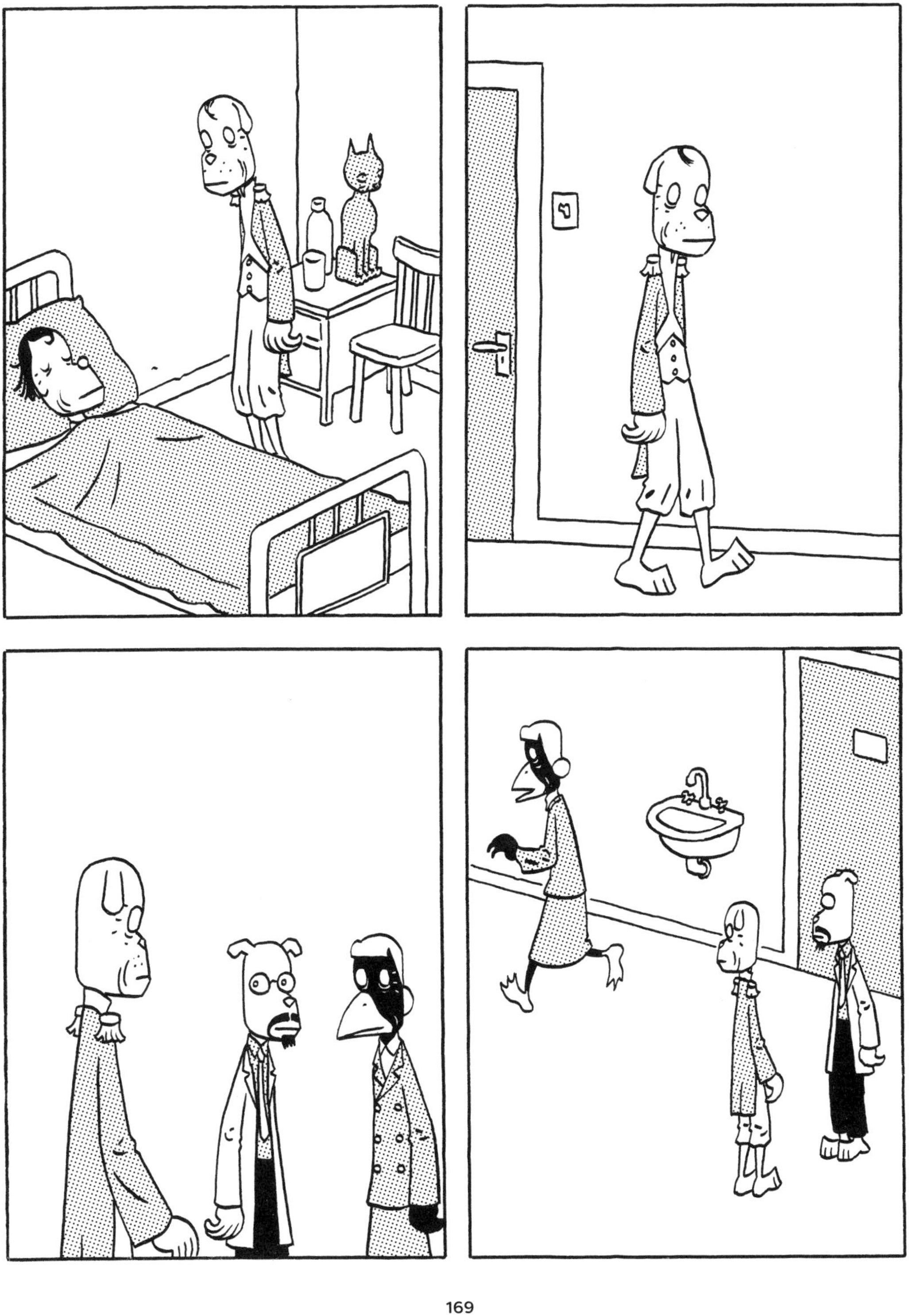

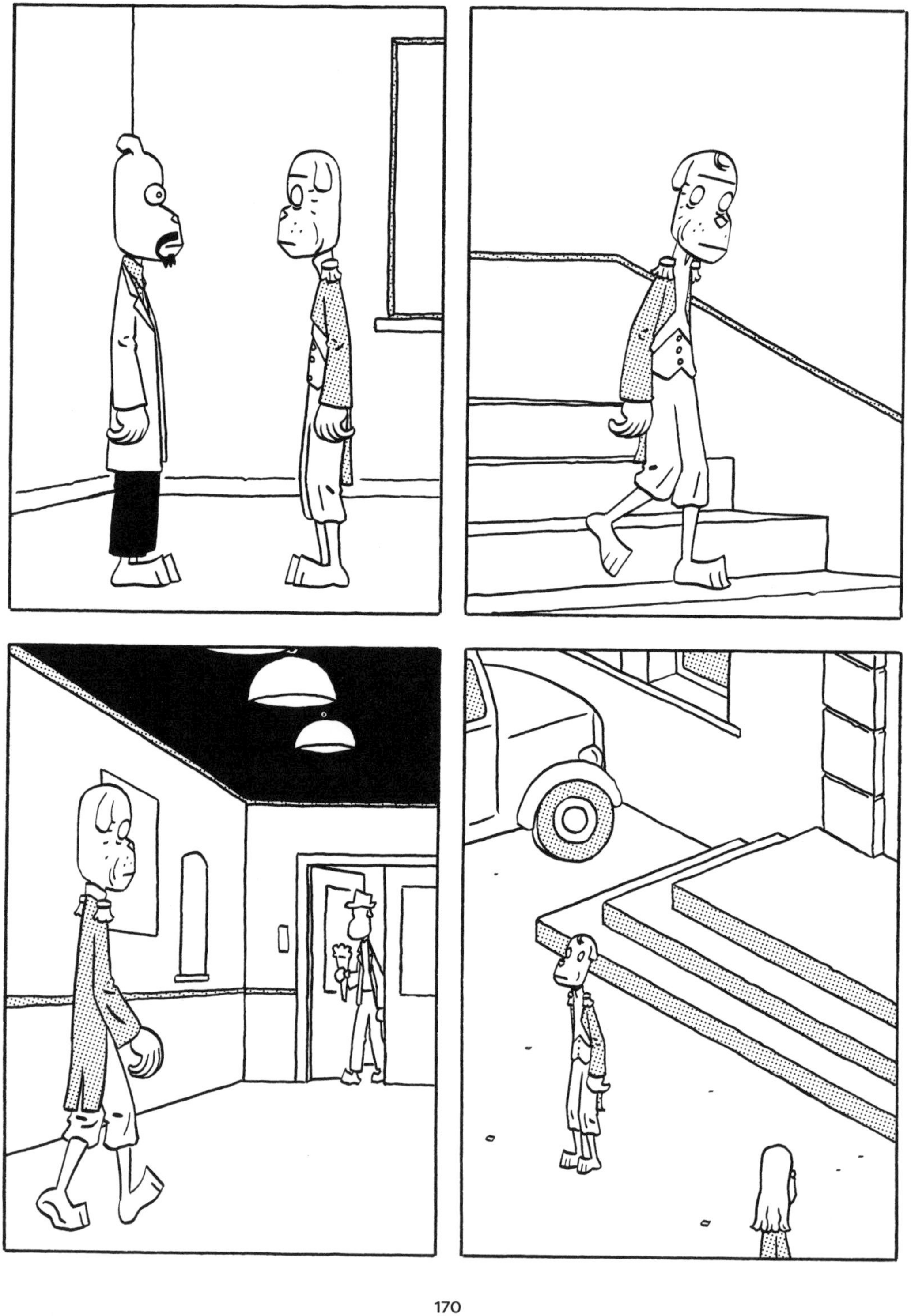

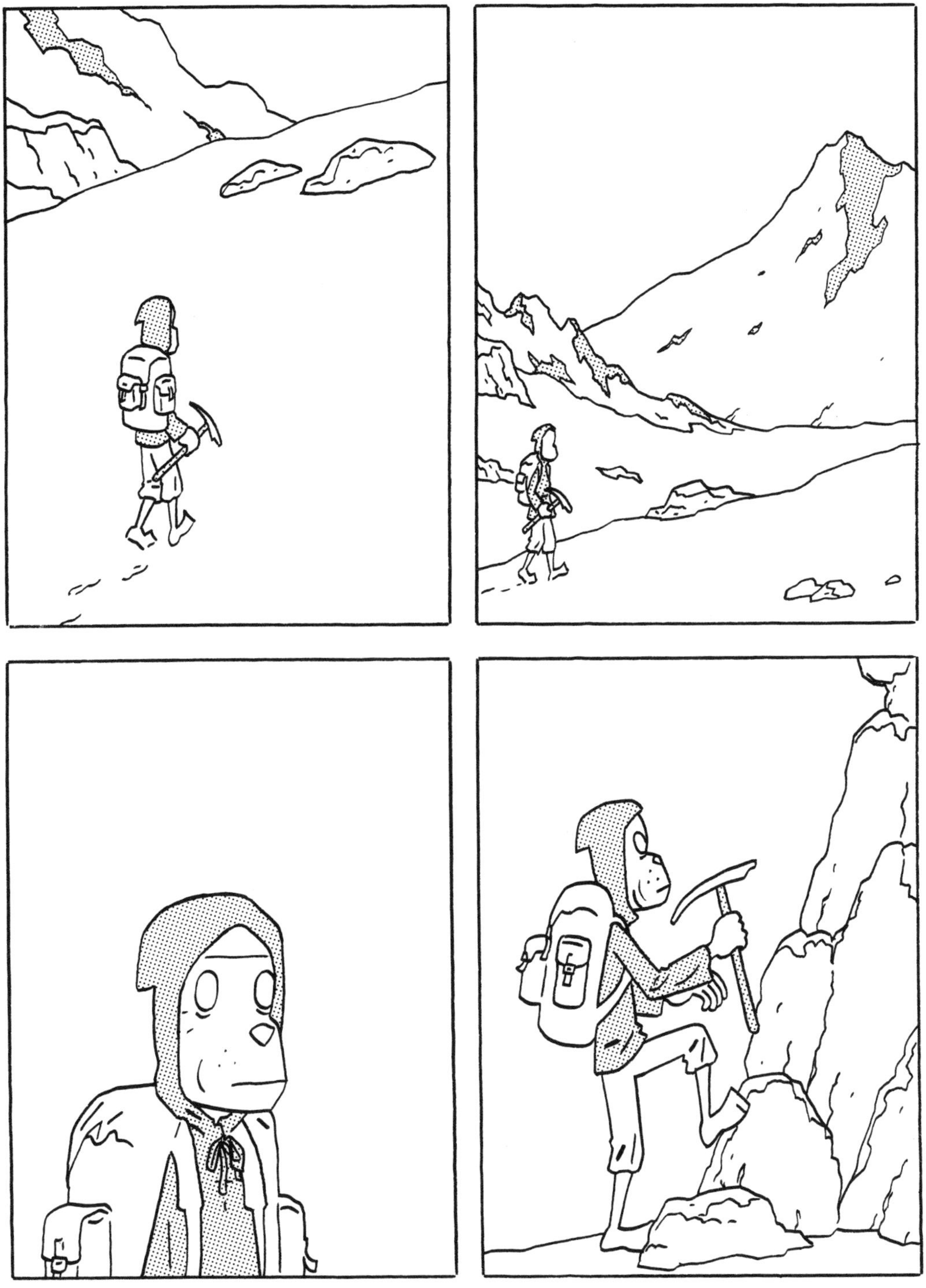

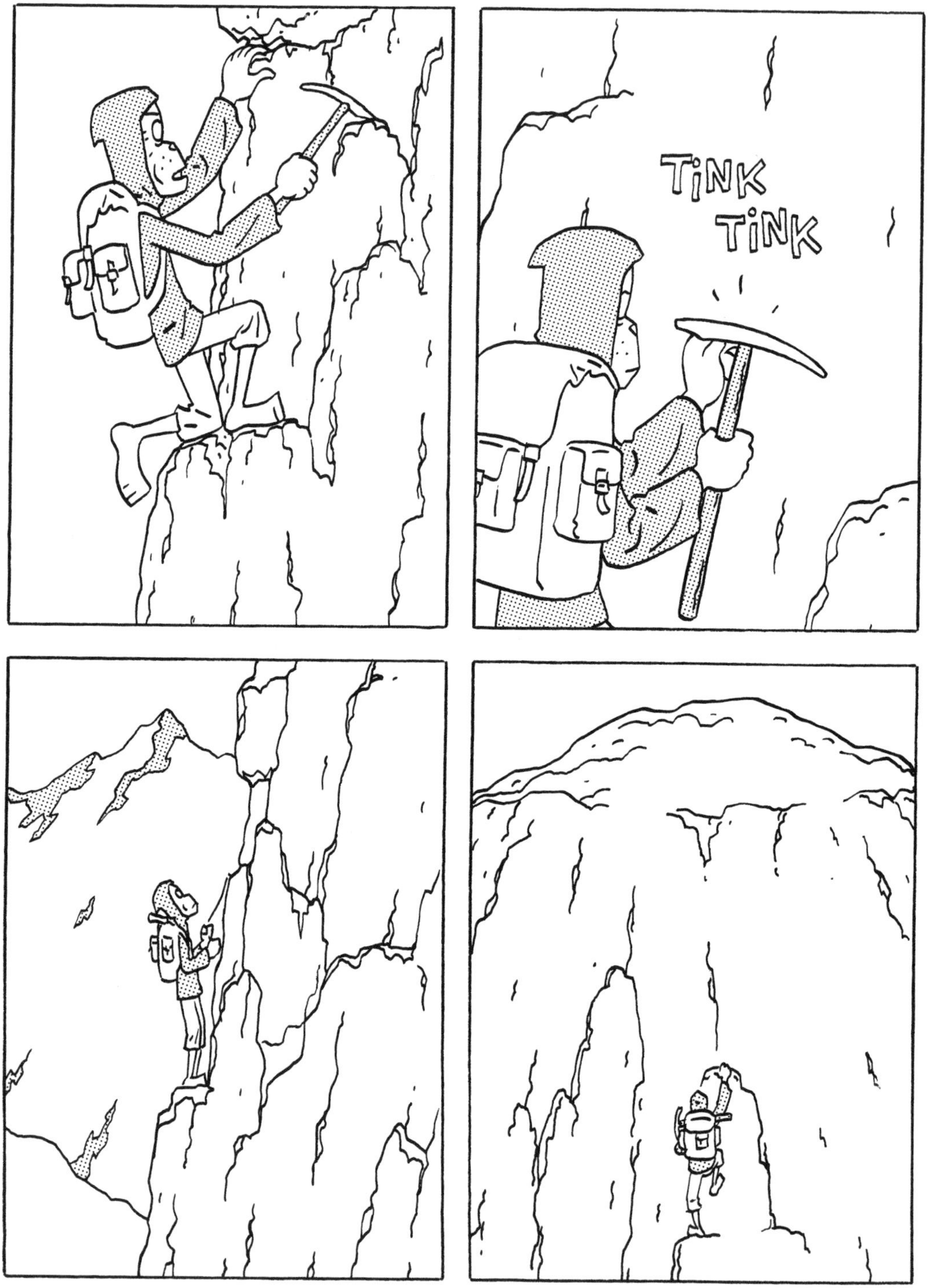
TINK
TINK

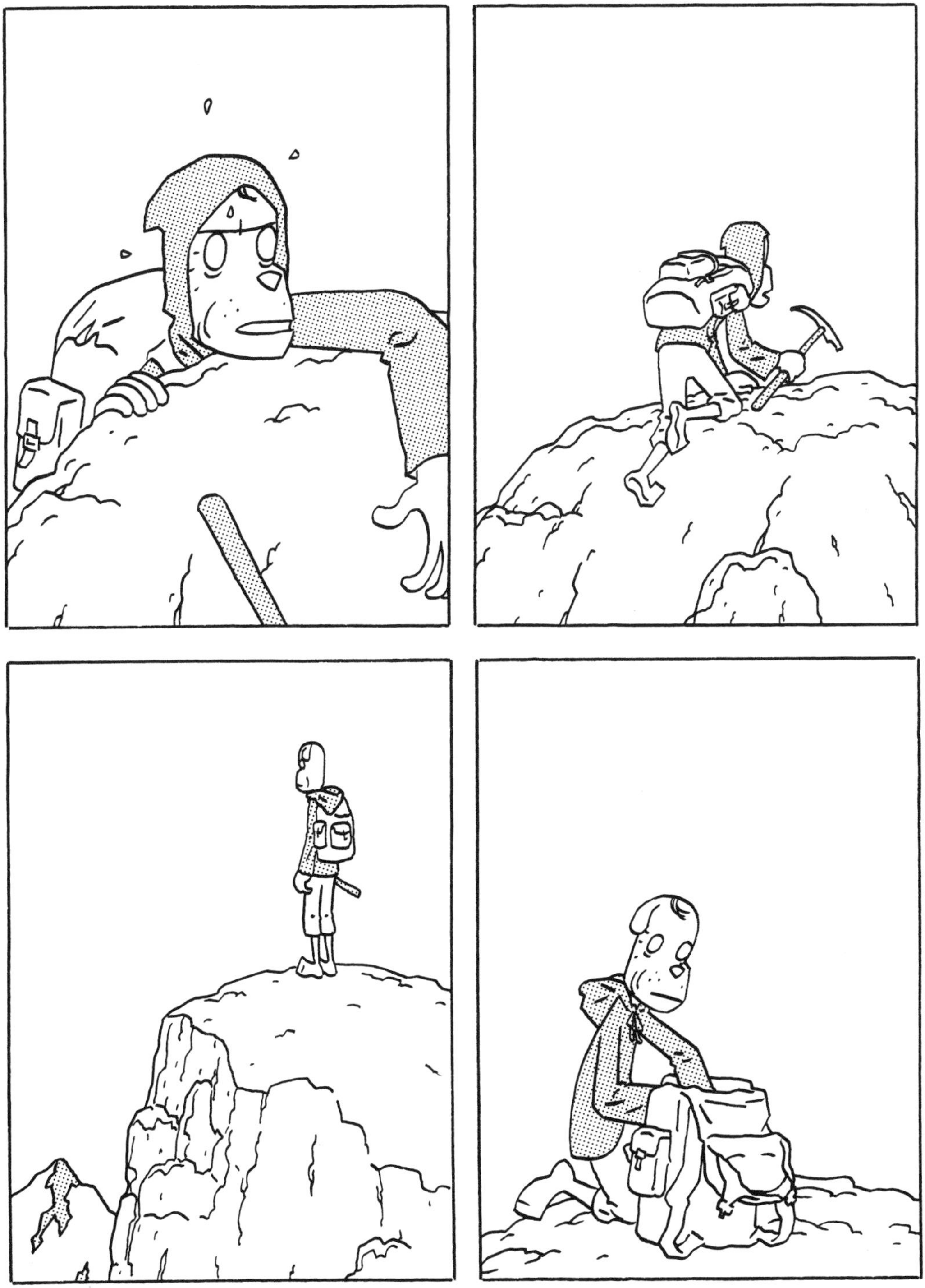

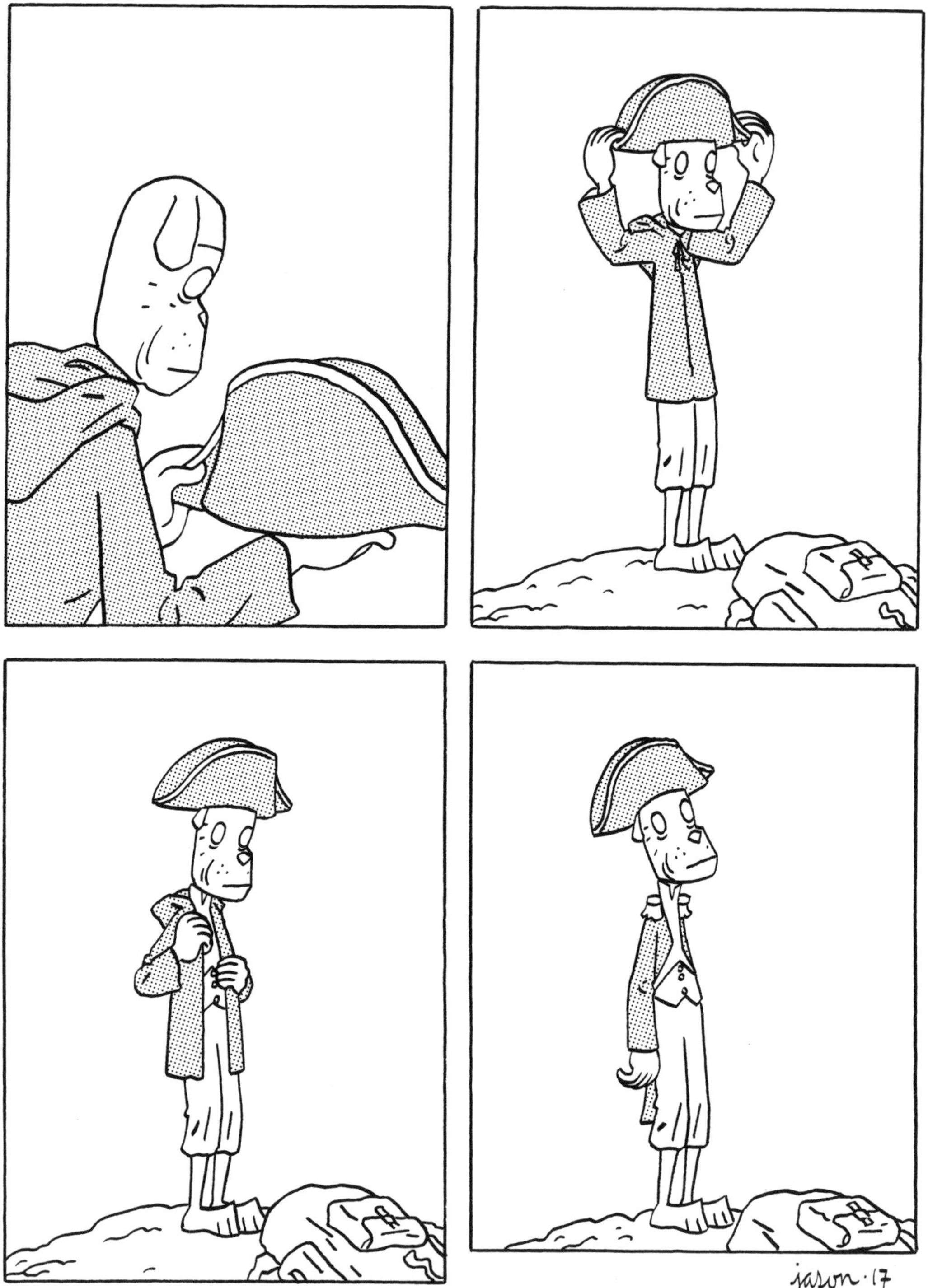

jason · 17

"Under the North sky will be born a man
who will tell strange tales in images and words.
He will be known by one name where he goes
and great confusion will rule the land."

-Nostradamus

OTHER BOOKS BY JASON

Why Are You Doing This? (2005) • *The Left Bank Gang* (2006)
I Killed Adolf Hitler (2007) • *The Last Musketeer* (2008)
Pocket Full of Rain (2008) • *Low Moon* (2009)
Werewolves of Montpellier (2010) • *Almost Silent* (2010 compilation)
What I Did (2010 compilation) • *Isle of 100,000 Graves* (2011)
Athos in America (2012) • *Lost Cat* (2013)
If You Steal (2015) • *On the Camino* (2017)